PROSPECTS

OF PEACE

By Thomas
Cross

Introduction

-

-

Late summer 2620 on the remote planet Molten, tucked away in deep space between two arms of the galaxy.

Thyatira is one of the states of the nation of Hoame. Firmly established there, the former traveller, Frank Thorn, is lord of his domain. With family, friends and a loyal population, things appear stable. Until, that is, a large heavenly body comes crashing through the atmosphere. It threatens destruction which puts into question the very existence of the planet's inhabitants.

Who will survive? What effect will it have on those who remain?

Life is rarely without incident on troubled Molten...

Characters by Region

Hoame, Keepers

Birkent, Count	Black, Keeper
Bodd Bodstein, Count	White, Keeper
Deistenau, Baron	Black, Keeper – "Junior," son of previous Keeper
Hass, Baron	Black, Keeper
L'Rochfort, Baron	Black, Keeper – Schail's nephew, Frank's ally
Mallinberg, Count	Black, Keeper – in charge of civil service
Moffer, Baron	Black, Keeper, youngest ever I.C. Black member
Raseberg, Baron	Black, Keeper
Schroder, Count	Black, Keeper
Tastenberg, Baron	Black, Keeper
Wonstein, Count	Black, Keeper

Hoame, Despots

Aggeparii	Jon Kagel
	Despotess Marie Claire Kagel
Bynar	Yannick Lovonski
Capparathia	Norbert Schmidt
	Despotess Rudella
Schmidt	
Dermback	Pieper
Gistenau	Loffer
Harradran	Sandhausen
Metzingen	Wonstein
Reichmenn	Vonberg
Rilesia	Lothar Heisler
	Despotess Magda Heisler
Thyatira	Frank Thorn
	Despotess Hannah Unit Thorn

(Ephamon Under Inner Council)

Hoame, Thyatira

Whites (all)

Azikial	Priest
Cragoop	Senator
Darda	Squad Leader (Castle)
Flonass	Saw mill worker
Gabriell	Priest
Hanson	Land owner
Illianeth	Teacher
Isaac	Priest
Japhses	General
Jonathan	Captain of Castle Guard
Katrina	Selerm owner
Keturah	Deejan Charvo's servant
Lydia	Selerm manageress
Matthew	Head of the Castle kitchen
Paul	Squad Leader (border)
Rodd	Captain of Border Guard
Saul	Senator
Sebastian	Deejan Charvo's heir
Stephan	Squad Leader (Army)
Tranis	Guardsman
Tsodd	Selerm owner
Vophsi	Chef

Drones

Alan	Senator

Blacks (all)

Deejan Charvo	Merchant
Hanz Drasnik	Senator
Gunter Ekker	Bishop
Leto Konig	Onstein's nephew
Walter Krenn	D C's assistant
Walter Onstein	Saw mill manager
Otto Ronenvink	Senator
Tristan Shreeber	Volunteer
Frank Thorn	Despot
Hannah Thorn	Despotess
Joseph Thorn	Heir
Emil Vebber	Senator
Karl Vondant	Senator

Senators

Alan
Emil Vebber   - land
Hanz Drasnik   - law and order
Karl Vondant   - defence
Otto Ronenvink   - accounts
Freidhelm Trepte - trade
(+3 other blacks)
Cragoop   - production
Saul   - health
(+ 2 other whites)

Foreigners living in Thyatira

Esther	Bishop Gunter's wife	(Ma'hol)
Muggawagga	Abbot	(Ladosan)
Harn'an-Fors	Consul to Thyatira	(Ma'hol)

6

Ladosans

Auraura	Eleazar's wife
Nonnagan Ba	Army NCO
Hallazanad	Army Officer - Captain
Charlotta Nazaz	Army Officer - Marshall
Panarez	Army Officer - Major
Quinty	Church member
Aylon Sedgula	Neo-Purple supporter
Vap	Army Officer - General
Zebulon	Church leader in Isson

Hoamen living in Ladosa

Eleazar	Missionary

Chapter 1

Flashback: mid 23rd century, the newly-discovered planet Molten. Many different groups of colonists have arrived there and a viable eco-system has been established. With conditions ideal for a normal life on the surface, Molten has acted like a magnet to would-be settlers. That is, until the mysterious Chang Tides out in space rendered communication and travel with the planet impossible. Those already there would have to fend for themselves.

In time, states would emerge from these disparate groups. For now, though, they were trying to establish themselves in a place where most, if not all, advanced technology had ceased to function.

One such band of people were desperadoes from a lost cause in a recent interstellar war. The 92nd Wing, 3rd Culper Fleet, would eventually form the nation of Hoame. At this early stage, however, they are still building what their commander hopes will be a Utopian society. The soldiers and their families will be the ruling elite, served by a genetically-modified underclass of 'whites,' so called due to their extraordinary, snow-white, wool-like hair, a by-product of the creation process.

In the north of the area that their expedition has carved out, lay a science research centre. The series of neatly-arranged, round-roofed huts were largely empty now. With most of the equipment rendered useless, the majority of personnel were redeployed. A mere two laboratories were still in use.

In one of these sat the distinctive, lanky frame of a resident junior science officer. All alone, he peered into an ancient microscope at slides he had meticulously prepared earlier that morning. Deathly quiet, he examined a specimen at length before making some notes with an old-fashioned pen on his paper notepad.

A visitor entered the room softly, but not too softly to be heard by its occupant, who turned round.

"Surprise!" cried the newcomer, shattering the silence.

"What are you doing here?" enquired the scientist. His tone was inquisitive, not unwelcoming, for the weapons officer was his friend. "The last I heard, you were going to the Citadel."

"And I did. The major's sent me back here again. I think there was a bit of a mix-up with the orders, but of course he couldn't admit as much. I've been reassigned here."

"Here?"

"Yeah."

"Oh. Doing what?"

"Research and development."

The weapons officer looked slightly embarrassed as he said this. His colleague knew that all particle charged weapons and laser rifles were now in storage. If they worked at all, they were now more of a liability to the operator than the target. Their few remaining battle robots were inoperable and were being dismantled. This new planet, which they had hoped would be their haven, was throwing up some nasty surprises.

Eventually, following an increasingly embarrassing silence, more information was forthcoming.

"I'll be in charge of developing a new range of weapons which can be relied upon. Tomorrow they're going to deliver me a contingent of white operatives to do the manual work. I've got a couple of other men to assist me with design and testing. The commander himself has provided me with some blueprints to work from, although I haven't had time to study them properly yet. They're all ancient designs by the looks of them; pretty crude."

By now the two men were sitting together on adjacent stools and the science officer had given up his work for the moment. He wanted to know more. A biologist by training, weapons were not his speciality, but he was amazed at how things had come to this. The sudden cutting off of advanced technology was effectively setting them back a thousand or more years. This was coupled with their commander's obsession with building a kind of medieval ideal society. It struck him as crazy. They might as well have all stepped back in time.

"So you're reinventing the bow and arrow?"

"Exactly right, I'm afraid."

"That's bonkers."

"Not if we're going to defend ourselves against the colonists around us. They got here before us, remember, and are all tooled up. There's no point in aiming a CX-9 at an enemy if the thing won't fire."

"Hmm..."

"So I'll invent the bow tomorrow and the wheel the day after."

His friend smiled. After all, they were all having to face new realities these days. He asked, "You mentioned wheels, how was your journey to the Citadel?"

"Slow and bumpy! I'd give my right arm for a working anti-grav engine right now. These dakks are utterly pathetic. We've lost loads of them through overworking. We've got strict new orders not to do so, but it does mean the wagons move not much more than a walking pace."

"Is that right?"

"It is. At least they seem to be able to retain stamina at that speed."

"But we'd be lost without them right now, wouldn't we?"

"I guess we would. It's as well we took some from the colonists early on. The one good thing you can say about them is that they breed fast."

"What?" enquired the scientist with a twinkle in his eye, "the dakks or the colonists?"

The other man laughed at this, but felt it was time to turn the tables and put the botanist on the spot.

"So have you created any more monsters lately?"

"You know I haven't; strictly forbidden now."

"So that chimera you showed me was the last."

"My lagua? I'm afraid so."

"Did you destroy it in the end?"

"Hell no!" the scientist looked hurt at the suggestion. "Not after all that hard work. No, I released him, watched him scuttle away into the forest. It was evening time. I felt a bit sad to see him go."

"It looked creepy to me, I wouldn't be sorry to see him go. How long do you think it'll live?"

"If it can hunt successfully... um, maybe 30 years. Could be more."

"Didn't you tell me that it could self-reproduce?"

"If I've done my calculations correctly, yes, but there'd never be many of them. I thought that..."

"Why couldn't you make something useful, like a horse for instance?"

Shrugging, and looking a bit guilty, the botanist had to concede that it would have been far more useful. "Too late now," he continued, fiddling with the pen between his fingers as he spoke, "no advanced genetic engineering is possible, even if the orders were rescinded. We're going to have to make do with dakks I'm afraid."

"Huh."

"Anyway, did you come by yourself, or with others?"

"It was something of a convoy actually, but no one interesting to chat with. Not like at the Citadel when I had a riveting conversation with a couple of... um, I'm not sure what they were actually, astronomers I guess."

"Go on, I fancy being riveted."

"Did you know that there's at least one other planet going round this star?"

"Um, I've been a little too focused to worry about such things."

"Yeah, it's a long way out, apparently."

"Inhabitable?"

"Oh no, a gaseous giant, far beyond where water can exist as a liquid. It has a gravity that'd crush you in an instant. These scientists were interested in it, 'cos they said it acted as a magnet for meteors. They reckon there's a belt of rogue meteors, or asteroids, in an elliptical orbit which intersects Molten's course round the sun. The large planet is sucking a lot of them in by its great mass, making us a safer place to stay."

"Safer, but not safe."

"Nowhere in space is safe, you know that."

"True."

"They reckon there was an intersection of Molten with these asteroids shortly before we arrived. The absence of any visible craters is a good sign, they said. Nonetheless, they reckon there's still a danger and are trying to estimate how frequently these intersections take place."

"What sort of timescale are they talking about: months? years? centuries?"

"I'm not sure, although I got the impression they're talking about fairly large timescales, every few hundred years. I don't know if they were trying to scare me, but they said a really big one could wipe out all life on the planet."

"Gee, you're the purveyor of good news this morning, aren't you?"

The weapons officer continued, "But it would depend on lots of things: mass, trajectory, that sort of thing."

"But they don't think anything's imminent?"

"I guess not."

"In that case," replied the science officer, finally putting the pen down on the desktop, "let's go to lunch."

Forward to the present day, over 350 years later, the Year of Our Lord 2620. From its origins as an escaping Culper unit, the nation of Hoame had developed. A federal form of government means that its eleven regions are each under the control of a resident despot. The sole exception to this is Ephamon, managed directly by the central governing Inner Council. They are housed in the very same Citadel built by the first generation settlers. Known as the Keepers of Hoame, the Inner Council members expect the absolute loyalty of the despots and can usually govern the country with a light hand on the tiller.

A single man holds joint positions of Keeper and despot. Frank Thorn has been on the planet 18 years and the last person who knows of his extraterrestrial origins has passed away. As well as Inner Council Member, he is despot of the northernmost region, or despotate, called Thyatira.

One day that he would never forget was that on which the superbolide struck. It was a perfect summer weather: warm, pleasant and not a cloud in the sky. He made his way from his resident Castle to the seat of local government, the senate building.

Several men were intent on intercepting him as he made his way across. Firstly there was Captain Rodd of the Boarder Guard, wanting to talk about refugees from the civil war in bordering Ladosa. No sooner had he dealt with him than he encountered Alan, friend and senator. Alan was a drone, the product of an illegal union between a member of the ruling black and subservient white classes.

The conversation was still young when another figure, a great deal larger in size, wanted his attention. Senator Emil Vebber had been despatched to negotiate the purchase of a large parcel of land from a neighbouring despotate. He was returning with the good news of a deal having been struck.

Alan had just told him of a major development in the Ladosan Civil War, when there was an earth-shattering "Bang!" and the whole building shook. At the same time they became aware of an intense bright light outside.

They shot out into the courtyard, along with a lot of other people. In the sky was a huge fireball streaking across in a north-easterly direction. It was so bright that it rivalled the sun in intensity. They shielded their eyes as they tried to observe it. The light was elongated, like a bright tube progressing across the heavens.

Some folk cried out in fear, but most were initially dumbstruck at the extraordinary sight. Once view of the phenomenon passed beyond the perimeter wall, many surged forward to continue observing it. Several around Frank speculated as to what it could be, but he felt certain it was a large meteorite falling to the ground. It was caught in the atmosphere and burning up. The longer that process continued, the better. He told the senators.

It was not going to land in Thyatira, that much was clear. It was heading over the mountain range and into Ladosa, but would it travel beyond that troubled country to the northern, icy regions? No one knew. The crowd watched it disappear from sight over the mountain tops in the distance, then stood around discussing what they had witnessed. With no sense of urgency, Frank slowly led his entourage out, beyond the wall, to join them. As they did so, there was a bright flash of light on the horizon.

"Oooh!" voiced the assembled throng, as if they were observing a firework display, then the chattering recommenced.

Putting civil war news to the back of his mind, Alan sought more of his leader's superior knowledge on what they had witnessed.

"You said it's a rock from space?"

"A big one, yes."

"Why is it on fire?"

"Friction with the atmosphere."

"And it could do a lot of damage?"

"If it's large enough it could wipe out all life on the planet. We'll have a better idea in the next couple of hours."

"Dear me!" exclaimed Emil.

They stood there for a few minutes in silence as the crowd began to disperse.

"I don't feel like working any more today," commented Frank.

He was going to say more, but then a deep rumbling came from the northeast, the same direction that the superbolide had gone.

"It sounds like thunder," observed the portly senator, although he knew it was not.

13

"Must be a long way away," Frank stated, more to himself than anyone else. Then, with a note of decisiveness, he addressed the black, "I'm delighted with the news about the land purchase, but it will have to wait until tomorrow... if there is a tomorrow. I'm going over to the Castle."

The Despot strode off, leaving the two senators amongst the thinning crowd. Alan realised that his news about the Ladosan Civil War would have to wait too.

People were returning to their normal duties by the time Frank entered the Castle bailey. Whatever the phenomenon was, it was all over as far as these people were concerned. He quickly made his way across to the keep and went swiftly up the stairs to the roof. A little too swiftly, for he was quite out of breath by the time he emerged back into the sunlight.

A pale, dissipating vapour trail in the sky was the only evidence of what they had witnessed such a short time before.

As he stood beyond the roof entrance, getting his breath back, he heard a couple of female voices. Taking a step forward, he saw his wife, Hannah, with a handmaiden.

"Did you see it?" he asked.

"Oh, hello, my dear. We didn't see it properly. We were in the living room when there was a loud bang and a tremendous light came through the window. We rushed to see it, but it wasn't possible from that angle. So we came up here, but barely caught the tail end of it going over the mountains."

"And the big flash of light over there?"

"Yes."

"You can see more from up here. Did you see the top of a mushroom cloud?"

"A mushroom cloud?" queried Hannah, it sounded a most odd expression.

"Um, yes, a big cloud like this," he tried to demonstrate with his hands. "I wondered if you could see the top of it."

"Nothing like that. I did hear a rumbling sound after a while, but nothing since. What is it?"

Frank explained about meteorites to the best of his ability. He was no expert, but he knew that the biggest impacts drew enough material into the atmosphere to turn day into night. So far there was no sign of that. He concluded by declaring, "I should have measured

14

the time between the flash and the sound. That would give us an idea of how far away it was. It seemed a long time, so I reckon it was a hundred kilometres away, or more."

"The Ladosans..." his wife, originally a native of that country, began, her face etched with concern. She trailed off, not finishing her sentence.

Checking the sky once more, Frank witnessed the fading vapour trail. Then, looking at the handmaiden, he gave her some instructions.

"Go and fetch Captain Jonathan and bring him up here straightaway. He was in the hall a short time ago; try there first."

"Yes, My Lord."

As the girl scooted off, her mistress gave a quizzical look, which called for an explanation. It was duly forthcoming.

"I'm going to get him to post a couple of men up here for the rest of the day. I want them to tell me straightaway if they see anything coming up from the horizon," he said, nodding in a northerly direction.

"Your mushroom cloud?"

"I'm not sure. If it's going to affect us directly I'd have thought it would manifest very soon. The mountains would have shielded us from the blast."

"And what are you going to do now?"

"Once I've seen Jonathan, I'm going to retire to the lounge."

Looking wistfully into the distance, Hannah said mournfully, "Oh those poor people, I hope they're okay."

The fate of the Ladosans was also on Alan's mind. He joined Frank that afternoon and spoke of his intention of going back there. He had spent much of the year across the border in the role of military advisor to the pro-Hoame, Neo-Purple faction in their civil war. Now, though, with this strange, little-understood development, he felt a strong urge to return without delay.

"I was always planning on going back there, but I need to see how they are. If they've been hit by this meteorite-thing, then I have to find out if they are still alive."

"Of course, I understand."

"I'll need to get my things together... I'll leave tomorrow if that's okay."

15

"Absolutely! Take whatever you need and send me back a report as soon as you are able to."

"From what you've told me, they could all be dead."

"Well, I don't wish to speculate too much. It'll depend on lots of things . The mountain chain has shielded us from the immediate after-effects, but what is beyond there......?"

"I'll set off tomorrow morning and send back a report at the first opportunity."

"Thanks," replied Frank. He wondered what his friend would discover in Ladosa. Had the land been devastated? Would their Hoamen military advisors be in one piece? Would their friends over there, Tristan and Eleazar, still be alive?

Earlier that day, Eleazar, missionary and former Bishop of Thyatira, had decided to take his family for a picnic. It was a fine, late summer's day and they could afford to take a day off.

Eleazar was a Hoame white who had met his Ladosan wife, Auraura, on a previous missionary expedition to the country, several years previously. After spending the first years of their marriage in Thyatira, they moved to the hill town of Isson, a few kilometres from the capital city, Braskaton. Now he divided his time between serving Zebulon's church in the richer, northern part of town, and the one he himself has set up in the poor area. Ably supported by his wife and with the welcome patronage of Quinty, a wealthy widow, things were going well, relatively speaking.

For these were times of conflict. The country was in the throws of a messy civil war, made all the more complicated by the number of different factions involved. The hill people were doing their best to keep out of it. Yet some reckoned that it was merely a matter of time before they would have to choose between them. While the local Rose and Buff factions slugged it out in the valley, Isson was relatively safe from conquest. Nevertheless, with the situation so fluid, the town's medium-term independence was not assured.

For now, life went on as normally as possible. This time of year the mountain passes to the remote eastern settlements were open, but it was quite a trek to go there. Meanwhile, a limited, cautious trade had been re-established with Braskaton, firmly under Buff control.

When he needed to unwind, Eleazar's favourite place was The Crater. A remnant of a long-extinct volcano, it was a uniformly round caldera with a three quarters of a kilometre radius. A wet climate ensured it was covered in lush grass, with the occasional bush within the rim. At the bottom, a lake was largely concealed by the huge amount of vegetation floating on the surface.

"The cucumber is in this one... and here are the tomatoes," Auraura directed.

The couple were perched, that bright, sunny day, on the external grassy bank down from the rim of the crater. Accompanied by their four children, ranging in age between four and nine, there were no other people in sight. In this fine weather, the vista was crystal clear to the horizon. The nearby town was hidden by the wood through which the family had travelled to get to the beauty spot.

"Eat it nicely!" Auraura told Lottie, their youngest. "There's a good girl."

Her husband, meanwhile, was tucking into a cheese sandwich. Once he had finished it, he commented, "I'm glad we came here today, it's ideal weather."

"Yes, quite beautiful. We need to make the most of it, we're probably not going to have many more like it this year."

"No."

"Did you tell me you've got the Sabbath off?"

"I'm leading the service, but Lawrence has agreed to come down and deliver the sermon."

"Laurence?" she looked surprised. "It's rare for him to deign us with his presence!"

"It's a talk he gave at St Mary's last week. I told him that it would be helpful to my other congregation."

"No doubt he enjoyed the flattery."

"Don't be unkind," he admonished her gently, "I welcome him coming to join us. It'll give them a change from my voice and I meant what I said, I think it will connect to them."

After a while, Eleazar brought up a fresh topic.

"The committee are talking about having an appeal for metal."

"I think you said."

"With the blacksmith needing all he can get for making weapons, it's..."

"Boom!" A gigantic explosion in the atmosphere, accompanied by the brightest of lights, stopped him in his tracks.

They could not help but look up to see what it was and got temporarily blinded by the intensity of the fireball. Blinking madly as he recovered his sight, Eleazar shielded his eyes from it, while trying to track its flight through the heavens.

The children were crying and Auraura gathered them to herself like a hen gathers her chicks. Standing up, her husband continued to follow the flight of the projectile until, in the far distance, there was a monumental flash of light and he turned his head away instinctively. When he looked back, he saw the most extraordinary sight. A doughnut-shaped ring of fire and smoke was emanating from ground zero. Struggling to take it in, he could see, far away, whole forests being flattened. It was like a giant hand knocking down matchsticks. On it came, expanding inexorably. Then realisation dawned on the Hoaman.

"Quickly, run, this way!" he cried as he indicated up the last part of the slope to the crater's rim.

Auraura knew better than to worry about the picnic things and, collecting up the children, made as fast as she could up the incline. Eleazar came over to help and, picking up their youngest, shepherded his family along. The elder two children forgot their crying and scrambled up the bank, their mother carrying the last one. Once at the top, Eleazar took a glance at the effect of the quickly advancing shockwave. Then, leading by example, he bundled down the other side, child clutched tightly to his chest. The rest followed suit.

They were almost a third of the way down and hiding behind bushes when the blast hit. Shutting his eyes, shielding his child and burying his head into the ground, Eleazar was stunned by the force of the explosion. The ground shook, debris fell all around and the noise was deafening. He stayed clinging to the bush as he was hit by assorted small branches and sods of earth. Holding on for dear life, he could not glance up to see how the others were doing. The wind roared over them, to be followed by a deathly silence.

Peering up, he saw a scene of devastation, with some large trunks and branches lying around. Mercifully none touched them and the family had escaped with minor cuts and bruises. If they had not reacted so quickly it would have been a different matter. Shaking dirt and twigs from his person, he went over to where the others were.

The children were not crying any more, but shaking uncontrollably with shock.

"Look!" demanded Auraura, indicating to the massive tree trunk which had landed right in front of her. "If that had hit us we'd all be dead!" As it was, it shielded them and debris was stacked up the other side.

She talked more, a lot more, to Eleazar, to the children and to herself. It was her way of coping with what just happened. Not that they actually understood what had occurred. All they were aware of was that they had miraculously survived a catastrophe.

After dusting the children down and checking there were no serious injuries, the parents sat down to collect their thoughts. All was deathly still, no bird was in the sky, no insect in the air.

"We must go back," Eleazar announced.

Auraura nodded and got the children to their feet. Lottie began weeping, but her mother barely noticed as she began making her way around the giant log and up the slope. The six of them picked their way through the debris strewn about and finally made it back to the rim. The adults feared what they would find when they got to the top. When they did make it, the scene was one of utter devastation.

Whole forests in the distance were flattened, the trees all facing in the same direction. Nearby, a high proportion of the trees in the wood they had earlier walked through had been knocked over. Interestingly, though, not every single one was horizontal. It was a testimony both to the resilience of the trees and the fact that the shockwave here was beginning to lose a measure of its power.

Nevertheless, much of the wood was laid waste. With a mangled mess ahead of them, it appeared to be an impenetrable barrier.

"We'll never get through here," the priest declared.

"There's no way round it," Auraura warned. "We'd have to go many kilometres out of our way and it would almost certainly be exactly the same as this. We've got to work our way through here."

So it began, the hard trek through, over and under the jumble of trunks, branches and foliage. It was extremely hard work and progress was slow. Much to their mother's relief, the children forgot their upset and cooperated to the full. Sometimes the parents had to lift the youngest two over obstacles, while the older pair found ways through the tangled mess that were too small for the adults.

It seemed to take an age, but eventually they reached the site of the wooden bridge they had crossed on their way to the crater. Only a few pieces were remaining and the stream was clogged with logs and broken branches.

"Come on, this way," Auraura declared, taking the lead as she scrambled down the river bank. "The water's not particularly deep this time of year."

Hesitating for a moment, Eleazar noticed that the trees on the other side of the stream were not nearly as badly affected. Then he remembered that they had, in fact, been travelling downhill to this point. It was easy to lose track of that fact whilst negotiating all the obstacles. The blast had hit the trees on the far bank higher up and a much higher proportion here survived as a result.

They could not see the town further down and he wondered what, if anything, was still standing. He said a silent prayer before moving once more. The family crawled across the stream without getting wet, for at this place the debris was stacked high across it and the water passed underneath. Once they had safely negotiated the water course, they took a breather before hitting the trail down to Isson. At least there was a recognisable path from now on, even if it was blocked at regular intervals by fallen trees. Eventually they reached the outskirts of town and the sight did not look hopeful. The first houses they saw were smashed to smithereens. A couple of timber buildings here had been wiped away completely and the stone structures were not faring much better, with barely one stone left upon another. People were milling about, some searching in the rubble, others standing or sitting around looking utterly confused. One thing they all did was ignore the family coming down from the hill as they passed by.

"We'll go to the church," Eleazar stated. He meant St Mary's, Zebulon's church in the richer, northern area. They would naturally arrive there before the other one, or their home in the southern sector, so it seemed like a sensible course of action.

The six of them passed many more structures badly hit by the blast. Yet these were not completely flattened and, as they progressed, they were heartened to find the damage lessening by degrees. When they arrived, they finally found familiar faces. Folk were on the lawn, staring at the remains of the steeple that had been knocked off and was lying there in several pieces. No one was actually doing

20

anything. Zebulon himself was among the group and he turned as he saw the family arrived and went to greet them.

"You're alive! Praise God. Where were you when it hit?"

Eleazar gave a brief report and then pointed to the church building. The wooden steeple was gone and some of the rest of the roof with it, strewn across the lawn for some distance. Notwithstanding, the spiritual leader was sanguine. With a smile, he said, "As you can see, the top's been blown off and the windows blown out, but it could have been a lot worse. A few people were hit by flying glass and Laurence has hurt his leg, but there have been no fatalities here."

"That's a blessing. What about the southern end of town?"

"I have no idea. I have a great deal to do here. There are many casualties according to the first reports. I need to drag myself away and start..."

He stopped when a breathless church worker came running up. Pausing to take in some air, he gave his urgent news.

"It's Quinty's house, it's been hit bad. A pile of rubble now! No one's seen her, I think she's dead."

The thought flashed through Eleazar's mind that having his benefactress killed would be a major inconvenience to him. He then dismissed such a selfish thought as he told Zebulon, "We are going to the other part of town to see how badly hit it is. Please send me any major news you have and I'll do the same."

"Good idea."

"And I'll see you again soon, once I know what is going on."

"Yes, everything is in chaos right now. We have to stand firm and show ourselves as strong leaders in the community."

The other priest looked at him, but did not reply. Instead he took Auraura's hand and led his family down to the southern part of town to find out the level of devastation there. What the following days held was anybody's guess. Right now all they could deal with were the immediate concerns of sheer survival.

A civil war was raging throughout Ladosa. Many different factions, born of their pre-existing political parties, were involved. The strategically important town of Wesold, many kilometres west of Isson, had been continually fought over since the inception of the conflict at the beginning of the year.

Wesold was a magnet which drew in no less than five armies. Three had either withdrawn hurt, or been annihilated, leaving the Neo-Purples and Buffs. The latter, which formed the government prior to the General Election, had been badly bloodied in the fight, but still clung to a substantial tract of land in the southwest. On the other hand, the Neo-Purples were getting stronger by the week and considering their offensive options. Wesold was mainly in Buff hands at this point, but government forces were depleted and spread thinly.

The Neo-Purple field commander had been murdered in a Buff act of treachery. Former civil servant, Charlotta Nazaz, quickly stepped into the breech. Aided by foreign advisor Alan from Thyatira, she oversaw a heavy defeat of Buff forces in the town. With the Hoaman taking a brief, well-earned break in his home country, Marshal Nazaz (as she had become) was preparing her forces for switching from defence to offence. She liked Alan's plan to surround Wesold in a pincer movement rather than assault the town head-on. Urban fighting would be costly and throw away the advantages so carefully gained in the fighting so far. Charlotta was learning from her chief advisor that patience and careful strategy were winning commodities in war. Bravery and commitment alone would not succeed.

Sitting by herself in her command post, she found her mind going off at an unexpected tangent. Up until now she had told herself that her sole motive in wanting Alan back soon was his battlefield experience. Now, though, she surprised herself by identifying a completely different motive on top of this. The man from across the border was a little older than her, but his experience and cool demeanour appealed to her. She had once set her sights on Baron L'Rochfort, but, for all his charm, he proved a disappointment. Alan was straight, he did not use flattery or flirtation. He possessed an inner strength of character as well as his physical bravery. A few weeks earlier she found it necessary to reprimand him for involving himself personally in a desperate street battle. It was a clear violation of the terms of the Neo-Purple / Hoame agreement. The worst thing that could happen was that an enemy faction capture a foreign advisor and parade them for the country at large to see. It would be a propaganda disaster at this stage for news of their secret pact with a foreign land to get out. Not just any foreign land either, but one still seen by many as their main potential enemy. Why had they entered into it? Due to a desperate need for weapons, military trainers and advisors. So far the deal was proving invaluable to the Neo-Purple cause.

Charlotta had not banked on a personal element complicating matters for her. When the time came, she found it hard to admonish Alan for his recklessness. The truth was that the counter attack he led was pivotal to the battle. It had tipped the balance in the fight when it was most desperate. It ensured that a major victory was theirs. His tactics, foresight and bravery had saved the day. What a man he was!

Her musings finally ended when her subaltern came in and reminded her that she was due to address a group of officers.

"Oh yes, of course. Thank you Alexannap."

She collected a few papers and went out into the open air It was a beautiful, sunny day. They were at a temporary command post established a couple of kilometres outside Wesold. Four huts had been set up there in a shallow valley between two tree-lined ridges. They were hoping that their counter-offensive would move them further west, so there was no idea that this place would be in any way permanent. Nevertheless, it was proving an effective station in the short-term. With the wounded Buff forces no longer trying to seize the Neo-Purple toehold in the town, the marshal did not feel a necessity to be on the front line.

This was the day that the superbolide struck. Charlotta stepped out at around the time as her Hoaman advisor was watching the blazing projectile disappear behind the senate building outer wall. A moment later, she and her subaltern were watching the same phenomenon passing almost directly overhead. There was the same loud "Boom!" and intense white light. Heading northeast, directly over the central Buff heartland, they watched open-mouthed, eyes squinting and hands raised to shield them from the brightness.

It was falling quicker now and the huge flash, after it disappeared over the horizon, was a lot less delayed than it had been for the Hoamen.

"Whatever was that?" asked one of several officers who had hurried out of the conference hut.

A second officer let out a string of expletives before he caught his marshal's eye and desisted. A third man, with a note of drama, announced, "It's an omen!"

"Don't be ridiculous," Charlotta snapped. She needed to show leadership and nip such silly talk in the bud. "Come on," she continued, striding towards the meeting place and leaving her retinue in her wake, "we have work to do."

One or two stared up at the thick, grey vapour trail in the sky and delayed joining those entering the hut.

Opening her mouth to speak, Charlotta did not get a word out before there was the most almighty "Whoop!" and the sound of stuff crashing all around. The whole hut seemed to explode and objects and people flew across the room. When she picked herself up, she was surprised to find the structure still standing, if precariously. Thinking of herself first, she scrambled through the wreckage and out through the door, the lintels of which were at a dangerous angle.

The personnel outside had been knocked off their feet, but most avoided serious injury. Two of the four huts were flattened, but the other two remained standing - just. The rest of her staff exited the hut she had been in. It was a rhomboid shape now, with the walls at thirty degrees. The only reason they had not all been swept away to their deaths was that they were a lot further away than Isson from the epicentre of the explosion. The shockwave was beginning to lose its previously irresistible force.

Naturally they were all in a befuddled state in the immediate aftermath. "I told you it was an omen!" the man from earlier cried out, but everyone ignored him.

"Is everyone okay?" asked Charlotta with a note of authority.

The people around her nodded.

"See to the injured; check the huts!"

They obeyed. Three had been empty at the time and no one was left in the meeting building. They escaped with contusions and a few gashes which nearby medical staff soon saw to.

"Oh my..." began Captain Hallazanad, one of the marshal's most trusted officers "... I reckon that was one of those shooting stars we've been seeing at night, but this one decided to come during the day. I've heard of such things before."

Charlotta replied, "Let's hope there aren't any more on their way. I reckon this one landed in the middle of Buff territory. I never thought I'd say this, but I feel sorry for them.

"Do you?" asked the captain, sounding incredulous.

"Don't worry, it'll pass."

An enormous "Crash!" made Tristan and Ayllom jump to their feet inside their living quarters. Dashing out the back of the cottage where they were billeted, they looked up at the roof, for the sound had come from above. Several tiles were missing and more were displaced, but that appeared to be the full extent of the damage. The thick hedge to the rear of the one-story property ensured that no windows were smashed.

The marshal had been wrong about ground zero. The remains of the superbolide had, in fact, exploded above the ground seventy-five kilometres northeast of the Buff region. This was in the more sparsely populated "northern tribes" area, but the force was such that a huge area of the country had been devastated.

Tristan and Ayllom were Neo-Purple medics on the Fanallon Front, more than a day's journey south of Wesold. The blast was petering out here and had but a tiny fraction of its original power. They were several hundred kilometres from the epicentre.

"It must be to do with the bright light we saw earlier," remarked Tristan.

"The fireball? I guess you're right. I hope the folks at the Mansion are okay."

"Yeah."

It was a reference to the converted country house that was serving as their side's major hospital on the Wesold Front. The pair had been stationed there together until recently. Things were currently a lot quieter in their current sector, but no one expected that to last forever.

The two of them had teamed up together as an ambulance crew in the early days of the conflict and swiftly become firm friends. Ayllom was the black sheep of the military careerist Sedgula family. Several of his close relatives were fighting on the Fanallon Front. He did not fancy fighting, but soon realised that being an ambulanceman was anything but a cushy number. He believed his crewmate to be a fellow countryman from the less densely populated southeast region of Ladosa. In that, he could not be more wrong.

For Tristan was a Hoaman. He had crossed the border as part of a foreign delegation to assist the one pro-Hoame faction involved in the civil war. This clandestine mission was known about only in the top echelons of the Neo-Purple setup. A supply of arms, plus combat trainers and advisors had been most welcome and were proving their worth. It was led by Alan and, being a close friend, Tristan cadged a lift. As a newly committed Christian and pacifist, he wanted to serve his fellow man as a medic. Along with his partner, he had witnessed more than a few horrific sights during the desperate battle for Wesold. Yet they came through unscathed and he was happy in his choice. Indeed the thought of returning home before the war concluded had never entered his head. With his elder brother and father both dead, and his mother locked away, there was little to tempt him back to his homeland. Neither did the thought often occur to him that he was deceiving his friend as to his origins. What did it matter? As long as they got on well together and worked as an effective team, he was every bit as committed as the native Ladosan.

"Actually, it's a stroke of luck," Ayllom was saying, still staring up at the roof.

Looking a bit confused at this remark, the other said, "How do you figure that?"

"Don't you remember? We've got the maintenance crew coming round later in the week to look at those soffit boards."

"Oh yes."

"They can do the tiles at the same time."

"Let's hope so."

"They'd better!"

"You could threaten them with the wrath of Major Sedgula if they don't."

"Hmm," Ayllom considered. "I hope it doesn't come to that. Anyway, this is our day off, let's go back inside. It's cooler in there."

"Sure."

"We should have some juice left for a drink."

"I hope so. We'll have to replenish our supplies."

They retreated indoors and did indeed find some practil juice to enjoy in their living room. The following day they would be back on duty and, although the front was currently quiet, anything could happen. Due to their previous experience, they were under no illusions. Therefore it made sense to enjoy the present moment.

It could have been for this reason that their conversation moved away from the heavenly fireball and its impact. Ayllom wanted to talk about lighter things.

26

"Have you seen that communications officer they have here? The slim one with the ponytail?"

"She's a bit old for you, isn't she?"

"You're forgetting, I like mature women."

"Oh, yeah."

"I had a dream with her in it last night."

"You haven't mentioned it before now."

"No... but it's true. We were sharing long, lingering kisses. It was a lovely dream."

"I thought she had a man in her life."

"One can still fantasise."

"Hmm... Your subconscious does your fantasising for you."

At this point, a group of men walked by, talking loudly. The sound of their voices travelled through the open windows quite clearly. Ayllom paused, which gave his friend an opportunity to raise his own topic.

"You remember that swordsman we treated the other day? The one with the broken leg?"

"The accident? Sure, I remember."

"He told me that he'd previously been in the Yellows' Army, as an officer. He'd been taken prisoner and, like several of them, was given the opportunity to carry on fighting against the Buffs in our army."

"Yeah? The Yellows have ceased to be, haven't they?"

"That's right, they were too small to keep going, they got caught in the middle between two larger armies. Anyway, like I said, he'd been an officer and now he was fighting alongside some of the men and women he used to command, as a common soldier, the lowest of the low. I thought how humiliating that must be for him."

"I guess it was better than staying in the prison camp."

"Even so... fighting alongside soldiers you used to command. I'm not sure many people would have done it. From something he said, I got the impression he found it humiliating, but..."

Ayllom interrupted, "At least this way he still gets paid."

"That's true," Tristan conceded. "He did say something about sending money back to his family. They're in dire need, apparently."

"An' I bet they're not the only ones. There'll be a lot more deaths and maimings in the war before the winter comes. You can quote me on that if you want."

"You're probably right."

"It'll take a lot more than a few fireballs to halt this madness, just you wait and see."

~ End of Chapter 1 ~

Prospects of Peace - Chapter 2

"Good morning, my boy! Ready for another day in the office?"

The speaker was Walter Onstein, manager of the largest sawmill in Thyatira. Now in his fifties, this gentleman, from the ruling black class, had moved there from the Rilesia despotate ten years previously. That was at a time of mass migration to the northernmost region. It coincided with Thyatira's borders expanding at the expense of her neighbours Aggeparii and Bynar. It was seen as a land of opportunity for new blacks and whites alike. Few found disappointment.

The sawmill was owned by Hanson, a local, reclusive man who somewhat defied the usual social structure by being a white of wealth. Mr O, as Onstein liked to be called, was not unduly concerned by this, as long as it gave him a job. He would have liked to have been his own boss, but he did not have the funds to set up in business. These days, after being in the post several years, he was largely left alone to get on with it. That was something he appreciated. The owner trusted him to bring in a profit each year, which he did. Mr O was diligent, thorough and scrupulously honest. He expected to find those qualities in other people.

On this morning, the one following the meteorite, he was addressing his office assistant, Flonass. This white had not been long in the job, but was showing early promise. He had sought out employment following a four year adventure to far off Azekah with his friends Darda and Vophsi. Childless Mr O liked to think of himself as something of a father figure to the former adventurer, but loved to hear tales of daring do when they were not too occupied by business in the office. On this occasion, though, he was wanting to share his experience of the previous night's colourful display.

"Did you see it? The sky to the north?"

"Er, no, I didn't. I went to bed early."

"It was an astonishing spectacle, the whole sky was aglow. I stayed up and watched it with my wife. It faded before dawn. Multi-coloured, it was."

Laying out his writing utensils and opening his ledger, Flonass tried to sound interested as he repeated that he had been abed.

"What a pity! It must have been connected with that bright light going across the sky yesterday, it's too much of a coincidence. But you were safely tucked up in bed, were you? When I was your age, I was up most nights drinking in ale houses..." Then he hesitated before adding in an absent-minded fashion, "Perhaps I should not be telling you that. I would not appreciate such behaviour from yourself. Then you are so much more responsible than I was as a youth."

"You mean leaving home without so much as a by-your-leave and travelling to the other side of the world?"

Mr O roared with laughter, before replying, "Ah, but you returned... and now you are my exemplary employee."

Blushing at the compliment, the exemplary employee buried his head in the ledger and silently got on with his work.

There was a string of people entering the office that morning. They were situated on the first floor and the means of entry was an external wooden staircase. No one could approach then unawares, for several of the runners squeaked when stepped on. Some arrivals were prospective purchasers, one a salesman and another complaining about a delivery. They kept Mr O busy, but he dealt with all the problems in a good-humoured fashion. Come lunchtime, he got Flonass to fix the "Not to be disturbed unless it is an emergency" sign on the door and the pair opened their food boxes and tucked in.

The white was grateful to secure a job with a friendly employer upon his return from Azekah. Onstein himself was equally pleased. Flonass' predecessor, David, was an older man whom he now realised he had taken on against his better judgement. He came from bad stock, a family of troublemakers who lived in the old part of Vionium. David's brother once spent time in gaol for damage to a neighbour's property and David himself possessed a temper. The employer had suspected that the man pilfered from the safe, but was unable to prove it. The miserable human being was given his marching orders for his incompetence rather than his dishonesty, for Mr O had not wanted to provoke retribution in the form of vandalism. All that was in the past now that Flonass was in position.

Nearly every visitor that day mentioned either the fireball, or the night-time pyrotechnics. It was getting a bit monotonous, so Mr O decided to chat about something completely different.

"Tell me about when you crossed the mountain."

It was a tale he had heard from the young man's lips before, but he wanted to hear it again. Flonass was not unhappy to indulge him.

"It was on the way back from Azekah. The three of us picked up a young boy and were taking him home..."

"This side of the mountain?"

"Yes. He knew the pass, so it helped us as well. It turned out to be a perilous enterprise, damn near cost us our lives."

He went on to recount how they edged along the ledge with the snowstorm gathering in intensity, how they sheltered in a shallow cave overnight. Mr O listened avidly, as if he had not heard the tale before. When it was over, he offered some of his own, less exciting experiences.

"I was brought up surrounded by mountains. Mind you, the mountains of Rilesia rarely have snow on them. They do have their own beauty, I believe, on a clear day. Not that there were many of those. The climate is a lot drier here in Thyatira."

"It always amazes me how much the climate can change in a relatively short distance."

"You're right!" Mr O declared enthusiastically. "Rilesia isn't a huge distance from here when you think of it. Its a world away socially as well as climatically. Despot Heisler is not a bad man, but he's not as forward thinking as Despot Thorn. There's more freedom here, it's... it's hard to define; more of a feeling than anything else."

"Have you met Despot Thorn?"

"I can't say I have. I've seen him from a distance."

"My friend Darda's gone to work for him."

"Ah, I think you mentioned something."

"He's up at the Castle, in the guard."

"How's he getting on?"

"Seems to have got off to a good start. *He's* certainly seen Despot Thorn, he works alongside him every day."

"It must be a bit tame after Azekah, I should have thought."

Flonass let out a guffaw, but did not answer. The daily routine of peaceful castle life was a universe away from the siege they had been involved in on the other side of the world. The memories of the desperate fighting were not merely fresh in him mind, they were playing out in his head every single day. The fear, the blood, the

31

physical excursion - these things could not simply be turned off. They would be with him for a long time to come.

Yet he did not object to Mr O bringing up the subject, it was cathartic talking about it. Better that, than bottle up the horrors within him.

Introspection was catching. The manager found himself thinking about a strange incident that had happened the previous winter.

"Have I told you about the strange woman with the torch?"

"No, Mr O, I don't think so."

"It was after we'd closed the operation down at the end of autumn. The snows hadn't begun and I was there after dark finishing off some paperwork. That was when your predecessor was still here..."

Flonass had met the man briefly and knew that he left under a cloud.

"... and I was putting some of his mistakes right. Anyway, I spotted a flaming torch approaching along the road. I thought it most odd at that time of night. As you know, it doesn't lead anywhere, so I figured they must be coming here. Something made me hold back and I blew out my candle and watched from this window. So I had a good view of anyone entering the courtyard. It was a woman and she was by herself. She was well wrapped up against the cold and she was wearing a bonnet. I could tell she was a black, but I didn't recognise her."

"What sort of height was she?"

"Quite tall, but definitely female. Most odd to be carrying a torch rather than a lantern..."

"She came to burn the place down?" asked Flonass. His tone was serious.

"I never got that impression, although her intentions to this day are a mystery to me. I stood mesmerised. It never occurred to me to ask her what her business was. At least it didn't for a long time. I finally got my wits about me, but before I made my move, she turned tail and fled, even quicker than she arrived."

"So you never got to speak to her?"

"I didn't."

"And you haven't seen her since?"

"I have not. The whole thing is a mystery to me."

The truth was that this nocturnal visitor had struck Mr O with her ethereal beauty and he enjoyed the recollection of her features. For him it made the mystery that much more enticing.

His employee certainly enjoyed the tale, although he could shed no light on it. He certainly could not offer an explanation.

"I suppose," concluded Mr O with a warm smile, "it will have to remain an enigma."

As he finished his sentence, they both heard someone beginning the stairs ascent. With a sigh, the manager announced, "Back to work, my boy! Kindly remove the notice from the door."

Leaping up, Flonass did it before the customer got there. It was back to business for sure. Busying himself with his figures, he thought about the conversations they had held that morning.

'I've never spoken half as much with a black in all my life. He's nice; I didn't think I'd ever say that about one of them! If I had to have a black father, it would definitely be Mr O.'

The late summer sun was obscured by clouds as Alan made the last leg of his journey back to Ladosa and the Wesold Front. He stopped briefly on the way to call in and speak with the Hoamen advisors on the southern, Fanallon Front. They exchanged stories of the fireball in the sky a week previously. Unaware that his friend Tristan was nearby, he had not looked him up. It was probably for the best, he must be careful not to blow his countrymen's cover. Besides, with the war in this region about to enter a new phase, there was no time to hang about.

He travelled with some Hoamen soldiers, disguised as Neo-Purple Ladosans, escorting a precious cargo. A gift to their political allies, these were two wagons full of armour-piercing arrows. Made from the finest steel available in Hoame, the tips had been forged by the master blacksmiths of Ephamon. Their effectiveness was guaranteed.

Having been told Marshal Nazaz's whereabouts, he slipped casually off the wagon and, heaving his large rucksack with one hand, gave the soldiers a wave goodbye with the other. It was but a short walk from the main road to the training camp she was inspecting that morning.

There was a slight twinge in his back as he adjusted the rucksack. At thirty-nine, his athletic body needed more maintenance to keep in tip-top condition than it had a few years previously. An early riser, he endured a punishing fitness programme each morning. He knew that his reactions were not as lightning fast as they were a decade ago. In combat this was compensated for by guile and moves perfected through experience. There would come a day when he would have to retire from frontline participation. That would be a sad one for him. For Alan still enjoyed the thrill of pitting himself against an opponent with sword and shield.

The trees lining the route were dripping rain from a downpour the night before. The occasional gust of wind brought more droplets down. There were puddles to be avoided along the track too. It was not possible to tell how deep some of the watery potholes might be.

Coming up fast on the camp, he noticed the marshal on a grassy patch, facing the other way. She was talking to a group of training instructors, half of whom both she and Alan knew were Hoamen incognito.

As he got close, several pairs of eyes looked up. Charlotta turned and, upon seeing who it was, her face broke into an enormous smile. In fact it was so extreme that he wondered if it signified relief at his return. Was there a crisis on? But everyone seemed relaxed.

So his opening words were, "Is everything okay?"

"Yes, of course," she replied, her smile not diminishing. She took a step closer to him before retreating once again. "I was obtaining an update on the training schedule," Charlotta explained as she became more businesslike. "It continues to be good news." Her respondent giving an encouraging nod, she expanded. "Up until a week ago we continued to get a steady stream of volunteers for the cause. These trainers are doing a fine job in preparing them for the rigours ahead and the supply of fresh blood is keeping us all busy."

"Up until a week ago?"

"The falling star."

"Ah, of course. We saw it go over and a white light over the horizon. What was it like here?"

That evening that Alan got his question answered. The marshal was currently billeted in a country house not too far from the frontline. There was a room reserved for the chief Hoame advisor and he had dumped his things in there before joining the others for supper. Come the evening, he was alone with Charlotta in her small, private lounge. Over a glass of wine, they exchanged notes on their varied experiences of the superbolide.

"For a short time it was as bright as the sun," said Alan, "but it moved across the sky quite quickly."

"You didn't experience an aftershock?"

"We briefly saw a bright light on the horizon, that's all."

Charlotta then advised in detail her own experience in the hut. Alan was amazed. She continued, "We're getting conflicting reports, but whatever it was, and most folk here are calling it a shooting star, it looked well northeast of here. Indeed it seems to be beyond Braskaton and Lefange."

"In the central Buff region?"

"That's right. Reports are sketchy and confused, but some are wild in the extreme."

"Like what?"

"Talking of unbelievable destruction. It's hard to know what credence to give them. It's noticeable that recruits have stopped feeding in from the north all of a sudden. I'm sure it's to do with the same thing."

"If the wind was strong enough to demolish huts and knock people off their feet where you are, it must have had even greater effect where it fell."

"Mmm. Our patrols north are showing signs of widespread damage, but I've warned them not to venture too far. I am reducing our presence to the north, anyway, as we'll need as many troops as possible for the up-and-coming offensive."

"You're still going with my idea for the investing of Wesold?"

Charlotta shuffled in the large, easy chair she was perching on the end of. It was not a comfortable-looking position. Her answer came, "Your idea has been fully sold to my field commanders. Intelligence reports since you left tell us that the Rose Army has been keeping the Buffs occupied. I've no love of the Roses, but they're doing us a favour right now. We're being careful to do our build-up out of sight of the enemy. If the Buffs are distracted, then our attack should have an element of surprise."

"Yeah. Given what I've seen today, I suspect they're unaware of our current strength."

"That's right, Alan!" she replied eagerly, moving across to the settee he was on. "We lost a lot of good people in those battles, but not as many as the enemy. We've been able to replace our losses, but as far as we can tell, they have been weakened."

"Good. The element of surprise will be a huge help if we can secure it."

"Yes."

"But I got the impression that your southern commanders are expecting to go the offence there too pretty soon."

"They're eager, it's true, but it'll have to wait a bit. Wesold is top priority; any southern offensive will come afterwards."

Alan was pleased at all this positivity. They experienced desperate times during the summer's Wesold battles. Victory had hung in the balance, but eventually the Buffs recoiled from the bloody nose inflicted on them. The Neo-Purples now wanted the tide to turn fully against their enemies.

"Logistics are key," Alan warned, "All these extra troops need feeding, for example."

"Don't I know it! Frontline soldiers consume food like nobody's business. We're having to source more of it from our heartland. Sacrifices are having to be made there."

As she spoke, her hand moved across to land on his. Maybe military logistics is not the most romantic of topics during which to make one's move, but Alan's hand darted back as if he had been bitten by a frass. As a drone, he had a lifetime's conditioning. It told him in no uncertain terms that he must have no dealings with the opposite sex. It was one of Hoame's strongest taboos. Yet now he felt guilty at his reaction. This woman was pleasant both in looks and personality, but it never entered his mind to consider her as anything but an allied military commander. Before he knew what he was doing, he reached out and took her retreating hand in his.

Charlotta did not have time to react to his initial recoil before his subsequent compensation meant they were holding hands together. Her heart beat quickly, it felt good to have his touch. All talk was over. Now was the time to move forward for a kiss.

A sudden knock at the door shattered the tension. Who would be calling at this hour? Was there an attack at the front?

Struggling to get the words out, the marshal told the messenger to come in. She was standing by the time the man entered and Alan's hands were firmly in his lap.

"I'm sorry to disturb you so late, Marshal, but Captain Hallazanad thought that you and Chief Advisor Alan would want to have these papers now."

"Papers?" she enquired, taking the folder.

"I understand it is the training schedule, a revised version."

"Very well," Charlotta replied, before dismissing the man.

Any possible atmosphere in the room was long gone. The man she desired had moved to an upright chair by the table. In a businesslike manner she asked him, "Shall we go through this now, or in the morning?"

Either way, there would be no more hand-holding that evening.

Heavy dews wet the tired-looking grass surrounding Thyatira's Castle. It was late summer and the dampness took longer to clear each day. The days were getting cooler and the nights beginning to draw in.

Three weeks had gone since the superbolide lit up the sky. The event was all but forgotten this side of the mountains. In the first few nights after the event, the northern sky was aglow with pretty lights. However, these soon faded, as did people's memories as they got on with their busy lives.

The Despot, though, knew that parts of Ladosa were devastated by the explosion and resulting shockwave. Information coming across the border from his right-hand man, Alan, and a few Ladosan traders, gave a uniform, if somewhat incomplete picture. He was receiving these accounts third-hand, for no one directly involved near the epicentre had turned up. Maybe anyone remotely close had been killed by the explosion. The reports spoke of widespread destruction in the northeast of the country. Whether it landed in the central Buff region, or beyond its furthest border, was unclear. Some said one, some the other. Either way, there was consistency with regards to their capital, Braskaton, having been hit hard.

Of primary concern to Frank was the effect on the civil war raging over there. Alan's despatch spoke of continued preparations for an offensive action. So there appeared to be no change in the southwest of the country. It was hard to believe there would be no repercussions nearer ground zero. He reasoned that the consequences for the central Buff area would be severe, but there was no hard information on that. And what of the northeast tribes? Alan had only just told him of the mustering of this new force, supposedly backed by a foreign power in the form of Oonimari, when the extraterrestrial body struck. Had this fresh player been able to muster themselves again? Were the Buffs gathering to repulse them? No one coming across from that troubled land seemed to have the answers to these questions.

Nevertheless, he felt that a communication to Hoame's ruling body, the Inner Council, was very much in order. Sitting alone in the Throne Room, off the Castle's hall, he bent over the table as he penned a newsletter to his fellow Keepers.

Eighteen years had passed since Frank first arrived on the planet. It was not long after that when he encountered his first Keepers. Count Zastein and Baron Schail had both passed away in the intervening period, but struck fear into the traveller's heart at that primary meeting. How ironic, therefore, that he himself was now a member of the same Inner Council. Not just any member either, but seen as the most powerful and influential one who manoeuvred his own men into position in the Citadel. Count Wonstein could be a thorn in his side with persistent criticisms. In reality, that man's power was limited, with most men in the august body firmly in Frank's camp. He had proved himself by decisive action in the past on more than one occasion and was seen by them as their best hope.

It was a major anomaly that Thyatira's despot held a dual role as Member of the Inner Council, it was a unique situation. He was spending an increasing amount of time in Thyatira, his trips to the Capital being rarer these days. With autumn fast approaching, he was not in the mood to attend any more meetings that year. It would be music to Hannah's ears, for she did not like it when he was away in Asattan. He felt there was no need, with matters quiet in the Citadel. He was better positioned where he was in Thyatira to keep an eye on events across the Ladosan border.

Hoame was actively, if clandestinely, supporting the Neo-Purples, one of the many factions involved in the civil war. He hoped they were backing a winner. While the help amounted to weapons, trainers and advisors at this stage, there was always a danger they might get sucked into the conflict.

Meanwhile, the despotate was home to something like five hundred refugees from the conflict. Made up of women, children, plus a few elderly men, these were confined to a specially built camp east of the Castle and no more were being allowed across the border. To Frank's mind, they represented a further complication in an already delicate situation. He looked forward to the day when they could be sent back.

His report on the meteorite was on the vague side, because the intelligence had been sketchy. He still felt it worthwhile to tell the Keepers what he knew. Once completed, he shouted, "Guard!" and almost immediately Squad Leader Darda appeared.

"Get a messenger to send this to the Inner Council," Frank commanded, handing over the sealed tube.

"At once, My Lord!" the soldier barked, before asking more quietly, "by superdakk?"

"No, thanks, an ordinary one will do."

"Yes, My Lord."

Darda was not long been in the post and still finding his feet. He had arrived back in Thyatira a few weeks before the superbolide incident and been given the job by the Despot himself. Prior to that he had been a member of a trio of whites returning from far off Azekah, the others being Flonass at the sawmill and Vophsi, now employed as a chef at the Selerm.

Castle life was taking some adjusting to for Darda. He found it an uphill struggle to gain the respect of the soldiers under him, most of whom were far senior to him in age. The fact that he had been an officer in an army on the other side of the world cut no ice with them. His guardsmen were either not interested in his tales, or simply resentful of having someone so young over them. He was trying to learn to be more circumspect. This did not come naturally to Darda, who was a joker by disposition.

On the positive side, the one Castle resident he had won over completely was the Despot himself. For some reason, he took a shine to the new recruit. Darda reckoned that if there was but one person on his side, he could do a lot worse than it be the man in charge. He hoped that he would win the others over in time.

Stepping back into the Throne room after delegating the message to one of the men in his squad, he asked, "Was there anything else, My Lord?"

Pausing for a moment before answering, Frank eventually asked, "Are you busy right now, Darda?"

"Um, no, My Lord."

It was true. The day was going slowly for both of them.

"Come in and sit down for a while."

The new squad leader did as he was told, sitting across the table from the most powerful man in Hoame. What had he done wrong? What had he heard?

"How are things going? How are you getting on here at the Castle?"

"Okay," came the wary answer.

"I expect it'll take a while for you to settle in."

"Yes, My Lord," Darda replied, still expecting the conversation to take a turn for the worse. He was convinced that Captain of the Castle Guard, Jonathan, resented him. Maybe words had been said.

"Good," continued Frank, still sounding genial. "Something you said to me when we first met... when you were in Azekah you got presented with some medals. Is that correct?"

"It is, My Lord."

"For bravery?"

"Yes," confirmed Darda, trying to sound modest.

"Tell me a bit more, I'm interested."

He certainly sounded curious, so the former crusader recounted some of what happened on the battlefields of Azekah. The Despot certainly enjoyed the last tale.

"You mean you went through the enemy camp naked?" he asked for confirmation, his tone a mixture of incredulity and amusement.

"Yes, My Lord. As I said, it was a night time operation..."

"This was before you were made an officer?"

"It was."

"Go on."

"We penetrated deep behind enemy lines on a reconnaissance mission. We discovered that the enemy was preparing for an assault on the city. It was essential to get this information back, but I found myself alone and on the wrong side of a river. I couldn't find a boat, so I had to wade across. I took off all my clothes except my underwear, but I kept my sword, of course."

Frank laughed; this young man was a breath of fresh air and his stories amusing in their absurdity. He stopped to say, "And they gave you a medal for that action."

"They did, My Lord, we were able to make a pre-emptive strike to neutralise the danger."

"I hope they allowed you to get dressed before trying to pin the medal on you."

Blushing, Darda was about to reply when there was a knock on the door.

"Come!" the Despot cried, unnecessarily loud. In stepped Captain Jonathan, frowning at the sight of his new, immature squad leader sitting and having a laugh and a joke with their ruler. Collecting himself, and concentrating his stare on Frank, he said, "I have the duty rota for the next two weeks to show you, My Lord, unless you are too busy..."

"Of course not, come in. Thank you, Darda," he added, his face still a picture of amusement.

"My Lord," Darda mumbled and shot out of the room double quick.

"Take a seat, Jonathan. Show me what you've got."

The following day was a fine one and Darda was with his men outside in the Castle bailey. Training often took place in the area outside the stables and a short distance from the new kitchen block. A new design of helmet was being issued to the Castle Guard and he and his men were to try them out.

Darda was first and he inspected the equipment. Conical on top, to deflect sword blows, it had an inner, flat top to help protect the wearer against a mace.

He put it on at an angle at first and a couple of his men began tittering. With barely a thought, he decided to play for laughs and turned his helmet completely sideways and began marching up and down. The men were much amused, but enough was enough and, after a short while, he put it on properly and the training session commenced. By the end, Darda felt it had gone well, unaware as he was of a certain observer.

"Darda, a word!" commanded Captain Jonathan as the squad leader entered the hall for lunch.

Led away to a quiet corner as the long tables filled up, Darda did not have to wait long to find out what this was all about.

"I watched your antics in the bailey. That is not the way for a squad leader to behave! You'll never get the men's respect by playing the fool. They were laughing *at* you, not with you. They might do that sort of thing in your mythical Azekah, but you're in a real army now. If I got my way, I'd replace you with a more suitable man."

Jonathan went on in similar vein for a while. It both shocked and hurt Darda and showed the depth of the captain's loathing for him. He realised that he had been trying too hard to be liked, and maybe

41

he was going about things the wrong way, but need Jonathan be quite so cruel? Tail between his legs, and close to tears, he slunk to the end of a table and ate his meal by himself. He wanted to succeed in this role, but he would have to try a different way.

The captain would indeed have liked to have him replaced, but, for some strange reason, the Despot had taken a shine to the young officer recruit. While that lasted, his hands were tied.

Meanwhile, the Despot himself was upstairs alone in his sitting room. On this occasion, he was leafing through his big, old Bible, thinking more about the book itself rather than its contents. After leaving the planet Eden, selling rare, collectable books provided his means of travelling between the stars. Rich bibliophiles were prepared to pay handsomely for the volumes he took with him in a special container with its own anti-grav unit. What a world away it was from this primitive backwater. Yet he was settled and happy here and he did not miss the civilized universe at all.

His musings were cut short by his wife entering the room. She had a purposeful air about her and, sure enough, there was something on her mind.

"I've been thinking," she began, then paused. He considered a witty response at this point, but instead waited for her to continue. "About the Castle Complex, it's quite a size now."

This was true. When he first arrived in Thyatira, the Castle stood majestically alone. Once the senate building was constructed, a few hundred metres outside the walls, private dwellings soon began springing up nearby. At first it was an exclusive area for wealthy black families, the senators and others. The place soon began expanding along the road to Vionium. Houses for whites, shops, a couple of schools, a small factory and other workshops, it was already a small town in all but name. This was Hannah's exact point.

"Where did the term 'Castle Complex' come from?"

He husband thought for a moment. He had no idea and admitted as much.

"No, nobody does. Someone coined it and somehow it stuck. It might have suited in the early days, but not now we have a proto-town on our doorstep. I don't mind it being there, most of my friends live there and are handy to get to. I was discussing it with Klara the other day and she agreed that the current name hardly does the place justice."

"Did she have any suggestions?"

"No, but I've been giving it some thought. It's not a radical idea at all, a mere slight alteration, but I think 'Castletown' gives it gravitas and heralds the coming-of-age of the place."

"Or... maybe we could simplify it to 'Castleton.' It rolls off the tongue better."

"I agree!" said Hannah, before trying it out for herself, "Castleton."

"All right. I'll announce it at the next senate meeting, later this week..."

"Good."

"And I'll make any usage of the old term punishable by death."

Hannah gave him a look; it was a strange sort of joke to make. Seeing as he had but recently abolished the death penalty in Thyatira, the single despotate to do so, she was sure it *was* a joke, even if an odd one. She let it go and brought up the second thing on her mind.

"I've decided to recommence work on my garden."

"The herb garden?"

"And other things. I want it to look good, a real splash of colour in the spring and summer. We'll have the best possible view from here in the Castle. So it'll serve a practical purpose and be pleasing to the eye at the same time."

A traditional Ladosan mixed garden, she had overseen the project with enthusiasm. Until, that is, the news came through that Frank had been kidnapped. It knocked her sideways and put her right off the garden idea. Beside herself with worry, at the same time she was determined to get her husband back unharmed. Fortunately she was successful in that, thanks to the Thyatiran and Bynar armies. Despot Lovonski of the neighbouring despotate, where the crime had been committed, proved a big help. Then he was under an obligation. It was Vanda Hista, insane daughter of the previous despot, who was behind the plot. Fortunately she was safely locked away again and the kidnapped man freed.

For Frank, the scars were not so much physical as mental. He had needed to talk, but there were few people he could confide in. Abbot Muggawagga was such a man. His wisdom and discretion had helped a great deal the last few weeks and Frank was starting to feel that he was finally recovering from the ordeal. The fact that Hannah was wanting to recommence her gardening project told him that his wife was getting over it too.

The following two days it rained solidly and there was no question of gardening in these conditions. Frank was inside the hall, never the brightest of rooms, even with freshly decorated walls. With leaden skies over head, it seemed as dark as midwinter in there.

He noticed Darda helping out by taking a supply of fresh candles through to the adjoining chapel. The young man had appeared melancholy earlier in the morning, so Frank decided to follow him in and engage him in conversation. It was a quieter than normal day and he had nothing pressing.

"Oh!" Darda jumped upon turning round after depositing his load.

"Helping with a delivery," observed the Despot, for want of a better way to start a conversation.

"Yes, My Lord."

Turning his head as he sought for something to say, he spotted the tapestry that hung on the wall. With its busy scene of men on dakks and various animals in a woodland setting, its title was clear to see: *The Hunting of the Lagua.* Pointing up to it, he asked, "Do you like it? There seems to be a lot going on in it."

"Yes, My Lord," Darda felt obliged to say, but then he added, "although the lagua doesn't actually look like that."

"Ah yes! I was forgetting you actually encountered one on your way back from Azekah."

"I did, My Lord. Well, all three of us did."

"In the report I heard it was you who actually killed the beast and severed its paw."

His tone was of someone impressed by such a deed. Frank was neither scoffing, nor sceptical.

"I didn't actually kill it. It was still alive when it sped off. A lucky swing of my sword did cut off the paw, though, that's true."

Frank liked his modesty, saying, "And is it true that you brought the paw back with you?"

"I did, My Lord. I smoked it first, to preserve it, but I did bring it home..."

"As proof."

"As a trophy, I guess. I'd never met anyone who'd seen one before and thought folk might find it interesting."

44

"I bet!"

"I've been offered a lot of money for it, but I'd never sell it."

"Hmm... where is it now?"

"Back home, My Lord."

"I'd be interested in seeing it."

"Oh, of course."

"But don't go especially. But next time you visit your parents, Vionium isn't it?"

"It is, My Lord."

"Well, next time you're there, if you don't mind and if it's not too much trouble, I'd like you to bring it up here for me to have a look."

"Of course, My Lord, I'll do that."

A few days later, Bishop Gunter was in his magnificent house, saying goodbye to Esther, his wife. She was going out for the day with a couple of friends to do charitable good works in Sardis. He was checking she had everything.

"And the leaflets?"

"Safely packed."

"Sufficient food?"

"The servants are seeing to that, I don't think we'll be going hungry."

"And you're taking the covered wagon? It looks like rain again."

"Yes, dear, it's sitting outside all ready."

"Good."

They said their farewells. She would only be gone a day and a half, but it was still a major enterprise for Esther to lead such an expedition. Gunter was confident that his popular wife would make a good job of it.

He looked up at the sky. Sunny first thing, but the orb was well hidden now and dark storm clouds were gathering quickly. The weather had been changeable the last few days as the season moved from summer into autumn. Nature did not wish to mark the transition quietly.

Soon his guests arrived for a scheduled meeting. Gabriell and Isaac were new priests to Thyatira, but both doing well. There had been a shortage of ordained ministers in the region and the pair were among the new ones coming online.

Gabriell, at forty-four the oldest of the new intake, was formally an established priest in his old despotate of Reichmenn. He chose to move to Thyatira for a multitude of reasons, a new beginning being the major one. Since arriving, he had taken an interest in the refugee camp for displaced Ladosan women and children. Now he ran a church for the poor whites in the newly renamed Castleton.

Meanwhile Isaac, at twenty-four a mere four years younger than the youthful, but experienced bishop, had taken a different route. He could also point to experience helping out at the refugee camp. Most of his time was taken up at his curacy in Setty, the town he grew up in. He had been in the post since the spring and was finding it challenging and rewarding in equal measure. The old priest there had begun by telling Isaac that he was never going to please all the people all of the time. Those words of wisdom were a great help to him when faced with criticism. He realised that it came with the territory. For the most part, things were good and he was enjoying the role. He had recently been involved in the huge celebration service to mark the safe return of the Despot following his kidnapping.

The bishop had a lot of people to see. He wanted to find out how things were going with these two individuals, then have a discussion with them both together. They knew each other and previously cooperated in the Church's mission to the refugee camp.

A report on Isaac's progress from his incumbent priest in Setty was highly complimentary. So Gunter's job was an enjoyable one in telling him he was doing well and to keep up the good work. Gabriell's interview was altogether different. It was more a matter of hearing how the new mission to the Castleton white community was going. The bishop's house was up the exclusive end, near the senate building and Castle. He felt that he did not know the poorer, white end as well as he should.

For the Church of Hoame was at the forefront of the social revolution going on in the country. For centuries, ever since the first settlement, the whites had been the despised underclass, lorded over by the blacks. Historically, the vast majority of whites followed the Christian faith, while their counterparts did not. Frank, first as the sole Christian despot and then as the most influential Inner Council member, sought to improve the lot of the whites. To some observers' amazement, he managed to take most of the Keepers along with him and certain antidiscrimination laws were passed. Hoame, with its federal constitution, found many of the despots slow to exact the legislation. Some ignored it altogether. Nevertheless, progress was being made and a token white Keeper, Count Bodstein, originally from Frank's Thyatiran despotate, was the most high profile member of his caste. He represented something for them to strive for.

In recent years there had been a surge in blacks becoming Christians. It was certainly not a universal phenomenon within the country, but in some black circles it was quite a trendy thing. Not all whites welcomed the development, but most Church leaders were wise enough to know that the first shall be last and the last first, and to welcome it.

It was hardly surprising that Thyatira, still with the sole Christian despot, was at the forefront of these changes. Nevertheless, Frank was sensible enough to ensure the pace of change did not get out of hand. If managed properly, people would get used to the new order of things and a counter-reformation avoided. So, for example, the Thyatiran senate's constitution was biased two to one in the blacks' favour.

One unintentional result in that northernmost region of the country was separate white and black congregations. Neither the bishop, nor Despot, felt this was desirable, but were loath to enforce compulsory mixing. Birds of a feather would always flock together . Many new black Christians would have baulked at the idea of having to sit alongside their white brothers and sisters in Christ. Frank had reminded the ecclesiarch that Rome was not built in a day.

Gunter, a former missionary to Rabeth-Mephar and chaplain to the Mehtar himself, was now, as a black Christian, fully committed to the Thyatiran Church as a whole. He bore in mind Jesus' words that he who would be the greatest must be the servant of all. He wanted both communities catered for equally and earnestly sought to expunge any latent prejudice within himself. Here he was, trying to learn about a white church from a white priest and finding it most informative.

"Bringing folk together is a real challenge," Gabriell told him. "The entire set-up is new. Fresh buildings are going up every week in that part of town. The school mistress is from Lowdebar, the butcher has relocated from Vionium. A good proportion of my congregation has migrated from other parts of the country in the past couple of years or so. We're working hard to get a community spirit going."

"I see."

"And many of them are poor. The subsidies you have allowed me have proved essential, but I must ask that they continue for the time being. We are not able to stand on our own two feet yet."

"Are you getting enough assistance?"

"The recent introduction of two lay ministers has eased my burden and is proving a big help. Not having to preach so much myself, I can concentrate on other things. I will want to go back to it; indeed I do keep my hand in, but it is good to have this aid while I am establishing other things, such as the after school Bible club."

"And is their preaching up to standard?"

"It is."

"Did you hear them last Sabbath?"

"I did, but I'd looked at their text beforehand. I make it a point of principle only to critique a sermon prior to it being delivered. It does not seem right to pull apart something that has already been offered to God."

This was a new way of looking at it to Gunter. He would defer to the more experienced priest. Their discussion on Gabriell's church was concluded soon after this. Then Isaac, who had been enjoying perusing the bishop's modest library, was called back in and the three of them discussed the Ladosan refugee camp.

To a background of a thunderstorm passing overhead. Gunter said, "As far as we are aware, the celestial object dropping on the Ladosans has not cooled their ardour for war. The fighting continues. We must expect the refugees to still be with us for some time."

"Another winter, then?" asked Gabriell.

"Yes. It can't be a pleasant existence cooped up within what is for them a foreign land."

Isaac offered, "They are improvising with fresh diversions. I know for a fact that a drama group has been set up, plus there is a poetry club. The foreigners are proving quite civilized."

"They must miss their menfolk," stated Gabriell.

"I think they value their safety more than anything else."

"They know they're free to leave us at any time."

The younger priest replied, "I visited Honey yesterday. Her attitude was that she was grateful at not being forced back into Ladosa."

"Some folk around here would like to see that happen!"

"I know."

At this point, the bishop stepped in, telling them that he had managed to have a brief discussion with the Despot on the subject recently. "He said that the refugees are a drain on our resources and he is pleased that the decision was made to cap the numbers allowed in. However, I have convinced him how meritorious it is, us maintaining the camp. I am as confident as I can be that there will be no forced repatriation whilst the conflict across the border continues."

As he spoke, the thunderstorm was moving away. The rumbles of thunder were getting fewer and farther between, whilst their intensity waned. The rain stopped and the sun burst through once more.

~ End of Chapter 2 ~

Prospects of Peace - Chapter 3

Bishop Gunter's predecessor now lived in the Ladosan town of Isson with his family. Eleazar much preferred the role of parish priest and was grateful for the change. Apart from anything else, relations with his wife, Auraura, were much improved. The job still had its stresses, but he felt more at home than he had as a bishop, even in this foreign land.

A few weeks had passed since the shockwave hit the town. Most of the cleaning up operations were concluded. Twenty-seven people had lost their lives and over three hundred injured, but it could have been so much worse. Isson's elevated position, and the presence of a large wood to the north had reduced the blow. Nevertheless, several buildings were flattened, while others lost their roofs.

One of the casualties was Church benefactress, Quinty. The top floor of her house had been completely sheered off and the poor lady killed in the process. Her body was discovered amongst the debris. Once the rubble was cleared, the remaining ground floor structure was found to be in surprisingly good condition. The new owners, whoever they were, could use it as the basis of a fresh building.

Before the war, Isson felt divided between the "haves" and "have-nots." Eleazar's mission to the poor was helping to dilute that feeling, while the conflict had certainly brought the two communities closer together. People who would never have dreamed of socialising now found themselves side by side, manning the barriers on the approach road.

The impact of the superbolide barely touched the southern, poorer area. It was almost completely confined to the richer area as the air wave appeared to have hit that before passing over the rest of the town. In the days and weeks following the disaster, the citizens' lives were taken up with funerals, clearance and re-building. Little time was available for considering the impact on the rest of the country.

Intercourse with the nearby capital city Braskaton was discouraged. It was a good fortnight before reports began filtering through from there. Established in the lowlands and without anything to shield it from the blast, tales came through of destruction on a colossal scale.

In fact the rumours were so extreme that they were met with disbelief. No Lowland traders came up the road since the impact, merely a few dazed Isson residents returning home. For all they were aware, the war in this part of the country had been snuffed out.

"'Tis an ill wind that blows no one any good," was the verdict of one of Eleazar's parishioners.

"You're right," he replied, "but I've got to go right now."

"Go?"

"I've been summonsed. Zebulon has asked to see me."

It was with some trepidation that he made his way towards the mother church in the northern part of town. With Quinty's demise, he was beholden to them for his living. The poor folk at his preferred, southern church could in no way finance his ministry. When he had first arrived, Zebulon made it plain that they could not afford an extra priest on their books. Yet his salary continued to be paid since the disaster. Eleazar weighed the odds as he approached St Mary's, but he knew speculation was useless. Surely he should be praying about it.

Scaffolding surrounded one end of the church while workmen constructed a fresh wooden steeple for the one blown off. The missing roof tiles had already been replaced. They were making quick progress with the restoration.

"Ah, Eleazar! Thank you for coming up," came the warm greeting. "Take a seat." As the Hoaman did as he was bid, the elderly priest continued, "Firstly, I was wondering if you could take the evening Eucharist this coming Sabbath. Laurence and I find ourselves otherwise engaged."

"Yes, of course," he replied eagerly; this was an opportunity to show cooperation.

They discussed a few technicalities surrounding the service before Zebulon brought up the key subject.

"We were all upset about Quinty's death. I thought Laurence did a good job with the funeral... such a good turnout too."

"Indeed."

"It turns out that she has left all her considerable fortune to the church."

"Oh," went Eleazar in the silence that followed, he was not sure what to say.

Then, putting the younger man out of his misery, Zebulon continued, "So we can continue to finance your mission to the poorer quarter..."

"Thank you. Thank you so much!"

"... because it's what she would have wanted."

The recipient of this news was greatly relieved, for it meant his future was secure, or as secure as anyone's could be in these uncertain times.

"Thanks again."

"You work harder than anyone, Eleazar, dividing your time between the two church communities. Don't think that it is either unnoticed, or unappreciated. I will continue with the same amount you've been handed the past few weeks, but if you need an extra amount for any particular project, don't hesitate to come and speak to me."

It was apparent that the church was going to keep a firm control, but it was still good news. There was more.

"Quinty's place has been cleared and, as you know, the remains have been found to be structurally sound. If we can rebuild it, we can have a facility and grounds for the church's use. This conflict cannot go on for ever, indeed the fireball may have knocked the stuffing out of the warmongers. I sincerely hope so."

"Would you use it to house refugees from the fighting?"

The suggestion was met with a frown. "No, I had other plans." Just then some loud banging from the steeple restoration began. The man continued, "I see it more as a centre to hold conferences. Church leaders from all around can meet to discuss the issues of the day. There will be a lot of reconstruction to do once all this nonsense is over. I mean peoples' lives, not merely buildings. Quinty's legacy will be something tangible and worthwhile. Her spirit of generosity will live on and be a force for good in Isson and also the surrounding area. In these dark days we need something positive, Eleazar. We must not succumb to negative thinking. The gospel is good news indeed and the population need good news more than ever."

"Amen to that," Eleazar replied with a smile.

Frank was in upbeat mood as he waited for the last few senators to join him in the chamber for the weekly meeting. The one seven days earlier had been cancelled due to the superbolide. The Despot was far too taken up with the possible repercussions of it to discuss other things. In the event, the phenomenon did not seem to be affecting Hoame at all, but at least he could concentrate on other matters now.

Most pressing was the purchase of a large tract of land belonging to the neighbouring despotate of Aggeparii. Even as the celestial body fell from the sky, Thyatira's chief negotiator, Senator Emil Vebber, had been breaking the news: Despot Kagel had accepted their eighteen grend counter-offer. It was the top item on the agenda and Frank was not alone in being excited about it.

"I will need to do a survey of what industry there is in the new land," said Cragoop. "I know that Emil's initial report touched on this, but we must have a breakdown of exactly what's what."

Karl's high-pitched voice was heard to add, "And I need to look into the defence implications. What army will we get? And equipment. Are there any castles in the new area? It will make our border a whole lot longer."

"We need a breakdown of the population there," another senator said.

Emil indicated to the Despot that he would like to have the floor. This was granted and the general hubbub died down as the others listened.

"Firstly, I think it will help if we have a name for the new tract that is soon to become ours. I'm told that the northern area of Aggeparii is often referred to as 'Norland' and I suggest that, for the sake of ease, we adopt this term for the entire piece of land that we are to purchase."

"Norland," the Despot tried it on his tongue before giving a nod of approval.

"Yes, My Lord."

"Very well."

"And while I don't disagree one bit with all the things being said in this room, I would advise that our top priority is that we send off the payment for the land as soon as possible."

"Before Despot Kagel changes his mind, you mean."

"Exactly that. I have his sealed note, but even so I will not sleep easy until the gold is transferred and the deal unequivocally completed."

"Very well."

53

"If we set about it, we can have the eighteen grend on the road before the end of the week."

"Phew!" Saul exclaimed, "it is a monstrous sum of money."

"It still represents a good deal," Emil promised him. "There will be a lot of hard work ahead of us. If the last expansion is anything to go by, then the work will be measured in years."

Frank stepped in with, "The first step will be to get the money convoy safely to Aggeparii City, then mark the new border actually on the ground."

"Yes, My Lord."

"We must make sure that their surveyor is present as well as ours. I want no dispute further down the line. Once it has been agreed, we can get the chain gangs to mark it with an earthen bank."

"Certainly."

"As for the gold, please liaise with Karl here, and General Japhses, about a suitable guard to travel with the convoy."

"I can organise that," Senator Vondant assured them, "we will take a large force in the circumstances."

"Good. And have you drawn any preliminary conclusions, Karl, regarding the defence implications of Norland?"

"I have a few initial thoughts, yes, My Lord. As you know, as well as the northern strip taking in the large towns, we..."

Interrupting him, Frank turned to Emil and said, "Remind me, remind us of the names of the major towns in the new... in Norland."

"Newton, Carnis and Felsham, My Lord."

"Hmm... sorry, Karl, please continue."

"Thank you, My Lord. As well as the northern tract containing those three towns, there is the western band of land. Almost as big in size, it is sparsely populated with no proper towns. In the event of a war, it would simply be impractical to defend that area. It would spread our army too thinly and lead us open to having our forces cut in two. The single practical way is to defend our existing Thyatiran borders plus the northern strip."

"Very well, that sounds sensible. We can discuss contingency plans further with General Japhses at a later date. There is currently no tangible threat either from the south, or the southwest, of course. Thank you for your thoughts, nevertheless."

Senator Trepte then asked if he could accompany Cragoop on the latter's fact-finding trip. "It makes sense to consider the trade implications for Thyatira, both within our borders and without, alongside seeing what this Norland actually produces."

"Of course," Frank agreed. "There will be plenty of work for all of us. For instance you, Hanz, will have to look into their justice system."

"Yes, m..." the senator cleared his throat before starting again. "Yes, My Lord, although I imagine they will be identical to the previous land we took from the Aggepariians several years back. As I recollect, we got several good ideas from them rather than the other way round."

"Ah, yes."

"But naturally I shall look into it and report back accordingly. The constables are sufficiently well organised to take over this Norland, I'm sure."

The Norland discussion continued for some considerable time, there were so many different facets to consider. Yet they had taken over other towns in the not too distant past. There was a general mood of optimism that they could cope with this new expansion. In fact the excitement in the room was palpable. It was the beginning of a new era for Thyatira; the region would be bigger and more prestigious than ever. Despot Kagel's profligacy would help their own status no end.

There were not many other items on the agenda which could not be put back a week, but Frank let Saul have his say about a pet project of his. The elderly, dour white's deep tones resounded in the chamber.

"Work has commenced on the new hospital building in Sardis. I have previously shown you the plans and it should be a fine facility once it has been completed. Extra medical staff are already being trained. The new building will give them a good base to work from."

"Well done," Cragoop led the congratulations. "We all know how hard you have campaigned for this to come about. Although it does raise the matter of medical provision in Castleton." He paused, pleased with himself for using the new term. "We all know how the place has got bigger, but it will soon need a hospital of its own."

The Despot perked up. "Really? That's interesting. Well, I think that is something you should look into, Cragoop. Well done for raising the issue."

55

The white looked across the table at the experienced Karl, who was smiling. They both knew that Cragoop had talked himself into an extra job.

Eleazar was not the sole person on Molten benefiting from a bequest. Flonass' manager, Mr Onstein, was also the beneficiary of one. He came into the office one morning with a broad grin on his face. Who better to share his good news with but his favourite employee?

"My late aunt left me a good sum. The poor old girl struggled for a long time; her death came as a merciful release. I knew she was quite fond of me, but it was still a surprise when I heard she'd left the bulk of her fortune to me."

Flonass was surprised at such candour. Did Mr O have no one else to share these details with? The black continued.

"Hanson has a buyer lined up for the mill, a Ma'hol would you believe?"

This was certainly news to the white, he had no idea that the owner was wanting to sell. He was shocked at the prospect of a foreigner coming in. What was the world coming to?

Continuing his thread, Mr O went on, "I must ask you to keep that under your hat; it's not general knowledge. I can't see the men being happy about it. I'm not sure I'd want to stay on. I wouldn't have to..."

"Oh!" went his assistant, involuntarily, for he was growing to like his manager.

"Don't you fret, my boy, I'm going to see if I can do something bout it."

It took several days to set up a meeting with the elusive Hanson, but eventually Mr O found himself closing in on his stockade in the old part of Vionium. Approaching with trepidation, he considered the matter. Usually for a meeting between a black and a white it would be the latter at a disadvantage, but there was nothing usual about Hanson. A white landowner with an extensive portfolio of properties was unique in Mr O's experience. He had never heard of such a thing either here in Thyatira, nor in Rilesia where he was brought up. Everyone knew that Hanson was a recluse who employed an exclusive, ultra-loyal army of servants who lived on site and communicated as little as possible with the outside world. Some of the rumours that abounded were utterly absurd, that the man was old beyond time and had sold his soul to the devil for a mortal life of ten thousand years. Apparently old folk in the town said that he had been around as an adult when they were mere babes.

Trying to dismiss these crazy reports as he neared the property, Mr O found his steps faltering. There seemed to be no one else about in the surrounding streets, in spite of it being mid-morning. His eyes scanned the top of the two-metre tall palisade that circumnavigated the property. Many of the wooden stakes were going green from the bottom and some even sported fungi.

His reveries were interrupted by a click of a latch and a large section of palisade began to swing out, allowing him to enter. He introduced himself to a dour-faced servant who, unexpectedly, showed a brief smile before bidding the visitor follow him.

Given the job four years previously without actually meeting his employer, this would be the first time.

Recent rain made the courtyard muddy. They were stepping out at a fast pace, but he was able to take in a number of sights on the way: what appeared to be a small blacksmith's near the entrance, a couple of men working on leather hides in a structure open to the elements on one side.

Hanson's dwelling was a large, round, wooden building in the middle of the compound. The visitor wondered if he would be kept waiting, but he was not. The man himself was sitting on one of two low-backed couches in the centre living room. Cushions abounded and a small, old-fashioned coffee table had to be negotiated as Mr O went to the rising figure. Handshakes were exchanged, introductions made and drinks ordered. Then the host got straight to the point.

"You wish to buy the sawmill yourself, is that correct?"

"It is," Mr O replied calmly, but inside he felt far from calm. He would have preferred some small talk to settle him. Besides, he was trying to take in the white's appearance. He looked so... ordinary. A neat haircut, unostentatious clothing and average height, but it was the cold eyes that hit you. Colder than ice they were and belied his reasonable tone-of-voice. Mr O tried not to be intimidated by them. One thing was certain, though, the figure before him was in his mid-forties. It must be his father, or grandfather, that folk remembered.

"I have a ready buyer, I thought you knew."

"A Ma'hol."

"Correct."

"May I ask if a figure has been agreed between you?"

"It has."

"Um..."

"Six hundred and fifty sten."

"I see. With a small loan I could match that.... if you would sell it to me."

The unspoken implication was that the property owner should sell to a fellow Hoaman rather than a foreigner, but this was not expressly said. Glancing into those piercing eyes, and remembering Hanson's reputation as a hard businessman, Mr O dare not spell it out. Besides, it might not cut any ice with this fellow.

"You are sanguine regarding your prospects of obtaining the loan?"

"Merely a top-up, yes, extremely confident. A mere formality, I'm sure"

Hanson hesitated. What the black did not know was that the Ma'hol buyer was procrastinating with the purchase. The current owner wanted the money sooner rather than later, to increase his residential property portfolio. There was greater profit to be had there. The income from the sawmill was steady and little risk involved, but a further move into housing would rationalise his empire.

"Can you guarantee raising the money within the next fortnight?"

"Yes, yes... I think so. I have recently come into a legacy. That would cover the vast majority. I can have the entire sum to you within the week."

There was no reaction at first. The receiver of this information was as still as a statue for what seemed an age. Mr O nervously took a sip of his drink.

"Acceptable," replied Hanson, snapping out of it. "We can do business."

Two days later, Flonass accompanied his manager as they made their way to Castleton. Mr O was beside himself with frustration and self-loathing the day after the Hanson deal, for he had got his sums wrong. Even with the legacy he fell a full one hundred and fifty sten short, a lot more than he had thought. He confided in his assistant who told him that all was not lost. "I'm sure you'll be able to borrow the balance," said Flonass optimistically.

So now they were on their way to see Deejan Charvo. Flonass continued his encouragement.

"We've got a good business plan. The work is steady and profits guaranteed. You'll get the funds, I'm sure."

Inside the big house, Mr O was ushered through to meet the financier, but Walter indicated that Flonass should wait outside. So he sat in the large entrance hall from which other doors led off. In the centre was an imposing staircase leading up to other floors.

The time passed slowly. He could hear talking going on the other side of the thick, botawood doors, but words were impossible to make out. After a while, a youth of similar age to himself appeared. Neatly dressed, he had a huge mauve birthmark across his face which the visitor made sure he did not stare at. Introductions were made.

"I'm Sebastian, Mr Charvo's son."

"Hi, I'm Flonass. I'm waiting for my boss, he's in there asking for a loan."

"Been here long?"

"Um, a while."

"I'll get you a drink," Sebastian announced cheerfully and shot off before the other could say anything.

True to his word, he came back promptly with a practil juice and then stood over the seated figure who duly sipped from the glass. Hovering there, he showed no sign of leaving. Finally he voiced what was on his mind.

"Are you the Flonass who went away on the crusade?"

Modestly, the other admitted that he was.

"Is it true you went as far as the other side of the world?"

"As far as I know, yes. It took us long enough to get there."

"And you joined an army there?"

"I did."

"Tell me about it."

Flonass did exactly that. It was a far more pleasant way to pass the time than merely sitting there. Eventually, though, there was a click at the door and the men began coming out of the room, chatting as they did so."

Sebastian's concluding remark was, "I wish I'd been an adventurer like you, it sounds brilliant."

The comment was met with a smile before Flonass downed the last of his drink and handed the glass back with a word of thanks. He looked round at his boss and was pleased to see a relieved expression.

"Shall we go?" asked Mr O, neither expecting, nor getting an answer before heading for the door.

On the way home, the assistant got to hear the outcome of the meeting.

"Mr Charvo has agreed to lend the money at an affordable rate. He questioned me at length about my business plan and other things, but was satisfied in the end. Crucially he can get the funds to me in time for me to get the full amount to Hanson. He even offered to lend me some bodyguards to accompany the payment."

"Did you accept?" asked Flonass, glad to be included in everything. He did not think it was normal for an employer to do so, but it was quite welcome. He liked the idea of Onstein owning the sawmill, loan or no loan. The job was enjoyable and his boss was treating him more like a son. He had landed on his feet.

"Will you stay for a drink?"

As the military commanders left the room, Alan hung back and closed the door behind them. The meeting had been held at Charlotte's billet, a quaint cottage a short way back from the line.

The plan was all in place, Alan's proposals plus a few modifications and refinements. Since the conclusion of the battles in and around the town of Wesold earlier in the summer, quiet reigned for several weeks. The initiative had swung away from the Buffs due to the heavy casualties incurred in their unsuccessful offensive. The Neo-Purples continued to build up their strength and were ready now for the counter offensive. Some officers favoured an assault on the town, but Alan's encirclement idea had won the day. It was designed to minimise casualties and preserve their strength for future attacks. With autumn fast approaching, there was limited time before winter brought everything to a grinding halt. Everyone knew that things came to a standstill with the first snows. The Neo-Purples would deprive the Wesold defenders of the ability to resupply and starve them into submission. It would not be easy, for their enemy would probably launch attempts at a breakout. Plus the besiegers would have to be on the lookout for attempts to relieve the garrison. A key part of the plan was to seize as much ground to north and south of the town as possible and put distance between the Buff forces.

Alan knew better than anyone how easily military schemes were blown off course. They had been through it all a thousand times until it was wearying. The attack would take place at dawn on the morrow. He was welcome for the distraction before him right now.

For Charlotta was indicating for him to sit next to her on the two-seater settee. He was happy to oblige. Being a drone, he had been conditioned from birth to the reality that he was not allowed relations with a member of the opposite sex. However, he was a long way from Hoame and he was starting to find this woman attractive.

"Drink!" the marshal commanded as she thrust a glass of red wine into his hand.

He drank.

"They like your idea. The commanders have bought into it."

"Let's not talk more about it, not tonight."

"No, you're right," she replied, taking a deep gulp of her drink. Charlotta was annoyed with herself for not having thought of a more neutral topic to raise. She wanted this man so much, his natural reticence was all the more enticing. "Do you like the wine?"

Nodding, he was about to take another sip before finding the glass being taken from his hand. Both drinks out of the way, she made her move. There was no more talk as their lips met. Gentle kisses soon turned to long, firm, passionate ones.

Approaching forty years old, he had never kissed a woman in earnest before. Nevertheless, he was a fast learner. It felt so good and soon her hand had found its way beneath his shirt and was feeling his chest. His own hand went to her knee, then approached her thigh. Desire was growing.

Pulling back for a moment, she said breathlessly, "Stay the night."

Her words had the opposite effect to that intended. For he also moved away, answering, "Best not, got to get up before dawn."

The spell was broken. She was more frustrated than ever and it showed in her face. He said, "If I survive tomorrow, I'll stay the night, I promise." Other than a perfunctory farewell, these were the last words between them that night.

Dawn seemed an age in coming. Heavy clouds did not help and the days were getting shorter anyway. Alan was crouching down at a small ridge beside Captain Hallazanad and a liaison officer, they peered through the binoculars in turn. No sign of activity in the enemy camp.

It had stopped raining, but conditions were wet and muddy. The military advisor glanced back at the large group of soldiers about to go over the top. The attack would be not be long now.

Alan was not supposed to get involved in the actual fighting, but had managed to persuade the marshal, against her better judgement, to allow it. He hated the thought of having to stay behind, preferring to be where the action was.

"That's the signal," the liaison officer announced, looking back at the flag waved by the coordination officer.

Hallazanad raised his arm and the trio moved forward, followed closely by their body of troops. They mounted the ridge and streamed down the other side. All foot-soldiers, there were no battle cries, for the element of surprise needed to be maintained as long as possible.

They advanced along the shallow valley to the north of Wesold. To the left, the town; to the right, a spinney already secured by an advanced unit who had met with no opposition. In front of them, the enemy position. A casemate formed from sturdy logs with firing loops for archers. In front of it was a line of sharply pointed stakes, angled against the attackers.

The Hoaman expected to see arrows whizzing towards them at any moment and men falling, he hoped not himself. The force moved forward at a steady trot, armour jangling and feet squelching in the mud. Two hundred metres, a hundred and fifty... the enemy would be crazy not to open fire soon. Yet, even as they got closer still, no projectiles came their way.

When they got within fifty metres, the attackers' horns sounded and they rushed forward with a roar and battle cries. Carefully negotiating the stakes, they hurdled up and over the casemate to find a handful of Buff soldiers rising from their slumbers. They gave up without a fight, none even tried to make a dash for it.

"There are only bloody six of 'em!" the liaison officer announced, smiling. He was also panting heavily, for running in full armour soon tired even the fittest man.

More would-be defenders were located in the barracks and these, too, gave in without a fight. It was an anti-climax, but the Neo-Purples told themselves to be grateful for an easy victory. There was a pause while the Buff officers were interrogated. Hallazanad threatened them with gruesome torture if they did not answer, but it was not necessary. The defenders seemed fully prepared to divulge the little they knew. The post had been on minimal rations for weeks and morale was low.

After gleaning what information he could, the captain told Alan, "It was odd. Their commander said that he'd been warned that an attack was coming. I asked him why he wasn't prepared for it."

"And?"

"He said there'd been so many false alarms in the past weeks that they no longer took any notice of them."

"That's a bit daft. It looks like the fight has been knocked out of them anyway."

The prisoners were not harmed and were led off to the Neo-Purple rear in the most docile manner.

Meanwhile, the drive forward continued, leaving a small force at the captured position. Having got his breath back, the liaison officer exchanged a few words with the captain and his Hoaman advisor. There was not a great deal to say at that stage. A swift advance ensued.

The rooftops of Wesold passed by in the distance and they came across another small wood in an otherwise empty area. No sign of further enemy activity.

"Look!" cried Alan, pointing to a body of soldiers coming up from their left.

Upon sighting them, the others held aloft their flags, purple ones.

"They're ours!" Hallazanad announced triumphantly. The link-up west of the town was accomplished, Wesold was surrounded.

With further vital operations to take part in over the following day and a half, it was late on the second day that Alan found himself alone once more with Charlotta in her base. Business came before pleasure and he was eager to summarise the overall operation of the last two days.

"It all went beyond our wildest dreams! We've pushed forward both sides of the town with ease and secured a new perimeter. We encountered little resistance. I reckon the Buffs have been so taken up with their fight against the Rose to the north that they took their eye off us. If we can establish our lines quickly against any counter thrust, we..."

"Alan, enough! We've been through it all a hundred times. If you must go through it again, leave it for the morning."

63

It was a mild admonishment, for she did not want to upset him. Sitting back on the couch together, she did not want to be disappointed yet again. He went to open his mouth, but she put her finger gently up to his lips and he stopped. Finally he got the message.

Kisses followed, lots of them. Then she invited him through to her bedroom. This time he did not pull back.

It was the Sabbath Day up at the Castle and the weather was fine. The weekly service was being held in the bailey, probably for the last time that year before they were driven indoors. The sky was blue, but with the sun lower on the horizon, most of the congregation was in the shade.

Hannah's handmaiden had been sent back to get her mistress a shawl, while her husband was starting to wish he had worn thicker clothing. Still, they paid attention as Bishop Gunter began his sermon.

"Jesus was fun to be with, he'd make any party go with a swing! A funeral wake? He'd bring the dead body back to life. The wine run out? He'd produce some more. Unfortunately, his critics were not impressed; this wasn't the way for a religious leader to behave! In exasperation, you can hear it in his voice, Jesus turned on his critics: 'There's no pleasing some people! John the Baptist came along, fasting and abstaining from wine, and you say he's mad. Then I turn up and you complain that I'm too much of a party animal. Well, you'll see, I'll be vindicated by my actions in the end.'

"Many earnest seekers after God found it hard to pin Jesus down. He didn't match their expectations. He came and told the Jews what God is really like, but they couldn't compute. It didn't match their preconceived ideas. The image of God that people had was vastly different from how God actually is. In effect, they were worshipping a false God.

"Unfortunately the same is true today. People believe in all sorts of images of God, many of which do not match the God that Jesus came to tell us about."

He went on to enunciate some of the false concepts of the Almighty. These ideas included the notion of a divine being who should always give what people ask for, or a god who wanted to make people feel guilty all the time. Gunter then began the conclusion to his talk.

"We have to grow up and discard these false notions. If you want to know the true nature of God, find out what Jesus taught. He showed us what God is like through the parables. He is like the Good Shepherd who will go out of his way to search out the lost soul. He is like the father who longs for his bad son to return so that he can pronounce forgiveness. He is the priceless treasure worth more than anything else.

"Faith through Jesus should be liberating and fun. There is no room for fear, or guilt. Jesus the partygoer freed us from our sin. We should be overflowing with happiness and an example of joyful living to others."

Following the service, the bishop and his wife enjoyed lunch up on the third floor of the Castle with Frank and Hannah. The conversation was light over the meal, but afterwards the two men sat alone to discuss more important issues.

"Rodd came to see me the other day," Gunter said. "They're still having to turn Ladosan refugees away at the border."

Frank was surprised. "I must confess I hadn't heard any more about that. I'd assumed that no more were trying to come across."

"Apparently it's a weekly, if not a daily occurrence still."

"Well, we can only take in so many. The refugees camp has been full for some time now and our resources are not infinite. We've got..."

"I know," Gunter took the unusual step of interrupting his Despot. "I understand why we can't reasonably take more people in. I support your policy, Frank. I have heard many moans from folk who think we shouldn't be 'wasting' *any* resources on these foreigners. No, I was thinking more about the border guard."

"Oh."

"It's not the nicest of jobs having to say no to desperate families and I know it's affected some. I've been thinking of starting a chaplaincy to the border guard; give them someone to talk to."

"I see."

"I wondered if the captain might pour scorn on the idea, but he was fully supportive. I'll have to run it past General Japhses, of course, I mustn't go behind his back. I trust you have no objections."

"Indeed not," Frank replied, "it sounds like an excellent idea. Have you got anyone in mind."

"It would not be a fulltime post. I've had a preliminary discussion with Isaac. He came to see me, in fact, after getting wind of my intention... I'm not sure how. Be that as it may, he is extremely keen on the idea and could incorporate it into his schedule as well as his current role."

"Which is...?"

"He's a curate in a church on the west side of Setty. So he would not be badly placed to visit the troops patrolling the border."

"I've met Isaac, an enthusiastic young man."

"I believe he's genuine. His father is a fletcher and served in the militia in the war against the Ladosans."

"Well, they say that a volunteer is worth ten pressed men. He might be the best candidate... unless you have someone else in mind."

Raising his eyebrows, the bishop confessed that he did not. He added, "There is still a lot of sorting out to do before it becomes a reality."

"Of course. Now, Gunter, what about you? Am I right in supposing your diocese is about to expand greatly?"

"When we take on this Norland you mean?"

"Yes."

"I watched the gold shipment departing the other day, it was quite a column. I can't see anyone wanting to raid that with the amount of soldiers going with it!"

"I certainly hope not. I'm looking forward to receiving a message that it has arrived safely and the deal completed, but I can't see anything stopping it now it's all been agreed."

"Nearly everyone I speak to seems pleased with Thyatira's expanding again. They believe it will bring greater prestige to the area and, with it, prosperity."

"Well, that's the plan! It will also bring its fair share of problems and challenges, I have no doubt. These will be ecclesiastical as well as secular."

"That's right," confirmed the bishop. "Aggeparii does not have its own bishop, an'..."

"Doesn't it?" Frank sounded surprised.

"Not every despotate does, you know."

"Oh."

"But it will fall under my remit now. I understand that three sizeable towns will fall within the new area."

"Norland."

"Yes."

"You're right, three towns plus their associated villages."

"Gunter admitted, "I don't know as much about the area as perhaps I should. I'm going to have to find out what organisation they have in place and how we can incorporate it into the rest of Thyatira. Personnel, buildings, liturgy, finances and a whole host of other issues are going to have to be gone into. The situation will have to be handled with sensitivity too. I've felt it wise to hold back until it was absolutely certain that the takeover was going ahead. Aggeparii has not had a bishop in office in living memory, so we will all have to do some adapting to the new situation."

"That's true. The senate are undertaking similar fact-finding missions, led by Senator Vebber. Sensitivity is a good word to use; it will be important. Thyatirans might be happy about the annexation of this Norland, but not all people living there are likely to have the same view. We will have to convince them that it is in their long-term interest."

"I am sure that they will benefit from having a new, wise ruler over them."

It was not like Gunter to issue such a gushing compliment and it took Frank by surprise. Then he hesitated. After all, he was being compared with the vain, profligate Despot Kagel. It was not the greatest of compliments after all.

As if reading the other man's mind, Gunter asked, "How did Despot Kagel seem during the talks? If you don't mind me asking... It can't be easy bargaining your land away."

With a shrug, Frank admitted that he had not seen his opposite number while the negotiations were on-going, continuing, "It was Senator Vebber at the sharp end and he did not talk much about the despot's disposition. I'm afraid all I was concerned with was getting the land once it was offered. Maybe I should have gone in person, then I would not have got into that little local difficulty in Bynar."

Gunter knew that this was a reference to the kidnapping and his leader's way of trying to play down what must have been a traumatic ordeal. Not certain what to say, he tried, "We all give thanks for your deliverance."

A faint smile flickered across Frank's face. It was best to move the conversation on. He said, "I meant it earlier, when I said I enjoyed your sermon."

"It's nice to hear you say so."

" I mean it!"

"It's rare for me to receive feedback. My priests do not feel in a position to."

"Hmm... well, you made a valid point that it's easy to get a false image of God. People should not fear the Almighty."

"Sometimes I wonder if the truth seems too good to be true. But if God cares when a sparrow falls to the ground, he certainly cares about us, for..."

At that point the womenfolk entered the room and the men stood up. Hannah was smiling excessively and Frank asked what was amusing her.

"Ah, Esther here has been telling me about a situation in a church in Setty. Apparently there is a woman there who sings as loudly as the rest of the congregation put together. That's not all, she is tone deaf and puts everyone off."

"Oh dear!"

"No one will say a word to her though."

"Are they too polite?"

"Esther tells me there's another reason."

"Oh?"

Hannah deferred and let Esther continue the story.

"The lady in question has been there a couple of years now and she is most generous in her giving. They dare not upset her in case she takes offence and goes elsewhere."

Frank smiled, but inwardly he was thinking about the financial resources that the bishop had at his disposal. No congregation should be held to ransom like this. Then he realised that he was taking the matter far too seriously and should simply enjoy it for the funny story it was.

The tale was already known to Gunter, who added, "I'm told that the priest in charge did have a word with her once, but it had no effect. They are lumbered with it."

"It's not your Isaac's church is it? You said that he is based in Setty."

"I understand it's a different one."

"Oh. I wondered if he was wanting to take up the other post in order to get away from this woman's singing!"

They all laughed. It was not long after this that the bishop and his wife departed. Hannah and Frank found themselves alone once more and the latter asked, "Where's Joseph? I haven't seen him since the service."

"I told you! He's spending the rest of the day at the Ronenvinks."

"Ah yes." This was good, a nice, upper class black friend to play with.

"I thought I might go and visit Wanda again next week," she said, then waited for a reaction.

If she wanted to visit her friend who was effectively gaoled for life for arranging he husband's death, should he complain? He saw Hannah as his equal and did not want to dictate to her. So in his sweetest voice, he replied, "That's nice, darling," and went to his chair.

Feeling a burst of energy, Hannah said, "Don't sit down! Come on, let's go for a walk outside."

"Um, okay, where to?"

"Nowhere in particular. Let's just go for a walk."

~ End of Chapter 3 ~

Prospects of Peace - Chapter 4

Tristan and Ayllom were relaxing in their digs behind the lines. All was currently quiet on the southern, Fanallon Front. The operation against Wesold to the north was not affecting them. As ambulancemen, they did their bit during the hardest fighting for the town. Now they were enjoying a well earned rest.

Not that they expected the current tranquillity to last. It was apparent here, as in the north, that the Buff forces were severely depleted. Constant battles against several other factions had drained them of personnel and resources. They were not able to get reinforcements from the Central Buffs who, in any case, were experiencing their own problems now following the fall of the fireball. Currently the initiative was fully with the Neo-Purples who were taking their time making preparations for their southern offensive.

The immediate objective was hardly a surprise. The town of Fanallon was twenty kilometres behind the present Buff frontline. A full scale attack would be launched to capture it. Preparations were in full swing, although a casual observer might have considered there to be a lack of urgency. It was certainly not going to take place any time soon. The local Neo-Purple commander was a meticulous individual who wanted to leave nothing to chance.

Meanwhile, the pair enjoyed the break. With a friend of Ayllom's in supplies (he seemed to have no end of connections) they were well stocked with food. One mild, autumnal morning, they lounged about in their living room waiting for a visitor.

"Another juice?" asked Tristan, reaching out towards a half-full jug.

"Naa, I'm okay," his friend replied lazily.

The Hoamen scanned the walls of this room. It was quite absurd. They had salvaged a huge number of classic paintings from their previous accommodation up north, artwork which would have been thrown out by the Philistine military authorities there. Not that the paintings appealed to him greatly. Nearly all were portraits of long dead Ladosan luminaries and they struck him as somewhat absurd.

70

Serious men and women in old-fashioned clothing, he could not take it too seriously. Salvaging them had been a wheeze and they were still something of a joke to him. There was a possibility that they were actually worth a great deal of money. Not that a buyer was likely to be found in these troubled times. Anyway, Ayllom got wind that a local Neo-Purple officer had been an art critic in his pre-war life. Kazzapaken by name, he was invited along that day to cast his eyes over them.

"I hope he comes soon," declared Tristan, "I'll be wanting to get lunch."

"Ah!" the Ladosan suddenly exclaimed. "There's been something I've been meaning to tell you. I heard some gossip yesterday. They were saying that Marshal Nazaz has taken a Hoamen lover! Would you believe it? It's that Alan and he's by her side at all times. What she does between the sheets is her own business, but a Hoaman?"

His secret Hoame colleague started back. This was not the usual easygoing Ayllom he knew. It was one suddenly affected by an inbred nationalism that he was usually immune to. Mercifully, before Tristan could think how to respond, there was, at that moment, a knock on the door and the two young men sprang to their feet. They went out into the reception area. Ayllom, his outburst already forgotten, exchanged a cheeky grin with his friend before opening the door.

The man outside was younger than they had envisaged, in his early thirties from his appearance. Short hair and a neatly-trimmed beard, his uniform was pristine.

"You must be Ayllom and Tristan."

"Yes, sir," the former replied, "thank you for coming."

"Not at all, I was intrigued," the man said pleasantly as he stepped inside, "and you can drop the 'sir' while we're back here. Now where are these... oh my goodness!"

The exclamation came as he moved forward into the living room. He could hardly believe his eyes. "Are these genuine?" he asked.

Ayllom shrugged his shoulders and said, "You tell us! I can tell you where I found them."

"Oh my goodness," Captain Kazzapaken repeated and went up close to the one nearest him. "The Pink Supremacy Collection!"

He spent a long time at the cottage. The temporary residents explained exactly where they had come from. They felt there was nothing to hide. Ayllom was equal with Tristan that the whole thing was a bit of joke and could not take it entirely seriously, even if, being a native, he had a greater appreciation of Ladosa's heritage. It had been fun salvaging them from the scrap heap, but he was not greedy with the idea of making money out of them, if indeed they were worth anything. It was a matter of honour to get them back to their rightful owner, if it were possible, after the war. He told the art expert, "We understand that the owner was a Buff supporter who fled."

"I know exactly whom the owner is," the art expert announced, not taking his eyes off the second portrait as he inspected it closely with a magnifying glass.

"Oh?"

"Former Prime Minister Banzarrip."

"Um... I might have heard of him."

"You should have! Although he retired several years ago."

They then remained silent for a while as their guest studied the works of art, muttering as he did so. Eventually they were able to sit down while the verdict was given.

"When I was told that you may have possession of a collection of portraits from the Pink Supremacy, I was highly sceptical. Sceptical, yet intrigued. With a bit of time on my hands, I was happy to come down and take a look."

"And?" asked Ayllom.

"They are certainly genuine, a fine collection."

"That's good."

"And they're worth a fortune."

"Oh."

"In the message you sent me, you expressed a desire to get them back to their rightful owner once this current mess is all over."

"Yes."

"It's a noble thing. There are not many of the Banzarrip clan left. I feel certain that if these paintings can be preserved in their current position, then, once sanity has returned to our stupid country, they will give you a substantial reward for their safe return."

Tristan beamed, exclaiming to his friend, "I told you it was a good idea to salvage them."

"I thought it was my idea!"

"Never mind," Kazzapaken broke in, "you did well to salvage them. In fact I find it unbelievable that they were going to be left to rot without your intervention. Correction: not unbelievable, for I can too readily believe that those idiots would do such a thing. We were lucky that they were saved for the nation. Well done, you two!"

"Thank you," replied Ayllom. It seemed the natural thing to say.

"I'm not going to broadcast my find and if you have any sense, you will keep quiet about them from now on."

After the expert was gone, the pair laughed and danced around a bit before reality set in.

"I think," said Tristan, "I preferred it when I wasn't sure they were worth a lot of money. We always knew they might be, but that's different from knowing for sure."

"Never mind," Ayllom replied, still sounding up-beat, "once the war is over we can make it our mission to find the owner. I made some notes. That'll be an adventure in itself. I mean, this war can't go on for ever. If we survive, it'll be fun restoring them to where they belong. A matter of national honour as well, that goes without saying. Naturally we'll split any reward fifty-fifty. I bet they'll be surprised."

Tristan returned his smile, but inside his thoughts were completely different.

'If I survive this conflict, I'll probably go back to Hoame. In which case I'm afraid you'll be on your own.'

A week and a half after his pleasant time with Gunter and Esther, Frank was sitting alone in the Throne Room. It was late morning and he was taking a breather. He had had a busy time since sunrise, but the good news was that the convoy taking the money to Despot Kagel had arrived back safely. The deal was complete and Norland was now officially part of Thyatira.

He wondered what the other despots made of it. This was the second time that his despotate had expanded at the expense of its neighbours. From what Frank knew about his opposite numbers, though, many were solely interested in being able to live self-indulgent lives. They pulled together at the behest of the Inner Council in times of national crisis, but most of the time they were an introspective bunch.

Still, there was no use worrying about them, there were a lot of things to think about with the acquisition of extra population. There were three substantial towns in the new territory. Indeed, Carnis was larger than any of the existing Thyatiran towns. In the previous annexation, Meshtam alone had formally been in Aggeparii. This expansion was bigger in scale and threw up many questions.

That was why he held a meeting with several interested personnel earlier that morning. Key amongst them was Emil, who was leading an integration task force, plus Karl. Karl's remit may have been defence, but Frank valued the opinion of this long-established advisor. Of all the current blacks from the old Thyatira, only the Despot had been there longer than Karl. He had stuck his neck out by emigrating with his family to what was then a backwater. He proved his worth many times over since then.

Yet it was Emil, who had successfully negotiated the deal with Despot Kagel in the first place, who was in charge of the project. He would be extremely busy for the next couple of years making the transition work. With limited opportunities to travel to Norland before winter, the senator felt it important to spend as much time there as possible now. An inventory of villages and businesses was a priority. A full census of the new population was planned for the spring. Industry, taxation, defence and many other issues would have to be ironed out. It would give Frank and the senate plenty of extra work for some considerable time.

"Nevertheless," Emil declared at the meeting recently concluded, "I got the impression from my previous visit that the change is welcomed in many quarters there. That was something of a surprise, for folk rarely welcome change in my experience. Yet they are hoping for greater prosperity in the future and the Mayor of Carnis was eager to stress his willingness to play his part. It certainly helped when I told him that we have no immediate plans for changing the current system of local government. I suspect he breathed a sigh of relief at feeling secure in his position. We will need to see how good a job he and his counterparts are doing. If Aggeparii is close to bankruptcy, and reports indicate it is (why else would they sell a chunk of their land?), then it is hard to believe the northern towns are doing quite as well as the mayor was leading me to believe. Yet our initial analysis is that there seem to be many viable industries in

Norland. Rest assured, My Lord, that I will leave no stone unturned as I delve deeper into the matter."

That was earlier. By now the good senator must be in his wagon heading off, for he said he wanted to leave as soon as possible. After all the chatter, Frank enjoyed merely sitting there lost in his thoughts.

'I know that Kagel is thought a fool by some of the other Keepers. If he's sold off his best industrial area for short-term profit then it is foolishness indeed. He's got a great deal of money for it, it certainly should be enough to keep himself in luxury the rest of his life. Maybe that's all he cares about.'

Just then, a visitor arrived at the door. Deejan Charvo would always be welcome, for he was someone Frank could have a relaxing chat with.

"If you're not too busy..."

"Not at all."

"I can't say I have any business matters to see you with."

"That's fine. I had a heavy meeting this morning, I wouldn't say no to a distraction. Would you like to go to my suite? I can order some drinks."

"I wondered," replied the moneylender, if we could simply go for a walk."

"An excellent idea," beamed Frank, moving into the hall.

"There will be few days as good as this one before the snows come."

"That's a bit pessimistic isn't it? We've still got the second half of autumn to get through!"

Deejan's reply, as they got to the entrance, was drowned out by some noisy soldiers exiting the stairwell. Frank let it pass. Before long, they were ambling up the track towards the Ladosan border. It was an increasingly well-worn track these days, with patrols being despatched for the border more frequently than before. It got extremely muddy after a rainfall, maybe they should consider laying hulffan tar and widening it. That would have to be a project for 2621.

"I spotted Joseph yesterday," the merchant said, "he's growing into a fine lad."

"He does seem to have put on a spurt recently."

"How old is he now?"

"Twelve. I'll have to have him sitting in on senate meetings soon. He's got to learn how to govern wisely. We are spending the afternoon together, I've promised him. It will be nice to have some time together, just the two of us."

"I'm sure," agreed the merchant. "Children are such a blessing."

He had adopted his own two children in recent years. Both teenagers, they were his pride and joy. Frank asked him how they were doing.

"Grand! They make my life a joy."

"They get on well together?"

"Katrina and Sebastian? Oh yes, they rarely argue. A few weeks ago I was with them as they braved brambles and nettles to pick blackberries. They collected a couple of large tubs full."

"Did you pick some yourself?"

"I didn't take a container, but I might have picked the occasional one to eat there and then." He said this with a twinkle in his eye.

"I bet you did."

"It was a sunny day and some of them were warm as you put them in your mouth - delicious too."

"You're making my mouth water!"

They left the track and continued to walk round the Castle from a distance. The grass had nearly dried off following that morning's dew.

Said Deejan, "Walter's away for a couple of days, visiting a relative. He should be back tomorrow. Meanwhile, we had a birthday party for Keturah. She's sixteen now."

"Is she?"

"Her birthday fell on the Sabbath. She's on the threshold of womanhood, but sometimes she seems like a little girl."

"I'm sure she'll grow up soon enough, don't rush it."

"You're right," the merchant replied with a sigh. "From time to time she comes out with words of intense wisdom. I believe she will go far in life."

"And Sebastian?"

"Quite the young man now. The transformation from the street urchin I once knew is remarkable."

"And thanks largely to you, Deejan, it was a wonderful thing you did in taking him in."

The other man tried to play this down, but it was nothing but the truth. Then, following a period of silence, Frank mentioned something that was on his mind.

"I've been hoping for a letter from Alan this week, but none has arrived. I'm sure he's been busy, that's all."

With a sigh, Deejan replied, "Alan's quite the adventurer. All these exploits abroad, both to the west and Ladosa. He's lived quite a life and I think part of me envies him. I've never been out of Hoame and it's a slight regret of mine that I did not do something like that when I was young."

"I can't imagine you swashbuckling your way through Ladosa," said Frank with a laugh.

Deejan took this in good humour, but came back with, "I'm sure you're right. But I've heard tell that you had your adventures in years gone by."

"Me?"

"Yes, a clandestine mission to Ladosa before the war, I've heard. Plus leading a cavalry charge in battle itself!"

"Who've you been talking to? On second thoughts, I think I'd rather not know. Well, I can't deny the charges. They might be hard to believe, but I confess they are true. A lot of water has gone under the bridge since those days."

They completed their walk in good spirits and, afterwards, Deejan made his way home. When he got there, he opened the door to find a concerned-looking Keturah waiting for him.

"What's the matter?" he asked.

"It's Sebastian, he's in his room."

"Go on."

"A client, a black from the Sardis Potters Guild, made a nasty comment about Sebastian's... you know what," she replied, pointing to her own face.

He immediately inferred correctly that she meant her brother's birthmark. Furious at this, he thanked her before storming up to Sebastian's room. He found him sitting on the bed. His eyes were red and he was wiping a final tear off his cheek.

The following morning, Walter returned and the other man told him about the previous day's drama.

"I had to try and get from Sebastian exactly what had been said. I wondered if it was a simple misunderstanding."

"And was it?"

"It seems that man was quite rude. There's no excuse for that. I am cancelling the Sardis Potters Guild account forthwith."

"It won't affect our business much," added Walter helpfully.

"That's not the point. I'm not going to have anyone think they can insult Sebastian and get away with it. It's simply not on."

His assistant knew better than to query this decision. The Sardis Potters would have to look elsewhere for funds from now on.

Hannah walked slowly back from the women's quarter at the monastery. She was returning from seeing Wanda Shreeber. Bricked up for the rest of her life, she usually showed great resilience. Not this time. She was in a bad way, tearful and angry. Nothing her visitor said had helped. Hannah came away feeling a lump in her stomach and a tear in her eye.

There were not many people about. Situated in the middle of Thyatira's western forest, the monastery was peaceful now that all the building work was completed. She went past a field with livestock in it, one of several owned by the religious establishment. Some heifers were walking along, parallel to the fence. They nodded their heads as they went which amused her.

Calling in on the abbot had been her plan, but, finding herself slightly depressed following her visit, she had second thoughts. In the event, when she spotted him through his office window, she made up her mind to do so.

"My Lady, how nice to see you."

The greeting was warm and genuine. Declining the offer of a drink, she sat down and asked how things were. It would be good to keep the conversation off Wanda if possible.

"There's always plenty to do, My Lady. I got involved in a dispute over a meat supply this morning."

"A meat supply?" she echoed.

"Yes, without wishing to go into detail, it wuz unhealthy and had to be sent back. Fortunately we're still in good time to have a fresh shipment delivered. It'll be salted for the winter. I don't normally have to get involved in that side of things, but an argument had developed. I don't like arguments."

"No, indeed."

"May I ask if there's fresh news from our homeland?" he asked. The reference being due to the fact that both of them originated from Ladosa.

"The war goes on, so I am told, in spite of part of the country having been devastated by that celestial thing falling from the sky."

"It takes a lot to end a war once it's been started," he said gravely. "Man's inhumanity to man shows no sign of abating."

She nodded her head in agreement as he continued.

"My father's brother was a lot older than himself, my uncle, of course. I was still little when he came back from war, a changed man. He wuzn't hurt physically, but it messed with his mind and he wuz never the same again."

"How terrible."

"All violence is terrible. I wuz sent off to school and got bullied a lot. I wuz different, see? I bowed on the outside, but inside I would not let them break my spirit."

Hannah changed the subject when she replied, seeking to make the conversation less personal. "Some say the fireball from heaven was a judgement on the Ladosan people, although I do not know the truth of it."

"I don't believe the Ladosan people are any more evil than anyone else. I'm not a subscriber to the idea that God sends thunderbolts from heaven to zap naughty people. God sends the rain to fall on good and bad alike."

"I'm sure you're right."

"Any further news from Ladosa in the past week?"

"Not in the last week, no."

"In any case, I should not concern myself with such things. I know I asked the question, but the truth is, it is a distraction."

"Don't be so harsh on yourself, Muggawagga," she said warmly. "You asked because you care. You are a caring soul."

In trying to cheer him up, Hannah found her own spirits lifting a bit. It was good to talk. Glancing at the papers on the table, she asked what they were.

He answered, "I am looking for a spiritual quotation to begin the meditation session this evening."

"Ah, I was thinking on my way here what a quiet place this has become."

"Now all the banging and sawing is over with, you mean?"

"That's right."

"There is a quality of peace, it's true. But we can all find our quiet places within us if we seek hard enough. The early Church desert fathers found tranquillity in the sandy, rocky places, yet a wise person will find such a place deep within them. Then you will have tranquillity wherever you go, even noisy, busy places. It is a state of mind."

"I like that idea," Hannah said.

"For it is in the quiet that we find God, not through dispute, arguments, or clever reasoning."

"We can't *think* our way to God," she offered.

"Exactly right, My Lady! Our minds are finite and God is infinite, so we must try a different approach. All we can do is to try and connect with him in love. If we connect in love, we connect with God, for God is love."

"Going beyond the intellectual approach then."

"Precisely! The intellect is ultimately too limited. That's not to say that the intellect has no function, of course not. It can lead us towards faith through reason and logic, but in the end we need to step beyond it. Take holy scripture, for instance. I love to read the Bible and learn from the scholars of the past about the society and culture of the times. It gives a deeper understanding. That all has its place. But on top of that, we can practice *Lectio Divina*."

"I'm sorry?"

"Divine reading. It is a complementary approach to the scriptures. In small groups we read a section before meditating silently on its meaning. No comment is made. That is followed by prayers and contemplation. We are not seeking to do a theological analysis of the passage, that would be for another time. Instead we focus on Jesus' statements, for example, and enter into them rather than dissecting them."

Hannah was trying hard to take this in. She asked for an example. The abbot was forthcoming with one.

"When Jesus gives his command to love one another, we dwell in that love in quiet contemplation rather than trying to work out with our minds the benefits of such love in the world. It is a non-analytical approach. Instead of looking at it from the outside, one dwells within it."

The Despotess left Muggawagga's room feeling happy and refreshed. As she approached her wagon, she saw her driver and handmaiden sitting there patiently. She felt guilty about having left them so long, but it was their job after all. Besides, he had fallen asleep and she had her nose buried in a book, so neither of them seemed to have suffered from the long wait. In any case, they jumped to it upon Hannah's approach and helped her into the covered compartment at the back.

Holding on due to the swaying movement of the vehicle as it got underway, she was soon lost in her thoughts. 'Muggawagga is such a tonic. How uplifting it is to be in the presence of such a holy man.'

Back on the Fanallon Front, the local Neo-Purples had continued their build-up ready for their autumn offence. It was to be a major effort and the local commander wanted to leave nothing to chance. He knew how such a push often broke down in the end due to an overstretched supply line. Vast stores therefore were assembled in preparation.

It took a lot of time and effort to get everything in place, but the commander felt it was well worth it. Until, that is, the Buffs made a pre-emptive strike. Taking the Neo-Purples completely by surprise, a cavalry formation suddenly rode in and set fire to huge stockpiles meticulously accumulated over the previous weeks. Two days of ferocious fighting ensued with significant losses on both sides. Then the Buffs retreated to their lines, leaving their opponents to survey the damage.

The commander and his local Hoaman advisor were red-faced. The offensive had to be postponed. With a limited number of autumn weeks remaining, it looked like the offensive would have to be put off until the following year. It was a major blow to their ambitions.

Tristan and Ayllom experienced a hectic couple of days, ferrying wounded back to the first-aid station. They were not called upon to dig graves on this occasion. Then the fighting ceased for now, as quickly as it started, and the pair were allowed back to their digs to rest.

The following day was a fine one. The sun came out from behind the clouds and it was pleasantly warm for the time of year. The two men enjoyed a lie-in, then surfaced mid-morning for a large, fried brunch. Sitting together in their modest lounge, still surrounded by the works of art and the fine furniture they had salvaged, it was good to talk.

Tristan remarked, "I've heard that the notorious Buff General Vap has been relocated to this front."

"Notorious? Why's that?"

"Don't you remember? He was responsible for that war crime, having our marshal killed when he was under a flag of truce."

"Oh yes, of course. That was him, was it?"

"Vap, yes. He's a nasty piece of work. I don't fancy his chances if our soldiers ever get hold of him."

"I guess that's war for you. In truth it's one big atrocity, I think."

"Yeah."

Suddenly changing the subject, and sounding upbeat, Ayllom declared, "I saw mother yesterday, briefly."

"Oh yes? And how was the major?"

"She and my brother had been involved in the fighting, but mercifully were not hurt. She didn't have a lot to say to me, she seemed distracted by her duties."

"Still, it must have been nice to see her."

"I suppose so. My mother never was one for small talk. When I was little, my family loved to engage in debates... like all good Ladosans," he added with a smile. "I was the baby of the family and usually sat there listening to the others. They used to get quite heated, or should I say passionate? But it was all good natured. They'd be arguing over which representative would make the best Prime Minister, or some such matter. They'd be shouting each other down, then, as soon as it was over, it was smiles all round and 'what's for dinner?'"

"Sounds like a normal Ladosan household," Tristan replied. If he knew anything about these people it was their love of political debate.

"Yes," agreed Ayllom, still smiling. "I guess I formed a lot of my opinions then. I was told that the Pinks are a bad bunch and I believed it."

"The Pinks *are* a bad bunch," the other said light-heartedly.

"Yeah, but maybe it's better to find out for oneself than take someone else's opinion in, even a family member."

"Actually," replied Tristan, becoming a bit more serious, "It's probably a good thing to try and keep an open mind as much as possible. But we find ourselves putting labels on groups of people, or whole nations. I hear people generalising, saying things like, 'All Sarnicians are lazy,' or whatever."

"Hmm, I've heard that."

"But it's not an intelligent way of looking at an issue. In truth, it's laziness, 'cos once you label a group, whether it be a political party, a nation, or whatever, you stop thinking any further about it. Your mind is closed to further investigation. It would then take a huge effort to change your mind."

"Because you've become prejudiced."

"Yes! I have come to the firm conclusion that folk are basically the same the world over. They have similar hopes, fears and ambitions for their offspring. If people of goodwill got together then all this war nonsense could be put to an end."

"Spoken as a true idealist!"

"Okay, so I'm an idealist, but I make no apology for that."

Ayllom was sprawling in his easy chair by now. If he moved forward he would be in danger of falling off. He considered the matter before coming back. He said, "It all sounds fine in theory, but have you been to Hoame, Rabeth-Mephar, or Sarnice? You might find that people are not quite the same after all. How much should we trust the Hoamen?"

His friend hesitated. He had been to Rabeth-Mephar and spent most of his life in Hoame, of course. He had also visited Karamonfor, West and East Torravis, although he had not set foot in Sarnice. However, he could not disclose any of this if he did not want to blow his cover. For a brief moment, he was tempted to tell the truth, but the implications of that revelation were too hard to contemplate right then. If he said nothing, he would come across as a rather ignorant young man and not merely an idealist. Concluding it was the best option, he fell silent.

With a guffaw, Ayllom resumed, "Don't look so glum! I wasn't trying to strike you dumb, or win an argument. I like it that you try to think the best of people, it's commendable. Do you think it's 'cos you're a Christian? I used to think that having a set of beliefs like that got in the way, stopped you from thinking straight, but now I'm not sure. It might be helpful after all."

This brought Tristan back into the conversation. He liked the way that his Ladosan friend was opening himself up and not merely trying to "win" the discussion. He replied, "I think I treat my beliefs as a kind of 'working hypothesis' in my life. It gives me a base to start from. I don't think it means my mind is closed. My faith is a code to live by and an ideal to strive for, making living worthwhile."

"I seem to remember you were shocked when I told you that I liked older women. I got the feeling you were judging me."

"I didn't mean to come across that way," said the Hoaman. "It's not for me to judge you. Besides, the sole woman I've ever fallen in love with was a lot older than me."

"That so?" Ayllom said eagerly, "tell me more."

"It was a few years ago now. She was a widow and we hit it off tremendously. I adored her and she told me she loved me. It's a wonderful feeling, being told that. We weren't together too long I suppose..."

"What happened?"

"An accident. She was crossing a gorge on an old footbridge which was in a poor state of repair. It sounds stupid now, but we were playing about and she rushed onto it. The bridge gave way and she fell. I tried to save her..."

"How tragic," his friend replied earnestly.

"It was a while ago now, I try not to think about it." Then, trying to lighten the mood, he added, "At least it proves you're not the only one who prefers older women."

Someone was at the door. They both moaned. With Ayllom showing no signs of moving, it was up to the other to go and see who it was.

He opened the door to a trooper who delivered his message verbally. "You're to report to Sector A headquarters immediately. There are two casualties to evacuate."

"Oh, more fighting?"

"No, they were working on defences and fell into a hole," the young man said without expression.

It was all Tristan could do not to laugh, but he thanked the visitor and told him they would be along straightaway. "Come on, lazy bones!" he shouted towards the lounge, "we've got a job on."

Emil was entering Newton, the smallest of the three towns being incorporated into Thyatira. Frank had insisted on him having a full squad to escort him, although he hardly saw it as necessary. Still, if the Despot himself could get kidnapped, it made sense even for a senator to take precautions.

The entire contingent consisted of Emil himself, four clerks, two servants, Squad Leader Stephan and eight soldiers. The big man was the single black amongst them. This was his first visit to Newton, a place which, like the other two formally Aggepariian towns, possessed a higher proportion of blacks in them than the more northerly conurbations.

Wagons and dakks stored safely at the stables on the western edge of Town, Emil knew from directions he had received that it was but a short walk to the mayor's office. First, though, some eating needed to be done. His large frame needed sustenance and it was lunchtime. Nothing must come before that. So, cohort in tow, Emil led them into the nearby restaurant area.

"No Whites," read a permanent sign outside one establishment. Despot Thorn would not stand for that. Anyhow, that was a battle for another day, so they walked on. A pizzeria proved the ideal place for the contingent to dine. The waiter was quietly efficient and not nosey enough to ask them their business.

Sitting at a table alone with Squad Leader Stephan, Emil tried to make conversation, but the pair had little in common.

"Have you been to Aggeparii before?"

"No, senator, I haven't."

"There's some fine architecture hereabouts."

The soldier glanced up from his food and nodded as he chewed. At twenty-eight, he was exactly half the age of Emil, so that was another barrier between them. Not that Stephan minded the assignment. Patrols along the Ladosan border were getting tiresome, particularly when they had to turn refugees away. This was a pleasant diversion and a change of scenery.

Time to move on. The town hall was an impressive structure. A large, rectangular building, it employed square-napped flints embedded in the stonework to an intricate design. Grey slates covered the roof. It was unlike anything Stephan and his soldiers had seen. The hall was situated with a large, cobbled area which was busy with people crossing it going about their business. Some benches, most of them currently empty, were situated within this space. The servants and military escort were instructed to wait there while the senator and his clerks entered.

"Ah, Senator Vebber!" gushed the mayor upon seeing them entering his palatial office. Fine frescos covered the wall and high ceiling. The man himself retreated behind his gigantic desk. A long business meeting ensued.

When it was all over, Emil came away considering it a success, or had the gushing mayor put up a front? Either way, one of the clerks had made copious notes and would be writing up comprehensive minutes of the meeting that very evening.

The mayor seemed cooperative, almost too much so. The visitor had hinted that the man's position was safe for the time being. That seemed to be the best strategy to ensure he was co-operative, neither over-confident nor having nothing to lose. In truth, from Emil's initial glance at the books it was apparent that the ordinary citizens of Newton were being stung by a local tax on top of the despot's. The proceeds of this were being used to feather the beds of the mayor and his cronies. That would have to stop, but subtlety was called for to achieve this goal without too much resentment from the local centre of power. Subtlety and patience.

At the last moment, Emil decided to take up the "No Whites" restaurant sign with the mayor. The local government leader could not have been more helpful. It would be taken down before nightfall.

'My report,' thought the senator as he left the building, 'will make interesting reading back home.'

Reunited with his escort, they passed on to their lodgings. The meeting had gone on longer than he expected and it was late afternoon. Entering a new district, they found the architecture quite different here, with whitewashed timber-frames buildings the norm.

The squad leader asked directions from a man crossing in the opposite direction, an extravagantly dressed individual. He was given them. The local added, "Although it isn't the best quarter of town to stay in, you know. They've been having a little... er, local difficulty of late."

With that, he was gone. Emil shrugged his round shoulders, he was starting to feel tired and he was not going to start looking elsewhere.

"I'm sorry, sir," the landlord said, sounding more officious than sorry, "but we only have the two rooms available."

Going red, Emil raised his voice as he replied, "This is unacceptable! We booked on ahead; four rooms."

"Again, I'm sorry, sir, but there was a small fire last week which ruined a section of the hotel."

Stephan felt his anger rise at this. After all, here was a Thyatiran senator no less. For half a sten he would have threatened violence. In fact he gave the landlord such a fearsome look that he said, "Okay, I'll see what can be done." He then studied the ledger again before miraculously discovering a third room was available.

It still was not enough, but Emil decided it would have to do. By rights he and the squad leader should have their own individual rooms, but in these brave new times it did not seem of prime importance. In a magnanimous gesture, therefore, he said that Stephan could share with him. leaving the other still seven to a room.

The chambers were, in fact, quite large and Emil fell asleep on top of his bed and enjoyed a nap before they were due to go out for dinner. The dining hall was across the road. Whether this was due to the fire or not they did not enquire. It did not seem to matter.

Smartening up as best as they could, the whole contingent traipsed across to the restaurant. There was lots of bunting across the street, two metres above their heads: penoncels coloured blue, white and red. It had been up there for a while and was in a poor state of repair, hanging down in places. Nearby, a group of black youths had nothing better to do than stand with their hands in their pockets and smirk at the party going by.

The helpful stranger's warning that this was not the most salubrious part of town was proving accurate. On the other hand, the restaurant turned out to be rather good. Wholesome foods at reasonable cost and with good service. They had no complaints.

"Tell me," said Emil, cornering a female servant between course, "what is all that bunting up in the street for?"

The woman, a white, was dismissive. "Oh, that there were for the Lord Mayor's Procession. That were weeks ago now, but no one can be bothered to take it down. I reckon it'll still be up there next year." With that, she carried on with her duties.

A delicious apple pie concluded a pleasant meal. They were the last diners to leave. As they were about to go, they heard a commotion outside. The same servant woman was going past and saw her customers' startled looks. She offered a few words, saying, "'Tis them poor black boys, ain't got nothin' better to do than make trouble."

Emil looked at Stephan. "Maybe we should delay our exit."

"You have us to protect you, senator," he replied. "We mustn't let some snotty youths disrupt our evening, must we?"

"If you say so," went Emil, looking less than pleased. He got up, nevertheless. As he did so, he noticed the soldier whispering some orders to his men.

They thanked the staff, Emil leaving a generous tip, and ventured out. The sky was dark, but torches outside both the restaurant and its sister hotel on the opposite side of the street ensured they could see well enough. See the group of youths for one thing. They were swaggering about nearby, swigging beer from bottles. Many of them were the worse for alcohol.

A great, ironic cheer went up from them as the visitors re-emerged. Emil hesitated, as did all the others apart from four of the soldiers who hurried across to the hotel on a mission. Then, before the senator could seize the initiative, the youths had moved across to block his path. Stephan felt down at his waist for something.

The leader of the gang, a fairly muscular individual with close-cropped hair, stepped forward. Bottle in one hand, he held the other arm out, palm outstretched, and shouted for his followers to hear, "And what've we got 'ere? A big fat man!"

A great roar of laughter went up from the youths and Emil said softly, "Move aside please, I don't want any trouble."

"Any trouble?" Gang Leader shouted. "Do yer hear that, boys? He don't want any..."

At which point the pommel of Stephan's dagger went crashing into his mouth. The youth staggered back, bent forward as he spat out teeth and blood. The others were momentarily stunned. Before they could collect themselves, the four guardsmen who had gone back to the hotel ran back out. Brandishing their swords, they placed themselves strategically both ends of the group, so that that none could escape.

"Arrest these scum!" ordered Stephan. "Use the bunting to tie them up."

While half the soldiers stood guard, the others tied up the miscreants with a quiet efficiency. A quick enquiry within the restaurant elicited the whereabouts of the town gaol. In fact the servant woman even volunteered to lead them there. It would be her pleasure.

Taking torches off the buildings to light the way, and with the prisoners tied up firmly, the soldiers allowed the woman to go at the front. Emil and his civilian staff, meanwhile, quietly made their way into the hotel and up to bed.

"Open up in the name of the Thyatiran Senate!" thundered Stephan once they had got to their destination. The noise shook the formerly quiet night air. It brought the white gaoler scuttling out of his den.

Faced with a direct order from someone so clearly in authority, in spite of him being a fellow white, he did as he was told. Besides, it was rather fun having some blacks to lock up, he did not get too many of those. The said blacks were as subdued now as they had been rowdy before. Their leader was moaning piteously at his injury, but no one paid him the slightest attention.

"What a shame," the gaoler remarked, not trying hard to stifle a smirk, "they will be very cramped overnight."

Stephan said that he would leave the matter for the local authorities to deal with, but that Senator Vebber would take an extremely dim view of it if he heard that they had been dealt with leniently.

The message was clear, they were under new management now and law and order would have to be properly enforced. Newton and the other towns would have to buck their ideas up. In time, the new Thyatirans would learn what their new social and financial responsibilities would be. The Despot was keen for this to be a process of implementation over a period of time. When pressed to be more precise, he had said two or so years. "For we don't want to come in like a whirlwind for one thing, but neither can we allow things to carry on in ways different from the rest of us."

A lot of the work would be resting on Emil's shoulders. For this period of time he was effectively the Minister for Norland. His other duties were having to be taken up by the other members during this transition period. This was an initial fact-finding meeting here in Newton. He would be back at the town hall in the morning for part two. This would include getting the mayor to sign the minutes of the first meeting. That way he could not turn round later and say that he did not understand the parameters of what was going on. Emil's efficient clerks would then begin the painstaking task of going through the books in detail. The mayor wanted to hold onto his job. He would do so, as long as he cooperated and came into line with the new directives which were coming his way.

The Despot, and the senate, believed that Thyatira should be a beacon for good local government. They wanted to set an example for the rest of Hoame. It would, in particular, mean increased rights for the white citizens of Norland. Many blacks would not like it and some would move to what remained of Aggeparii. Some, but not most. The majority of blacks would comply, even if they moaned to themselves, for this was the new future and they would not be allowed to hold back the tide of time forever.

~ End of Chapter 4 ~

Prospects of Peace - Chapter 5

Esther loved her husband, the bishop. He was so kind to her when they first met at a church in Krabel-Haan. A native of the city, she had never met a Hoaman before Gunter. He led Bible classes while she sat at the back and listened. It had been lovely to see his sheer joy when she fully committed to the faith. Most importantly, though, he never condemned her for her dubious past. At her baptism, Esther took on that new, Christian name and became a fresh person in more ways than one.

Her relationship with him developed first into friendship and then love. She knew that it was real when, after he took up the position of Mehtar's chaplain, he made every effort to escape the Phalebine and visit her regularly. When, eventually, he asked her to marry him, her joy was complete.

To go with him, when he went back to Hoame, was a huge step for her, but there was no question of her doing otherwise. Now she was ensconced in a magnificent house within the exclusive end of what was now being called Castleton. Moreover, as the bishop's wife she was in a position of respect within the community. Pretty amazing, she considered, for a former pagan temple prostitute.

Her decision to get her former life out into the open soon after arriving was a bold one. Yet it was also shrewd, for it meant she had nothing to hide and no one could blackmail her should they find out. It certainly caused a stir at first, but folk long since stopped talking about it. There was always a new scandal to provide fuel for gossip.

Naturally shy, she fought against her reserved nature in order to throw herself into the role that was expected of her. Women's groups, attending all her husband's services and other duties, she had enough to keep her busy.

Life was not all duty, however, and, when she got the opportunity, she would love to go out and draw. Charcoal was her preferred medium, although the paper here in Thyatira was not of such good quality as that obtainable in Rabeth-Mephar. She made enquiries about importing some. In the meantime, she made do and found herself adapting a style more attune to paper with little wood flakes in it.

Having servants at her beck and call was something else that had taken some getting used to. Wary of a foreign mistress at first, they warmed to her once they got to know her. They were kept extra busy one particular morning though. For she had an important visitor due early afternoon, one who did not visit often.

"Hannah, do come in. I'm glad you could make it."

The Despotess had been kindly disposed to the Ma'hol all her life. Her parents had been personal friends of the current Mehtar and his father before him. So when Esther, the week before, had told her she was working on a miniature bell cradle, Hannah was keen to see it.

Large bell cradles were to be seen throughout Rabeth-Mephar. A set of four (it was always four, the traditional Ma'hol holy number) bells of varying size were set in a row within a wooden framework. Sometimes it was as long as six metres, but often half that. The idea, as old as time, was that the bells must be struck in a special sequence to ensure longevity and good health.

Esther's was altogether on a smaller scale, measuring no more than thirty centimetres across, but it had been intricately made. Set within an "A" frame, the tiny bells were multicoloured and the smallest one exactly half the size of the largest.

"It's beautiful!" Hannah enthused. "It must have taken a while to get them set so finely. It reminds me of ones I've seen in your country - full sized ones, I mean."

"I've been doing it in my spare time. I got the inspiration when I came across the bells on a market stall up at the Castle."

"One of the Ma'hol traders?"

"Yes, of course."

"And does it work?"

"Bring people good luck, you mean?"

The Despotess laughed, although she was not sure if the other woman had been joking or not. "I mean, can I sound them?"

"Oh, yes."

Pausing for a moment, then showing concentration, she hit them with the small stick provided in the sequence 1, 4, 3, 2; 2, 3, 4, 1. Then she added, "That's right, isn't it?"

"According to the main Bon school, yes, but there are other schools who dispute this sequence."

"Oh."

"I hear that the Church over there is seeking to have them based as superstitious throwbacks to the old religion."

"Are they?"

"Which I think would be something of a shame. After all, it's merely a bit of harmless fun, isn't it?"

Hannah was not sure and, rather than commit herself, asked, "Does Gunter approve?"

"He doesn't mind. He said that superstitions only have a hold on you if you allow them to."

With a giggle, Hannah tried them out again. She considered that it would be a shame if such an innocent thing caused arguments over what was right and what was wrong. She mused, 'People don't like to compromise when they think it's something important, like religion. Then an argument ensues. It's a shame that there are so many divisions in the world by opinion, whether it be religion, politics or whatever. So much fussing and fighting...'

Mid-morning and Muggawagga was returning to his office after a meditation session. The following day was been designated a Quiet Day. No visitors would be allowed and the whole period from dawn to dusk was given over to contemplation. Not that they would be sitting down the entire time, for two sessions of walking meditation were set into the schedule. A luncheon, during which no talking was permitted, would also break up the day. The abbot was looking forward to it.

Today, as normal, he found he had one foot in the secular world. He had just been told that a pair of agitated parents had asked to see him. Picking up his pace as he spotted the couple waiting outside his office, he wondered what they wanted. 'I presume they are a novice's parents, I'm not sure which one.'

They certainly did look concerned, he noticed, as he got close and gave them a cordial greeting. Her face sported a deep frown and her husband was wringing his hands. They started speaking as soon as they were seated.

"It's our son," the husband began, then paused as if he expected the abbot to work the rest out. Strangely enough, he could not.

"Your son?"

"Yes, we're extremely worried about him."

93

"He's one of the novices here?"

"No," the man replied, looking puzzled at the suggestion.

"Be he ill? Have you come for prayer?"

"No, it's not that at all. He..."

"Tell him, John!" the wife interrupted.

"I will. He's got it into his head that he wants to be a monk."

"Is that such a bad thing?"

"He's our only child!"

The mother joined in, "He's got it into his head, wanting to do the religious life. Talks about 'testing his vocation,' I don't know where he even got the word from, it certainly weren't from us!"

Calmly, Muggawagga replied, "Perhaps it might be best for all if he did just that. Not everyone who comes here, stays." Seeing the grave faces before him, he added, "Or maybe he should come and see me, alone, and we can talk about it. If you simply forbid him, it could have the opposite effect to the one you want."

"Come and talk to you, alone?" the mother said incredulously.

"Yes."

"But he's only seven years old!"

It was all Muggawagga could do not to burst out laughing, but he restrained himself. This was clearly no laughing matter to these people. Nevertheless, it did mean a change of tack in his approach.

"I think, perhaps, your concerns are premature. He's very young. You will probably find that this is merely a phase that he grows out of. My advice would be to let him work through it in his own way. Like I said, it's probably merely a phase he's goin' through. At the end of things it's in God's hands anyway."

A couple of days later, the abbot was up at the Castle with Frank. The two of them were in the Throne Room and Muggawagga could not resist telling the tale of the worried parents. He felt a bit guilty about breaking a confidence, but the listener found it extremely amusing.

"Seven years old? Oh that's too funny!"

"I'm sorry, I shouldn't have said anything, but I know it won't go any further."

"Don't worry, I'll keep it to myself. You must get a varied selection of problems and ethical dilemmas at the monastery."

"You can say that again, me ol' bucka!"

94

"I remember our ethics module," Frank said wistfully as he remembered his time at the university on Eden, so many years previously. "I always found it frustrating, because the object was never to come to a conclusion. We had to compare situation ethics with... oh, I can't remember half of it now. We'd talk about scenarios such as: if it is wrong to use violence, what should I do if someone was about to attack my family? The debate would go round in circles like smoke from a fire and eventually dissipate in much the same way."

"I never had the benefit of such classes," replied Muggawagga. Then, looking thoughtful, he continued, "Mine is a simple philosophy. I don't think it pays to be too inflexible. My reading of the gospels is that we should approach each situation with Godly love in our hearts. Allow God to speak to us and do whatever the most loving thing is."

"Hmm, that sounds like a pretty good philosophy in life. Our Lord was flexible at times, wasn't he?"

"He wuz indeed; like with the woman caught in adultery."

"As long as we don't throw all our morality out of the window."

"Our Lord did not condone the adulteress' sin. He told her to sin no more. Yet neither did he condemn her."

"No."

"You see, it's all well and good considering scenarios of what might happen, but it isn't real life, is it? I firmly hold that we should enjoy the present moment. We shouldn't spend our lives waiting for some future which may never come. That's not living."

"You're right, Muggawagga. The present is the sole opportunity we have to actually live in. The past is the past and the future is a dream... Do you want another drink?"

Eleazar and Auraura were struck dumb as they walked slowly through central Braskaton. They had witnessed some of the damage to northern Isson, Zebulon's church and Quinty's mansion amongst other casualties, but nothing could prepare them for this. Ladosa's capital city had been absolutely flattened by the superbolide's explosive force.

The whole place was a mass of rubble, with the occasional sturdy building still standing, often with its walls at an angle. There were no streets as such, but narrow paths had been cleared through the debris.

95

The main impression was of mounds of bricks interspersed with timbers and other wreckage. A closer inspection revealed odd items such as a child's toy here, or a broken chest of drawers there.

Frasses skipped amongst the ruins and the smell on a warm day was quite revolting. At first there did not appear to be any living souls about, but once their eyes got accustomed, they could see signs of life. A dust-covered man of indeterminate age was sifting through what was left of his demolished house, searching for something. He was oblivious to the couple slowly walking past. They moved on in silence. At the base of a large building, two walls of which still partly standing, was a mother with a couple of children. They were squatting over a small fire and looked listless.

"Have you noticed people's eyes?" whispered Auraura.

"Yes, they look dazed, even after this time."

In the few weeks since the impact, the couple had been busy helping out in Isson. There were people to comfort as well as practical help with reconstruction. Zebulon and Laurence were seeing to the replacement of the church steeple and the repairs to Quinty's house now bequeathed to them. Eleazar's poor church in the southern part of town was unaffected by the blast. He found his work cut out in stopping his flock gloating over the damage to the rich people's houses and not their own. Indeed he found it essential to come down hard on the pernicious doctrine that it was God's will that the rich should suffer. He had even managed to get a team together to help with manual work in the affected area. It was the least they should be doing considering the assistance given to them over the past year.

What of the surrounding area? Reports came in that it had been devastated on a scale immeasurably worse than Isson. All the same, the hill folk were an insular people at the best of times, few wanted to descend to the plain and help those there, be they Rose or Buff supporters. After all, up until now the outsiders had wanted to take them over.

It is an ill wind that blows nobody good. News was that the Badlands to the northeast were affected worst of all. That meant that the uniting of the tribes there, along with their foreign backer, had been nipped firmly in the bud. There would be no army of Oonimari on the march in Ladosa. Exactly what had happened to them was unknown, but it appeared to amount to annihilation. One less enemy to worry about, maybe more. The eastern Rose enclave was close to the epicentre and ceased to exist. The main Buff area was also hit hard and the northern Pinks had not escaped unscathed. The civil war in this side of the country had been cast aside by a bigger enemy that gave no regards to persons or property.

Tales of Braskaton's fate pricked Eleazar's conscience and, discussing it with his wife, he found that she too felt that some form of help should be sent. They had discussed it with Zebulon's church members, but met with a lukewarm response. "We've been hit hard ourselves!" they complained, "we can't be bothering about them." Charity, it seems, began at home.

So the duo had set off by themselves. Now they were in the centre of the city. Or rather, former city, for it bore no resemblance to a functioning metropolis. Lefange, another large town to the northwest, had also been hit, if not quite so badly. The natural phenomenon left Braskaton looking like they had been atom bombed.

Laybbon, to the west, was in a better state, thankfully for them. Local government officials dispatched soldiers to the other two conurbations to help them. Burial of the dead was a high priority for obvious reasons. There were many of them and the scale of the operation was so enormous that they felt overwhelmed. The one good note in all this was that none of the other sides in the conflict was taking advantage by invading the central area controlled by the Buffs. Maybe taking over ruined cities did not appeal to them. In any case, the only factions carrying on the fight - the western Rose, the southwest Buffs and the Neo-Purples - were too engaged with each other.

On the day Eleazar and Auraura visited, there were no helpers from Laybbon to be seen. The pair had been put off taking food on the grounds that unruly people might steal the lot before they could distribute it fairly. All they had were a few blankets which, looking at the scene of utter devastation, seemed inadequate to the point of being pathetic. For two coins, Auraura would have dumped the blankets, but she did not. Seeing a couple of children playing amongst the piles of rubble, she felt an urge to go over and comfort them. Then she spotted a woman, presumably their mother, scowling at her and went back to Eleazar.

"Look at it," she said softly, scanning the entire scene, "nothing but destruction as far as the eye can see."

"I know; the casualties must be enormous."

They walked on, heading vaguely for a large, square building that had fared better than most, but was still an empty shell with the roof gone. A couple of families were sitting there listlessly. A half-hearted attempt had been made to clear the inside, but it was still a chaotic mess with broken timbers all over the place.

Trying not to be put off by the initial hostile looks, the husband and wife team entered the building.

"We were wondering..."

"Go away! We don't want your sort around here," cried one of the women. The rest of them, a mixture of adults and children, looked decidedly unfriendly. Before her husband said anything, Auraura pulled him away and he complied. They withdrew a safe distance, where she said, "Let's go home. These people are not ready for help yet." Without a word, he followed her back along the track and they started heading in the direction of home.

A little further on was another small group of children and the visitors fairly dumped the blankets on them and walked away at a faster pace. As they did so, they noticed a man making a beeline for them, moving along another track which intersected theirs further up. He was alone and his body language was not threatening. However, as they got closer, they saw he had a Buff official's uniform on and the couple slowed and tensed up.

"Welcome! My name's Martyn Dupont..."

It was a cheerful greeting and his name was clearly not a Ladosan one.

"... have you come all the way from Hoame?"

Eleazar chortled before saying, "My hair is a bit of a giveaway! I am from Hoame originally, of course, but I am currently living in Isson."

This was followed by introductions, during which Martyn explained that he was part of the mission from Laybbon.

"My colleagues are helping out in the north of the city today and I'm rather left on my own. I saw you give those children the blankets; that was kind."

"Oh," went Auraura, "it was the least we could do."

"They might not need them now, but once the colder weather sets in a warm blanket will be like gold dust in these parts."

"It's so overwhelming."

"It is. I've been here a week now and I still can't take everything in. Those who survived are in a state of chronic shock. A lot of our time has been spent locating and burying the dead.... those we can find, that is. Also clearing tracks through the rubble."

"Will it ever be rebuilt?"

"Braskaton? It seems unthinkable not to, but what a task! It's hard to know how many people were killed, for those survivors with families elsewhere have left the devastation. We were swamped with wounded, but have dealt with them the best we can. There's a field hospital set up in the west of the city, several in fact, but they're overflowing."

Eleazar explained that unfortunately there was not much sympathy amongst the hill folk for their brethren's plight. "Maybe if we took in some of the wounded it might soften their hearts."

"So it's been a Hoamen and a non Isson lady who have taken the initiative." Then, in response to Auraura's quizzical expression, he explained, "Your accent gives you away. I'd say you're from the northwest - Tracana?"

"Very good!" she responded, well impressed. This man was most pleasant, unlike a normal Buff official. Maybe they were nicer when met on a one-to-one basis. Returning to the business in hand, she said, "The scale of it all is simply overwhelming, what can we do?"

"You could tell the good citizens of Isson about the desperate plight of so many down here. Pull a few heartstrings and appeal to their humanity. If your hospital could treat some injured, help them convalesce, it would be doing good on more than one level. Now the war is over we need to rebuild bridges."

Eleazar and Auraura came away from the encounter with renewed hope. They would certainly be telling the Committee about conditions down here and press for some help to be organised.

"Our visit hasn't been a failure then," Auraura remarked once they were back in the countryside and hitting the road home.

"No, indeed."

"I'll never get over the first time we saw it, though."

"We experienced the power of the fireball up at the crater. It's not surprising it could do this to a city."

"Maybe not, but even so... The death toll must be appalling."

"Mmmm."

"He mentioned Tracana, I wonder how they've fared. I've still got friends there."

"They're a long way away. I expect they will be all right."

"Nevertheless, I'm tempted to travel there to see with my own eyes."

"Across the country at this time, when for all we know there is no law and order being maintained?"

"Hmm, it *is* a long way. I'll have to think about it."

The sawmill was proving a most profitable enterprise. Mr O paid off Deejan Charvo's loan early. It was only now that Onstein realised quite how much money the dishonest, former employee, David, had been creaming off. There was no absolute proof after this time. The best thing was to put it behind him and move on. What mattered was that business was booming and he was becoming wealthier by the week.

Flonass got into the office early as there was some catching up to do. This time of year, with the days getting shorter, working hours were from shortly after dawn to shortly before dark. He had set off when the sun was still below the horizon and admired the beautiful sky as he walked to the sawmill.

He was trusted with his own key and got it out as he ascended the external staircase to the first floor office. There was a lot of work on currently as the end of season accounts had to be reconciled. The white did not mind, for he would rather have too much work to do than too little. At the present rate he would have plenty to keep himself occupied well into the winter season when a lot of normal activity ceased.

These quiet, early hours were the most productive he found and his enjoyment of the job came hand in hand with being conscientious. His parents could tell that he was establishing himself in this position and were pleased to see it.

On this occasion, Flonass had not been in long before Mr O came breezing in. He liked his manager and was a lot more relaxed in the company of the black these days. Onstein clearly enjoyed the company of his personal assistant and spoke freely to him on nearly about every topic under the sun. In fact it was a bit disconcerting sometimes how much he would confide in the young man, but he seemed to have a need to speak to someone. He chatted freely and Flonass was not going to betray any of the confidences given him.

"Look what I've got, my boy!" he exclaimed, waving some papers in the air triumphantly. "The ownership documents have finally come through. Every last 't' is crossed and last 'i' is dotted. The mill is all mine now and no mistake."

"Congratulations, Mr O," Flonass exclaimed cheerfully.

"Cheers, thank you. The deal was done a time ago, but this paperwork has been taking an age. It's a mere formality, I know, but I can relax now it's completed. I thought we might celebrate. I have some Ladosan wine to share..." and he produced a bottle and a couple of glasses from a bag. The white had tried some wines when in Azekah, but he had not liked them much. "I know what you're thinking, how did I get hold of such a rarity? But I can tell you it predates their civil war by some years. I've been holding on to it for a while now, looking for an opportunity to celebrate. The wife doesn't drink alcohol, you see, but you'll join me won't you?"

It was not an offer to be refused. He took the two-thirds full glass and took a sip. It tasted at least as bad as the Azekah stuff to his pallet. He tried not to show his distaste, but without much success.

"Ah, not for you?" his boss said, before carefully taking his first sip. He played with the liquid in his mouth for a short while before swallowing. Looking hard at his glass, he went on, "I see what you mean, not quite as good as I'd been expecting. Oh well, never mind. You don't have to finish that if you don't want to."

"No, it's okay," Flonass lied cheerfully as he did not want to cause offence.

Mr Onstein, though, was lost in his thoughts now, which he proceeded to reveal at length. "We're no longer beholden to Mr Hanson, that's the truth of the matter. It gives me a great sense of freedom to say that. I know it's been a while, but it only seems real now the paperwork is completed. I have some plans... I've had them for some time, actually. With this new situation, this extra territory coming into Thyatira, I see opportunities for the future. My spies tell me that there's but one sawmill in this Norland and it's technologically behind us. Our steam-driven saw is not up to maximum capacity. I reckon, come the spring, we can increase

101

production and sell more down there. I've priced things up and we can undercut them an' still make a profit."

"I see."

"I'm not sure I'd ever have been able to persuade Hanson of the merits of this plan. He was all for the status quo. A funny man, I always had to deal through an intermediary which slowed communication and added an extra barrier to getting things done."

"Everyone knows Hanson is a recluse, Mr O."

"They do, my boy! That they do. For why? When I finally saw inside his stockade it was an anticlimax. He does not live in a palace. 'Tis a wooden structure of considerable age from the looks of it. If he has all this tremendous wealth, and that appears to be the case, why does he put up with it?"

"I don't rightly know."

"Me neither. I've never heard of a white landowner before, neither in Rilesia, nor Thyatira... nor anywhere else for that matter. And his name... 'Hanson,' what sort of name *is* that? It's not a white's name, nor a black's."

"Nor a drone's," Flonass added helpfully.

"No, indeed."

"There have always been stories about him, that he practices black magic to keep him from getting old."

"What, sacrificing young virgins?" the older man said in mocking tone. Flonass shrugged his shoulders before Mr O continued, "I'm surprised the Church hasn't got involved. Then I guess that if he keeps himself to himself there's no need to."

"But you got to see him."

"I did indeed."

"An' is he a white?"

"Most certainly... and not as old as I expected either. Anyhow, I should not complain, for he sold me this place at a fair price - more than fair - and with a minimum of fuss."

"I was wondering if he was a drone."

"Certainly not! It's always struck me how few drones there are in Thyatira, ever since I came here. There were a lot more in Rilesia."

"Were there?"

"I remember once, when I was a young man about your age. We came out of a local tavern, I was with a few friends and we met a drone lying in the street. He'd been attacked and I administered first aid. There was a lot of blood, I ended up with it on my hands and clothes. He'd been robbed and left for dead, but thankfully he didn't die. In fact he made a full recovery. Valentine was his name, an arrogant fellow and leader of a guild squad there in Rilesia. I got precious little thanks and no reward for my assistance."

Into the silence that followed, Flonass asked, "Did you do it for the reward?"

"Help him?" asked Mr O for clarification. His tone was more of shock at the suggestion rather than offence. "No, of course not," he replied, "but it would have been nice to have received recognition."

"I don't think I've ever spoken to a drone. My friend Darda told me he's spoken to Alan up at the Castle. He's not a normal drone from all that I've heard about him."

"Quite the hero, I gather, and the Despot's right-hand man, yes. He must be the exception that proves the rule."

"What rule is that, Mr O?"

"The thing that people say about drones."

"I'm not sure I rightly know."

"That they're a bunch of effeminate ne'er do wells!"

At this, they broke into laughter, just as the first customer of the day entered the office. A mature white man from Vionium, he looked shocked at the frivolity. The proprietor immediately became serious and asked what he could do for him.

Flonass got back to his numbers following the distraction. Future plans, Hanson and drones, his conversations with Mr O were nothing if not varied.

"You can't be everywhere at once, Muggawagga."

"You be right, but this wuz the first time I be there in a long time."

The abbot was visiting Deejan Charvo up at the latter's Castleton's residence. The two of them were alone in the merchant's spacious study.

"Anyway, how did you find the refugee camp?"

"Things be a lot more static these days. There've been no new arrivals for several weeks. Those who are there have made a community life for themselves. They have an art group, weaving, even an amateur dramatics group. It keeps them occupied."

"And a political debating society, no doubt."

"I don't think so. They may be Ladosans, but they can see that division has caused the war over the border. They don't want politics causing arguments in the camp."

"So it's a bit of a taboo subject then?"

"That be right."

"Are most resigned to a second winter in Hoame?"

"I'd say so. It's a good thing those cabins were built as sturdily as they waz. If I said they're resigned to it, I'd be giving you the wrong impression. They're merely being realistic about it. That's why they're organising all them groups."

"You have to admire their resilience."

"Our mission at the camp still finds itself fully occupied. A lot of counselling takes place there. Most of the refugees are from the southern part of Ladosa. But a few are from father north, nearer to where that there thing hit them, the thing from the sky."

"A meteorite, the Despot informs me."

"But we're not getting solid news from them parts. Plenty of rumours and nothin' good."

"What about you, Muggawagga, your family? I hope they are okay with all the turmoil going on."

"They were well, the last I heard, me old bucka! My parents don't want to get involved in the conflict; they try to bend with the wind. I pray for them every day."

"Of course."

"But they're over to the west of the country, where I understand they were safe from the meteorite. I hope so. Contact is well nigh impossible these days."

"The war still carries on, the Despot informs me," said Deejan, before taking a large gulp of his drink of water. "He's being kept informed by Alan. The lines of communication through the Mitas Gap are still intact, I gather, but we only get reliable information about the south of the country."

"Hmm," the abbot sounded thoughtful. "My former countrymen are certainly suffering, one way or another."

Then, seeking to lighten the mood, Deejan asked, "Did you sell much in the way of autumn fruits up at the market this year?"

"That we did, both in Vionium and up here at the Castle. We're goin' to see how the weather goes, but I reckon we'll be able t'sell some meat come the spring. I want us to be self-sufficient in the long run. Despot Thorn has been most generous with grants. They've helped with a lot of the building work, but we're entering a new phase now. An' he's going to need his money for this Norland takeover. From what I hear, some parts are a bit run down and'll need bringing up to speed with the rest of Thyatira."

Deejan smiled, saying, "You have to be good with finances as well as the spiritual side of things."

"As innocent as doves, but as wise as serpents."

"That's right."

"But I'm wanting to extend the work that the monastery does in the community. Our prayer life, plus our extended periods of meditation, are vitally important to form a foundation for our spiritual life, but as well as..."

Muggawagga broke off there, because Keturah had quietly opened the door and come in. It was during her free time, for her working day had long finished.

"And what can I do for you?" her father said amiably. Neither man was perturbed by the interruption.

The girl spoke, "I could not help hearing your conversation from the hall. I wondered if you wouldn't mind if I sat in and listened. Deejan looked at his guest who shrugged and said it was no problem as far as he was concerned. So she gently sat down on a chair a little to one side and observed the other pair in silence.

The abbot spoke for a while about his plans for the monastery to reach out to the wider community. This would take several forms.

"Since we started, we've had two families... I hesitate to use the word 'dump,' but in any case two families have left their mentally retarded children with us. I thought it wuz an imposition at first, but the nuns have taken them under their wing and they are doing well. I'm not convinced they will ever be equipped to live in the outside world, but I am hopeful they will be able to make a contribution to the life of the monastery, in more ways than one."

They discussed ways in which the institution could be used to provide care for more people with mental illness. All the time, Keturah sat their quietly, taking it all in. After a while, Muggawagga brought up another idea.

"I believe it would do good if we can enter the local economy more. I've already mentioned us bringing our surplus meat and vegetables to market. We've been selling our honey for years. It all takes a good deal of organising and I must not lose sight of our primary spiritual purpose. The produce side of things is a bit haphazard at the moment, although I do have a vision. I do like the idea of us helping in a practical way. We are in the world, whether we like it or not, and helping the wider community thrive comes under 'good works' in my books."

"You could do with a business manager."

Both men turned to Keturah, surprised. Encouraged by this, she spoke further.

"If you employed a dedicated business manager, he could take care of the secular side of things while you concentrated on the holy ones."

"You're right!" confessed Muggawagga, impressed by the maturity she was showing. He had set up the monastery from nothing and it was still very much his child in his eyes. Yet there was much wisdom in the girl's suggestion. Rather obvious in fact, but he had not seen the wood for the trees. Delegation was not his greatest skill, but he would have to learn to apply it.

"I could do it... one day," she added.

After exchanging glances with Deejan, he replied, "I dare say you could. I think I'd better find someone else in the interim. It's not that we don't already employ folk on the non-spiritual side, because we do. But a manager to oversee matters and give us an overall strategy, now that would be a step forward. Thank you, Keturah."

She looked down and blushed, but he added in humorous tones, "You haven't any more ideas have you?"

Starting slowly, she said, "I have been thinking..."

"Yes?" he wanted to encourage her.

"How about hosting a festival in the spring? Something to raise people's spirits following the winter. There could be a feast, music and you could put on morality plays to entertain and educate them at the same time."

"Mmm, that's an idea an' a half, me ol'.... I think I should get you to come and organise it."

He was joking, of course, but he was mightily impressed by the teenager's ideas and was certainly not dismissive. The three of them discussed the festival idea at length. Later, on his way home, he considered the encounter with Keturah.

'Not for the first time, she has shown extraordinary maturity. The girl is wise beyond her years. The festival idea is inspired. I'd have to run it past the Despot first, but with some publicity here and there, it could prove extremely popular. It would take some dedicated organising....'

Coming off the main road, he walked along a shortcut to the monastery. The nettles at the side of the path had died back, while the blackberries were well over. The air possessed a chill and, with the pale, overcast sky, it was clear that winter was round the corner.

'Why has no one at the monastery suggested a manager to organise these things? It's pretty obvious when you think about it. Maybe I was too closely involved in matters to see it for myself, but other people... Am I that unapproachable? I hope I'm not too overpowering. I'll have to give it some thought... and a lot of prayer."

A few days leave was usually a welcome break. Yet for Darda it had not gone well. He had been hoping to meet up with either Flonass, or Vophsi, or better still, both of them. They were so busy with their own lives, though, that it was not possible on this occasion. Staying at his parents' house for a few days, he managed to have an argument with them which soured the air. It was over such a trivial thing too. Then, to cap it all, he was having to sleep in the living room, because his bedroom had been promised to visiting relatives.

On his last night, he lay awake in the dark, looking forward to daybreak when he would return to duties up at the Castle. He shifted on the settee. It was short in length and he had to have his feet on a stool. The nights were getting colder, but his body was well wrapped up in blankets.

He heard a shuffling sound, that would be his aunt who did this most nights.

"It'll be through 'ere," whispered a male voice.

"Go on then," came a reply.

In his dozy state, it took a moment for Darda to work out what was going on. By the time he realised that a burglary was in progress, two men were entering the room he was in. They carried a small lantern which gave out a mere fraction of light, but it made a big difference in the otherwise pitch black.

Without stopping to think, he leapt off the sofa and went straight for one of the tall, brass candlesticks above the fire. Before the leading intruder realised what was happening, he was being struck by a heavy object. Later, over breakfast, Darda told his parents what had happened after that.

"There was a scuffle and the light went out. It was all chaotic really. I got shoved and the one behind pulled away the man I'd hit, I think. Before I knew it, they'd gone."

"And left blood all over my living room!" complained his mother. It was a gross exaggeration, but there were a few, small splatters here and there.

"Be thankful it was his blood and not mine."

Father then piped up, saying, "I never heard a thing, slept through the lot."

Mother continued, "It's plain why they came. It's that there silly lagua trophy. We never had burglars before. Not got anything of value... except my candlesticks and you managed to dent one of those."

"It was already dented," Darda complained, but it was no use, he was already in his mother's bad books. He returned to the Castle early.

Meanwhile, Frank experienced a funny morning incident of his own. Lying awake in the middle of the night, he had got so bored that he decided to get up. In utter darkness, he groped his way to the door and, operating the latch as quietly as possible, went out. Once in the corridor, he reached out blindly for the tinderbox which was always kept on the table outside the door. In recent years he had become quite proficient at igniting the char cloth in order to get a candle burning. Yet on this occasion he reached out and knocked it off the table. The fire steel landed on his bare foot and it was all he could do not to shout out at the pain. At least it did not made as much noise as if it had landed on the floor. He felt around on his hands and knees, but apart from the steel itself, he could only locate the tinderbox lid. He probed some more, but it was a helpless task. In the end he had to admit defeat and crawled back to bed.

"Hey, sleepy!" cried Hannah, "are you coming down to breakfast?"

Frank woke to find it was well past dawn. Recalling the night's mini-adventure brought a smile to his face until the bruise on his foot registered itself.

"You look tired."

"It wasn't the best night's sleep, but at least I've made up some hours now."

"Do you want your breakfast brought up?"

"No, no, I'll get up and join you."

After getting washed, he heard female voices the other side of the door as he got dressed."

"What's all this mess?"

"I don't know, My Lady, I've this moment come on duty."

Shoeless, he hurried for the door and opened it, keen that his wife blame no one else for his clumsiness.

"It was me, last night."

He gave a full account of what had happened over breakfast in the hall. It gave Hannah an early laugh that day. Further up the table, old Castle stalwarts had chosen to eat there that morning. Eko, Natias and Laffaxe were engaged in conversation. The retired physician looked awfully thin to Frank's eyes, but he did not say anything.

After the meal, he decided to go to the chapel for a short time of prayer. He did not have an early appointment and it would calm his mind in preparation for the day.

The noise in the hall was dying down as people dispersed to go about their business. Inside the chapel he found Squad Leader Darda taking a keen interest in one of the wood carvings on the wall. Upon seeing his Despot, he looked guilty, apologised and began walking out, but stopped when Frank addressed him.

"Good morning, Darda is everything okay?" he asked. For the young man's demeanour was melancholy, as if he had his own personal cloud hovering over him.

"Yes, My Lord."

"Are you sure?"

"It's nothing."

"Tell me about nothing."

So the two of them ended up sitting down on a bench in the chapel, Darda telling him about the attempted burglary and his mother's reaction. When it was over, Frank quizzed him.

"They didn't manage to take anything?"

"No, My Lord."

"But you're pretty sure it was the lagua's paw they were after?"

"I think my mother's probably right there. It's becoming a burden. Maybe it's my own silly fault for talking about it in public. I should have thought. It's attracted a lot of interest; too much interest."

"I'm going to get the constables to investigate this. It's totally unacceptable to have burglars around." Then, flashing a smile, Frank came out with an idea that had suddenly occurred to him. "How about if you bring it up here to the Castle? We have the tapestry here, *The Hunting of the Lagua*, it could be placed in a display cabinet above there. I can order one to be made to measure. It will still belong to you, but be on view to the public and safe. No one is going to try and steal it from here! What do you say?"

"Thank you, My Lord, that's a great idea."

"Good. Bring it here and we'll take the measurements. We can get a piece of good quality glass cut especially for the front."

'That will not be cheap,' thought Darda, before giving his thanks once again and asking, "Shall I bring it in next time I have some leave?"

"Oh no, go back and get it today. I'll explain to Jonathan if I see him around. We'll keep it safe until such time as the cabinet is completed. It will still belong to you. I'll get a plaque written to that effect."

Darda left the room feeling a whole lot better. He felt grateful to have a despot, no less, who was concerned for his welfare and willing to put himself out for him. Captain Jonathan had not told him off recently either. Things were looking up.

~ End of Chapter 5 ~

Prospects of Peace - Chapter 6

The first snows came to Ladosa. Most of the country was covered in a white blanket, but it had not lain thick. A sharp drop in the ambient temperature coincided with a secession of snowfall and the ground was easily passable.

Following Eleazar and Auraura's visit to the remains of Braskaton, it was arranged for twenty-five injured people to be transported to Isson's main hospital. It was a drop in the ocean, they knew, but the pair were not alone in hoping that the gesture would help build fences come the peace. While there was no more fighting in their vicinity, reports were coming through of continued hostilities elsewhere in the country. It was highly unusual for war to be pursued once winter arrived, but nevertheless it was happening.

Having moved south to the Fanallon Front, where the action was, Marshal Nazaz was briefing her officers. Alongside her stood chief Hoame advisor, Alan. She pointed to a large-scale map laid out on the table.

"In the first week of this winter offensive," she said, "four out of five objectives have been achieved. This village, Taldor, has not yet been secured, but Captain Hallazanad is hopeful of being able to do so within the next couple of days. A contingent of diehard Buffs are holed out there, but I don't see that derailing our general plan."

The commanders stared hard at the map as Charlotta continued.

"The element of surprise has run its course, but with continued attacks along these points we can keep them off balance."

"Surely it's obvious," one officer pointed out, "that our chief goal here is Fanallon. They must know it's the prize we seek."

The speaker was Major Panarez. Recently arrived from an administration job behind the lines, he seemed keen to earn his spurs in real combat.

It was Alan who responded. "They will think that, yes, but as previously mentioned, we must not use that mindset. The destruction of the Buff army is our main objective. Indeed, our sole objective. Once that has been achieved we can walk into Fanallon, or any other town in the southwest. Don't let's get fixated about Fanallon. If the

Buffs want to do that, it will help our cause, but only if we continue to be unpredictable in our attacks."

Charlotta took up the theme. "The Buffs still have considerable resources to use against us. They are a lot weaker than when the conflict began and we have grown stronger, but the need to avoid a war of attrition remains. We must to remain smarter than they."

"It's working!" declared Alan. "Fifteen hundred prisoners taken in the first week. Yes, things are slowing down a bit now, but the initial push is always the deepest."

Then Charlotta went over the objectives for the coming week. The plan involved more thrusts into enemy territory and enveloping Buff units by swift pincer movements wherever possible. The current weather was thought to be in their favour.

One officer asked, "Is it true that intelligence reports are saying that Buff General Vap is opposing us on this front now?"

"The Butcher of Wesold? Yes, our council has put a price on his head. We want him captured alive so that he can be put on trial for his war-crimes. He must not be allowed to get away with it."

The marshal's predecessor had been murdered whilst under a flag of truce, thanks to Vap. All the people present knew this. She went on to a fresh topic.

"We are indebted to certain of our agents for supplying us with inside information from the enemy camp. Their job is dangerous, but vital in keeping us ahead of the game. Unfortunately it is getting increasingly difficult for them to get messages through to us. One of our agents was discovered recently, we don't know how. The enemy are putting more resources into counter-intelligence... or maybe it is a matter of them being more aware. Either way, things are harder than ever for them."

Then Alan spoke up again, "Are you going to mention the possible security breach?"

All eyes turned to Charlotta. She had not been sure whether to mention it, but now she was put on the spot.

"We're not quite sure it *is* a security breach, but one of our reconnaissance patrols recently had a lucky escape. They were ambushed and it occurred to the commanding officer that the enemy was waiting for them. I mean, it was as if they had prior knowledge of the operation. The quick actions of the commander ensured that they managed to give the Buff devils the slip."

"Casualties?" asked a voice from the back.

"None serious, fortunately. All relevant parties have been interviewed and nothing concrete has come up. The same feeling was experienced by more than one member of the patrol... namely that a trap had been set for them."

Major Panarez commented, "Ambushes happen in war, it does not necessarily mean a breach of security. It could be for another reason."

Not wanting to extend what would have been a pointless conversation, Charlotta said, "I merely mention it. It does no harm to remind ourselves of the need for care. Only divulge information when there is a direct need to know."

"Naturally," the major replied.

"Good. I know that the people around this table are my most trusted advisors, but vigilance is important. Now Alan has something to say."

Taking centre stage, the Hoaman began. "So far, the offensive has gone well. The enemy was not expecting a major attack in these wintry conditions. Yet the snow is still not deep enough to hamper our operations. There is every reason to continue while we still can. The Buffs are a tenacious enemy, but signs are that they are not the force that they once were. Without doubt, constant operations against multiple adversaries have weakened them. We have the Rose army in the northwest to thank for tying up a sizeable force of Buffs away from here. We must make the most of this opportunity."

He went on to show on the map where the next Neo-Purple thrusts would take place. The plans were discussed in detail before Alan said, "We will be keeping up our deep penetration patrols. These are more important than ever now that our own agents, as you heard, are experiencing difficulties in getting their messages through. Knowledge of the enemy's movements are essential if we are to keep them on the hop and retain the initiative. If we can drive through the enemy here to the Rabeth-Mephar border, they will be cut in two. It will be a significant step towards victory over our most powerful foe."

"What of the Rose, then?" asked Panarez. "Surely they have a presence near Wesold."

"They do, but so far there are no reports of them having come into contact with our units. The Rose seem content to fight the Buffs for the time being and that plays into our hands. There's every sign that the war in the northeast of the country has come to a halt due to the fireball. If we can secure a victory here before the Central Buffs regain their composure, it could be a step towards us winning the entire war."

Time would, of course, show whether such an optimistic assessment was accurate or not. For now it did not matter. The Neo-Purple commanders knew the plan and their part in it. They would do their best to see it was carried out.

The following few days saw fierce fighting along several stretches of the front. The Buffs possessed fewer troops here in the south and initiative was with their increasingly confident adversaries.

Alan did not like being out of the action. As an advisor, he was not supposed to get involved in the actual fighting. That rule had been strictly applied at first, but now it was loosening. With the central section of the southern front showing signs of an imminent breakthrough, he got permission to don uniform and equipment and join the fray.

This occurred as a unit of veterans, led by Captain Hallazanad, was about to storm a large, isolated building. The soldiers were observing their objective when the Hoaman joined them and exchanged greetings with the captain. The latter was not sure about protocol and asked, "Are you taking command of this operation?"

"Oh no," Alan was quick to reassure him. It would not be right to do so. It was not clear where amongst the ranks "Chief Advisor" fell, but Alan had no intention of disrupting Hallazanad's command. He continued, "I'm here to tag along," and gave a cheeky grin.

In response, he was told the situation. From the cover of a clump of trees, four hundred metres from their objective, the captain explained. "We believe this to be some sort of Buff H.Q. There could be some senior officers there, maybe Vap himself."

"But you're not sure."

"No, we've advanced ahead of our reconnaissance units."

"Really?"

"There were none present, anyway."

"So it is a surmise that this is their H.Q."

"We have no binoculars, but there has been limited activity since we got here. There are definitely uniformed personnel around the building."

114

Taking a good look, Alan could see the objective clearly. A square, four story structure, the architecture left a lot to be desired. It had obviously been a country estate in peacetime, the formal gardens in the middle-ground proved that. The building itself showed sharp lines and its multiple, oblong windows possessed no decorative gables to break up its harshness.

In front of the soldiers was a stretch of flat, open ground before the gardens started. The bushes there were islands of green in a white landscape. The snow covering was thin, so moving should not be a problem.

The captain was trying to stop himself from shivering The cold was starting to get to him.

"There's no way of getting round to look at the front?" Alan enquired.

"They have a sentry on the roof and they'd spot us in an instance."

"So what's the plan?"

"There's another unit due to join us any minute. Then we continue to wait."

"Wait?"

"Until dusk. We'll speed across the open ground, traverse the gardens and enter the building simultaneously from front and rear. I'll give a full briefing once the other unit arrives. It's important that none of the enemy escape. Timing will be vital; if we're too early, they'll spot us as we break cover. Too late and we'll be groping in the dark."

"Lanterns?"

"None that work. Speed, discipline and timing are going to be essential if the plan is going to work."

Alan surveyed the scene again, careful to stay behind the screen of trees. The ground was hard, the air cold. If they could spend the night in that conquered building it was going to be a whole lot better than stuck out here.

The winter sun was dropping to the horizon when the reinforcements arrived. Hallazanad retreated back from the trees a short distance into a wide ditch. There he gave the extra troops a thorough briefing, clouds of water vapour coming from his mouth as he spoke. By the end of it each soldier knew exactly what the mission was and their part in the scheme of things. Alan was impressed and could not think to recommend any amendments to the captain's plan. All they could do now, as the man in charge said, was wait.

Dusk came early this time of year which was a relief to the attacking force. Inactivity had chilled them to the marrow and, still hidden from view, they did exercises in the snow to get the circulation going again. Helmets were put on, the metal cold even through gloved hands. This time of year a lot of the armour was leather rather than steel. Strips of light, but tough halku wood had been carefully sewn between the layers for extra strength.

Before the light failed completely they filed out of the wood and lined up in open ground. They would be extremely hard to spot by a sentry. Forward they moved at a fast pace.

Alan was striking out with the captain. He would be amongst the force storming the front door. It felt good to get his muscles working again. Colours quickly disappeared and the bushes were grey now. They traversed these and the differently-assigned units split up.

Skirting round the side of the structure, they could see orange glows from lanterns in many of the windows. Eventually they were in position at the front. Before they could strike, though, they heard a commotion which appeared to be coming from the rear of the building. The others had attacked prematurely. There were no two ways about it, they had to go in. Without a fuss, Hallazanad led his troops forward as they made their way across a courtyard to the front door. The area was gravelled, but their boots made little noise due to the stones being frozen together.

No sentry at the front door, so they stormed forward. Alan noticed a couple of wagons stationed nearby with white awnings. The dakks coughed at the sudden intrusion, but it was too late for the defenders. The Neo-Purples burst through the unlocked door into a large reception area... to be confronted by a startled-looking man in a white coat.

Stretchers propped up against the wall on the left, so sign of a guard, Alan exclaimed, "It's a hospital!"

All psyched up for a do or death struggle, the attackers took a bit of calming down once it was realised that a fight was not going to take place after all. It was indeed a military hospital, one that had been evacuated the morning before of all except the worst injured. There seemed to be plenty of these and they were being cared for by a skeleton medical staff who had opted to stay behind even as their front moved backwards. The sentry on the roof turned out to be a dummy.

A guard was put on all exits, but a lot of the soldiers, once they had composed themselves, congregated into a single room. There they got a large supply of cut logs and fed the fire until it was roaring away. Downing hot drinks and eating food stolen from the kitchens, they settled in for the night.

Hallazanad met up with Alan following a discussion with the head surgeon. "A lot of soldiers here are weak with sickness and diarrhoea. It's a good thing ours are keeping out of the way. When the sick are well enough, we'll take them back as prisoners."

"We must be ready for any counter-attack."

"True, but the front seems to have folded in this sector. If there's sickness going through the enemy camp it explains a thing or two."

"Yeah."

"The surgeon's complained about looting, but I told him it's only a bit of food. My troops were hungry, I don't mind them taking that."

"And our main army?"

"They'll arrive tomorrow with a bit of luck. We'll be vulnerable to a large-scale counter-attack until then. I'll send out patrols first thing, see how the land lies west of here."

"There's still a long way to go," stated Alan, talking more generally, "but we're making good progress."

Following a lull in the conversation, Hallazanad asked, "Do you think the war will be over soon, in the spring?"

With a chuckle, Alan replied, "I'm not in the business of making predictions. Who knows? We still need to keep the enemy off balance as long as possible. As long as the weather holds, we should press on with this winter offensive."

Late morning saw Tristan and Ayllom taking a well-earned break. Thirty kilometres away from Alan's current position, they were attached to a forward field hospital. Under canvas, in a snowy field, it was a world away from the mansion they were stationed in at the beginning of hostilities. The pair sat on a fat, mossy log, a short distance from their tent.

Their art collection was still at the cottage, now a full day's journey back from the line. When they had rescued it from the elements, it had been something of a joke to them. Now they were concerned for it.

"I don't want someone looting it while we're away," Ayllom commented.

His colleague replied, "Not many people know about it. That caretaker chap said he'd look after the property."

"I hope so."

"What you're saying is, you don't want anyone to steal the stolen artwork."

"I'm not a thief!" the Ladosan said with feeling. "I have every intention of returning them to their rightful owners after the war."

"You might get a reward," Tristan replied, but the comment went unanswered.

They were both wrapped up warmly with many layers of clothing, but Ayllom still stomped on the ground to try and stop his feet from going numb with cold.

Tristan was chewing a faltice root. It tasted vaguely of liquorice and was not unpleasant. With dinner still some time away it kept his mouth juices flowing.

The current action had seen them busy without being overworked. A steady trickle of casualties was being sent back from the fighting and the pair were being called upon regularly. With the front moving ever forward, it would not be long before the tents would have to be taken down and re-sited further west. They would help with that operation as they had done the previous three occasions.

Trying to recommence their conversation, Ayllom struggled to get his words out and ended up making an "F..f..f..." sound. This set his friend off in hoots of laughter which must have been easily audible within the nearby tents. The Ladosan found himself joining in.

Once this was over, he could not remember what he had been going to say in the first place. His friend kicked the dirty snow in front of him and unearthed an old fir cone. This got him reminiscing.

"I remember when I was a little boy, I tried out an experiment. I'd gone out with my mother and grandmother, but was on my own at the time. Victor wasn't there."

"Victor was your brother?"

"Yeah. Anyway, I lost contact with the others and was alone with lots of trees around me. I picked up a cone and dropped it to the ground. I told myself that whichever way it pointed, my mother would be there. I'd walk in that direction. I tried it... and it worked! I went straight to them."

Trying not to sound too sceptical, Ayllom asked if he had tried the trick since then.

"No, only that one time. I guess having a one hundred percent success rate I don't want to threaten that record."

"Hmm, you have a point there. I guess if I ever get lost, I can give it a try."

"I'm sure it was simply a coincidence."

"You seem to think it worked."

"On that single occasion, yes it did."

"Maybe if you believe in something strongly enough it can actually come about."

"You reckon?"

"I don't know, but your tale prompted a long-buried memory of something I did as a kid. I'd read a story about a man who could wish away a cloud in the sky. All he'd use was concentration and willpower and the cloud dissipated there and then."

"And did you try it?" asked Tristan.

"That's the thing. I did... and it worked! There were three clouds and I chose the one in the middle. I looked at it and it slowly disappeared while the other two remained. I was with my parents and I told them."

"What did they say?"

"They humoured me; I'm sure I'd have done the same. But, like you, I never tried it again as I didn't want to fail on a second attempt."

"You could try now," smiled Tristan as he looked up at a sky which was uniform white.

"Ha ha! I think it would take both of our willpower, then a bit more."

They were enjoying the conversation, but then a sound drew their attention back to the camp. The captain was calling them. Hurriedly they got up and trotted over to him.

"Come on you two, there's work to be done."

"Yes, sir!"

"Two casualties up at the crossroads. They need bringing back here, quick as you can."

The ambulancemen made a dash for their vehicle and were soon speeding towards their rendezvous. Boyhood tales were forgotten for the moment.

As 2620 came to an end, Frank found himself in reflective mood. Sitting alone in his living room on the third floor, he thought back on what might prove to be a significant year.

It all started with the proposal from Despot Kagel to sell off part of his fiefdom. A deal was struck, but Frank was wise enough to know that was but the first step. There would be a lot more hard work before the new land and its people were assimilated. He felt confident that Senator Vebber was the right man to oversee the transition.

Meanwhile, what had been social unrest across the border finally spilled over into a full Ladosan Civil War. The biggest consequence for Thyatira was the refugee camp for displaced persons. The move proved unpopular in some quarters, but a positive response from the Church was helping to turn that around.

Frank's friend and closest confidante was spending more time than ever abroad. His reports were getting fewer and further between. As long as Alan was safe, and the conflict not spilling over the border, those were the things that really mattered.

The most traumatic event for him personally, of course, was the kidnapping. It had been a frightening ordeal and he was not sure that he handled it particularly well. Still, it was over now and the outpouring of good wishes upon his return had been heart warming. There was so much to be thankful for.

Once piece of recent good news was that a couple of burglars had been caught in Vionium. They were found trying to break into a private property. Under questioning they confessed to the intrusion into Darda's house. They were both in the local gaol now. The young squad leader was pleased to hear it.

Looking out of the window, Frank saw a patrol making its way up the slushy track to the border with Ladosa. The snow on the general landscape was shallow with tufts of grass sticking through it. There had been no fresh snowfall in the past week. It was a mild start to the season in northern Hoame.

Feeling better for his period of contemplation, Frank made his way downstairs. Breakfast was long over, he had eaten in his suite, and

120

there were few people about. A servant was scrubbing the long tables in the hall and a small group of workmen were doing something in the chapel. His attention, though, was drawn to the figure entering the room from outside. Bishop Gunter was well wrapped up against the chill and there was a spring in his step.

"You look happy, Gunter!"

"Yes, My Lord, I've received some uplifting news."

"Oh, come in here," Frank replied, stepping towards the Throne Room. Then, addressing the servant, he said, "A couple of hot brankees in here, please."

"Yes, My Lord."

Unseen, Gunter had a little smile to himself. No other despot would say "please" to a white servant.

"Right, do sit down. You've got some good news?"

"It's about Paul, the builder in the Cast... um, Castleton."

"Oh yes," responded Frank, trying to sound like he could remember the case. He was far from convincing, so Gunter explained further.

"The one who fell off the scaffolding and broke several bones."

"Oh yes, he's doing well is he?"

"I should say! His recovery is little short of miraculous. Immediately after the accident, it was touch and go as to whether he'd live or not. The physicians have done their best, but they admit that his improvement is beyond their most optimistic forecasts."

"That's wonderful."

At this stage a servant girl arrived with the drinks. Gunter took his in both hands to soak in the warmth from the mug. He had more to say about Paul the builder's case.

"The family were all at the Sabbath service yesterday, giving thanks to God. The Church has been praying hard for his improvement and his good progress has been seen as an answer. They were rarely, if ever, seen at services before, but they turned out in force. His wife was talking about their going regularly from now on. It seems that something good has come out of a bad situation. No one wants a person to suffer such terrible injuries, but if an extended family come to faith as a result, then it's marvellous, isn't it?"

Frank pondered the matter, he was not fully convinced. "It's obviously good that this fellow is recovering well and I don't doubt that God's hand is in it. Yet, is this the right type of faith? What happens when something else bad happens and their prayers are not answered quite so spectacularly? God sometimes says no. Will their faith evaporate as quickly as it sprung up?"

"But..."

"Even though he slay me, yet shall I praise him," Frank quoted from scripture.

"That is the voice of a mature faith. Their faith is still in its infancy. If the incident can open their eyes to the spiritual world, it is surely an unmitigated good. In time they can mature into a deeper understanding of God's ways. I see it as an awakening to new life for them. They will learn more. Early shoots can be grown to a thriving plant; where there are no shoots, there is no life at all."

The Despot hoped that the speaker was right and assured Gunter that he would hold this Paul and his family in prayer.

"But I must away," the visitor suddenly declared. "Esther told me that we're having something special cooked for lunch today."

"Is it that time already?"

They emerged back into the hall and, as the bishop departed, Frank found himself cornered by one of the workmen.

"The cabinet's all in place, plus the plaque as you ordered, My Lord."

"Ah, the lagua! Lead on."

A quick walk to the chapel and there, above the tapestry, was Darda's lagua paw in its shiny new cabinet with a glass front. Such good quality glass was as rare as it was expensive, but he had been happy to authorise the purchase. He would have liked to have said it showed the trophy in all its glory. However, it was somewhat gloomy in there on that overcast day. 'Well, it retains its mystery,' was the spin Frank put on it.

The plaque was readable enough. "Paw from the Lagua slain by Darda." Straight to the point, even if somewhat inaccurate. The hero himself admitted that the beast was still alive the last time he saw it. Still, it sounded good and there was no doubt that it was a genuine body part.

After thanking the craftsmen, he asked, "Where *is* Darda?"

They were unaware, but a guardsman who had come in to have a peek said that he was in the bailey, adding helpfully, "Would you like me to fetch him, My Lord?"

"Um, no. He's a modest lad, I don't think he'd like the fuss."

Emil Vebber had taken a gamble. He would not normally have travelled this far in winter in case he got cut off by a heavy snowfall and could not return home for a while. The winters were increasingly mild, he figured, and an extra trip into Norland before the year was up would be most beneficial. Two clerks and a small military escort accompanied him.

He settled into a hotel in Carnis, the most central and largest of the three major towns recently transferred to Thyatira. The establishment was on four floors and both larger and grander than anything in the north of the despotate.

This town was not far from Aggeparii City itself. Emil considered that if Despot Kagel carried on like this he would have no territory left to hand on to his heir. He was not aware of any other, similar land transactions between Hoame's regional rulers. Still, he considered, Despot Thorn, being a member of the Inner Council as well as a regional despot, was the most powerful man in the country and could do as he wished. The other Keepers had not expressed alarm, as far as he knew. Then northern Aggeparii seemed distant to those bodies in the Citadel at Asattan.

The day before, Emil had toured the site of a malting house on the outskirts of town. It had recently been re-built after burning down. Indeed it was deliberately sited away from other buildings due to the high fire risk.

A large steeping tank was where the barley grain was soaked to provoke germination. As he watched, several sacks full were emptied into it.

"They will be left in the water for four days," it was explained to the observer.

The germination process was halted at its early stage when the grain was taken out of the tank for drying. The owners proudly showed the senator the newly lain clay working floor. Yet the heart of the facility was the new kiln. Made of daub and covered within a spacious wattle and daub structure, it had a drying floor above the heat source. Here the grain was laid out to be dried over a sustained period. It was a slow parching to stop germination on the one hand, while not destroying the grain on the other. Large quantities of barley were processed over time.

"But that not be the sole use," the potbellied, black, kiln foreman announced. "There's the wheat harvest to dry as well. They've

123

missed us while we were out of operation. We'll be good for next harvest though."

Later, the senator was taken to a brewery within Carnis itself. Another escorted tour commenced. It had, he was told, begun in a small way twenty years previously. There had been no particular intention to expand out of all proportion, but success meant the facility was large by any standards these days. Emil quite enjoyed a nice beer, not a popular drink in Castleton, and had a good time sampling the wares. The enterprise was exactly the kind of success story that he wanted to hear about. It would be another positive mark in his final report on Norland. They could do with more such businesses.

Today it was a roof tilers' factory on the other side of town. Met at the entrance by the manager, a balding, short man with a paunch, the senator was amazed at the size of the factory.

"How many people do you employ?"

"Over two hundred and fifty now, men and women."

"My goodness, it's quite an enterprise."

"We've expanded over the years."

The manager was keen to show his important visitor some of the processes involved. He took him to an area where a long line of employees were working orange clay with their hands.

"They have to knead it with water to make it malleable. The process here is called wedging and is used to remove any air bubbles. Otherwise it will explode inside the kiln."

Emil watched as the skilled craftsmen formed their lumps of clay into cubes before working them in a rhythmic way with the heels of their hands. They pushed down on the closest edge before rocking the further edge forward and doing the same with that. Over and over they went through the process, making sure any bits of clay that stuck to the table were taken up. By the end of this stage, the substance was highly malleable. It was then transferred into individual moulds.

"Are all the tiles you make the same size?"

"Three hundred and fifty by one hundred and fifty millimetres; that's the standard size."

Showing great dexterity, the tilers cut off any excess clay into buckets provided. These were taken away at frequent intervals by child employees to be used for the next batch. Meanwhile, once pressed down into the wooden moulds and settled to the craftsmen's satisfaction, the frames were removed. This revealed the damp tiles-to-be which were placed horizontally on racks.

The manager explained, "These will be taken away to a special room to dry out. Once they are dry, they are able to be loaded into the kiln."

"I see," replied Emil, fascinated to observe another factory process.

"These are the plain peg tiles which are most popular."

"They're attached to the roofs with nails?"

"That's correct. Copper nails forced into timber battens. They provide a long-lasting, watertight roof at a cost affordable by most. In another part, we have the ceramic tiles finished in a variety of colours. They are far more expensive; the wealthy alone can afford a roof covered in them. You may have noticed the town hall, that was one of our jobs."

Emil wished now that he had paid more attention when he had visited the local seat of government. He would have to look at the roof next time. They moved on to another part of the factory.

"This is where we make the ridge tiles. They are designed to cover the ridge-line of the roof. Sometimes a customer wants these decorated in a certain fashion. All sorts of different designs have been used in the past. These terminal crests are visible from a long way away."

The senator noted the triangular design that would stick up along the apex of the roof. He asked, "Has it got a function?"

"Not at all, purely decorative. It indicates the status of the house owner."

"Because folk know they can afford it!"

"Exactly."

In the last part of the guided tour, Emil was shown the area devoted to slate tiles. A craftsman was punching holes into them. Using a slater's axe, he gently, but firmly, struck the desired spot several times to produce each hole. He did not break any and made the operation look simple. The observer felt sure that if he had a go he would make a hash of it.

The manager said, "We get our supply of slate from a quarry in the south of Aggeparii. I hope that's not going to be a problem now we're no longer in the same despotate."

"I don't see why it should be."

"It's in the southwest, near the border with Rabeth."

"Is that so?" Emil responded triumphantly, "that border area also falls within the expanded Thyatira. I didn't know there was a slate mine there. I'll have to investigate that on a future trip."

After the tour, they retreated to the manager's office and spoke some more over a hot drink.

"I will have to take a closer look at the town hall the next time I go past."

"It was a big job for us that we completed last year. The mayor certainly did well out of it."

"I'm sure it's a fine roof."

"That's not what I meant. We had to pay him four hundred sten to secure the contract."

"A bribe, you mean?" asked Emil, shocked.

"That's the long and the short of it. That's the way we have to do business here. We still made a profit overall."

The senator then delved deeper into what had taken place. He questioned the manager in detail. It turned out that public funds had paid for the work, but the mayor made a large sum for himself in the process. That would have to stop, Best to have a word with the Despot first.

Not wishing to sour what had been a pleasant visit, Emil decided not to say more for the time being. He parted from the manager on good terms and determined to write up his notes that evening in the hotel room.

Emerging once more into the street, his two clerks in tow, Emil noted the gentle snow falling. Small flakes, but from the look of the sky there was plenty more up there.

'I think it's time to say goodbye to Norland for now and return to Castleton. I think I'm starting to understand the culture down here. A few key changes will have to be made.'

Light snow was also falling in Ladosa. Slowly, silently, the flakes descended and lay on the ground, waiting for more to join them. Fortunately for the Neo-Purples, it turned out to be a mere flurry. There was not a big enough fall to hamper their military operations.

Alan had managed to persuade Charlotta to let him lead a deep reconnaissance patrol. It was a small-scale venture, comprising of a sergeant, a corporal and three swordsmen as well as himself.

The winter offensive had punched a hole into the enemy's territory, resulting in a sizeable bulge in their line. It was considered essential to probe into the northern flank of this salient. If they detected any build up of Buff forces there, they would have to report it urgently.

A flat, white landscape was before them as the patrol set off. A rural area, the only buildings visible were the occasional farmsteads. All the ones they came across that morning were long abandoned. The temperature had dropped further, round about the time the snow stopped falling and the air was stinging cold. Above, unbroken pale cloud-covered the sky. The soldiers were well wrapped up against the elements which was just as well.

"No sign of life here," the corporal announced as he led the men back from a search of some agricultural buildings.

'The whole area has been made a wilderness thanks to the war,' thought Alan.

Then the sergeant suggested they strike north where, a few kilometres away, smoke could be seen rising above the trees.

"Good idea," replied Alan and they set off along the edge of a field by a hedgerow. The snow was still shallow, in spite of the fresh fall. Lumps of dark brown earth showed through it.

They walked for what seemed like an age. They were not due to return until the following day, so they were not unduly concerned. Taking a rest in a spinney, one of the foot soldiers volunteered to scout on ahead.

"Okay, but whatever happens make sure you're not seen."

"Yes, sir," the eager young man replied and disappeared between the trees.

The rest of them waited in silence. It was a fair time before the volunteer returned. 'At last!' thought Alan as the man reported.

"No sign of enemy activity, sir. There is a river a couple of kilometres north of here and a homestead on this side. I drew this sketch which may be of assistance."

The Hoaman took the pad with the illustration on it. Far from being the brief diagram he expected, it was an elaborate drawing of a tree-lined valley with a broad stream at the bottom. It was something of a work of art, but totally absurd in the current context. Alan toyed with telling him off for wasting all their time, but relented.

"Okay," he finally said, "we'll head up there and see what's what."

There was still sufficient daylight for them to make it without difficulty and they set off at a relaxed pace. Walking with another field demarcation to the right, a dry stone wall this time, they were suddenly startled by sounds the other side. Swords were drawn and a bow and arrow produced before you could say "knife."

More, low noises from the other side of the wall and the corporal leaned over to investigate.

"It's a pig!" he exclaimed and they all laughed as they relaxed.

The bowman came forward and declared, "I can kill it."

"No!" said Alan firmly. "The last thing we need is a wounded pig squealing the place down. Put it away."

Obeying, the bowman joined the rest as they moved on. Soon the farmstead with wisps of smoke rising from the chimney was in their sights. Two men were sent to skirt round the property and they returned to say that there was no sign of activity. So, leading the entire group, Alan cautiously approached the front door.

There was no response to his knock at first. He was about to try again when it was opened by an elderly gentleman with a ruddy complexion. Upon spying the purple armbands on the soldiers arms his face lit up and he welcomed them in. Before they knew it, the soldiers were sitting round the table in his warm kitchen, sipping hot drinks and eating sweetmeats. The paltry fire was brought alive by the addition of logs chopped and brought in from the yard by the soldiers. Their host was delighted at the company.

"Bless my soul," he enthused, "you're a sight for sore eyes. All I ever seen the last year is them Buff bastards. Damn near cleared me out of house and home they did. I've got good at hiding things from their thieving hands, I have."

The man went on to explain that he had farmed these lands for many years and was not going to be driven away by a mere war. He favoured the Neo-Purple cause and proved this by giving as much intelligence as he could about the enemy's whereabouts. There was no substantial force in these parts to the best of his knowledge. However, there were still Buff patrols about. The last one he had spotted was two days previously.

Obviously delighted to find such a good informant, Alan produced a few silver coins and handed them to the farmer to say thank you. It took some persuading before the man accepted them, but in the end he did.

"You're welcome to spend the night in one of my barns if you want."

"Most kind, but we must move on."

Alan's troop was less pleased at their commander turning this offer down. He did not have to explain his reasoning to his subordinates, but he nevertheless did so.

"A barn is one of the first places the Buffs would look for us if they catch wind of our presence in these parts. We'd be like rabbits in a trap. I'm sorry, but you'll have to wait a further night before you sleep on straw."

They still had time to reconnoitre the valley bottom and the stream. It was wider than it looked from a distance. Its fast flowing current ensured that it had not completely iced over. The water still felt bitterly cold; refreshing to drink, but numbing for anyone entering it.

"Look!" cried the corporal, some boats."

There were indeed a couple of canoe-like vessels up on the bank, seventy-five metres downstream. Alan had not previously intended to cross over, but they might as well check out the boats.

"They're no good," one of the soldiers said when they got close.

It was an understatement. The bottoms had been deliberately holed by someone and they were utterly worthless.

"Never mind," said Alan. "We've seen enough and gathered plenty of intelligence. We'll head back now. If we make good progress, we'll cross our lines again before midday tomorrow."

"How did it go?" Gunter asked as his wife moved further into the reception area.

A servant shut the door and silently took her hat as she replied, "I *think* it went well."

"Come on through, sit in front of the fire."

Esther did as she was bid and soon she was recounting her trip out.

"Gabriell's church doesn't look much from the outside, but it's got a special charm once within. I was helping the other ladies put flowers round to make it look nice for tomorrow."

"Flowers? This time of year?"

"Holly, calabies... maybe not flowers as such, but decorative foliage and the like. One woman was working with twigs and bare branches, her decoration was one of the best. I do love the vivid greens and red together this time of year."

"Were there many people there?"

"Not at all, half a dozen of us at most. One woman left the group in a huff last week apparently."

"Oh, why's that?"

"She wasn't being given enough thanks for decorating the church."

"Is that so?"

"That's what I was told."

"So her motive was more to do with getting praise from her peers rather than honouring God."

Esther replied, "I did not know the woman. The others told me about her. She wasn't too popular by all accounts. They certainly found plenty of nasty things to say about her."

"Some Christians can be incredibly unchristian at times!"

"Do you mean the woman wanting praise, or the others saying nasty things?"

Hesitating to answer at first, Gunter eventually said, "One doesn't like to judge, but it sounds like both parties need to examine themselves."

The fire crackled in the grate and a burning log rolled before settling again.

"Oh, look!" cried Esther, pointing at the window, "I only just made it in time."

Outside it had begun to snow heavily.

"Yes, it's settling. If it keeps this up then roads will be impassable by the morning. It's been threatening for a long time, but it looks like the proper snow is finally here."

~ End of Chapter 6 ~

Prospects of Peace - Chapter 7

Experiencing a woman's love was a new experience for Alan. Charlotta was as passionate as she was persuasive and in the end he succumbed. She showered him with compliments, kisses and a good deal more. He had recently moved in with her and their relationship was anything but a secret. Not that it mattered to the Ladosans. If their commander wished to take a lover, even one known by some to be foreign, it did not matter as long as military operations were not affected adversely.

As for Alan, he was not sure what he felt. 'Is this love?' he considered in his occasional times alone. It was not the overwhelming feeling that he had been led to believe. The physical side of it was extremely pleasurable, that was for sure. At thirty-nine, he was a little long in the tooth to be losing his virginity, but, he reasoned, better late than never.

He justified breaking the strictest of Hoame taboos by reasoning that he was not in Hoame. Neither was he with a woman from Hoame. When he went back, all this would be left behind him. But would that break her heart? He was getting ahead of himself. The way that she looked at him, that longing in her eyes, made it clear that she was smitten. She touched him at every opportunity and even his slightest witticism was laughed at. In the end, he reasoned that he would simply have to stop analysing it and live for the day.

Outside it was snowing again. It lay deeper now and that was having an adverse effect on the winter offensive. Fanallon was tantalisingly close, its spires were visible in the distance. There were no two ways about it, though, the Neo-Purple attacks were petering out. It was difficult getting supplies up to the front and the troops were exhausted.

With some difficulty, Alan managed to persuade the marshal that he should lead one last patrol that year. Their leaving time was delayed by a day due to a blizzard, but eventually he set off early the following morning.

Wading through fifty centimetre deep snow, he led a small party consisting of a corporal, two male swordsmen and a female bowman.

Snow clung in clumps on the bushes, while the trees looked stunted with their lower sections hidden. The utterly white scene possessed a monotony, or a beauty about it, depending on one's opinion.

The sun was barely up and still hidden by trees on the horizon. Everything around them was deathly quiet. Nature was at rest. All they could hear as they struggled forward was their heavy breathing and the muffled sound of their steps through the snow.

"This is a bit daft," grumbled one of the swordsmen. The words were barely above a mumble, but easily audible to the whole group in these conditions.

Alan flashed him a sharp look and the man looked away. Yet the Hoaman was starting to wonder if the fellow was right. He halted and they all caught their breath, the sweat on their faces turning to ice. Alan glanced back and was pleased to note their starting point was no longer in sight. They had come further than he realised.

"We'll go as far as that ridge and have a scout round before reporting back," he announced.

This was well received, for the ridge in question could not be more than four hundred metres ahead. In the middle distance, and slightly to their right, was a burnt-out farmhouse with its roof caved in.

They started off again, the soldiers pleased that their objective for the day was in sight. Everything was still until Alan noticed something move in the farmhouse. Too late. A large group of Buffs came storming out from behind the ruins. Before they knew it, the enemy was between them and their escape route.

In the middle of the Buffs there seemed to be a giant of a man armed with a large wooden club. The others did not appear half as daunting, thin and hungry-looking. Yet the Neo-Purples were outnumbered four to one, not nice odds.

'It's as if they were waiting for us,' Alan concluded, but his thoughts were cut short by their leader addressing them.

"If you surrender," he shouted, "you will be taken prisoner and treated well."

"I doubt that," said the corporal flatly.

There had been too many tales of atrocities in recent weeks. Bodies were discovered tied up and clearly showing the marks of torture. A tense standoff followed during which Alan noted that none of the enemy appeared to be sporting bows. That was a good thing, because they could easily have been picked off under no cover and not being

132

able to move freely in the deep snow. This reconnaissance mission was proving to be one too far and a rare, but fatal error of judgement on Alan's part.

The deadlock was broken when the giant made the first move forward. Alan was keen to fell him, but the corporal was nearest and, with a great battle cry, surged at the advancing figure. His sword blow was parried by a swing of the giant club. Then, sickeningly, a second swing crashed into the corporal's head, crushing it and sending blood and brains splattering across the snow.

Alan stepped towards the enemy champion while the others joined the fight. He noticed a Buff fall with an arrow in his chest and heard shouts and the clash of metal against metal. Alan brought his sword down as hard as possible at the giant. The latter parried it with his club and the blade stuck firmly in the wood.

"There, grab him!" came a cry.

Before he knew what had happened, two other Buffs were upon him. Yet rather than hit him, they bundled him over and held him firm. He could not see down there what was happening, but soon the sounds of fighting ended and he was hauled up.

"Bind him fast," ordered the leader, "and the others."

The bowman lay dead, sinking slowly even as the prisoners were taken away. The two swordsmen had survived, for the time being at least, although one of them was hurt.

Nothing more was said until they hit a well used track on the way back to the enemy camp. Then the leader could not resist gloating.

"So you are the mighty Alan! How good of you to step into our little trap." He then laughed at his captive's look of surprise.

'How does he know my name? He didn't seem surprised to see me. I didn't realise I was so famous around here. Were they expecting us?'

No further information was forthcoming until they arrived at the Buffs' base. An unusual looking building was surrounded by defensive earthworks. Snow-tipped wooden spikes reached outwards at a forty-five degree angle. A good number of personnel were about and appeared busy. Some were loading some wagons with equipment. Buff headquarters in this sector looked like a farmhouse in some respects, but it sported both a tower and a small moat. It appeared to be a mishmash of styles.

His architectural observations were cut short when a score of people in uniform, men and women, poured out of one of the subsidiary structures nearby. They cheered and jeered in equal measure.

The column came to an abrupt halt at the door and the leader headed inside. He emerged almost immediately, alongside him an important-looking personage flanked by guards. The latter were sporting top quality armour and, unlike the first captors, well fed. It took a moment for Alan to recognise the smarmy, grinning man before him. Then the penny dropped.

"Ah, Director Vap."

"Field General Vap, if you please," came the exaggeratedly polite reply.

"A thousand apologies, Field General," Alan played along.

The smile disappeared from Vap's face as he commanded, "Bring him in!"

"Um, w-what about the other two?"

"Oh, kill them," the general ordered, trying to sound dismissive.

Alan began protesting, but was smacked hard in the face by one of the escorting soldiers for his trouble. Reeling from the blow, he was dragged into the building to the sound of renewed cheers from the baying crowd outside. He was taken downstairs to the basement which had been cleared for use as a dungeon. With a quiet efficiency, the guards manacled their prize prisoner to the wall. There was no sign of Vap now, which came as some surprise. The soldiers spoke not a word and soon Alan was left alone in the dark to consider his fate.

'No doubt they will not take long before beginning interrogation. They will want to start while the intelligence is still fresh. I've never been tortured before. Oh well, this seems to be the year for new experiences.'

The black humour helped a bit, but there was no one to share it with. Black was the operative word, for there was no light there and his future looked black indeed.

Most Thyatiran households had a siege mentality when it came to winter. For many weeks before the snows came they were busy stocking up on food and fuel for the long, dark nights. In a normal winter there were quite a few days when they could not venture far from home due to snowdrifts and inclement weather.

It was true that there were more mild winters these days, a phenomenon which was welcomed. Nevertheless, they knew that a bad one could still hit them, so the preparations were much the same. The current one had started late, but several heavy snowfalls in the past week made travelling extremely difficult.

Senator Vebber had arrived back from his latest Norland trip just in time. He was happily back home in Castleton. Meanwhile, another resident of that fast expanding settlement was trying his best to make the season as enjoyable as possible for his household.

Life for Deejan Charvo was utterly transformed compared with a few years previously. His new Christian faith gave him something worthwhile to strive for every day, while his adoptive children gave him joy on a different level. They played many board and parlour games together when the weather was at its worst and the business was on hold. Even stuffy Walter found himself joining in for a while. Until, that is, he would remember a certain ledger that needed revising.

One day, the assistant was walking past the living room when he heard Deejan and Sebastian laughing away inside. Poking his head round the door, he saw they were building a tower with wooden bricks. Such a childish pursuit for a youth and a grown up man, but what did it matter in the greater scheme of things?

"Where's Keturah?" he asked, aware of the young woman's conspicuous absence.

"She's with Daniel," answered Sebastian immediately.

"Who's D...?"

"Her pet dakk," came the answer to the unfinished question.

"Pet dakk?!" Walter responded in bafflement.

Deejan enlightened him. "I'm not sure one could describe him as a pet, but he pulls the wagon, second on the left normally. The one with a smudge on its nose."

The assistant frowned. Names for dakks? A black knowing where a particular beast is usually harnessed? This was absurd.

"We had the vet out the other day," offered Sebastian. "He's been off his food for several days now. She was up most of the night with him."

Not knowing what to say, Walter simply stood there. Dakks were merely working beasts, nothing more, nothing less. Still, it showed Keturah's big heart and he found himself smiling.

Just then, the young lady herself came in the side door. She was in floods of tears. One did not have to a genius to guess what had happened. In between sobs, she explained, "Daniel's dead!"

Sebastian and Deejan took it in turns to hug her as Walter entered fully into the room. Before he realised it, he was giving her a stiff hug as well.

Accepting a warm brankee which a servant fetched her, Keturah sat down and explained.

"The vet said he had an enlarged heart and there was nothing more that could be done for him. Daniel coughed a few times and then he was no more."

"Oh dear," her father said in his most sympathetic tones. "At least he's not suffering any more."

Keturah sobbed some more and Walter finally sat down on his comfortable chair.

"He was my favourite," she explained, although it was a fact they were well aware of.

Her father replied, "He was one of our eldest dakks, you know. There's a foal that's set to join our regular team come the spring. We can call him Daniel as well, if you like."

"Two."

"I'm sorry?"

"We'll call him Daniel Two," Keturah announced, still not looking up, but inspecting her sopping handkerchief.

"Very well, Daniel Two it shall be."

Deejan looked up and caught Walter's eye and they exchanged a look. Even Walter's life was affected by the big changes around him. His once hard heart, driven entirely by the need for profit, was seeing how good things could not be measured in monetary terms.

"Daniel the Second," he muttered, smiling and shaking his head at the absurdity of it. Absurd, but rather fun.

Charlotta was beside herself with worry. Three days since Alan's patrol set off and there was no sign of them whatsoever. The weather remained quiescent, so it was not as if a storm had driven them under cover. There was no word; no member of the group had returned. Nothing.

It was hard to hide her growing concern from her officers and they knew she was upset. Captain Hallazanad volunteered to lead a larger group to go out and search for Alan and she readily accepted. A further, even bigger force was being assembled to probe the area where the lost patrol had set off for. With widespread fatigue, and increasing cases of frostbite, this operation was not starting as soon as she would have liked.

"We must take advantage of the current break in further snowfall," she declared, "for one last operation this winter."

Yet she was meeting with resistance from some of her commanders.

"Our troops are exhausted!" exclaimed Major Panarez. "It would be folly to extend winter operations."

Overruling him, she ordered that preparations for this final attack of the year to be speeded up.

"I want the assault to commence first thing tomorrow morning. Every last able body in the sector must be mustered for the fight."

At least it would make her feel like she was doing something. She needed to keep busy with her lover missing, presumed dead.

Back in his dungeon, Alan had been given precious little to eat since his incarceration. He was therefore extremely hungry. Worse still, was the thirst. Resorting to licking the condensation on the wall, he found it tasted horrible and gave up. Yet to be interrogated, this was something of a surprise to him. Maybe they were waiting until he was weakened physically, or would offer him food and drink in exchange for information. He had not seen a soul for... goodness knew how long.

Therefore it was with something of a start that he heard the latch click and a whole posse of people pour in, two bearing flaming torches. These were used to light the static ones on the wall opposite. Alan squinted in the light and it took a while for his eyes to adjust.

Vap was in front of him, sickly smile in place. The others were all soldiers, except for a nervous-looking youth holding a metal mug with shaking hands. The general was there to gloat, but he spoke abnormally quickly and had the air of someone who was in a hurry.

"We have our man Major Panarez to thank for our guest here."

When Alan did not speak, he continued, "That's right, he has been supplying us with some useful information as of late."

Still no response from the captive, so Vap decided to lecture him on the bigger picture.

"Before you die, I want you to learn some truths about the armed struggle before us. For the strength of a people lies in their inner values and these can only be fully exposed in a time of tremendous trial. Its ultimate expression is found in blood and iron, the will made solid in the army. The eternal values of the people are forged by the hammer blows of history. A nation never became strong by avoiding battle. If we are cast into the furnace we are forged into something far stronger and more durable. Neutrality and non-aggression pacts are for cowards. A people can only rise through the impetus given by conflict. They rise to the challenge and do not cower away like pathetic inhabitants. I understand these things. Ladosa needs intelligent state leadership and I am the one to provide it."

One of the accompanying soldiers, an officer, appeared to be agitated, as if he wanted to move the proceedings on. He whispered something in the field general's ear. All Alan could glean was the word "hurry."

Vap had leaned towards the soldier to hear him and now stood up straight to address the prisoner again.

"It seems we cannot tarry, more's the pity, but it can't be helped." Then, looking at the prisoner's cracked lips, he said with false sympathy, "Oh dear, are we a bit thirsty? Would you like a drink?"

The captive was not going to give him the satisfaction of a reply and he was certainly not going to beg. Besides, he felt sure that Vap would use the old psychological trick of holding the mug near his lips, before pouring the water at his feet. Instead of this, he nodded to the youth to give him the drink.

Coming forward hesitantly, the water carrier appeared worried. Did Alan have such a fearsome reputation? The mug went to his lips and he drank eagerly, although the youth pulled the receptacle away before he could down the last and stepped backwards.

"Good," proclaimed Vap. "Now, I am afraid, we have to leave you. I would have you paraded through the streets of Braskaton if I could. Show everyone the Hoame support for the Neo-Purples. But events have dictated otherwise. Come, my people, we must go."

He took a pace towards the exit, but stopped himself and turned back. With glee in his eye, he told the prisoner, "Oh, did I not mention? You have just drunk poison. Don't worry, you have a while yet to live. Your limbs will lose their feeling, starting first at the extremities, then it will spread to the rest of your body until your heart stops beating. Enjoy the last moments of your life alone, Hoaman!"

While he was still speaking, an adjutant entered the room and announced that their enemy's forces were less than three kilometres away.

"By the forefathers!" exclaimed Vap, annoyed that his moment of triumph was being compromised. Then, turning to the woman on his left, who was his second in command, snapped, "You must speed up the evacuation!"

"I still don't know why we can't make a stand here. We've prepared a good defensive position."

"I'm not going through this again," her commanded retorted petulantly. "We're too exposed here. We need to pull back to the river. Make sure nothing useful is left behind."

"Shall I finish him off?" another soldier asked, nodding at the prisoner.

"No, he's dead already, he simply hasn't realised it yet. Let him stew."

Even as he completed his sentence, another soldier burst in and announced that the general's wagon was ready.

"I'm coming, I'm coming! Leave him, come on."

The torches on the wall opposite were kept burning, but Alan was soon alone again. His mind raced. So that was why they had not bothered to interrogate him. Panarez was a double agent and they already knew what was happening in the Neo-Purple camp. He had been feeding details of the patrols. He had betrayed Alan personally. But why was Vap hurrying away? Would Charlotta learn exactly how he died?

So many unanswered questions which he would never receive the answers to. 'What a pathetic way to go out!' he considered. 'I'd much rather have died fighting. Alone, in a dungeon, having been given poison? An ignoble end.' He wondered if the minstrels back home would sing a song about him. It would be better if they made up a death worthy of him. 'He fought against impossible odds right to the end...'

The dying man could not help a little chuckle. Even as he did so, he felt his fingers and toes going numb. The poison was working.

"Ah! A letter from Alan," cried Frank triumphantly as he tore at the tube to get the contents out as quickly as possible.

He was in his suite with Hannah. A fire was roaring in the grate and they were well wrapped up in any case.

"Oh, it's quite an old one by the sounds of it," he continued, looking disappointed.

"Be grateful it got through at all this time of year."

"You're right, the messenger should get a medal."

"Hmm."

"It's not his usual informative missal anyway. He seems to be mentioning Marshal Nazaz most of the time. I suppose that's to be expected if she's his commanding officer. Although it does..."

He stopped talking when Joseph entered the room. Their son was clutching a book which Frank recognised as one he had managed to procure the year before. It was good that Joseph was reading for pleasure now. Robin Hood was a classic tale and exciting. The edition was, Frank estimated, at least a couple of hundred years old, but tantalizingly he could not find a date in it.

"Are you enjoying your book?"

"Yes, father," the lad replied as he came and sat down, "but it is a bit confusing."

"Oh?"

"It says that Robin Hood does a lot of kind things by taking money from the rich people and giving to the poor. But isn't that still stealing?"

"That's right, it is."

"But he has lots of friends and the whole story is on his side."

"It's a legend, not a true story as such."

When Joseph frowned at this, his father explained further. "I suspect that there was a man in history who was a robber and the common people got to rather admire him, because he tended to rob rich people rather than go for the slender pickings from the poor houses. There was a lot of resentment against the rich, so people liked the idea of them getting robbed. The story was told and gradually it became romanticized until he was portrayed as an heroic figure."

"So it's not true?"

"It's a story, so no, it's not true. It was probably started by real events which changed over the years. So now he is made out to be a noble fellow which, in reality, he probably wasn't."

Hannah looked concerned and chipped in, "Don't spoil it for him! It's a fun tale; Joseph doesn't need a social analysis on its origins."

"Oh, sorry..."

"It's okay, Father, I'm still going to enjoy it," the boy said as he got back on his feet and skipped out.

The adults waited until he was out of the room. Frank then forestalled what his wife might comment by exclaiming, "I was simply saying!"

Hannah bit her lip before going back to their previous topic and asking what Alan had to say about the war.

"He's a lot more cagey than usual. Presumably something is brewing, or else he would not have written this way. In any case, with the snow there's no doubt that operations will have closed down for the winter."

"May I have a read?"

Passing it over without a word, her husband waited patiently for her to complete the letter. She took her time and, when she finished, she handed it back, asking, "What do you think will happen?"

"In the war? Goodness knows! I never thought it would come to a war in the first place. Now they seem locked in a do or death struggle. If that meteorite can't make them stop and see sense, then I'm not sure anything can."

"Are you going to send another report to the Inner Council?"

"And tell them what? I found it hard to glean much information from this latest offering from Alan. Or did you find something I didn't?"

Shrugging, Hannah replied, "It isn't his usual style. He implies a big operation is being planned, presumably for the spring. It's not exactly news. He's obviously spending a lot of time with Charlotta."

"The marshal?"

"Yes. You don't think he's romantically involved, do you?"

"Are you serious? Alan?" Frank's face was a mixture of ridicule and utter disbelief. He added, "If she's the one I'm thinking of, she

141

had a tilt at L'Rochfort during the negotiations. Maybe she's a man-eater."

They left it there and, after an early lunch, Frank decided to take a stroll across to the senate building. Not that much went on there this time of year, but it would get him out into the fresh air for a while.

It was no colder than expected once he stepped into the bailey. It was also dry. Guardsmen had cleared most of the snow away from within the wall and kept a walkway to the entrance salted. One or two soldiers were visible, going about their duties. Other than them, the only people about were a small number of white children standing in the middle of the enclosed area. They made a strange sight, standing silently in a circle and he could not help pausing as he went past.

Earnest expressions, they posed with arms outstretched. Upon seeing the Despot observing them, the eldest explained, "We're angels." That was a good enough explanation for Frank who smiled and let them get on with their game.

Fortunately the guards' snow-clearing activities extended across to his destination and he was able to make it to the senate without much effort. Ascending the steps, he noticed no one about and inside there were but a couple of secretaries busy with their duties.

He peered inside Hanz and Emil's offices, but neither were in. They were not supposed to be, so it did not matter. Entering the office reserved for himself, he was surprised to see a despot's message tube lying on his desk. As he picked it up, he wondered if it was from Kagel, but no, it was from Despot Lovonski of Bynar, his other Hoame neighbour.

Deciding to read it back at the Castle, he took it in hand and stepped out of the room. As he did so, a secretary walked past.

"When did this arrive?" he demanded. It was not right for such a communication to be left there.

The secretary was about to answer, but upon seeing Senator Vondant approach, left it to him.

"Hello Frank," Karl greeted him cordially. "It arrived a short while ago, I was about to bring it over myself."

"Oh," he went, then in less abrupt tone, said, "I wonder if it is something important, sending it this time of year." As he spoke, visions of a Ladosan army forcing the Mitas Gap formed in his imagination. "Maybe I should open it here and now. Come in with me, Karl... sit down."

So with his secretary of defence waiting, he opened the tube and read its contents. Anticlimax followed. No war, but that was hardly a bad thing.

"It's merely chit chat, although he does mention refugees," was the reader's initial assessment. "A bit strange to risk a messenger for that."

"Maybe he was bored," the senator's high-pitched voice spoke. "Ah, what's this?"

Karl waited patiently while the other man re-read the final section of the letter. He exclaimed, "Oh, good heavens! He's had the people involved in the kidnapping executed."

"I should think so!" the senator replied firmly, "and not before time."

"I suppose you're right."

"We can't have people committing such an act of terrorism not being properly punished."

"But he appears to have had their families executed too. If I've understood the letter correctly, that's what he's saying."

"He has to set a deterrent. We can't have people doing such things. This will put any others off."

"I suppose you're right," Frank said weakly. He almost added, "But it does seem a bit harsh," but managed to restrain himself. Instead he asked the whereabouts of the Bynarian messenger.

"I believe he's here in the building."

"Please don't let him go until I've written a reply. It'll be tomorrow now. He can stay in the Castle overnight."

"Right."

With that, he made his way back, clutching the tube. The sky was getting darker, but no snow had fallen that day as yet.

Back in the bailey, the children had found a new game. As he walked past a little girl hiding behind a barrel within the courtyard, their eyes met. He winked at her, but did not give her place away to the boys fifty metres away searching for her. He was a few paces away from the keep entrance when a guardsman stepped up to him.

"Do you wish me to clear the children away, My Lord?"

"Oh no, let them play, they're not doing any harm."

143

Soon he was back upstairs with Hannah, who was reading Lovonski's communication and he sat with his hands round a warm drink.

"Quite right!" was her verdict. "About time too."

"That's what Karl said," he replied, somewhat surprised at his compassionate wife's attitude in this matter. 'Then,' he considered, 'I didn't have my spouse kidnapped and locked away in a darkened room. I did not spend sleepless nights wondering if I would ever see them again.'

"He doesn't say what he's done with Vanda Hista," he commented.

"No. If she hasn't been executed then I hope she's been locked up for good and the key thrown away!"

"I did ask him to deal with her leniently."

"You're too soft, my love," was her verdict.

He did not reply, but at this point Hannah felt it might be a good opportunity to sow a particular seed.

"I was thinking about Wanda Shreeber," she said tentatively, but he made no response. "The woman has long repented of her misdeed, committed in the heat of emotion when she was not thinking straight. I was wondering if she might be released one day as an act of clemency."

Still no reaction, so her words hung in the air. Hannah knew that an act of clemency for the murderess was undeserved, but Madam Shreeber was a friend and she did not turn her back on friends.

Unfortunately, though, her husband merely sat there stony-faced. She knew it would not be a good idea to press the issue, so she let it drop for now. Maybe she *had* sowed the seed of an idea. Maybe on a future date, when he was in a better mood, he would suddenly come up with the idea as if it were his own. If that happened she would not disillusion him.

Following a protracted period of silence, he did speak, but on a different matter.

"I don't think I'll write to the Inner Council about the latest information about Ladosa; it doesn't add up to much. On the other hand, I will do a short one to the Ma'hol consul. Best to keep our allies abreast of what we know."

"Okay."

144

"Oh and more urgently, I need to pen a reply to Lovonski. I suppose I should thank him for his efforts. I'll keep it fairly general and I won't ask for further details."

"You know," his wife replied, "you need a personal secretary."

"Hmm," was all his response.

"I know it's been mentioned before. If you had someone with the right skills it would take a lot of mundane work off you. You aren't supposed to do all this stuff yourself, you know. I'm amazed that you still do it. With us swallowing up Norland, the work is going to get bigger still."

"I do have help from the secretaries in the senate building," he protested.

"Yes, but what you need is a dedicated personal secretary to help organise your days and do jobs for you such as letters to Lovonski and company."

"I'll think about it," he said dismissively.

In this mood, she knew better than to keep on at him. So she left it there for the time being.

Work had been stopped for several weeks at the sawmill. All the annual reports were completed and Flonass did not have any work to do. With all that free time on his hands he should have been happy. Instead, he found himself at a loose end and rather bored. Living with his parents had its compensation, but he would like to buy his own place one day. His savings were coming on, if still far short.

Darda was up at the Castle most of the time and apparently still enjoying military life. Flonass did not have a girlfriend and his experience of the Azekah Crusade created a gulf between him and most of his peers. Vophsi it was, then.

Vophsi might be a decade or more older than him, but they had that important experience in common. It created a bond that would not be broken.

The snow on the way to the Selerm was not too deep. In fact it was dirty and ugly and far from the thing of beauty when it first fell. There had been a sharp frost and the puddles were frozen. The ice was not too thick, though, and water was visible underneath. Flonass could not resist putting his foot on it, he liked to hear and see it crack under the pressure.

Mid-morning and the chef was busy preparing food for the evening. He had been alone and did not mind the intrusion at all.

"You sit over there, and..."

"I won't be in your way?"

"Not if you sit there, you won't. You can talk to me, I'll be listening, but working at the same time. Ah, and I suppose I should get you a drink."

"It doesn't matter."

Very much in busy mode, Vophsi ignored the last comment and sorted out a drink for his friend before getting on with his work. Skilful hands produced banak pies and sandwiches at a prestigious rate while his friend talked.

"Mr O has big plans for the mill. He likes to use me as a sounding board for them, although I don't know enough about the business to comment a lot of the time. I think he knows what he wants to do, but wants someone to say it to out loud to. I feel lucky, 'cos my job looks secure right now."

"Mmm," went Vophsi, to show that he was listening.

"Which is more than can be said for the twins working for the cobbler in the old part of town. He's given up the business, the old man, and the new owner said he's got his own employees, so they're not needed any more."

"Mmm."

"I saw Darda last week. The lagua's paw's been put on permanent display up at the Castle. I haven't seen it myself. He said it's all dried out now and has shrunk a bit. It's attracting quite a lot of attention apparently, although I guess that'll go down when folk get used to it. I was brought up to believe that a lagua was like a unicorn, a mythical beast. I never thought I'd actually see one, but I have!"

"A unicorn?" asked Vophsi, not too busy to tease his friend.

"No, silly! A lagua."

"See it? It darn near ate you for lunch!"

"Yeah. We had some adventures, didn't we? Fighting battles, crossing over mountains..."

"Learning Pythagoras' Theorem," said the chef, going back to his work.

"You're in a funny mood!" declared Flonass, half smiling, half frowning. "What's new with you? What are Tsodd and Katrina like as employers?"

"They're extremely good, I've no complaints. Tsodd was furious a few days ago when we had to chuck out a whole load of meat. It was covered in maggots. A complete waste, but he realised it wasn't my fault, so his wrath was directed elsewhere."

"Good!"

"I don't see much of Katrina, actually, she takes more of a back seat in the business these days. I've heard plenty of tales about her though. Not the kind of person you'd want to cross, I gather."

"I think I've seen her from a distance."

"Did you know that the original Selerm was in Ladosa?"

"What?" asked Flonass, surely he had not heard correctly.

"Yes, years ago she had gone over the border, long before the war started. She managed a place like this over there and it gave her the idea of setting up a similar one over here."

"Well I never!"

"She even gave it the same name. That was in the days of the old Upper Village."

"Oh."

"Anyway, things are quieter this time of year, as you'd expect. Tsodd does have his cronies round quite a lot of the time. That's what these are for," he added, indicating the food he was preparing.

"You must know what they like."

"Um, yes. Reuben and Amos are here regularly. Reuben likes my pies and never seems to tire of them."

"That's good."

Vophsi then asked to be excused as he left the kitchen for a short while. The visitor sipped his drink and scanned around at the huge amount of specialist equipment contained in there. On one wall was a set of brass pans with wooden handles, arranged neatly in size. The largest, he considered, would need two people to carry it. Nearer was a selection of ladles hung up on a bar, no two of which appeared exactly the same. Apart from the immediate area in which his friend was working, it all looked immaculate without so much as a teaspoon out of place.

It was extremely quiet in there, so he heard Vophsi returning from some distance away. As he re-entered the room, Flonass struck up conversation once more.

"You don't miss Azekah then?"

The chef looked round to see if the other was joking, but it did not appear so. He replied using an Azekah expression, "A hundred say no! It was fun while it lasted, at least some of it was, but I wouldn't go back even if I could. I have a lot of memories of that adventure, but that's all in the past now. I've got a good position here and everything I could wish for."

"I'm sure you're right. I shouldn't complain either. Mr O is good to me, I've never got to know a black before. Still, part of me wishes to go on another crusade somewhere..."

"Really?" Vophsi sounded incredulous, then remembered that his pal was still only nineteen years old.

"I'm not sure. I do feel this way sometimes, when things are quiet here. I guess I should be grateful for the life I've got."

Halting what he was doing and paying full attention, Vophsi said, "It's easy to look back on Azekah through rose-tinted spectacles. But there were some harsh, dangerous times there. And don't forget how they spat us out at the end when we were surplus to requirements. We'd risked life and limb for them and how did they thank us? By kicking us out on the street."

"Okay, maybe not a full crusade. A little lagua hunt maybe... I don't know."

Vophsi shook his head and got back to his work.

It may have been late in the season, but continued winter operations had been keeping Ayllom and Tristan busy. A steady flow of casualties from the front ensured plenty of business for the ambulancemen. Then, when it looked like the offensive was petering out, Marshal Nazaz ordered a fresh resumption. The pair went about their work with an efficiency forged in three seasons of continual battles.

It was therefore with some relief when the fighting actually did die down. Soon afterwards they were given a four day furlough. Back in their digs, amongst the now familiar artwork and antique furniture, they were able to relax and put the horrors of the conflict to the backs of their minds for a while.

Their first full day off happened to be the Sabbath; not that it meant much to most people in the middle of a bitter civil war. Tristan, however, found a local church to attend that morning. It was an old building which miraculously escaped serious damage as the armies passed through. He walked there on what was a milder morning than of late. The surrounding countryside had seemed deserted, but a healthy congregation, most of it elderly, somehow come out of the woodwork to attend.

No priest was available and the woman who took the service had not given a talk. It did not matter to the Hoaman, who was happy to join in with the prayers and songs of praise, most of which he knew. After it was over, the gathering melted away and he found himself wandering back to his digs alone, but in cheerful mood.

Ayllom had prepared the meal. Through a contact he managed to procure a lovely joint of beef and the meal turned out well. Once it was over and everything cleared away, they slumped in the chairs in the cottage living room. It felt good simply to relax and do nothing. A roaring fire in the hearth kept the room warm enough.

Religion was not a topic often raised between them. The Ladosan possessed no faith himself, but he was somewhat curious about his friend's. If one of them was going to raise the subject, it was more likely to be Ayllom.

"Why do you think God allows this war to go on?"

'Oh dear!' thought Tristan, 'that's a tricky question.' Not that he minded discussing theological matters with the present company too much. Ayllom did not have entrenched views and his mind was open. Tristan was more concerned that he might not do the cause justice. He was, after all, still fairly young in the faith. A simple, straightforward answer might be the best idea.

"God gave us freewill. People started the war and they keep it going, not God."

"So the war is against God's will?"

"Of course. Jesus told us that the highest ideal is to love our enemies."

"But what's the point of having a God if people can flout his wishes?"

"What's the alternative? A race of slaves who can only act in a certain way and have no minds of their own?"

"Does God care?"

"Of course he does! I'm sure this war grieves him greatly."

"But he can't stop it."

"Not directly, he won't. He can influence people to do good."

149

"So what's the point of following him if the bad people can do whatever they want?"

"There are lots of reasons, but it's important to remember there's a reckoning. When we die, our souls have to give account for our lives, the things we've done. Bad people will then suffer the consequences of their actions."

"And the good people?"

"They will be rewarded in the afterlife."

"Okay, I can see a certain logic there," Ayllom came back. He was not trying to trip his friend up, but to understand his position. He asked, "But I thought that Christians were taught that bad things won't happen to good people, 'cos God will protect them. Using that logic, if bad things *do* happen to good people, this protecting God does not exist."

"I am not sure if I've heard anyone say that he won't ever allow bad things to happen to good people."

"I'm pretty sure I heard it as a child."

"Everyone knows that bad things sometimes happen to good people; that's life. To say that it means there's no God is nonsense. God never said that bad things won't happen to good people, or folk who follow his ways. The Bible is full of bad things happening to good people, from Cain killing Abel to the martyrs in the Book of Revelations.

"Jesus warned his apostles that they'd be persecuted. He never said thy would not suffer, quite the opposite. Then there's Jesus himself. He was the ultimate good person and he suffered tremendously with his scourging and crucifixion. To know that and then say that God won't allow good people to suffer is complete nonsense."

"Hmm, that's a good point."

Warming to his theme, Tristan continued, "Whoever told you as a child that God will protect you from all suffering was, was..."

"An ass!" the other finished his sentence for him.

"Yes; well said."

"Hmm, I hope you're right. We've seen too much suffering this year."

"And no end in sight."

Tristan got up to put a couple of fresh logs on the fire. Outside it was snowing hard. Ayllom slipped out and got himself another drink which he returned with and sat back down. It was obvious which way his mind had been working when he came out with a fresh question.

"Okay, so as a believer in God, do you feel his presence around you all of the time?"

"Um... not exactly. I don't doubt he's there. I mean, I *believe* he is around me the whole time, but I'm not always conscious of it. It would be a bit weird if I was on Cloud Nine the entire time. Sometimes I feel him more than at other times."

"Okay."

"I mean, you don't ever say, 'Isn't the temperature in here normal today!' do you?"

"I suppose not, but it's still based on faith."

"Sure; and there's nothing wrong in that."

So Christians have this faith that God is with them the whole time?"

"Not necessarily."

"No?"

"No, some of the greatest Christians have had periods where they did not feel him close at all. They didn't doubt his existence, but lamented the fact they could not feel him near. You only have to read the Psalms where this comes across."

"But you haven't felt that yourself?"

"I wouldn't say so. To be honest, I don't think I'm advanced enough. I'm a simple person with a simple trust."

"So," Ayllom continued, "it's the more advanced Christians who sometimes don't feel God's presence? That's a bit odd."

"Maybe a child in the faith like me needs it more than them. They are being tested. Maybe my time will come, I don't know. I've told you before that I don't know all the answers."

"Yeah," said his friend with a smile, "and that's what I like about you, your honesty. I'm far more likely to be converted by you than someone who reckons they know all the answers about God."

"When the war is over I'd like to spend some time with wiser, more mature Christians. They probably don't know *all* the answers, but they'll know lot more than I do."

"Maybe, but if your infinite, omnipresent God does exist, surely it would be a foolish person who claimed to know *all* about them."

~ End of Chapter 7 ~

Prospects of Peace - Chapter 8

It was a grim-faced Charlotta who sank back into her chair in the Strategic Planning Room. More often simply called the War Room, she was alone now that the meeting was over. In the face of a united front from her commanders, there was no alternative but to give way.

"The troops are exhausted!"

"We'll face widespread desertions if we carry on."

"They need a rest; we all do."

"It's madness to carry on in these conditions."

She glanced out of the window at the large, damp snowflakes falling past. Offensive operations were over now until the spring. If they could have just continued a little bit longer... They might have taken Fanallon; they might have learned Alan's fate. But no, the answers if they ever came, would have to wait.

Rest and recuperation, it was something they all needed. The winter offensive, her Hoaman advisor's brainchild, had been a triumph. A large tract of land passed into Neo-Purple hands and prisoners and supplies captured. In her heart of hearts she knew that her commanders were right, but when you are in love it does affect your judgement.

A knock on the door was not welcome, but when she saw Hallazanad's face she relented somewhat. As a captain, he had not been present at the senior commanders' meeting, although no doubt he knew its outcome.

"May I sit down?"

She gestured for him to do so and he spoke again, his tone soothing.

"Don't be harsh on yourself, marshal; the winter operation's accomplished all we could possibly have hoped for. We've got the Buffs at a disadvantage now and can finish them off in the spring. Cut off from the central area, they won't be able to replenish all those supplies they captured."

"It was his brainchild, you know."

"Alan's? Yes, I do know. If, as I expect, it proves crucial in our victory over the enemy here, that will be his lasting legacy. We won't forget the contribution he made."

The man knew that, for Charlotta, this was more about losing her lover. The resuming of the winter offensive had been a last desperate bid to find out what happened to him. It failed in that objective.

She said, "I haven't broken the news that we've halted operations to Captain Wulf yet. He'll be the chief Hoaman advisor now. Our allies won't be pleased when they hear of Alan's death."

At that point there was another intrusion. Her intelligence officer was excited about something and had a broad smile on his face. Hallazanad made as if to leave, but Charlotta bid him stay.

"I have some good news, Field Marshal!"

"Yes?"

Producing some scraps of paper, he exclaimed, "You remember that farmhouse with all the abandoned defences that we took over?"

"Yes."

"It was their headquarters for a while and we made an important discovery there. It is excellent news."

"Go on," Charlotta said, thinking, 'There's no doubting the man's enthusiasm at least.'

"We had a good search of the building and..." and then he started coughing.

Trying to be patient as possible, Charlotta eventually asked, "Would you like a glass of water?"

"No, thank you, I'll be all right. I'm sorry about that. Anyway, this is we found there." Placing partially-burnt papers on the desk, he explained. "Upon analysis, we believe we have uncovered evidence that the Buffs were negotiating to bring in an army of Sarnician mercenaries. It appears that talks broke down simply because they did not have sufficient funds. The fact that they were trying to bring in foreigners is something of a coup, don't you think?"

Charlotta held back her enthusiasm, asking, "These are your preliminary findings?"

"They are."

"You must keep them to yourself for now. Do me a full report which I can present before the Committee. I the meantime it is best that this information does not leak out. Do you understand?"

"Yes, Field Marshal."

"We need it to have maximum impact, so it must be handled the right way and not get out in gossip."

After the intelligence officer had left, Hallazanad observed, "You do not seem to share his enthusiasm for this revelation."

Looking stern, she replied, "We have to be careful how to handle this. There has to be a possibility that Alan has been captured and recognised for who he is. They will then parade him through the streets as proof that the evil Hoamen are conspiring with the Neo-Purples. If that happens it would then be the best time to release news of Buff collusion with the Sarnicians. I don't want to do it prematurely."

"I'm sorry," said the captain, "but if Alan had been captured, I think we would have got word of it. Besides, which streets would they parade him through? There are but two sizeable towns held by them in the southwest. One of them is under siege and the other has their enemies at the gates."

Deciding not to respond to this, Charlotta peered out of the window and was surprised by what she saw.

"Look! The snow's turned to rain. That'll melt it quickly."

"And turn the roads into muddy morasses," replied Hallazanad, wanting to curtail any renewed thoughts of winter operations."

"I know, but it heralds a new beginning."

"Ah, you're back! Come and sit down, your supper's ready."

Auraura went to the stove where the stew was simmering. It was late and the children had all gone to bed. When her husband had been Bishop of Thyatira, she possessed servants to do the cooking and other chores. It seemed like a long time ago and she felt a lot happier these days. That position had, in her opinion, made Eleazar stuffy and boring, not the bold man she fell in love with. She was pleased to have that previous person back, not afraid to go on a mission to Braskaton and face all kinds of dangers that they could only have guessed at. She went with him, of course, but she would not have gone on her own. Now they were safely back at home, engaged in the church's community work.

Their mission to the capital was an isolated event. Most of Isson's inhabitants wanted to continue the state of self-imposed siege going as long as possible. It was solely due to the missionary's personal popularity that a token number of injured lowlanders had been taken in at the hospital. The door was effectively slammed shut after them. The many post-storm refugees, who had lost house and home, were not going to be helped in this quarter. It was a theme that Eleazar took up after finishing his meal.

"There was a little old man moaning about the assistance we're providing. He reckoned that charity begins at home. I got the impression that charity began and ended with himself. He went on and on until I finally snapped and told him what I thought of him."

"Did you?" asked Auraura, both amused and surprised.

"I'm afraid I did. He said that he was deeply offended by my comments and would not be coming to my church any more."

"Oh... and what's his name?"

"I don't rightly know, but I've never seen him here anyway. He said he'd tell all his friends to boycott our church too. At this one of the other men there said that the fellow possessed no friends, so I need not worry."

They both laughed.

"But," Eleazar continued, "some of the intransigence I met with is amazing. Some of them have raised it to something of an art form, decrying any sort of change and certainly aid to people outside the town. They take their mistrust of outsiders as a badge of honour."

"Yet we're outsiders and we've been accepted."

"Yes, I suppose you're right. I can't complain."

The truth was that the couple were highly respected in the community, but that was because they had earned it. Through their social welfare programme, hard work and willingness at one time to man the barricades, they were not seen as "outsiders." Eleazar's conversation having run its course, Auraura brought up something she was wanting to say.

"Nathaniel came home upset."

"Crying?"

"Nearly. He'd been teased because of his background."

"We always knew it was going to be tough for them here. In Hoame they'd be bullied for being half Ladosan, here it's because they're half Hoamen!"

"I don't think this was bullying as such, more of a tease."

"What did you say?"

"I told him not to let it get to him. He should be proud of his heritage. More practically, though, the teasing will soon stop if they find out it doesn't niggle him. If he passes it off with a smile they'll soon grow tired of it."

"Let's hope so."

Auraura had finished clearing up by now and was sitting with him in their tiny kitchen. They were both tired, but moments alone together were worth a great deal, so they talked some more.

She said, "Going back to your incident today, it's not as if the town has taken on a large burden of help. Those injured people we have brought in are merely a drop in the ocean, as we saw with our own eyes when we visited the city."

"Yes indeed, I'll never forget the sight. Mind you, having, with my own eyes, seen it flattening the entire countryside on the way to the crater, I'm not surprised. By the way, the expression you used, 'a drop in the ocean,' do you think they actually exist?"

"Oceans?"

"Yes."

"I don't know. I've never seen a sea, only heard about them in stories. I've always presumed they do exist, but I've never met anyone who's seen one."

"I once met a man who claimed to have visited the far north and seen broad rivers of ice. He swore by it, said it was blue in colour."

"How can it be a river if it's ice? It wouldn't move."

"It moves extremely slowly."

With a laugh, Auraura said dismissively, "Now you're teasing me."

He beheld his wife. How beautiful she was still. She had felt a little unwell the day before, but seemed fully recovered now. His mind wondered back to some of the earlier topics they had covered.

"As far as I know, no one has heard anything about the folk who live on the other side of the mountains since the fireball."

"No. I don't know much about them."

Zebulon told me about them soon after I arrived. He said that they make a lot of wine and exported it through the mountain pass to Isson."

"Have you met anyone who's been over there?"

"Yes, Zebulon himself, he said he did so as a youth. Mind you, that must have been a long time ago now. I hope that they weren't as badly hit as some parts of the country."

"Sure."

"We haven't been back to the crater since that day."

156

"I should think not. Both Nathaniel and Phillip experienced nightmares about what happened."

"Not still, surely."

"No, but I wouldn't want to set them off again. Besides, even if all the snow's cleared now, I reckon there'll still be a tangled mass of branches and tree trunks between here and there."

"At least the church tower's been fully mended," her husband said cheerfully, looking on the bright side.

"They got on with that quickly."

"There will be a lot of work needed to be done on Quinty's residence come the spring. They made it waterproof after the disaster, but there is a tremendous amount to do."

"Did you tell me it'll be the church's conference centre from now on?"

"That and other purposes, yes. It has extensive grounds. I can think of half a dozen uses that we can put it to. I'm sorry that the lady was killed, it was a tragedy, but at least her legacy will live on."

A couple of days later, Captain Hallazanad was back with Marshal Nazaz, making a request.

"The spirit of the troops is much improved."

"Why, because the offence has been called off?"

"I was referring to this morning's shipment."

"The salted beef?"

"Yes, rations have been a bit sparse lately, but now a better line of communication has been set up with our bases at the rear, I'm hopeful that supplies will be more regular."

"Good," Charlotta replied. She was trying to sound upbeat as she got over the death of her lover, but it was not easy.

"And the sergeant has been to see me about organising some entertainment to take their minds off things. As morale officer, I was hoping to second this NCO to my sub-committee. We need people with ideas and he is some..."

He stopped and they both pricked up their ears at the sound of cheering outside.

"Not another shipment?" joked the captain. It would take more than food to provoke the increasing racket coming closer with each moment.

157

A large number of footsteps were approaching the door and the two of them stopped to watch it open and in step... Alan!

"Hi," he said casually as he walked into the room, closing the door behind him. The noise outside died down. Charlotta and Hallazanad, their jaws dropped, watched speechless and frozen to the spot.

"Have you missed me?"

It was all she could do to restrain herself from throwing her arms around him, but she did manage to splutter incredulously, "Where have you been?"

The marshal bid him sit down and some hot soup was brought. As he finished this off, the whole story came out. The ambush, his incarceration, the poison. "...And they left me there alone while they evacuated. I thought my time was up, but it can't have been long before the worried-looking youth came back. He turned out to be one of our agents and he administered the antidote. Even so, I still felt absolutely terrible. The place had been evacuated and the two of us were alone. He took me back to his house where he lived with his grandmother. It was quite nearby. I was in and out of consciousness for... I don't know how long. Even when that time passed, I was still pretty sick for a couple of days."

Hallazanad quizzed him about where the fortified farmhouse was before declaring excitedly, "I'm sure that's the one we overran, the one where we got the papers about the mercenaries!"

They discussed it some more before Alan said, "Vap was keen to get as much men and materiel evacuated as possible. He seemed in a hurry with our forces advancing on the position. Had that not been the case, then I would probably have been kept for interrogation, torture, or goodness knows what."

"So our prolonged offensive operations were a help," Charlotta stated, more for self-justification than anything else.

"I'd say so."

"I'm... we're glad to have you back," she said with feeling.

"You're a hero!" declared the captain.

"No I'm not. Don't get carried away. I should never have set off on that damn foolish patrol. I got those soldiers killed!"

"Don't be harsh on yourself," Charlotta told him, "casualties are unfortunate, but they are part of war. Besides, two of them surrendered, you said, and were murdered in cold blood. When this war is over, we shall put Vap on trial for his war crimes. He must not be allowed to get away with it."

"I'm not sure I finished the story."

"Oh, go on."

"The youth did tell me his name, but it escapes me now. My head was pretty fuzzy in any case. Anyway, following my recuperation, he led me back to your lines before melting back into the woods. He saved my life. Make no mistake."

Charlotta repeated her declaration of relief at his safe return, adding, "We've suspended operations until late spring when the troops are rested and the ground firm. You will have plenty of time to recuperate."

"Yeah? I've decided that will be my last patrol. It's darn silly my going out like that. I'm not as young as I was and it puts the whole Neo-Purple cause at risk if I am captured again."

The marshal was visibly relieved at this. In fact she was trying to think of a way to dismiss Hallazanad so that she could be alone with him. Alan, however, needed the captain to stay.

"Before I went, you were worried that there was a leak of information to the enemy, correct?"

"That's right, they seemed to be intercepting some of our patrols far too easily. We haven't found the source yet."

"Would you like me to tell you who it is?"

It was hardly the time, or the issue, to tease them with, but he certainly got their attention.

"Vap took delight in telling me when he thought I was about to die."

"Go on then!"

"Major Panarez."

"What!? the other two exclaimed in unison.

"Unless it was a trick to divide us, but why lie when he was talking to a dying man?"

Following this revelation, the major was arrested and an investigation launched. Panarez, of course, denied the allegations and at first no evidence could be found to back up the charge. Hallazanad led a second search of the suspect's quarters and finally, behind a hidden panel in the wall, incriminating papers were discovered. Marshal Nazaz lost no time in having the enemy agent executed. The consensus in camp was that Alan's mission had been a success insofar as it exposed a scoundrel and blocked a dangerous intelligence leak. Alan himself did not witness the execution, because he was in bed recovering from the ordeal he had been through. Unsure of his feelings for Charlotta, and with a lull in the fighting, he lay there considering whether to stay, or head back for Hoame.

Azikial the priest originally held reservations about taking up the post as chaplain in the hospice. To work in a place where several people died each week would surely be a depressing thing to do. Yet he felt God's call in it and, as his faithful servant, he knew he had to obey.

Now that he was well established in the role he discovered the wisdom of it. Strangely enough it was not a depressing place at all. Of course the residents only had a limited time there, it would be foolish to pretend otherwise. Nevertheless, it was often a happy place, for acceptance was the order of the day. There was no use pretending the residents were going to live for ever; these people came here to die. So it was a place of realism where platitudes and false hope had no place. This in itself was refreshing.

The priest learned like never before quite how precious life was. These people had not long to go and cherished every single moment. He also discovered that to look on death as a kind of defeat was extremely foolish. After all, the one certainty about life was that we all die in the end. It was a simple fact that, for the people there, the time was close. They made the most of what they had and even laughter was not an unfamiliar sound in these corridors.

Then there were the staff. How he had been humbled by their example of Christian devotion. They cared for their residents with patience, love and attention. What a vocation!

Of course there were sad days. Some people's passing affected him more than others and it was not always clear why. However, he grw to embrace sadness as another God-given emotion, not one to be bottled up or denied. St Francis had known what he was talking about when he called for God to be praised through Sister Death, from whom no one living can escape. Blessed are they she finds doing your will...

One day, late in winter, there was a visit from Bishop Gunter. It had been arranged for some time (weather permitting) so Azikial was ready for it. It was not the first time the bishop had been there by any means, but he was still taken on a tour of the wards and the pair ended up sitting in the chapel together for a discussion afterwards.

"You know," said Gunter, "that I think you're doing a wonderful job here."

"That's very generous of you, but in reality my staff seem to run themselves. They now exactly what they are doing and most were working here long before I arrived."

"But you provide a focus for them. I believe the team is stronger under your guidance and leadership."

The recipient of this praise felt uneasy, because he did not want to be tempted into pride. So it was with some relief that he witnessed one of the nurses enter the chapel. Appearing not to notice the existing occupants to that gloomy room, she came in, said a little prayer to herself and then left. It all seemed so natural, a routine act of devotion within her day.

Azikial commented, "The chaplaincy is as much for them as it is the residents."

"For the staff?"

"Yes. They are so open about everything and that openness helps keep us all sane, I think. It does not do to suppress one's emotions."

"I can see that."

"Do you know where the word 'compassion' comes from?"

"Um, I do not."

"Com: to be with, plus passion: someone suffering. So compassion is the byword for staff and chaplains alike. It is the key to how the place is run. Our faith helps us throughout each day. Without knowing God's loving presence here it would be bleak indeed."

The conversation then turned to practical matters. The bishop wanted to make sure the hospice was well stocked with provisions and fuel.

"We have not needed to burn quite so much fuel this winter," the chaplain informed him. "It has been a milder one."

"Yes, it has."

"And that's kept the death rate from soaring over the past weeks. I understand that has happened some years."

They went on to talk about the new area that the bishop had taken over pastoral responsibilities for.

"We haven't wasted any time in trying to find out the state of play in Norland. It's not a pretty picture I'm afraid. I suppose I'm used to a Church with the full patronage of the despot. We are unique in that respect, of course. I'm not saying that Despot Kagel is anti-Church; I suspect he never gives it a thought. There is a higher proportion of blacks over there and few, if any, are believers."

On the face of it, this was rather an odd way for a black (Gunter) to talk to a white (Azikial), but the bond of their faith transcended even this deeply engrained social distinction. The speaker continued.

"As a result, the members there seem to be in the shadows rather than prominent in the life of the community. They are poor, with few buildings set aside exclusively for worship and those in a bad state of repair. A great deal of work is needed."

"Surely Despot Thorn will release funds to assist with the cost of materials."

"The central funds have had to pay out a great deal to acquire the Norland area, so they are not so well placed. Besides, I don't want to be seen running to our Despot at the first opportunity. I think it best if we see how much we can accomplish with our own resources. They're not inconsiderable now."

"Ah, I can see the sense in that."

"At a later date, I might invite Despot Thorn to see if he can release some central funds for our cause. He, and others, would then see that we have not merely sat on our wealth, but used it to help our brethren down there."

"So you're saying it's one step at a time."

"I am. As for Norland, even more alarming than their physical deprivation is their spiritual poverty."

"Oh?"

"Our investigations to date are showing a worshipping community with worryingly little depth. Biblically they are lightweight. They have few copies of the scriptures and the knowledge of their faith is sadly lacking among the clergy there. A huge job lies ahead of us in changing their culture."

"It sounds like it."

"Frankly, Azikial, if it was not so obvious that you are fulfilling God's will here, I'd ask you to take charge of the project."

"Are you asking me anyway?"

162

"No, no," the bishop assured him, "but your prayers to get the right man for the job would be appreciated."

"Of course you will have them."

"And another thing: the congregations there seem to be split on the lines of their different forms of worship. The singing, for instance."

"Don't we have that here too? I've come across more arguments in church over the style of music than anything else!"

"Ah..." Gunter sighed, "human nature. I wonder sometimes how the Almighty puts up with us."

"You're right, God would have given himself a much easier time if he had left out the freewill bit," Azikial said cheekily.

The other man sighed before relying, "Easier, but without a challenge. Our lives are worthwhile because we have the daily challenge of trying to behave correctly. God's life is worthwhile because he has the challenge of having to put up with us."

Work started picking up at the sawmill even as the last snows were melting away. "We're going to have a busy year," was Mr O's prediction, "and if it's as profitable as last year, then we'll be laughing."

It did not take long for the mill owner and his assistant to get back into their routine. Flonass worked hard, but it was not unusual for him to have to stop and recount details of his time in far off Azekah to his fascinated boss.

"The winters there? What were they like?"

"They weren't as bad as the ones here."

"Really?"

"It could get pretty cold, and we had snow, but it never lay as deep as it does here. The rivers didn't freeze over as much as they do here either."

"Did life carry on as normal then?"

"Not exactly. The pace did slow down, both the fighting and the normal living, but folk didn't bunker down the same as Hoame."

"You mean Thyatira; the climate's a lot warmer down south."

"Oh yes, so I've heard. I've never been there myself."

"Despotates such as Capparathia and Gistenau are particularly hot in the summer and their winters milder."

"I hope we've seen the last of the snow here for this winter."

"I think we have," Mr Onstein declared firmly. Then, with a change of tone, he said, "I'm expecting a visit from my nephew, Theo, later today, I don't think you've met him."

"No, I'm sure I haven't."

"He's one of my sister's boys, works at a quarry south of Lowdebar. It's a dangerous job and I know his mother worries about him the whole time. She doesn't want to lose a second son."

At that point there was a rap on the door and a potential customer came in and began conversing with the mill owner. Flonass got back to his work, but was able to add up the figures and, at the same time, think about what he had heard. He already knew that Mr O's sister suffered from mental problems and fretted a great deal. What he did not know was that she had lost a son. That, surely, would be enough to push someone over the edge.

Quite a lot of business was got through during the rest of the morning. Come lunchtime they took a break. Mr O was his usual chatty self.

"I hear that those two burglars have been given exemplary sentences."

"The ones who confessed to raiding Darda's home? Yes, I'd heard. There was a spate of break-ins from last autumn and the constables want to deter other would-be robbers. I've no sympathy for them."

"Of course not."

"And they're going to be asking for volunteers to form a force to patrol the streets of Vionium at night."

"I hadn't heard that."

"That's what my father said. I don't know if it's going to come about."

Once lunch was over, the conversation dried up and the assistant got his head down. It was some time later that Mr O's nephew arrived and the owner got up to greet him. Flonass was finishing a piece of work and only looked up when the young man, a little older than himself, was introduced.

"Theo, this is my able assistant, Flonass."

The visitor was surprised at the cordial way his uncle was acting towards a white, but went along with it and shook his hand. Unlike the older man, Theo had not noticed Flanass' strange reaction upon seeing him for the first time.

"What is it, my boy?" Mr O asked once business was concluded and they were alone together again.

"I'm sorry?"

"I saw your face. You looked like you'd seen a ghost when I introduced him to you."

"Um, it's nothing," Flonass replied, trying to be dismissive, but Mr O was not to be put off so easily and pressed him.

"Come on, it must be something."

"I don't know, I'm probably being silly... but your nephew reminded me of someone I've seen before."

This was not a satisfactory explanation, because his reaction had been far too extreme. In the end, he had to tell the full story.

"On the way back from Azekah we stopped in a tavern in... West Torravis I'm pretty sure it was. There was a man at the bar there and he stared hard at us before promptly leaving the room. He didn't even finish his drink. I remember his face extremely well, because it unnerved me at the time and I wanted to move on."

"And?"

"And that man looked so like your nephew Theo. I realise I'm being silly. I wouldn't have mentioned it if you hadn't asked. It obviously wasn't Theo."

"No," said Mr O slowly, for he was hanging on every word, "but it could be his twin brother Leto."

"Your sister's lost son?"

"It is. He gave up a perfectly good job a couple of years ago and announced that he was travelling to Rabeth-Mephar."

"East and West Torravis are on the other side of Rabeth."

"So I understand. Can you swear they looked the same? They are identical twins."

Flonass thought for a moment. Before he began working at the mill, he would probably have said that all blacks appeared alike. Yet even at the time, the young man at the bar had appeared distinctive. He looked more like a Hoaman black than someone from Torravis. Since the autumn, he had come into contact with many more blacks. None looked particularly like the one he had seen abroad - until today. "Yes," he eventually confirmed, "I would swear to it."

"Thank you, Flonass, thank you." Mr O said with passion. If he could give this news to his sister, it would give her hope where little existed at that moment. "I shall be leaving early today. I will leave you to lock up."

"Yes, Mr O."

Frank welcomed the milder weather now that winter was ending. The days were starting to lengthen and soon the trees would start budding. It was time for optimism, although he did wonder what the coming year held in store.

Another year, another birthday. He was only a year off being sixty, a fact which he found hard to sink in. 'I don't feel any different inside,' he told himself. His general health was still pretty good. People did not live as long on this planet as in the civilized universe. Seventy was old in a world where hard manual work and crude living conditions were the norm. The poor, in particular, suffered during the long, hard, damp winters. Most folk on Molten grew up quickly and died early. There was a big divide between the vast majority and the few rich people who were able to have a level of luxury. The Despot was, of course, numbered amongst the latter, but even he had spent the coldest periods of the season huddled in front of the fire with a blanket over him.

Would he be visiting the Capital again soon? The idea did not appeal to him at all. He would keep them informed of foreign events through correspondence. It was amazing how much influence he could exert from afar. With the possible exception of Count Wonstein, the Keepers were remarkably acquiescent. It was in the black culture to follow someone perceived as a strong leader. Not that Frank always got his own way, but on the most important issues he could carry the Inner Council with him.

If the domestic scene was peaceful, what of abroad? Things had been extremely quiet in Rabeth-Mephar since the end of the Chogolt War. That event hit the country hard and it would take a while to recover. Meanwhile, there was social upheaval there with the change of the official religion to Christianity. The Mehtar was far more introspective these days, he was studying Church doctrine and ritual. Frank did not anticipate much change there as long as that country's absolute ruler maintained his health.

Which left Ladosa, still locked in its bitter civil war. It was not clear, at this distance, what effect the superbolide had had on that country. Rumours of another foreign power, Oonimari, becoming involved ended with the impact.

Frank was getting far more information from the southwest of the country where even the winter had not halted the fighting. The indications were that the Hoame-backed faction, the Neo-Purples, were doing well. He hoped that would continue. What extra aid would they require this year? How would the conflict develop? These were big, currently unanswerable questions. Hoame would continue to monitor the situation over there extremely carefully.

"Having a daydream, are we?"

He glanced up and saw his wife grinning at him. She came and sat down near him by the modest fire in their living room. Mid-morning and it was cool, but not exactly cold.

Hannah indicated to the tube on the table next to him and asked who had sent him a letter.

"Harn'an-Fors called by yesterday and delivered it in person. It's from the Mehtar."

"And when were you going to tell me?" she enquired accusingly. After all, she was a long-time personal friend of the Ma'hol ruler and he knew that she liked to be kept abreast of events over there.

"I'm sorry! You can read it if you like, there's not much information in it. The consul was quite chatty for a change. He even mentioned a Sarnician circus that's on tour in his homeland."

"Oh... is he is a fan?"

"He said he saw a circus from Sarnice when he was a boy and was enthralled by it. I think he'd quite like to invite them over here."

"What did you say?"

"I've never seen a circus, so I had to ask him what it was all about. I wouldn't want anything here that might corrupt our people. He did say there were some scantily-dressed female dancers and performers, but I suppose we could put up with that for a limited time."

"Or we could make them cover up from head to toe," his wife teased.

Frank let the comment pass and moved on, saying, " Harn'an-Fors said that the Mehtar is delving deeply into his new faith. He is studying the doctrine of the Trinity now, apparently."

"Good luck with that!" said Hannah with a smile.

"I know it's hard, but then most rewarding things require some effort being put into them."

"Yes, dear," responded Hannah, realising that her own flippant mood was not matched by her husband's. "Anyway, the Royal Family are well, I hope?"

"Indeed. All quiet on the Ma'hol front."

Later in the day, Frank went up to the roof to inspect the view. It was becoming one of his favourite places to be alone and undisturbed. On this occasion, if he was hoping for solitude, he did not get it. A veritable army of workers was up there scrubbing the stonework.

"Come on, put your backs into it!" he heard Darda's distinct voice commanding.

'Oh, so they're not volunteers then,' Frank quickly concluded.

They were, in fact, minor offenders who were being put to work rather than face a fine or other penalty. They had committed offences which did not warrant gaol and the work detail were not chained. They were part of an initiative instituted by Senator Drasnik; indeed it was his latest flagship policy. If the present scene was anything to go by, it was a good thing.

"Is everything in order, My Lord?" the concerned squad leader asked.

"Very much so by the looks of things. They're doing a good job. Well done, Darda."

"Thank you, My Lord."

Then, while the offenders worked round him, he peered out to the west and north of the Castle. There were a few tiny patches of snow clinging on, but much of the view was brown. The track up to the Ladosan border appeared extremely muddy.

The Despotess' garden was not its prettiest this time of year, but would brighten up come the spring. The sky was grey and uninteresting. A chill wind was getting up and he decided to go back downstairs.

"May I ask you something, My Lord?"

"Yes, Darda."

"I was wondering if I could organise a football match for the lads during a break. I believe it would be good for morale."

Kindly disposed to the idea, Frank replied, "I don't see why not. Where were you thinking of holding it?"

"Er, maybe down there beyond the wall."

"The ground's awfully soft there. It would become a quagmire in next to no time. What about in the bailey?"

"I'm not sure there's enough room... and the kitchen block's there."

"All right, the courtyard then."

"The market is recommencing there this week."

"After they've packed up for the day?"

"It'll be nearly dark, My Lord."

"Um... what if you do it on the Sabbath when there's no market? If you have a game following the church service, that will be fine. You have my full blessing. After all, the Sabbath should be a time for enjoyment and it's pretty quiet here most of the day."

"Thank you so much, My Lord, I'll organise it."

"Well, don't let it get out of hand. I don't want half the castle guard reporting themselves injured the next day!"

It was settled and Darda initiated a Sabbath football event which was to run for many years subsequently.

Frank had one more encounter that day when the priest Gabriell came to see him. They spoke in the hall early afternoon.

"I would have seen Senator Vebber, but he is tied up with the Norland business right now."

Pleased that he was not deemed unapproachable, Frank asked him what was on is mind. It turned out merely to be permission to extend his church in Castle. Apparently they were operating out of a converted house and with the building next door coming available, they wanted to take it over as well. As far as Frank was aware, they did not require permission. The priest did not seem to be asking for funds towards it. In the end, he merely gave his blessing and that appeared to satisfy the petitioner. So, with a new year beginning, life was currently peaceful in Hoame. He prayed that it would continue that way and that 2621 would see an end to the civil war raging across the border.

Mr O's facial expression as he entered the office was hard to interpret. A cross between excitement and seriousness, he had something important to say to his assistant.

"Good morning, my boy. I spent the evening with my sister and Theo. From what I told her, she is convinced that it was Leto whom you saw in West Torravis. Between you and me, my sister is not the most stable of people at the best of times. She reached fever pitch

169

last night, I could tell you! The three of us discussed it at length and..."

'Why is he stopping?' thought Flonass, who raised his eyebrows in anticipation of what was coming next.

Sitting down, Mr Onstein resumed hesitatingly, "Theo said he won't go. He kept making excuses, but at the end of the day it was apparent that he simply does not want to go. But you're an adventurer! You've been there before, you know the terrain, the local customs, the exact place that Leto is holding out..."

"You want me to go and get him," the white came straight to the point.

"Er, yes. I've discussed it with my sister and we're prepared to offer an award of two hundred stens for his safe recovery. You can split it with your friends."

That was a huge amount of money to a young white. By 'friends,' he clearly meant Flonass' fellow crusaders. But would they want to leave their jobs to go on another journey? West Torravis was not nearly as far as Azekah, probably less than a quarter the distance. 'Also,' Flonass considered, 'I like Mr O a lot and this would be doing him a favour. A further adventure; it would be like old times.' Helping his employer and being paid a large sum of money into the bargain; he made up his mind quickly.

"I'll do it! It's the right time of year, or rather it will be by the time we are all prepared. I'll have to persuade Darda and Vophsi, but I'm sure their employers will let them off for the few weeks the operation will take. We'll skirt round the south of East Torravis to avoid that and then move north. I will need extra funds for provisions for the three of us."

"I will leave the details to you, but of course I will provide you with additional funds for the trip itself. You can take whatever you need."

With mutual enthusiasm, the pair discussed the matter further. Flonass would take a letter from the mother to hand to her wayward son. Carried away by the excitement of it all, any idea that Leto would not succumb to gentle persuasion was not given much airing. Mr O had already decided , although he did not mention it, that he would give the travellers a substantial, if reduced award for trying unsuccessfully. He wanted them to succeed, though, for the sake of seeing the sister he loved smile once more.

As for Flonass, the prospect of a further adventure enthralled him. He could not wait to see his confederates again and infect them with the enthusiasm that had suddenly taken him over.

~ End of Chapter 8 ~

Prospects of Peace - Chapter 9

Tristan and Ayllom were hitting the trail back up north to the Wesold Front. They presumed that they were again being sent to the sector where they were most needed. It did not strike them as being an efficient way to manage things. In fact they felt they were being shoved from pillar to post.

The thaw, combined with the early spring rains, turned the roads into a muddy morass and progress was slow. They were careful not to tire their dakks out, for they had no spares. What was normally a day's journey was taking four.

Ayllom's fighting family were being left behind. His mother, the major, plus her subordinate husband and other son were as committed to the cause as ever. He was simply glad that they were all in one piece. That being said, he felt some relief at increasing the distance from his fanatical relations.

Once more the ambulance was piled high with the works of art and antique furniture in their safekeeping. It had taken an age to get it all aboard and stowed safely. Tristan, unlike his colleague, was starting to get a bit fed up with carting it all from one war zone to another. It meant a great deal more to the Ladosan, being his country's heritage. In fact Ayllom was as determined as ever to track down the rightful owners once the war was over, Buffs or not. For now it was important to him that they were kept safe.

One mid-morning, the pair were taking a break, sitting on a waterproof tarpaulin they had placed on the damp, grassy bank on the side of the road. The dakks had struggled through the first section of muddy track they travelled that morning. They were currently untethered and eating grass a little further up. The men were confident that they would not stray far.

A flock of starlings flew overhead and, unusual for this late in the morning, a small herd of deer could be seen on the edge of a wood in the middle distance. The pair had not seen another human being since the previous afternoon. The few farmsteads in this region were all abandoned due to the fighting.

The road here was straight and lined with poplar trees. The well-drained, cobbled surface which meant the ambulance made a lot of noise as it progressed, but it was easier going than the sticky goo mud they had recently been through.

Chewing a faltice root, Tristan did not notice the small clumps of snowdrops beside where they were sitting. He was too busy looking at a pile of neatly stacked logs on the opposite bank. A long distance from the nearest habitation, that got him thinking.

"Why do you think they've been left there?"

"What has?"

"The logs," he replied, indicating towards them.

"Who knows? The logs are rotten in the middle. Look, they've got big holes in them. They probably thought they weren't worth taking home."

"Hmm. Whoever it was, they stacked them carefully."

Ayllom shrugged his shoulders. There seemed no point in speculating about something they could never discover the truth about. So instead, he asked his friend a question.

"What are you going to do after the war?"

"Um, I'm not sure. I haven't thought about it. I'll probably go home, I suppose. I'm the only one left in my immediate family. That must make the house mine, but I'm not sure what I'd do with it, or even what state of repair it's in."

"If you don't want it, maybe the local committee would take it over. Do you think they would?"

The question meant absolutely nothing to the Hoaman. He hedged about in his answer, which surprised Ayllom even more. 'Surely he must know about local committees?' he pondered. In the end he gave up, putting his friend's ignorance down to a southeast thing. He knew they were a pretty backwards lot in the part of the country he supposed Tristan to come from. It was not worth pursuing.

Deflecting attention away from his ignorance, Tristan asked, "What about you? What do you want to do?"

"I guess I'll have to find myself a job. I was content to lounge around before I joined up. I guess the war has changed me. If I'm going to make anything of myself I'll have to try to work hard. After all it can't be harder than what we've been at this past year."

"A post in a hospital?"

"Naa!" responded Ayllom with feeling. "Something sedentary like a civil service position, there are always loads of those. A lot will depend on the political make-up of the country when the fighting's all over. And what about Braskaton? They say it's been flattened by that fireball. They'll have to make a decision as to whether to rebuild the place or not."

"The reports sound exaggerated."

"That's true, but we can only guess at what state the country will be in when the war is over."

"When do you think that will be?"

"The end of the war?"

"Yes."

"No one but a fool would predict that. Folk are saying that the Buffs are a spent force, but time will tell. I've got a nasty feeling that when the armies take to the field again they'll be as strong as ever. All the predictions I've heard about the war so far have been wide of the mark. No one knows."

"And Braskaton, do you think it's been as badly hit as they say?"

Ayllom did not even bother to answer that. Tristan pondered the matter. A tale of the Ladosan capital's devastation was not the sole news to have reached them at their previous digs. One of the Hoamen trainers told him in private that Alan was missing in action, presumed dead. It knocked him sideways and he felt on the brink of slipping into a deep depression. He had suffered from the condition before and knew the initial symptoms. The report still let in a glimmer of hope that his friend might still be alive. He clung to that while on the brink. If he lapsed into profound depression, he knew, he would be no good to anyone. So far he had managed to hide his inner turmoil from Ayllom, or at least he hoped he had. He felt that he was pretty good at putting on a front. The matter would come to a head, one way or another, when they reached their destination.

Back on the road, the ambulance clattered along the cobbles. The noise was so bad that it prevented any meaningful conversation. A fresh piece of road, a wide cinder path, came as a great relief.

"If the front has moved on," Ayllom speculated, "then we'll probably find ourselves based at some forward post in a tent. I don't fancy that prospect."

"Wesold had still not fallen the last time we heard."

"Yeah, but the combat area proper is well beyond that siege now, so they say."

"Hmm... we've been told to report to the Mansion in the first instance in any case."

It was the following late afternoon that they arrived back at the base where the two had first met. There was a fair amount of activity going on, with vehicles coming and going and personnel about the place. Yet there was not the frantic pandemonium that accompanied heavy fighting.

Tristan was at the reins and he drew their vehicle up at the front of the building, a little to one side. No one was paying them much attention. Their dakks were tired and in need of a good rest.

Jumping down, Ayllom called out, "I'll report in; you stay here."

"Okay."

Sitting back on the bench, he watched the world go by. Conventional wisdom was that any new, large-scale fighting would be impractical until the ground had hardened a bit. They should therefore get a breather over the next couple of weeks. It would allow them to reaccustom themselves with the area. If they did have to join a more forward post, then...

His musings were blown away by a sight so unexpected that it took a few moments to register. Two men were walking across the front of his vehicle, talking to each other. One he did not recognise, the other was...

"Alan!" he shouted and vaulted off the bench. He ran the short distance and gave him a huge embrace. "I was told that you were missing, presumed dead. Oh, it's so wonderful to see you alive."

"I nearly wasn't," confessed Hoame's chief advisor who then turned back to the man he had been conversing with. "We'd just about finished, hadn't we?"

"I believe so," the Neo-Purple officer replied with a smile. He was amused at the ambulanceman's enthusiasm.

The two Hoamen were left to themselves in the courtyard of the mansion, oblivious to other people going by.

"Yes," Alan confessed, "it was a close run thing, but, as you can see, I'm very much alive. I've relegated myself to duties well behind the line. If I hadn't, I'm sure Marshal Nazaz would have done so."

"I'm so pleased to see you!"

"And me you."

"You don't know how much," Tristan said with feeling.

Trying to lighten the mood, Alan continued in flippant tone, "If we can survive the warlords in Torravis and that mighty explosion in Karamonfor, then I'm sure a little local civil was isn't going to hold us back."

With a beaming smile on his face, Tristan felt the gloom clouds around him blow away. He was deliriously happy... until he turned and saw Ayllom standing nearby, listening to his conversation. He did not look happy.

"Will you excuse me?" he asked Alan.

"Of course," came the reply and he moved on.

Stepping towards his Ladosan friend, Tristan wondered how much he had overheard. He did not have to wait long to find out.

"You're a Hoaman!"

"I..."

"You've been lying to me ever since we first met."

"It wasn't like that."

"You've deceived me."

"But I had to..."

"No wonder you didn't know some basic things. I always gave you the benefit of the doubt. I've been taken for a fool. All our friendship has been based on a lie."

"It's not like that."

"I'm not listening! I'm going to tell them I need a new partner. I can't work with someone who has deceived me like this."

Ayllom turned and stalked off, leaving his erstwhile friend standing alone. Emotions were going haywire in his head. How could someone go from a low, to a high, to another low in such quick succession?

There did not seem to be any point in running after him. He would have to wait until he calmed down. Ayllom seemed so furious though that he doubted if he would come round soon, if at all. He looked up at the sky and saw that it would soon be sunset. Deciding to grab a meal, he went for the early supper sitting.

More staff attended the later meal, so it was not crowded in there. Certainly no sign of either Ayllom or Alan. He ate alone at the end of a long table, pondering his future. Maybe he should pray about it.

Unwelcome company came in the form of an orderly who brought his tray to the table and sat down opposite. Tristan was eating the last of his meal as quickly as possible.

"Haven't seen you about," the unwelcome man observed in friendly tones. "You new here?"

A grunt for a response did not put the fellow off. "An ambulanceman, I see. I hope you have a long and industrious career here."

"Actually, I'm leaving tomorrow," Tristan found himself saying.

The words had shocked himself, but not the other man. Still cheerful, he responded, "Even better!" which struck the Hoaman as an absurd thing to say.

He was still chewing his last mouthful as he got up from the table. His subconscious had made his mind up for him, he was going home. Whether that was Asattan, or the Castle Complex, he would have to figure out on the way. For now all he knew was that he could not wait another moment to depart. His lips had said tomorrow, but if he was deserting it made sense to move out while it was dark.

The kitchen staff always allowed him to take some food for a pack lunch when on operations. He went there in hope and spoke to a young woman he recognised from his previous stay at the Mansion.

"I've been told to grab myself a packed lunch for tomorrow," he told her as casually as he could.

She merely nodded and turned away, leaving him to his own devises. Bread, butter, some pies, a few yackos... he realised that he did not have a receptacle to carry them in.

"Here," said the kitchen head, holding out a bag. So she had been paying attention to him.

"Thank you," he said as sweetly as possible as he took it, feeling himself blush as he did so.

He loaded himself up with enough food to feed an army and scuttled out of there before anyone else turned up and began asking questions. Grabbing a lantern from the supplies, he was soon outside.

It was getting dark quickly and he experienced some difficulty in locating his ambulance. Eventually he did, parked round the side, minus its dakks. Illuminated by the lights in the mansion, he did not have to use his lantern to see. He procured his rucksack and pitifully few possessions from the back of the vehicle. All the artwork was still in there, he was happy to say goodbye to it and leave it in Ayllom's keeping.

The road away from the Mansion he must have travelled back and forth hundreds of times. Yet with the last vestiges of light disappearing, he had to get his lantern going in order not to walk off the edge.

'Am I deserting?' he asked himself. 'I am merely an ambulanceman and a volunteer, I never signed anything... Still, I would not trust myself to Neo-Purple mercy were I to be caught. Should I go back? Am I merely giving up due to a spat with a friend that will be forgotten in the morning?' The memory of the look on Ayllom's face told him otherwise. 'They might ask for papers if I try to use the Mitas Gap. My best bet will be to cut across country and cross over the mountains into Thyatira. It's going to be a long walk, but I'm committed now. I hope I've made the right decision.'

Flonass was in optimistic mood as he strode out for the Castle. A prison work detail was beavering away on the road at the exclusive end of Castleton. The mud had been swept off the surface and they were filling in the potholes that had appeared during the winter. The pungent smell of hulffan tar hung in the air as he passed.

He had not actually made an appointment and was not sure precisely where Darda would be. The two had seen less of each other since the end of autumn, but that was to be expected with the weather.

In the event, he found him easily. Darda was sitting alone on a barrel within the bailey taking a break. He was eating a couple of sweetmeats and offered one to Flonass.

"No thanks. I see you're enjoying the easy life here at the Castle."

Feigning mock offense, Darda replied, "I'll have you know I work extremely hard!"

It was true. Things had been going well of late. He still tried to keep out of the way of Captain Stephen as much as possible, although things seemed to be somewhat better between them these days. He certainly still felt that the Despot was kindly disposed towards him, while the Sabbath football matches were proving popular with the men.

"Things are picking up at the mill again."

"Are they?"

"Yeah. I'm told this is a busy time of year as folk see to house repairs. Plus there are the bigger regular orders which have to be seen to."

"You're enjoying it then?"

"I am. I get on well with Mr O."

"You've told me that before; I reckon he sees you as a substitute son."

Laughing, Flonass replied, "I've never spoken with a black half as much as I have him. In fact it's about that I've come to see you?"

"Oh?"

After whetting his friend's curiosity, he told him all about Mr O's prodigal nephew and the plan to travel to West Torravis to try and entice him back. Darda had not expected the other to want to go on another adventure, at least not this soon. The conclusion came as an even bigger surprise.

"So I've agreed to go there. After all, it's a tiny distance compared with the trip to Azekah. We'd be back well before summer is over."

"We?"

"You'll come with me, won't you, Darda? It'll be like old times, particularly if we can get Vophsi to come along as well."

The hearer was incredulous. He asked, "You're serious?"

"I am!"

"I don't want to go. I'm carving out a new life for myself with this job."

"Think of the adventure!"

"I'm not in a hurry to experience half the 'adventures' we had on the way back from Azekah: getting shot at and starvation to name but two."

"This would be different," Flonass came back, his enthusiasm undiminished. "Mr O has agreed to provide sufficient funds for us to have plenty of food and drink. It's not that far and we know the way."

"But I'm enjoying it here. My parents are proud of me for the first time in my life and I even get on well with the Despot himself."

"There's fifty stens in it for you if we succeed. If you get on so well with the Despot, as you say, I'm sure he'll grant you leave of absence. And you'll be fifty stens better off. Think what you could do with that."

However, Darda's mind was made up. The money was no enticement either. He could have been offered a grend and the squad leader would not have been tempted. He had only recently got his feet under the table here and he was enjoying the role immensely. A whole career was ahead of him and he was not going to throw that away on a fool's errand.

"I'm sorry, but you'll have to find someone else to go with this time."

Flonass very nearly accused his friend of suddenly becoming extremely boring, but managed to stop the words from coming out. It was clear that his friend's mind was made up and there was no point in falling out over it.

Just then, a trio of soldiers approached their position and Darda said he would have to get on. Putting a brave face on it, Flonass said a cheerful goodbye and departed.

It was not too long a walk to Vionium and the Selerm where Vophsi worked. He would use the time wisely by deciding the best words to use to persuade him to join a quest.

'I didn't think I'd have any difficulty in getting Darda to come. He was always up for adventure. He's changed; this new position has gone to his head. A few compliments from the Despot and he doesn't want to do anything interesting any more. I was relying on him to say yes. I thought he'd be easier to convince than Vophsi who, after all, is a lot older than us two.'

Re-energising his enthusiasm, he entered the back door of the Selerm. It was lunchtime now and Vophsi was in the middle of a dozen tasks in the kitchen.

"You can speak to me as I work," the visitor was told, "but I can't stop what I'm doing. Don't worry, I'll listen."

The visit was therefore similar to Flonass' last one in this respect, except that the chef was twice as busy and had an under-chef present whom he was having to direct. The would-be adventurer made his sales pitch and finished while his friend was busy chopping up some roots.

His concluding words were, "So it would be a crusade all over again, but on a smaller scale this time. If we can get the three of us together again - you, me and Darda - it would be like old times. But this time there would be none of the hardships. It's not nearly so far, all our expenses will be met and you'll get sixty stens into the bargain. We'll all be winners!"

Finally the chef paused long enough to break the disappointing news.

"Listen, Flonass, I'm flattered that you've asked me, but you and Darda will have to travel without me on this occasion. My days of adventure are over. From what you've told me, I'd only be holding the two of you back anyway. If it's not too far, and you're merely going to see this one fellow, you don't need me tagging along. This black would probably be put off with the three of us all staring at him. You and Darda go... and tell me all about it when you get back."

Flonass' strategy of not informing Vophsi that Darda would not go had emphatically backfired. He was not going to tell him now. The chef had put on quite a lot of weight since he started this job. When he considered the matter, Flonass doubted the older man would make West Torravis in any case. So he left the chef to get on with his work and said goodbye.

'I'm not giving in!' he told himself as he walked back. 'I'll simply have to get some new people to go with me... but who? I could probably pick up a couple of men to go with me in an evening at the Selerm. But how reliable would they be? Would they change their minds the following morning? Would they take our food money and leave me high and dry? I owe it to Mr O to try... and two hundred stens is two hundred stens. I'll have to sit down and consider the matter. I need someone with me who has got a good reputation and will see the matter through. Theo has already said he would not put himself out for his brother. Besides, would I want to travel with a black? I need to consider all the options...'

Several weeks passed during which time the weather in western Ladosa was unseasonably warm for early spring. Some folk said it hailed a beautiful summer, while others, more experienced heads, said it meant nothing of the sort. Time would tell, but it did mean that the ground dried up especially early. In fact, before they knew it, the mud became hard-baked in the sun.

Marshal Nazaz hoped that this would work in the Neo-Purple's favour. She saw the need to seize the initiative once again in their military operations. Her troops were rested from their labours. With their commanders telling them that the end of the Buffs in the southwest was near, they were eager to get on and finish the job.

Some still expected an effort by their enemies to regain some of their lost territories, but it was not happening. Captain Hallazanad, now the marshal's liaison officer, asked her in a quiet moment why the Buffs were not putting up a better fight.

She answered, "We know that sickness was rife in their ranks during the season past. Another factor has been continual pressure from the Rose Army north of here. They've kept the pressure up on the Buffs, drawing substantial forces away from us. They're struggling to fight on two fronts and they certainly haven't been able to break through to their comrades in the central area.

"That's good for us."

"Mind you, if Braskaton has been even half as devastated by the fireball as the reports suggest..."

"I've heard it's terrible."

"...then the Central Buffs would be in no position to assist in any case."

"So we continue to press the Buffs here, westwards, right to the Rabeth-Mephar border?"

"Of course; we need to knock them out of the war before they can recuperate."

"And then it's the turn of the Roses."

"That, captain, remains to be seen. There's been no love lost between us and the Rose in the past, it's true. But things have been changing; the war has seen to that."

"How so, marshal?"

"The Neo-Purples were a bit-part player before the last election, let's be honest. As the tide of war has gone in our favour, so has our importance. The Rose will have seen that. Their main enemy was always going to be the Buffs, as has ours."

"So it's the old adage of 'my enemy's enemy is my friend'!"

"It's not quite as simple as that, we can't take anything for granted. The Roses aren't stupid. They know they've been helping us by incessant pressure on the Buffs here while avoiding contact with us. They also know that we'll be aware of those facts. After our final victory over General Vap and his forces, I want to put out an olive branch to the Rose. The fact that our armies have not engaged will facilitate this. We must make it work in our favour."

"Strange bedfellows, the Rose."

"We have to be pragmatic. I'm hoping they will see it the same way. Not that we'll take any nonsense from them, they will have to respect us as equal partners."

"What are the chances of a deal?"

"Impossible to say at this stage, captain."

"What will you do with General Vap if we manage to capture him?"

"He will have to be tried publically as a war criminal. He must not be allowed to get away with what he has done."

So even as the conflict continued, Charlotta was trying to see the bigger picture and looking to a post-war scenario. There were so many uncertainties, but she would need Rose support to crack the Central Buffs. If was not wise to get ahead of oneself, though, for there was still a job to be done here. That having been said, over the next few days she put out feelers to the Rose Party and their initial response gave her grounds for hope. From civil servant to army commander to politician, Charlotta Nazaz was proving to be an adaptable lady.

In her personal life, she had had to leave her lover behind as the front advanced. There would be time to pursue that relationship once all the mess of war cleared up. For now there was a job to do.

Wesold was proving a thorn in the Neo-Purples' side. Substantial forces still invested the town, but everything indicated that it would fall soon. The garrison commander had sent out an envoy asking for terms. Unconditional surrender were the only terms that the Buffs there could hope for. Meanwhile, the front moved well beyond that place which was looking less strategically important by the day.

Then, further south, Neo-Purple morale took a huge boost with the fall of Fanallon, the second largest town of southwest Ladosa. The day he heard the news, Ayllom was driving an ambulance at the end of a convoy heading west.

A long trail of vehicles moved barely above walking pace along a dusty track bordered by abandoned fields. Ayllom and his new partner wore handkerchiefs over their faces to keep out the worst of the dust being licked up. They looked like outlaws from the old Wild West.

His new right-hand man may have been a genuine Ladosan, but he was a taciturn soul and conversation was at a premium. He tried not to think about Tristan, whom he expected had gone back to his homeland. At least the artwork was safe, squirreled away in an upper room of the Mansion under the guard of the new janitor there, a relation.

"How far do you think it is to the Rabeth-Mephar border?" he asked Tristan's replacement.

Before the man could answer, if indeed he would have made the effort, a major came into view from beside the wagon they were following.

"You two!" he ordered. "jump down and help these men."

They halted their vehicle. As the dust settled, they saw the scene by the side of the road. About half a dozen bloated corpses were lying about in the field. A large number of frasses were feeding on the decaying flesh even as a platoon of soldiers advanced on them. Repulsed by the sight, one got a bow and put an arrow through the middle of a particularly large specimen. The others scattered as the troops got close.

The major continued, "Take those shovels and dig a pit for these bodies and shove them in. We don't want disease spreading, you know."

Grabbing the instrument, Ayllom obeyed orders. He, for one, would be glad when the war was over.

Alan, meanwhile, was back at the Mansion. Not allowed anywhere near the fighting, he knew that a room here was the most luxurious he could hope for in the present circumstances. The marshal obtained it for him, so he was secure there. They had enjoyed a final night of passion before she moved out with the army. He was having to stay behind.

It was a good opportunity to get letters off to Frank and Baron L'Rochfort of the Inner Council. He wrote the latter first, because he would enjoy writing to Frank more. It had been far too long since he sent his friend a message.

The lines of communication to Hoame were more secure than ever, but he did not want to include sensitive information. 'Mind you,' he considered, 'I'm getting further out of touch with the situation by the day.'

He certainly was not going to tell either recipients about his close brush with death. There was no point. In his second letter he paused to consider his situation as he wrote.

'I'm starting to doubt my purpose here now. In the early days there were real operational decisions to be made. Anyhow, events are taking on a life of their own. Our enemies in this region are crumbling before our eyes and the single 'strategy' is to hunt them down. I have received reports of widespread sickness in the enemy camp. That won't help their cause. It's probably caused by their diet, or lack of it. All the indicators are that their supplies are running dry.

'I am increasingly detached by what is happening now and am receiving reports third or fourth hand. I'm not sure what my purpose here is any more. I guess it's the training role, although we have not had many new recruits since the autumn.

'There is a whole year's fighting ahead. Once these Buffs are dealt with, there is likely to be a short pause to collect ourselves before hostilities resume against the other remaining factions. Having been here so long, I'd like to see the matter through. So I'm sorry, Frank, but you won't see me for a while yet.... but I do plan on going back home once this business is over.'

Once completed, he rolled the letter up and placed it on the table. A messenger would be setting off soon, heading southwards to Hoame.

Later that day, Alan was in the canteen finishing his meal when he was approached by a bald-headed figure who stood stiffly to attention, saluted and announced, "Corporal Ba reporting for duty, sir!"

He knew Ba from the ferocious battle for Wesold the previous year. Now, following recuperation from injury, he had been reassigned to training duties. A large proportion of the Hoame contingent was involved in the training, but that operation had not been so busy during the winter.

"At ease, corporal, sit down."

"Thank you, sir."

"And how are you now, the wound?"

Ba was not used to his superiors speaking in such relaxed tones towards him. He was not even sure if it was right. Yet he knew that Alan was a fighter like himself and he respected him highly.

"The leg is comin' on, thank you, sir."

"Good. I'm not sure there's a great deal for us to do in the way of training right now."

"I don't understand, sir," replied the corporal, looking confused.

"Why? What are your instructions?"

"To assist you with the basic training, sir. We've had a large number of volunteers enter the camp.

"I didn't know."

"They arrived today, after passing scanning by them intelligence officers. A mixed bag by the look of it: men and women. Some 'ad been in other parties before joinin' us, others none. They seem as keen as anything, sir. We'll soon knock them into shape!"

"That we will, corporal. Thank you."

'So the flow of volunteers has recommenced with the good weather,' Alan mused. 'There's nothing that succeeds like success it seems. The better the Neo-Purples do, the more people will flock to our cause. It is a good thing on so many different levels, not least because it gives me a purpose to live out here while the conflict continues."

"Will that be all, sir?"

"For now, corporal, yes. I'll see you outside shortly to meet the new recruits and discuss training schedules."

"Very good, sir," Corporal Ba barked and marched off, limping slightly.

Frank took a circuitous route to the senate building for the regular meeting there. It took him by a striking magnolia which was a blaze of white flowers. This was before the deciduous trees had got their leaves.

Gaining his seat at the end of the table , the Despot scanned the faces present and saw that all the expected senators were already there.

"No Emil today?" squeaked Karl.

"Not today, he's in Norland."

"Again?"

"I think he's going to spend a lot of time there this year. He's currently organising a census of the whole area; it'll be a big job."

"A good idea."

"Essential, I'd say. We need to get a full picture of what's out there. So far we have been getting odd glimpses here and there, but we need an overview of Norland."

Hanz said, "I've heard reports of some strange goings on over there, bribery and corruption they say."

"I'm not sure we need to bandy about provocative words, but we will have to bring their local councils into line. Inevitably, having been part of a different despotate, they have a somewhat different culture. It's more a matter of education than anything else. I'm hoping that following the census we'll be better positioned to work out an overall strategy. It is early in the process. After all, this time last year we had no idea we would be taking this on."

"It strikes me," Saul's dour tones filled the chamber, "that we still don't know what we're taking on."

The white had never been in favour of the takeover. Frank was about to respond to the comment, but decided to leave it and move matters on. "Hanz, may we have your Law and Order report please?"

Senator Drasnik's staff had been busy working out facts and figures for him. The senators got a full dose of them, sitting there in silence. When it was over, Frank asked why the current number of prisoners in gaol was on the low side.

"There are a number of factors, My Lord, but several prisoners have recently completed their sentences and had to be released."

"I see."

"I expect the number to rise again during the year."

"Oh, any particular reason, Hanz?"

"No," the man came back, looking a little surprised at the question. "It is simply the way of things."

Later in the same meeting, Senator Saul talked about a pet project of his.

"I can report that work on the new hospital building in Sardis has commenced. This is as per the schedule. It has been a long time in the planning and we want to get it right. The old facility has been there since Sardis was founded as the Talton village. It is woefully inadequate considering the size of the town nowadays."

Freidhelm asked, "Which part of the town will the new hospital be situated in?"

"On the western outskirts. A great deal of care was taken in choosing the site. At one time we were going to demolish some buildings near the centre and build it there. Apart from the disruption, it still would not have been a large enough site for what we hope to accomplish. So it is being built on what were fields. As some of you know, we have employed architects from Ephamon and they were able to plan the facility with a completely blank sheet of paper. We..."

"Yes," Frank cut in, "I remember you showing us the plans that year."

"That is right, My Lord. The new hospital will not be completed this year, even with the large number of workers on the project."

"I heard that some labourers were taken off the cathedral site."

"That may be so, My Lord, but I'm not sure they were required there currently."

"Well, we don't want to upset the good bishop."

The earnest Saul did not reciprocate Frank's smile, but continued, "Some of the workforce is from Bynar and beyond. Things have got well underway with the bad weather over. I shall keep you all informed of progress."

"Thank you, Saul."

"Although I do have one longer-term concern."

"Oh yes?"

"We will need extra medical staff to fill the new facility, over and above those currently in the old building."

"Are you organising the recruitment of some experienced personnel, or training some up from scratch?"

"Somewhat premature for the former, My Lord. Some training is already underway, but it takes time. Nearer the completion date we will have to try and get skilled staff from outside the despotate."

"Oh."

"Ephamon is our best bet, so I am told."

Re-entering the conversation, Freidhelm suggested something more radical. "What about the Ma'hol? We're always told that their medical expertise is second to none. It could only help to strengthen our alliance."

This last sentence was obviously included for the Despot's benefit, for everyone knew his desire to look for such opportunities. On the other hand, Saul was less than impressed with the idea.

"You may not know this," he said, looking straight at Freidhelm, "but there is still a sizeable proportion of Sardis' residents who consider themselves Taltons. Former slaves of the Ma'hol, it would not be well received to have medical staff from Rabeth-Mephar there."

Senator Trepte had to concede the point, but he did have a related issue to raise.

"Talking of hospital facilities, we could do with a hospital of our own here in Castleton. The population continues to grow and medical facilities in the western section..." (he meant the less affluent white area) "... are almost non-existent. It is most unsatisfactory."

Frank had been listening carefully to this and he replied, "I'm glad you've identified this need, Freidhelm."

"Thank you, My Lord. Whilst we are at it, I could mention the poor state of some of the new housing on the outer, western fringes."

"Of Castleton?"

"Yes, they are fairly being thrown up. In a few years from now I can see this turning into a slum area. The building regulations are not being adhered to strictly enough. We could use some central funds to extend the drainage system too."

"I thought it had been extended."

"Extended further, My Lord."

"Oh."

"It is an on-going requirement while Castleton continues to get bigger."

"Of course. Well, in Emil's absence, Freidhelm, I think that you have talked yourself into a job."

There were smiles around the table, but the senator did not mind. Something needed to be done about this and it was something he had a passion for. He was certainly the right man for the job. He therefore asked for extensive powers to proceed as he saw fit without recourse to consult the senate. As they considered it to be a good distance away from their own fine residences, this proposal met with no resistance.

The Despot concluded the item by thanking him, adding, "You're quite right that even the western area needs to live up to a certain standard."

Senator Cragoop then made an announcement. "I am happy to inform you that the highway to the border with Rabeth-Mephar has been completed. Along its entire length it has been widened and surfaced with hulffan tar."

His moment of triumph was soured slightly by Hanz, who pointed out that the project had been scheduled for completion the previous autumn. Before Cragoop could respond, the Despot had his say.

"Well, it's finished now and I'd like to thank you, Cragoop, for keeping your eye on that. It's given me an idea. That track that the guard patrols take to get up to the Ladosan border... it's in a bit of a state: narrow, sunken and muddy. That could do with some attention. I'm not saying make it into a highway, but if some hulffan tar can be spared for that then I think the soldiers will thank us for it."

The last item discussed that day was Frank giving an update on the civil war in Ladosa. It was with some relief that he received Alan's latest message that morning, although it was short on hard facts as to the conflict's progress. One of the men present asked if much intelligence on the subject was being received from Rabeth-Mephar. Frank had to admit it was not.

Karl said, "The Mehtar seems more concerned with internal issues these days."

"That's not a bad thing," Saul mumbled under his breath.

Choosing this time to conclude the meeting, Frank was the first one out of the door. It was all very well putting Thyatira to rights, but it was mealtime and he was looking forward to steak and kidney pie.

Nevertheless, seeing Cragoop's wife waiting on the steps outside, he made a point of speaking to her.

"Hello, Illianeth, how are you?"

"I am well, thank you, My Lord."

"And the school, is that all right?"

"We had a few boys absent today. It's lambing season and they have taken time off to help their parents with that."

"Ah, yes. Well, we have to get our priorities right, don't we? Education is all well and good, but we mustn't let it get in the way of the lambing, can we?"

Not waiting for an answer, he moved on, leaving an amused Illianeth still waiting for her husband to emerge.

~ End of Chapter 9 ~

Prospects of Peace - Chapter 10

"My boy, I want to take a trip out this morning," Mr O declared.

It was a long while before Flonass eventually responded, "You do?"

"Yes," confirmed the black, keen to share with his young assistant. "I want to see that moneylender fellow again, Deejan Charvo. I understand that if I deposit some of my money with him, he will look after it and add interest to it. With the business going so well, it makes sense. I've made an appointment to have a chat with him. I need to understand all the ins and outs before I commit myself."

"Don't worry, I can hold the fort."

"I think it's going to be a quiet day here. I wondered if you'd like to accompany me."

"Of course!" responded Flonass. A trip out would be refreshing.

So, leaving the fort in the hands of the foreman, the pair set off in a rather superior wagon that Mr Onstein had recently purchased.

The weather here was pleasant for the time of year, but not as hot as further north in Ladosa. The daffodils in the hedgerows were past their best.

"I'm expecting a visit from Theo tomorrow," said the sawmill owner. "He wants to go through the specifications for the quarry order. It will be a major one, one of this year's largest."

Flonass listened, nodding. He had already told his employer that he found noone to go to West Torravis with him. Mr O had been most understanding and took it well, in spite of knowing that his sister would be disappointed. Flonass felt bad about it, but was not sure he could do anything more. Going by himself was out of the question. Mr O toyed with the idea of hiring some men, but did not like to do so. Righty or wrongly, he felt that they would not be as reliable as volunteers. He simply had to put the matter to the back of his mind and move on.

"Here we are," he announced as they drew up.

Before long they were being ushered through to Deejan Charvo's office where the man himself was waiting. He greeted them cordially, but it was not long before they got down to business.

Onstein's fortunes had been such that he progressed from needing a loan last year to being in surplus this year. Not wanting to spend it for the sake of it, he felt that a deposit with interest was just the thing.

Flonass sat a short distance back from the two blacks and listened for a while. When it started to bore him, he found his mind wandering.

Then the door opened and in stepped Sebastian. Flonass recognised him from their previous visit.

"Excuse me for interrupting, Father," he began. His speech sounded slightly affected to those not used to it, as if he needed to make an effort to produce such clipped words. "Those boxes you ordered are being delivered. You asked me to let you know."

Deejan did not appear annoyed by the interruption, although he briefly apologised to Onstein before replying, "Get the servants to bring them indoors. They can put them in the drawing room for now."

"That's all right," the youth replied, "I may as well do it myself. They're not heavy."

Before he had a chance to shut the door, Flonass shot up and cried, "I'll give you a hand!" When no one objected, he went out with Sebastian.

It was a fairly easy task, but Flonass was pleased to have a break from hearing about percentages and compound interest.

"How are you finding the work at the mill?" enquired Sebastian as he placed the final box down.

"It's okay, but not as exciting as it was going on the crusade."

"I bet!" came the enthusiastic response. It was then that Flonass remembered how enthralled this other young man had been last time, when he told him about the crusade. An idea quickly formed in his head as he said, "I'm thinking of setting off on another adventure."

"Not to Azekah?"

"Not that far. To West Torravis, the other side of Rabeth-Mephar."

Then he told the whole story about Mr Onstein's nephew Leto missing and their conviction that he was the man that Flonass spotted in a tavern in West Torravis. He concluded, "So I'm seeking someone who'll travel with me and try to persuade this Leto to return home."

"Why doesn't his brother go?"

"He's made it plain he doesn't want to. No love lost between them, I gather."

"And this Leto has no friends prepared to help his mother?"

"Apparently not, but I've told Mr O that I'm ready to go. I just need someone to go along with me. What do you think?"

"Me?" asked Sebastian, incredulously.

"Sure; it would be a great adventure," the other replied. He mentioned the fifty stens reward, but it was apparent that this young man had fallen on his feet and did not need money as an incentive. No, It was his sense of adventure that appealed to him. Flonass pressed, "Think about it, crossing Rabeth-Mephar, going through Karamonfor and West Torravis. Different cultures, different scenery. Have you ever been abroad?"

"No, I came from Aggeparii."

"There's a whole world out there waiting to be explored."

"But it's a fool's errand, surely, why would a black listen to a couple of whites?"

"We'd take a letter from his mother with us."

"I thought he was trying to get away from her!"

"There was a family argument, apparently. I don't think he fell out with his mother as such. Time cools tempers, Mr O says. He's hopeful his nephew will come round if someone else makes the first move."

"And you think we'd find him?"

"Yes, I do."

Noises were coming from the other room. Before the men got to them, Sebastian said, "I'll have a word with my father and see what he says. He never says no to me... not that I have to ask for much. Anyway, I'll speak to him and let you know. I'll send word to you at the mill."

Hope once more filled Flonass as he went back in the wagon with his employer. The latter had concluded a cordial and productive meeting with Deejan Charvo and would be depositing some money on a regular basis from now on.

"And you got on well with young Sebastian by the look of things."

"I did indeed," came the reply. "We hit it off brilliantly," he added, without giving more away until it was a certainty.

That evening, Sebastian found it extremely hard to get time alone with his father. After the meal, Walter was with him, then Keturah.

He was careful not to mention it to his sister. She would be too wise and cautious to give such an undertaking her blessing. Eventually he managed to get his father to himself in the drawing room and tell him all about the proposed enterprise and his desire to go on it. He finished, "I've been promised that we will be back before the summer is over. It's not nearly as far as Flonass went before. He is an experienced guide and we could even take one of the servants for protection."

Deejan was horrified at the very idea and would not listen to reason. "I totally forbid it, Sebastian! No, no, no! It is a crazy idea, a fantasy. They have warlords in Torravis, everyone knows that. Fierce tribal leaders with capricious natures. It would be far too dangerous for you to go. I'm sorry, Sebastian, but I absolutely and categorically forbid it."

Bishop Gunter originally intended to make his visit to the Castle a fleeting one. Instead he got involved in a protracted conversation with Frank in the chapel there. He ended up recalling an incident when he had been a priest in a church in Krabel-Haan, capital of Rabeth-Mephar.

"I was trying to organise a service. There was an argument over the music for a certain worship song. I was not directly involved at first, but then the warring parties asked me to adjudicate. I found myself supporting the woman whose role it was to organise the music. It meant my having to go against my friend who'd objected to the proposed tune, but it was important to follow my conscience..."

It made Frank think back to his days on the planet Eden. As his bishop's personal assistant he spent much of his days organising special services and events. It felt a world away now, which of course it was, a world and half his lifetime ago. A planet run by what turned out to be a corrupt church institution. Such a pity, such a lost opportunity.

"...but it's important that we remember it is for God's glory," Gunter was still speaking.

"Er, yes, of course."

"The recognition should go to the right place. It should never be about human glory and our reputations."

"Of course not," Frank replied. Then, with a complete change of direction, he said, "Rodd came to see me yesterday."

"Captain Rodd?"

"Yes. I say he came to see me, in fact I think he was merely passing by. Anyway, he took the opportunity to say a few good words about the new army chaplain, Isaac."

"He did?"

"He was most complimentary, saying he's doing a good job. That means quite a lot from Rodd, because he's not what one could call the religious type."

"It's nice to know that Isaac's ministry there is being well received. It is not an easy role."

"Indeed."

"I have an appointment at the refugee camp tomorrow," the bishop told him.

"Oh yes? We don't hear much of them nowadays."

"Things are in a routine now. I think they're glad that the spring weather is well and truly with us, as are we all. They plainly want to return to their homeland as soon as they can, but I understand there's fighting on the other side of the border currently, closer than ever before. A few are afraid it might spill over."

"It's for Captain Rodd to ensure it doesn't do so. He also told me yesterday that a group of Ladosan soldiers offered to surrender at the border, but had been sent back. They'll have to rely on the mercy of their opponents rather than involve us deeper in their dispute."

"Has that happened before?"

"What, soldiers as opposed to civilians?"

"Yes."

"I don't think so. Maybe it's a sign that matters are drawing to a conclusion over there. I hope so."

"I pray so too."

Deejan Charvo suffered a bad day and two restless nights since laying down the law to Sebastian. The second night had been full of bad dreams. Felling rotten the next morning, he decided to cancel all his business engagements. In need of sage advice, he turned to the wisest member of his household: Keturah.

She was studying her Bible in her room, making notes as she did so. It was still early and this was her quiet time before her duties began. Looking up, she was surprised to see her adoptive father and was concerned at the state he appeared to be in.

"Are you not well, Father?"

"I fear," he began, stepping in and closing the door behind him, "that my affliction is more moral and spiritual than physical. May I speak with you?"

It seemed strange for him to be asking a sixteen year old for advice, but he knew that Keturah would be both wise and discrete. He, therefore, explained the situation with Sebastian and his firm words two days previously. He concluded, "If I am so sure I'm right, why do I feel so bad about it? After all, I merely want what's best for him."

Keturah blushed, she did not quite share his assessment of her powers of profound wisdom. Nor was she convinced that she was the right person for him to be talking to. Instead, she passed the buck.

"I would have thought that there is someone else you should be asking for advice, Father. Abbot Muggawagga; you always say that he speaks a great deal of sense. Why not seek his counsel?"

Not for the first time, she had come up with the goods. He chastised his own stupidity as he saw it. In his distress, he had not thought straight. Nevertheless, he put a positive gloss on it. It took Keturah to point out what should have been obvious to him.

"*Of course*! I shall go along there this morning, without delay. In fact, I shall go straightaway."

"It might be an idea to get dressed first."

Her cheeky comment brought the first smile from Deejan.

"A good idea!" he replied.

"And have something to eat as well," she advised. "You'll think better without hunger distracting you."

Sage advice indeed and he took it. Later that morning, he was waiting in Muggawagga's Spartan office. It was quite a wait, for the man was taking a service. Yet it gave the merchant time to collect his thoughts and soon enough the diminutive figure was seen approaching.

"Deejan, me ol' bucka! 'Tis nice to see you... but why the long face? Not bad news, I hope."

Then the full story came out. "My head tells me that I am being a good father by saying no. It's an absurd notion to head off to foreign lands with someone he barely knows, even if I insist on a couple of servants tagging along. He's been doing so well in the business, but this idea has turned his head. Ever since our confrontation, I have

196

seen how upset I have made him. I have tied to explain my reasoning to him, but he does not want to know. If only that silly lad from the mill had not come and turned his head with tales of adventures - lagua and fairy castles or whatever. Things were going so well. Now I fear that I have turned him against me. I'm rather late into this fatherhood business, maybe I have been doing it all for the wrong reasons. Maybe all I ever wanted was a younger version of myself who would be content with studying ledgers all his life. I..."

"Don't be ridiculous," Muggawagga's words brought him up sharp. "You are the best father to those two that a man could ever be. Now you hold your tongue while I think the matter through."

Somewhat startled, Deejan perched on the edge of his chair, quieter than a church mouse, hardly daring to breathe. The abbot sat with his eyes tightly shut. It was as if he was in communion with the Holy Spirit Himself. After what seemed like an age of utter hush, Muggawagga whispered an inaudible prayer to himself before returning to the land of the living. Fixing the petitioner in a firm stare, he spoke slowly.

"No one will say that you are being a bad father. So let's nip that nonsense in the bud. Sebastian is not stupid either, he knows that you are motivated out of care for his safety. But you say he has his heart set on this. He is of that age, of course, when most young men dream about foreign adventure. I know, I did myself."

"Mmm," responded Deejan, to whom even as a youth the idea of a foreign adventure was anathema.

"This Flonass does not sound like a bad character. He appears to be motivated by a desire to help his employer. That is commendable. He's not doing it for anything as tawdry as money. So his heart is in the right place and he is experienced, having been that way twice before - to and from the crusade. Plus you could insist, as you say, on Sebastian being accompanied by a couple of servants."

"You're saying I should let him go?"

"Not to do so may cause resentment, drive a wedge between you. You will demonstrate your love by granting him the freedom to explore. Ultimately parents need to let go. If you do that, he will come back. If not, a barrier will come up that might never be broken down."

"But he might get hurt," Deejan protested.

"He might get hurt crossing the road. We have to trust to God to protect him, pray hard every day. You say he should be back before summer is over in any case, so it can't be too far."

The two of them discussed it further, but the abbot's advice was unequivocal. It was not what Deejan had hoped for, nor expected. Yet he determined to follow it, even if it went against all his instincts. Walter would not be happy either.

Not wanting to end their meeting on this matter, Muggawagga gave a bit of news of his own.

"Following your Keturah's suggestion, I am appointing a manager over the secular side of things here at the monastery. That will release me to concentrate more on the spiritual. I will not need him to report to me over day-to-day matters. It was a good idea and I am indebted to your Keturah. She's a good 'un. As for idea of a festival, with everything else going on, I have shelved it for the time being. I can always get it back off the shelf for next year. Maybe I should get Keturah to organise it."

"I'm sure she'd do a good job," Deejan replied, feeling a little better that when he had arrived.

On the ride home, he went through in his mind how he should tell Sebastian about his change of mind. It should not be difficult, after all, for he was telling the lad what he wanted to hear. However, he would deliver the tidings with a raft of conditions. Sebastian had said that it would be a one-off and that he would return to his job afterwards. His father hoped so. At the very least it would destroy his spring and summer, worrying sick how this young man, who was nothing more than a street urchin when he discovered him, was fairing. Strange are the ways of love. He passed a giant magnolia which, a week before had been full of bloom. Now all the petals were fallen round the base of the bush and they carpeted the ground. It seemed to match his mood somehow.

Back home, and with a heavy heart, Deejan called his son in to give him the news. He could have the freedom to go on his adventure with his father's blessing.

Tristan wondered how much weight he had lost on his journey back to Thyatira. He had certainly experienced long periods of hunger in the last few weeks. The supplies he procured from the Mansion did not last as long as he hoped. Standing within the edge of a wood, ahead of him were the mountains which marked the border with Hoame.

He had managed to avoid Ladosan military patrols up until this point and he did not want to spoil that record now that he was so close to his goal. As far as he knew, the Buffs still controlled the border area, although bumping into a Neo-Purple patrol would have also meant difficulties for him.

For most of the time he completely avoided human contact. The one major exception being the four days he spent at one of the few inhabited farmsteads in these parts. The lady farmer had been alone and she appreciated his manual labour in return for food. That was not the only thing about him she appreciated and in the end he found it necessary to move on sharply to avoid her amorous advances.

Scanning the open ground between himself and where the mountains suddenly rose from the plain, he saw no signs of life. It was not so long ago that robber bands roamed these parts, but they had been driven away. Now though, with a possible breakdown in law and order, they might have been tempted to return. He wondered whether to wait until dusk before dashing across. It might be safer, but then he would be in the middle of the border range when night fell. It that case he would have to wait it out until dawn. The prospect did not appeal to him, so with the warm sun fairly high in the sky, he emerged from the trees and, at a brisk trot, made for the hills.

The farming lady had provided him with a new set of clothes and he looked every inch the Ladosan. New shoes were a blessing, scrambling up the scree as he began his ascent. Weakened through lack of food, it was hard work. Yet in his determination it did not take too long before he was at the ridge that ran along the top. Peering back into Ladosa, he observed the panoramic view. It appeared tranquil, with fresh, spring green as far as the eye could see. Who would guess that a bitter civil war was going on down there? It was a conflict he had decided to leave.

He found plenty of time to contemplate his decision the last few weeks. Was it silly for him to leave simply because of a tiff with a friend? Yet Ayllom was deeply hurt to discover the Hoaman's real identity. The look in his eyes had been of someone who felt betrayed. The thought of staying on with a new partner, while being avoided by his former friend, was too much for Tristan. 'Besides,' he told himself, 'the decision has been made and there's no turning back now.' It was an amazing experience and he felt sure that he had done some good. 'But it is over now. I must pull myself together again and look to a future career closer to home.'

The descent down the other side of the mountain was easier. He still had to watch his footing, but the sheer physical exertion was a lot less. Not long now.

Even as he considered this, a Thyatiran patrol of six men came into view. The ground was less rocky now and the traveller broke into a run, each long stride taking him towards his countrymen.

"Stand guard!" a shout went up and the soldiers adopted a defensive position. What was this lone foreigner doing approaching them at speed?

With heavy steps, Tristan came to a halt a couple of metres away. There he stood for a moment, trying to get his breath back. As he did so, he scanned the faces for any he might recognise, but there was none. All of them were whites and seemed to be without their squad leader.

"What is your business here?" demanded one of the guardsmen abruptly.

"I'm a Hoaman! My name's Tristan Shreeber, I've come back."

His fellow Thyatirans were not immediately convinced and escorted him back to the border post. They eyed him suspiciously, but did not try to restrain him in any way. Fortunately, Captain of the Border Guard Rodd was present on this occasion and recognised him.

"It's okay, I can vouch for him," he announced and the men relaxed immediately. Shortly afterwards, Rodd was sharing a drink with the new arrival. The two did not know each other intimately, but had met on several occasions during the time the black worked in the senate building.

"Would you like something to eat?"

"Yes, please!" the reply came with feeling and he was soon tucking into a pork pie which was manna from heaven to him.

"How come you came to be in Ladosa? Are you part of Japhses' spy network?

Swallowing hard, Tristan replied, "No, I was in Asattan when I got wind that Alan was forming a group to go over there to help out the Neo-Purple faction. I volunteered to help."

"Has there been a disaster? Are the others okay?"

"They were fine last I saw them. It was a personal decision for me to come back early."

"I see. I'm certain the general will want you to give him an update on what you know. I'm not sure where he is today, to be honest, but you'd do well to seek him out tomorrow and tell him everything you know."

Following a short period of rest after his meal, Tristan made his way down, along the track towards Castleton. It was mid afternoon by now. He had turned down the offer of an escort. In fact he decided to avoid human contact for the rest of the day if possible, so he skirted round the Castle. Its sight was so familiar it made him smile. This was home.

He thought about what Rodd had said. He did not feel like contacting General Japhses either that day or the next. Besides, any intelligence he possessed was well out of date and pretty worthless.

Walking down the lane in Castleton, his foreign clothes attracted a few enquiring glances. He did not see anyone he knew. He was making for his parents' house which, as far as he knew, was now his property. What state of repair he would find it in, he had no idea. Maybe it contained new residents.

The latter prospect turned out not to be the case, he surmised, as he got closer to the building. Boarded up and with tall weeds in the small front garden, it was obviously not in use. The property looked an odd sight with creeper growing over its unfinished extension. Broad planks were nailed diagonally across the front door. In the absence of any tools, he pulled feebly at one, to no effect.

Glancing back up the road, he noticed a parked wagon. Its driver, a Ma'hol, was watching him. Feeling he had nothing to lose, Tristan walked up to him and explained the situation. The foreigner was easily convinced, not thinking anyone would try to break into someone else's property in broad daylight. He kindly offered assistance and produced an iron bar from his wagon. With that, he had the boards off in next to no time.

"Thank you so much. I'd give you something for your trouble if I had something to give."

"No need," the foreigner said with a warm smile, "I'd rather do it for nothing."

As the wagon driver walked back, Tristan watched him, thinking, 'There *is* kindness in this world; it simply doesn't get reported.' Then he turned once more and gingerly entered the house.

Everything was as it had been the day his mother was taken away to serve her life sentence. No burglars had been in to rob the place; that was a relief. Everything was extremely dusty and the back garden overgrown, but there was nothing that could not be put right fairly easily. With water from the well he undertook a good wash and he trimmed his beard. Searching around, there was no money and no food. He did find some of his old clothes which still fitted. At least he looked like a Thyatiran once more. All he needed was a job.

He made up his mind there and then to try and settle down there. Maybe a post was available in the senate building. He had been a senator's assistant before, so he had the experience. Prayer was called for: to thank the Almighty for safe passage through war-torn Ladosa and for the house being in a sound state. Then a petitionary prayer for the means to live.

Laughing to himself, Tristan recalled another homecoming he had experienced, following a previous foreign adventure. On that occasion he had given away a fortune to a church in Krabel-Haan. How he could do with that money now! Maybe God would reward his former act of generosity with a job now. 'Only I'm pretty sure that life doesn't work that way,' he told himself.

Sitting down on one of the easy chairs in the living room, it felt soft and comfortable. He considered his state of mind and concluded it was not bad. Having suffered from mental illness in the past, he was always on the lookout for a recurrence.

Earlier, one of the soldiers at the border happened to let slip the fact that the following day was Easter Day. So there would be no job hunting on the morrow. No food either, unless he could beg a meal from someone. He would go along to the service up at the castle in the morning. Feeding his spirit was as important as his stomach and he had missed good Christian nourishment while in Ladosa. He was still a babe in the faith and it would do him good. Besides, it was a good opportunity to see people he knew.

Thus, poor in more ways than one, he possessed hope. Reaching in his pack for his Bible, he felt drawn to the Sermon on the Mount. "Blessed are the poor in spirit, for theirs is the kingdom of heaven..." He smiled and felt that all would be well.

"What wuz the disciples first reaction to the news that Jesus had been raised from the dead? They thought it was nonsense! That might sound a bit extreme, but that's what the gospels tell us. 'But they did not believe the women, because their words seemed to them like nonsense.' Why wuz that? After all, Jesus had told them in plain language what wuz going to 'appen?"

Muggawagga was in full flow and his audience attentive. The Easter Day service up at the Castle was major event in the calendar and this year the weather was perfect for it. A few small clouds scudded across an otherwise deep blue sky. There was a slight hint of a breeze which stopped it getting too hot.

The congregation filled the Castle bailey and anyone who was anyone was present: the Thorns, the senators with their families plus the other important blacks from Castleton with their servants. Not every senator had given his heart and soul to Christ, but the Despot still made it quite plain that he expected them to attend on this Sabbath.

The bishop usually gave the address, but this year Gunter had invited Muggawagga to speak. He needed no persuading.

"It wuz far beyond the disciples' comprehension at the time," the abbot continued, now in full flow. "There were several things which Jesus said that they only understood *after* the resurrection. It is made plain in St Mark's gospel that the disciples were so in awe of Jesus that they were sometimes afraid to ask.

"At the arrest of Jesus, the disciples scattered. We know that Peter and John stayed in Jerusalem and kept an eye on events. John was at the foot of the cross, but of the other disciples we hear nothing for the next few days.

"They may have well retreated to their base at Bethany, a few kilometres outside Jerusalem, filtering back into the city over the next couple of days. St John's gospel tells us that they were gathered together there that evening, behind closed doors because they were afraid of the Jewish authorities.

"Certainly the Resurrection triumph of their Master was the last thing they had envisaged. So when the first witnesses reported back, they thought that the report was crazy."

Frank was listening attentively, but his eyes caught sight of a figure, a young black man, shuffling his way sideways through the crowd. He looked vaguely familiar... then he lost sight of him. Muggawagga was still talking.

"The evidence for the resurrection, for those with open minds, is quite remarkable. More than a few people have set out to discredit it, only to find themselves convinced of the truth. The evidence is many-fold. The tomb was empty; never once did the anti-Christian forces say otherwise. The accusation that the disciples stole the body and then claimed Christ is risen is clearly absurd. They did not expect the resurrection and were surprised by it. They were willing to be martyred for proclaiming this doctrine; there's no way they would have done that if it was all a hoax. There are many recorded sightings of the risen Lord, one even to a crowd of five hundred people."

Towards the end of the address, the abbot mentioned some of the subtleties built into John's gospel.

"In the beginning, Jesus asks the would-be disciples, 'What are you looking for?' By the end, when the truth has been revealed in his person, the question has been changed to, '*Whom* are you looking for?' And, in the garden after the resurrection, he says, 'Mary,' for the Good Shepherd calls his sheep by their name. And he is calling each one of us by name. This Easter, as we commemorate and celebrate Christ's resurrection, let our ears hear his calling in our lives. Jesus is alive today and at work in the world if we let him. Let us heed his voice. Amen."

The service ended with an up-beat song of praise. When it was over, people hung about and chatted in the open air. No one seemed to be in a hurry to leave that morning.

Deejan Charvo, his children beside him, was talking with Senator Vondant.

"Have you any plans for the rest of the day, Karl?"

"We've got my wife's brother and his wife staying with us for a few days. If the weather stays like this we'll go for a walk after lunch, but don't have anything exciting planned. Yourself?"

"We'll be going home for a meal shortly. Then in the afternoon, I think Sebastian and Keturah here are going to rope me in for a few games."

Karl was about to answer when he saw a young black man hovering nearby, apparently wanting to speak to him. He felt that he should know him.

"Excuse me," he said to Deejan, before turning to address the stranger. Deejan staying close by.

"Can I help you?"

"Senator Vondant, I don't know if you remember me. My name's Tristan Shreeber, I..."

"Ah yes, Tristan, of course!" the senator's high-pitched voice exclaimed. Then, following a slight pause, he added, "I was sorry to hear about your father."

Tristan thanked him for these condolences and was about to say something more, but the other man got in first.

"So where have you been? Asattan, I thought I'd heard."

"Yes, I was there for some time, but I've recently come back from a spell in Ladosa." Faced with a surprised expression, he continued, "I was with Alan."

"Ah, our military advisors."

"Yes," Tristan confirmed. There was no need to go into details.

"I believe the Despot's recently received another message from Alan. You didn't deliver it, did you?"

"Er, no, that wasn't me."

"I see. He's promised to share its contents with me. The senate is keen to keep abreast of developments across the border. Is there anything that you can tell me?"

"Probably not. I haven't been near the action for several weeks. All I know is that the Neo-Purple offensive continues... I mean, that's my understanding."

"Good, good! It seems we've backed the right runner. With the weapons we've provided, plus the expertise, they're doing well."

"Plus a lot of Ladosan blood," Tristan would have liked to have added, but thought better of it.. Instead, he decided to make the most of this opportunity.

"Senator Vondant."

"Yes."

"I hope to be back for good now. I was wondering if I could take up a position as a senatorial assistant here in the Castle Complex again. I have the relevant experience, having done the job before."

"Hmm," went Karl, pulling a slight face. "There are no vacancies currently, I'm pretty certain. We're under instructions not to take any further staff at present in any case. The annexing of the Norland area is proving an expensive business. Not only the initial purchase, but if

205

we're going to get the whole area up to scratch, it is going to cost a lot of money. So we're on a bit of an economy drive. I'm sorry."

The young man looked crestfallen and Deejan, having patiently observed the entire conversation from close range, felt sorry for him. He said, "We're about to go home for lunch. You're welcome to join me if you like."

"Oh, that would be most kind," Tristan replied. Without two stens to rub together, a free meal was almost welcome.

"We'd better be going then," the merchant said warmly. Saying goodbye to Karl, he led the way, followed by Sebastian, Keturah, Tristan with assorted servants in tow.

"It's a special Easter Day meal," Sebastian explained to their dinner guest. "I think you'll like it."

At that point, Tristan would be grateful for any nourishment. In the event, he found himself round the table eating a meal as delicious as it was large,

Walter was present and, sitting opposite him, asked about his time at the Capital.

"I was working in the civil service, based in the Citadel itself."

"A fine building, I've only ever seen it from the outside and that was a while ago."

"It's magnificent inside, it's vast scale is amazing. There's no end to the corridors, stairways and rooms. It took me a while to find my way about; I got lost quite a few times early on."

"But you gave up a good job there to go adventuring in Ladosa," Walter stated, his tone-of-voice difficult to interpret.

"I gave it up because I became ill," Tristan corrected him.

"Oh, I see," the money man retreated.

"I was feeling better round about the time I heard of the Hoame delegation's mission abroad. I hoped that I could do some good by volunteering for it."

"Commendable!" Deejan declared. He was in the best of spirits that day. "Most commendable, doing your patriotic duty like that. I heard you say that you're looking for employment now. I wish I could help, but I can't say I have a suitable post I can offer you."

"It's all right, I did not have any such expectations."

"A pity," added the merchant, although he did not look too downcast. Inside, he was still on a high, because of what his son had told him the day before. After careful consideration, Sebastian concluded that he did not want to go adventuring to West Torravis, Rabeth-Mephar, or anywhere else for that matter. He realised what a wonderful life he already enjoyed and wanted to stay at home. Deejan was delighted with this perfect outcome, as he saw it, and grateful for Muggawagga's advice. Sebastian had asked for his freedom, been granted it, then exercised it by staying. His father thanked God for this wonderful blessing.

It was then Sebastian's turn to address the visitor.

"You're looking for a way to earn money?"

"I am."

"Isn't it true that you've already adventured abroad?"

"I have."

"I wasn't referring to your recent time in Ladosa; didn't you go westwards with Alan once?"

"I went with my brother. I ended up in West Torravis."

"Wonderful!" Sebastian exclaimed with a note of triumph. Then, while his father engaged Walter in a separate conversation, he told Tristan about Flonass' need for someone to accompany him. Here was someone who was used to foreign travel and actually visited the country in question before. He might be a black, but Flonass would be crazy not to want him as his partner.

"It's perfect timing, your coming back now. All expenses for the journey are to be met and there's fifty stens in it for you if you're successful." Then he explained where this Flonass could be contacted. Fifty stens would certainly be a help to Tristan in his current situation, but the thought of facing further foreign adventures did not exactly appeal to him. Still, he realised that beggars cannot afford to be choosers. Besides, the timing was quite a coincidence; maybe God was behind it.

"I'll seek him out tomorrow," he replied.

The guest stayed for the afternoon having been invited to play card games. Walter made his excuses, but Deejan joined in until a servant appeared and told him that he had another visitor. The Despotess, no less, was giving him a call regarding a church initiative they were involved in. Tristan continued the game with Sebastian and Keturah. They played, they laughed, it was a most peasant distraction.

Meanwhile, Frank was entertaining the abbot up at the Castle. Muggawagga had joined the Thorns for lunch and now the two men were enjoying a private conversation together in the Despot's third floor suite.

"Yes, it's true," Frank was saying, "with this Norland thing I have more work than ever. I wouldn't mind taking a break from it, but I'm not in the mood for one of my trips to the Capital."

"You need an assistant," replied the other man, "a personal secretary."

"Ah, that's what Hannah keeps telling me." The comment was dismissive, for he was keen to move on to more interesting topics. He commented, "Another Easter Day, a lot of people say this is their favourite time of year with fresh, new growth. Easter is like spring, a message of fresh growth out of what appears to be death."

"No, me ol' bucka! I can't agree. Spring is predictable each year; we know it's going to come. But Easter wuz unexpected and provoked astonishment, even incredulity. St Thomas took a lot of convincing. He wuz a practical fellow, he would not have been surprised by the arrival of spring."

"Point taken," Frank replied with a smile.

"We look at Easter from a position of retrospect. It wuz not the same for the disciples. They were taken by surprise and it wuz a while for their joy to be complete. Even at the Ascension some were doubting."

"Yes, how bold of the gospel writers to record that!"

"It were a gradual growing process of illumination. The full significance took years to sink in. That's why I love St John's gospel, he wrote after decades of contemplating these things and showed his deep understanding."

"That's right, such matters are profound and need to be thought through. It can take time for people to fully comprehend the goodness of God; for hope to fully take root and the reality of our being forgiven."

"It is so. I still have folk come to the monastery on a regular basis who feel the weight of guilt on their shoulders. Their self image is all wrong, way too negative. It doesn't do to concentrate on all the bad bits within us."

"No," confirmed Frank.

"Jesus said we will be like gods; that we will do great works like what he did, but even better. These be amazing promises."

"Jesus tended to use hyperbole to get across a point."

"Precisely right, me old bucka! He wuz trying to impress us to have a positive image and not to dwell on bad things. After all, he did say that the Kingdom of Heaven is within us, we..."

"Yes, yes!" Frank enthused. This exchange was taking him back to his university days and the kind of conversations he used to hold with his friends Patel and Nakajima. He said, "I remember our tutor telling us about that text once. Sometimes it is translated as 'the Kingdom of Heaven is *upon* you,' but he said that the best rendition of the Ancient Greek is certainly 'within you.' That has huge implications."

Completely on the same wavelength, Muggawagga came back, "It does. If we have the divine breath of life within us, and the Kingdom of Heaven is within us, we must believe in our innate goodness. Of course we all have the capacity to sin, but our real destiny is in the opposite direction. We are children of God and need to dwell on that. For what gets contemplated, gets strengthened. If we are constantly thinking of ourselves negatively, we will conform to that image."

Muggawagga nodded while Frank continued his train of thought. "And if we think of ourselves in a positive way, then we are more likely to be good."

"Yup; so in a good way we can be the masters of our own destiny."

Their theological deliberations were halted at this point by the arrival of Hannah, back from Deejan Charvo's. She was not alone, for she had a young man in tow.

"Don't get up," she said before introducing Tristan to her husband.

"Of course," said Frank, "we've met before." He, for one, was not completely surprised that Tristan was back in Thyatira, for Alan had predicted as much in the communication recently received. In it, the drone asked Frank to give some financial aid, writing, 'It is the least due to him for the sterling work he has done over here. So if (as I believe he will) Tristan does turn up, please give him some help.'

"Good," said Hannah, "because he is going to be your personal secretary."

"He is?" Frank asked, surprised at this news.

"Most certainly. He has relevant experience, the brains and expertise to assist you. He can start work tomorrow."

Hannah on a mission was an irresistible force. Her husband did not try to resist, but wisely submitted. Tristan would not be joining Flonass' adventure. He had landed a plumb job at the heart of the

209

Thyatiran government. His hope, it turned out, had been well founded.

~ End of Chapter 10 ~

Prospects of Peace - Chapter 11

The siege of Wesold had gone on long enough. The Neo-Purples strategy, as recommended by Alan, was to contain the Buff garrison and not engage the defenders in costly street fighting. It was not clear as to whether this plan was working or not. There had been no further communication with the garrison since the unconditional surrender demand.

Eventually the besieging field commander decided enough was enough. Without recourse to Marshal Nazaz, an all out bombardment of the town was commenced. For two whole days, boulders and incendiaries were hurled into the already war-torn streets. Fires were started the length of Wesold. The Neo-Purples possessed a large stockpile of ammunition and this was now used with gusto. Weeks of frustration were released and the morale of the attackers rose by the hour.

Captain Hallazanad was reassigned following a spell as Charlotta's liaison officer. She respected his wishes to be where the action was. The Fanallon Front activity was drawing to a close with mopping up operations being the order of the day. He was therefore posted further north. Almost immediately, he found himself in charge of a heavy assault platoon about to enter Wesold. Their existing commander had been taken sick and Hallazanad was put into the post at the last minute. He needed to get to know the personnel as quickly as possible. The orders were to go in the moment the bombardment was lifted the following morning.

The projectiles stopped going overhead as the sun first came up on the third day of the bombardment. Crossing open countryside to get to the first buildings, the heavily armed force was relieved to find they did not come under counter-fire.

Always on the lookout for ambushes, he led his force up a main street in the commercial quarter. Advancing past warehouses set on fire, they gave them a wide berth due to the intense heat being given off by the flames.

"A vision of hell!" exclaimed the Corporal Siannarad, but the captain did not reply.

211

Each building had to be checked for enemy soldiers, but for a long time that morning they did not see a soul. The civilians were long gone and there was no sign of the defenders.

"It seems," said Hallazanad, "that they've abandoned this sector. Presumably they intend to take a stand nearer the centre of town."

One of his men kicked open a door and peered inside a building. The roof was missing and there was no sign of life in that empty shell. Still Hallazanad insisted they advance with caution. It got to the stage when they began not to expect to find any Buff soldiers in each place they checked.

It therefore came as a surprise when, after they had been going for some considerable time, they entered a small, relatively unscathed warehouse and found it full of full of enemy personnel. Only these were not offering any resistance. Wounded and ailing soldiers of both sexes lined the walls on either side, mostly on the floor.

"It's a bloody hospital," declared the corporal.

Whilst it was full of Buff wounded, the term "hospital," even a makeshift one, was inaccurate. These soldiers had been abandoned by their comrades and there appeared to be no medical personnel helping them at all. The assault troops were shocked at the spectacle. Many were weak with sickness and diarrhoea. Some of the wounds were gangrenous and the stench inside was horrendous.

"I'm surprised we didn't smell it coming down the road," the NCO commented.

"The prevailing wind was behind us," the officer replied. He then continued, "These poor sods are no threat to us. It's not our job to see to them. Have a couple of soldiers stand guard and direct the follow-up troops to see to them. The rest of us have got to move on."

"Yes, sir!"

Hallazanad sought out a Buff officer to extract information from. One was found in the form of a surprisingly youthful major sporting a leg wound. This character was exceptionally cooperative and when he said that he simply wanted the fighting to stop, Hallazanad believed him.

"The remnant have withdrawn to the central, town hall area," he advised. "There aren't many of them."

"Are they fanatics? Will they put up much of a fight?"

"They're ordinary soldiers... as for what sort of fight they put up, I wouldn't like to say. They'll be tired, like the rest of us, but we held out against the odds far longer than we thought we would."

The Neo-Purples could have told him that the town would have fallen a lot earlier if they had chosen to launch an all-out assault sooner. They were not there to engage in general conversation though. Hallazanad led his force outside, away from the smell. There they took a well-earned breather. It was not long before the back-up soldiers came to view, along with some medics. They left the Buffs in their charge and pressed on.

At the edge of the commercial area they passed the last of a series of identically constructed warehouses. All were damaged, a couple completely burnt out. The road was paved with large, stone slabs which were covered in the debris of war: discarded weapons, bits of armour, wrecked wagons, burnt timbers and shattered brick fragments.

"What a mess," was one of the soldier's opinions.

No sooner were the words spoken than an arrow passed millimetres in front of his face. They dived for cover and a trio entered the building where the shot had come from.

"Bloody sniper," snarled the corporal who found himself following a female swordsman up a metal staircase to the top floor.

They found themselves in a large, rectangular area which had been stripped of its contents. Two rows of round pillars went up the room and they took cover behind the nearest one. The female soldier peaked out from her vantage point and had another arrow fired at her for her trouble. The projectile hit the pillar and deflected away at an angle.

Silently the attackers scuttled forward from pillar to pillar, minimising their exposure as much as possible. They had nearly got to the far end of the building when the lone sniper decided to surrender. The female soldier got to him first and grabbed his arm. She was amazed at how young their captive was, a boy.

"He's alone. We'll take him to..."

Her sentence was cut short by one of her confederates who, without ceremony, ran his sword through the heart of the prisoner.

"Why d'yer do that?" she asked accusingly as she let the dead youth slip to the floor.

Withdrawing his sword, her colleague replied dismissively, "He tried to kill us. He's got to learn he can't do that."

Rather than point out the obvious fact that the lad could learn nothing if he was dead, she led them back without a word. She was cross, but there was no point in arguing about it.

"Building cleared?" enquired Hallazanad when they emerged once more.

"Yes, sir."

"All right, proceed."

No further resistance was encountered until they reached Wesold's central square. In happier days this had been a lush, green area with grass, bushes and strategically-placed trees with a fountain in the middle. Now the fountain was smashed, the bushes uprooted and the trees felled for barricades.

On the opposite end of the square was the town hall. Central to a row of buildings, it was less damaged than most. Four stories high and with a neo-classical frontage, it was built to impress.

The platoon was under cover, spying out their objective. Scouts were sent to skirt round and see the situation at the rear and others were seeking weak spots at the flanks. As a result, the captain's force was spread thin. He was with a small, advance group, lined up behind a convenient, low wall. They were passing their one set of binoculars one to another. The only enemy soldiers visible were a group on top of the main building. If the Neo-Purples could see them, then it was pretty obvious that, in turn, they had been spotted.

"How many of those buildings contain enemy, do you think?" enquired his lieutenant.

It was, of course, an impossible question to answer. Several hundred could be holed up in and around the square, although the captured major suggested that there was not a large force here. Either way, Hallazanad decided it would be prudent to await reinforcements. He spoke to his officers and NCOs.

"We're attacking the town on all four points of the compass, but it seems we've got to the centre first. We won't want to assault this last bastion until we know they're completely surrounded on all sides. Siannarad, I want you..."

"Captain; look!"

He stopped in response to the corporal's cry. A delegation of Buffs, led by a tall woman holding a white flag, was approaching them.

"Let's hope this means what I think it does," Hallazanad said softly.

That evening, after dark, the captain was sitting writing his report, up on the third floor of the town hall. His soldiers were around him, most getting some sleep. It was good to be under cover, especially with the penetrating drizzle falling outside.

It was the end of an historic day, the fall of Wesold. Critics of the containment policy were proven right about the size of the defending Buff force. In fact now the truth had come our regarding how small their opposing force had been all along, some Neo-Purple officers found plenty to complain about.

"It was a skeleton garrison."

"They've been playing us for fools!"

"We should have launched the attack ages ago, then our forces would not have been tied up for so long."

"It was that Hoaman Alan's silly idea to wait it out."

Wiser heads would come to understand the truth of the matter in time. Whilst it was true that the Buffs garrison was somewhat smaller than expected, the weeks of hunger, illness and inactivity sapped morale and degraded their fighting potential. A lot of lives had been saved through the chief advisor's counsel.

Nevertheless, the Buffs had successfully carried out the first part of their strategy, namely to withdraw troops to use elsewhere. Their original idea had been to launch a surprise counter-offensive against the Neo-Purples. Yet, as so often in war, events overtook them. Continual pressure from the Rose army on the northern front meant these reserves being needed to hold the line there.

Sitting on a wooden box inside the old town hall, Hallazanad wrote a report for Marshal Nazaz which would be delivered at first light. She would receive many such reports to help her build an accurate picture. Towards the end, he gave a big yawn, for it had been a tense, tiring day. The lantern went out of its own accord, just as he was finishing his conclusion. He would complete the final couple of lines in the morning.

At daybreak, he awoke, stiff but otherwise refreshed. The report was completed, but he held onto it. Word that morning was that the marshal was coming up to Wesold to see the place for herself. He joined his troops for a breakfast from the rations they carried on their persons. The captain was then called to an officers' briefing from which he returned to his unit with orders for the day.

"Apparently the northern, residential area still has civilians within it. There are reports of minor disruption between them, also of looting taking place. We're to go there and keep the peace."

His soldiers took the assignment stoically and buckled up their armour as they prepared to move out.

"What," asked the sergeant, "are our orders if we catch any looters?"

"Use your discretion."

"Execute the bastards!"

"If that's going to deter others, then yes."

Hallazanad led his force down to ground level and, emerging from the building, was pleased to find the rain stopped. They moved out in a northerly direction and found themselves met by other soldiers on the same mission.

In the event, things had calmed down in the northern part of town and there was little to do. Then a colonel came up with the bright idea of searching peoples' houses for valuables in case they had been stolen. That only resulted in looting by certain Neo-Purple soldiers, although Hallazanad made it perfectly clear that he would not stand for such behaviour from his own unit.

"We've got one, we've got one!" a couple of more excitable swordsmen cried out as they dragged a hapless, balding, middle-aged man through the rubble of a demolished house. They dumped him at the feet of their officer and explained.

"In his house we found these - look!" and they brandished a couple of ornate, metre-long silver candlesticks, plus a cross of equal length. "These were hidden under the stairs, but it didn't take us long to find them." There was a note of resounding triumph in the voice of the soldier who announced this. Then he added, "May I execute him, sir?"

With a frown, the captain fixed his eyes at the pathetic figure kneeling before him. Worried expression, he was dressed simply. The man seized the opportunity to explain.

"I'm the warden at St Barnabas', the local church over there," he began, pointing vaguely in the right direction. "When the siege started, I took these for safekeeping. I was going to return them once the fighting ended. I don't want them for my personal use."

While the silver content was probably worth a great deal of money, Hallazanad was fully convinced of the truth he had just heard.

"Release him!" he ordered, "and return these things... take them back to his house. We'll do no more house to house searching, it's absurd. I'm going to talk to the colonel.

The would-be executioner and his mate obeyed their orders without a word and the church treasures were made safe once more.

Next day, Marshal Nazaz entered the liberated town and was debriefed in person by her senior officers, although Hallazanad was allowed to sit in. In turn, she shared news of the bigger picture of what was going on in southwest Ladosa.

Neo-Purple forces were continuing to sweep westwards, towards the Rabeth-Mephar border. Buffs were surrendering in numbers and would soon be a spent force in this part of the country.

One frustration for her was that enemy General Vap had not been apprehended, in spite of her slapping a large amount of money on his head. Still, in the greater scheme of things, this was a minor irritant. It was plain that the end of the southwest Buffs must come soon.

Along with the Neo-Purple Central Committee, Marshal Nazaz had been discussing the next phase of the conflict. Pre-war there was no love lost between them and the Rose Party. However, things change and there was no doubt that, in practice even if not in planning, the two forces had cooperated against the common enemy. As the last of the Buffs between them crumbled, the Neo-Purple standing orders were not to engage the Roses unless first attacked. No reports of fighting between these two factions were yet to be reported. Charlotta, with her old negotiator's head on, was keen to see if accommodation could be made. Ideally, both should combine to invade the Central Buff territory, but some intricate bargaining would probably be needed first.

As for the rest of Ladosa, news was sketchy. There were constant reports that the fireball had wiped out the northeast tribes and their foreign backers, if they ever existed. The phenomenon also struck a severe blow to the Central Buffs in the region of the capital Braskaton. It affected the Pinks to the north too. The marshal wondered at the tremendous force involved to achieve all this death and destruction.

Meanwhile, if she had not been fully in love with him, she could easily have forgotten Alan with everything else going on. As it was, she kept her messengers busy with communications to the Chief Hoame Advisor. Knowing that he was restricted far behind the line

217

these days, she was happy at the thought of him being safe. Once this terrible war was over, there would be time and opportunity for the two of them to be together.

Tristan turned and glance at his Castleton home before going off to work, clutching a leather document bag. Two weeks into his job and he felt that he was getting fully into the role. It was a new post and there was no job description as such, so really it was up to him to make it something beneficial.

The remit given by the Despotess was to ease her husband's administrative burden and he aimed to do exactly that. And how generous was his new employer! A substantial lump sum to start off with, followed by a generous salary. He had never heard of such a thing, but then he did not know about Alan's letter to Frank asking him to help the man out financially.

It was but a quick walk from his house to the Castle. Otherwise he might have had to move into one of the fortress's rooms. As it was, he was able to live in the house left to him by his parents and afford to have it cleaned and the garden tidied. A future aim was to get the half-built extension completed. He would have to save a lot of money before he was able to afford that.

There were fresh neighbours next door from the last time he lived there. They seemed a little cold at first, but had begun to thaw out over the last fortnight. Of all the Castleton residents, it was Deejan Charvo whom he saw most of in his spare time. Tristan took part in the midweek Bible study group held at the merchant's house. Sebastian and Keturah were always there, plus the occasional other neighbour, so it was on an extremely small scale. It was fun, with the philosophical discussions invariably going off at the most extraordinary tangents. No one tried to dominate the proceedings and everyone was given their say.

Once he had been offered the secretarial role, there was no prospect of him going off on a further adventure to West Torravis. So when, through Sebastian, he received a formal invitation from Flonass to discuss such a thing, he turned it down straightaway.

One dry, warm morning, Tristan made his way to work. The air was still at this early hour. Passing the senate building, he saw a number of clerks, as well as Senator Ronenvink, entering the complex. He had his own office within there, but his destination was further on and looming large in his sights. For the Despot liked to meet his new secretary in the Castle Throne Room more often than not.

The day before saw the weekly senate meeting, only the second one he had attended. While there was an official minute taker, Tristan sat in and made his own notes. He had been called on yesterday to clarify a point before the senators. No doubt there would be more of that to come. The main thing, as far as Tristan had been concerned, was that the senators made him feel welcome.

Entering through the Castle entrance, one of the soldiers on duty gave him a nod. He gave a faint smile by way of response, then wracked his brain as to where he had met the man before. It came to him before he reached the Castle keep. They served together briefly during the Chogolt War. How nice to be recognised.

"Good morning, sergeant!"

"Good morning, secretary. Going to be a nice day by the looks of it."

"Yes, indeed," he replied before taking the staircase two at a time.

A sudden flashback to his youth came to him. Victor and he used to try going up the stairs to their bedroom two at a time. They even tried three, but it had not proved practical. Their mother told them off for being so silly.

Mother... now bricked up at Muggawagga's monastery. Should he visit her? Could he bring himself to? It was not a prospect that he looked forward to. He certainly would not be doing so this day.

There was a lot of noise coming from the hall and he found that breakfast was still in full swing. Having eaten at home, he was not tempted even by the delicious smell of fresh bread. Noting that the Despot was not at his usual place in the large room, he made straight for the Throne room. Opening the door, he found him already seated and pawing over some papers.

"Oh, I'm sorry, My Lord, I didn't..."

"That's all right, come in."

He was in cheerful mood - good. Tristan sat down alongside his new employer and emptied out the contents of his document bag.

"I felt that the meeting went well yesterday," Frank offered.

"The senate meeting?"

"Yes."

"I thought it was productive, My Lord. I have some action points to go through as a result of it."

"Shall we order some drinks first?"

A short while later, with the drinks before them, the secretary went through some items.

"If you remember, My Lord, Senator Drasnik asked that you attend the ceremony being held in the senate building later this morning."

"Ceremony?"

"The award for the constable for his act of bravery."

"Ah yes."

"While Senator Drasnik is happy to give the speech, he felt that your presence would add to the dignity of the occasion."

Frank nodded. His face was serious, but inside he could not help but chuckle to himself. The former second-hand book salesman's presence would add to the dignity of the occasion. Well, that was a long while ago. His time in the Despot's role was longer than he had travelled in that other capacity. Nevertheless, he found the current meeting taking him back to Eden. As Cardinal Rouse's personal organiser he filled a role similar to that which Tristan now held. Frank had been more than a little scared of the cardinal, he hoped the young black before him did not feel the same way now.

"My Lord?"

"Yes?"

"Does that meet with your approval?"

"Me to stand and look regal while Drasnik spouts forth? I think I can manage that." Then, when he saw Tristan's shocked expression, he added, "I'm sorry, I'm being flippant. It is right that we acknowledge acts of bravery by our constables trying to keep law and order. What did the man do, anyway?"

"I believe he disarmed a maniac with a knife who was threatening... either his family or his neighbours, I forget which. I can find out for you."

"No need; I'm sure all will be revealed later this morning."

"Yes, My Lord. Then I have allowed some time afterwards for you to meet the constable and his family. I am sure that will go down well."

"All right."

"And immediately after lunch there's the meeting with the Mayor of Eshtaol who's visiting Castleton, and specifically the senate, to see how things operate here."

"Not straight after lunch, I hope," said Frank. Then , when the secretary did not respond, he added, "I do like to have a little rest after lunch these days."

"Of course!" Tristan exclaimed loudly. He must not forget that the Despot need his post lunch nap. It would not do for him to drop off while the mayor was talking. "I shall schedule the meeting with the mayor mid-afternoon. Shall I send a messenger up to you shortly before it is due to take place?" He was careful not to say, "To wake you up."

"An excellent idea, thank you, Tristan." Here was someone who was responding to his needs.

"And, if you remember, it was agreed at the meeting that a newsletter to the Inner Council needed to be sent. Giving an update on the war, it was best coming from yourself."

"Oh, yes," Frank replied, showing less enthusiasm.

"If I may possibly borrow Alan's letter, I can concoct a draft communication to the Inner Council for you to approve before it is sealed and sent off."

"Excellent! I think I have it here actually... yes, here it is. If you do me a draft, like you said, I can cast my eyes over it before anything is sent off." He continued talking while scanning the paper. "Alan's communication was somewhat vague when it came to actual news. In fact he does wonder if our advisors are being sidelined now that victory in the southwest looks assured."

Frank held back the final page which was all personal information, including the bit about Tristan. He was glad that he had not simply passed it over.

"So our communication to the Keepers can be in similar vein, giving a general feel for events rather than specifics. It is nearly all good news, so they will not be too disappointed at the lack of detail."

"Thank you, My Lord," Tristan replied, taking hold of the pages offered to him.

The Despot and his secretary continued their meeting. It was a good arrangement. The former got the assistance he badly needed and the latter got a well paid, varied and responsible job. Both had a lot to thank Hannah for.

People in the know did not underestimate the role that Deejan Charvo played in the Thyatiran economy. The fabulously wealthy financier provided a lot of the means for local businesses. Wanting to set up a new, viable enterprise? Go to see Deejan Charvo. Wishing to expand one's factory? You know who to turn to.

He was in a much better position here in Thyatira than in his previous base in Aggeparii. The biggest factor behind this was his relationship with the local ruler. Despot Kagel made no attempt to hide his contempt for the moneylender, even as he used his services shamelessly. Despot Thorn was a friend, particularly now Deejan embraced the faith.

The two men had an excellent working relationship too, an understanding which worked. The merchant would not charge extortionate rates of interest and the Despot would help him with bad debts by getting the constables involved. Not that every debt was recoverable, of course, but shirkers were brought to heel.

Since seeing the light, Deejan's attitude towards wealth had fundamentally changed. He no longer coveted money and what he held, he saw as something to be used for the community. It was merely in his safekeeping. The Charvo family certainly never went without, but he was not one for ostentatious living.

One day, Walter came to see him with a problem.

"It's the Sardis Weavers' Guild," he stated.

"Oh, them?" asked Deejan, looking concerned. "What have they been up to?"

"Four weeks overdue with their repayments."

"Four weeks?" came the surprised retort. It was not like Walter to be so tardy.

"The guild leader has the gift of the gab, but nevertheless I've spoken with Constable Kitel."

"And?"

"That was a fortnight ago. The constable has been dragging his heels. They're supposed to support us."

"Indeed they are."

"I'm asking you to see the Despot," Walter stated.

If his assistant was having this much trouble, it must be a bad case. He could go to Senator Drasnik, but an appeal to the top was the

222

most effective way to get things moving and Deejan was the man for the job.

"All right. Pass me the file, Walter. I'll have a look at it before arranging a meeting with Despot Thorn. I suppose I'll have to go via our friend Tristan now."

Fortunately this did not mean much of a delay and the following afternoon the merchant was explaining the situation to Frank in the confines of the Throne Room.

"And our repeated warnings have fallen on deaf ears. Walter has appealed to Constable Kitel to enforce the repayments, but he does not appear to have done anything. It is extraordinary, because from what we can tell, the Weavers' Guild in Sardis is not doing badly. I don't know what they're playing at."

Frank listened carefully and took a few notes as he did so. If there was anyone he would like to assist, it was his friend Deejan Charvo.

"Leave it with me," he told the financier. "I'm going over to the senate building in a little while. I shall speak to Senator Drasnik myself and make sure something is done without delay. You can rely on it."

"Thank you, Frank, thank you so much."

As the Despot's friend he was allowed to call him by his Christian name in private, it was an honour he was glad to have.

"So how's the family?"

"All well, thank you. We recently bought a baby dakk for Keturah to keep after her old one died."

"Oh, sorry to hear that."

"It had been ill on and off for some time. The new one is a character. Still unsure on its feet, he does tend to stumble a lot."

"Really? I never thought of dakks as having character."

"This one seems to. Keturah's brought it out of him."

"How sweet."

"She's fond of animals. I suppose Sebastian is too, in his own way."

"Is he?"

"With the nicer weather he's been outside more. Last year we got a pond dug at the back of the garden and he likes to watch the frogs and other creatures."

Frank laughed at the idea, then remembered his own childhood. "My father built a pond when I was little. He liked the fish."

"Fish to eat?"

223

"Oh no; ornamental. Looking back, Frank only now realised what a lot of his father's life had been merely to make ends meet. The pond had been a distraction from this. As the Despot's cover story was that he was a prince from Oonimari, this is not something he could mention. He continued, "I can't say I took much of an interest myself, they just swam round and round."

"Maybe your Joseph would enjoy a pond."

"Maybe! I'll have to ask him. He could do some frog spotting with Sebastian. He's currently outside with Hannah."

Joseph was indeed outside the Castle walls with his mother, but it was getting a bit breezy. The Despotess had her hair cut earlier and she was not sure it was totally dry. She tried to dismiss the thought and concentrate on the business in hand.

For Hannah found herself re-inspired with regards to her garden. This project had begun the previous year, a traditional Ladosan formal garden, a stone's throw from the Castle. As well as general workmen and gardeners, she employed the services of some volunteer Ladosan refugees from the refugee camp. The enterprise was suddenly suspended at the news of her husband's kidnap. When that crisis was finally over, all her enthusiasm was gone, she no longer found her heart in it.

The site was allowed to go back to nature. With the exception of the herb garden, it was untouched for a whole year. Supplying assorted herbs for the Castle kitchen had been the impetus behind the original idea. The formal garden notion grew from it, before to be abandoned.

Another year, another spring. Fresh growth, fresh shoots, fresh impetus and the impulse to resurrect the project. Only this time the personnel was different. For one thing, the Ladosan refuge women were no longer willing to take part. It was nothing that the Despotess said or did; they had no argument with her. During their time in and around the castle, they experienced low level, but persistent harassment from the locals. It was usually in the form of snide, anti-Ladosan, and in particular, anti-refugee comments by some of the Hoamen whose path they crossed. It had had a cumulative effect and, after a full year back in the camp, they did not want to volunteer again. Not that they told her the reason. She formed the impression that they had become so institutionalised that they no longer wanted

224

to leave their quarters, 'Whatever will become of them once the war ends?' she wondered, but she did not press the issue.

Hannah's ideas for the project were moving away from a traditional Ladosan formal garden in any case. Rather her thoughts were for introducing other, different elements. She now favoured a wildflower section and a labyrinth for a more original creation.

The area was back to being a hive of activity, with thirty or more men and women toiling in the pleasant weather. The site had become overgrown over the last year, but that was now cleared away. One group of men were currently sinking in long posts for what would be a pergola next to the central walkway. Another group of mixed men and women caught Hannah's eye. They were sitting next to a huge pile of flint stones and were washing mud off them in buckets. With Joseph in tow, she went over to their supervisor, a skinny, black gentleman with a ruddy face.

"What are these people doing?"

"Ah, My lady... um, this was the foreman's idea. These flints were taken off the fields following last autumn's ploughing. They were going to be used for walls outside Vionium, but were surplus to requirements. He had the idea of using them here to help define the borders."

"I see.." Hannah replied, taking this all in. She continued, "It sounds like a good idea. But who are these people?"

"Um..."

"I don't recognise any of them."

"No, My Lady. These are miscreants who have fallen foul of the law. Their crimes are not deemed serious enough to warrant gaol. Instead, they help out with public works for a period of time."

"The Despot mentioned this to me, one of Senator Drasnik's initiatives, I understand. A good idea." She studied the labourers as she spoke, but none of them raised their eyes. She was impressed by this articulate supervisor, almost as much as she was by Hanz's community service scheme. These were not the hardened criminals let out of gaol temporarily and chained together. Rather they were a mixed bag, exclusively whites on this occasion, who worked away quietly at their simple task.

The man added, "The flint stones will be laid out at a later stage. As you can see, many of them were caked in mud and need a good clean."

"Very good, thank you," she responded before moving on, her son still at her side.

As they made their way back to the Castle, Joseph asked, "Will it be finished this summer, do you think?"

"I hope so, although a garden is an on-going concern. We need to employ some workers permanently to keep it looking nice."

"We'll be able to look down on it from the Castle!" he added excitedly.

"Of course. As the flowers grow it should brighten up the view. I hope so."

One morning, Frank left the Castle for a meeting in the senate building. Although quite early, with the days lengthening the sun was well up and the sky bright. In fact the temperature seemed a lot warmer outside the keep than it had done inside the thick-walled building. He wondered whether the coat he was wearing was strictly necessary, but then it was only a short walk.

Ever since Tristan took on the new role as the Despot's secretary, Frank found a shadow following him everywhere, or so it seemed. He told himself not to complain and that Hannah had been right to appoint him. After all, the young man was making a difference. When he held a meeting, many of the action points were taken up by the assistant now.

He was rather looking forward to the meeting he was currently heading to. Emil Vebber was back from another fact-finding tour of Norland. It was an on-going project, but the Despot was keen to hear the latest news before the senator disappeared again.

He found the large gentleman alone, waiting for him in his office.

"Don't get up, Emil. You already know Tristan, I understand."

"I do. It's nice to see you again."

Tristan replied by way of a polite nod and took his place to one side.

"Excellent," announced Frank. "You arrived back last night?"

"Late afternoon. I thought that you'd want me to go through my findings before tomorrow's senate meeting."

"Indeed. So which parts did you visit on this occasion?"

"The two towns of Carnis and Newton. On my next visit I plan to travel down to the southwest."

"The strip that borders Rabeth-Mephar?"

226

"In theory, yes, although there is a huge, impenetrable forest along most of the frontier, plus some swampland."

"All right. And beyond the very bottom... remind me what that borders on, please."

"The Rilesia despotate."

"Despot Heisler in charge?"

"That is correct."

Frank felt pleased with himself. Even after nineteen years in the country, he still knew some parts a lot better than others. He had never been to the western area that was Rilesia and had only met Heisler briefly. Realising that he was straying from the issue at hand, he asked Emil how his visit had gone.

"I found it most productive. The Mayor of Carnis in particular was eager to keep me in harness throughout my visit to his town, but..."

"'His' town?"

"I think that's how he sees it. Anyhow, I did manage to break away and visit some of the less salubrious parts."

"And?"

"As I have found elsewhere in what was Aggeparii, the differences in the standard of living is much more pronounced than here."

"Between blacks and white, you mean?"

"Largely, yes. I had some difficulty in gaining the poor whites' trust. Then I suppose some resistance was to be expected. Nevertheless, some were forthcoming after a while. I think they were more helpful than they realised. Once they got talking to me, the truth came out. There is terrible poverty in parts of these towns. It's far worse than anything in the 'old' Thyatiran ones. One woman with a large brood of children was telling me that they have to take turns to use the bath water with their neighbours. I suppose the fact that they have a bath at all is a plus. They sleep several of them in a tiny bed. The children became involved in telling me."

"Did they?"

"Yes, they were laughing about their congested bed space and inability to turn over!"

"It seems you gained their trust."

"I hope so. I will be recommending poor relief for these areas, although I know that money is tighter than it has been in the recent past. I don't want to say too much to the senate until my fact-finding is complete. The census will help once we get the results in and I hope to give a projection for the cost of improving their lot."

"I see."

"Of course I am talking commercially as well as socially. Both will need a major overhaul to even begin to bring it into line with the rest of Thyatira. That has always been your aim, hasn't it?"

"It certainly has, although I recognise - now more than ever - that such a goal will probably take a number of years to achieve."

Emil continued, "In general, though, people there are still welcoming the change from Aggeparii to Thyatira."

"People welcoming change?" Frank responded with a smile. "Now that's something unusual!"

The senator could have said something about the citizens' relief at getting away from Despot Kagel, but passed over that. Still, the big man came across as optimistic for the future of Norland as part of their despotate.

When the meeting was over, Frank (plus shadow) sauntered back to the Castle to take lunch in the hall. He had been expecting Hannah to be there, but she was late. 'I expect she's got carried away with her garden,' he speculated. He let Tristan go and finish off a report he was writing.

Lunchtime in the hall was a lot less busy than usual and, sitting by himself, Frank's mind wandered.

'There are several despotates that I've never been to. Then if I have difficulty in visiting all the towns in Thyatira, I can hardly spend the time needed for a grand tour of the whole of Hoame. It would take all year! Of course I did visit the southernmost one of Capparathia with Alan many years ago. That was when old Schonhost was in charge. It must have been a dozen or so years ago now. I wonder how Despot Schmidt is getting on down there...'

"Hello, my darling!"

"Oh, hello Hannah. It's lamb, are you going to join me?"

She did and they found plenty to talk about over the meal.

"I was at the garden this morning when an old woman from Lowdebar visited the site. She gave me a donation of flower seeds which I thought was sweet of her. Although she couldn't name the species, she said that they were extremely colourful. I thought I'd incorporate them into the wildflower section. It was kind of her."

"Yes, it was, I..."

He broke off at the sight of a messenger coming from the main entrance. Making a beeline for the Despot, he was holding a message tube, one from another despot by the colour of it.

'Oh dear,' thought Frank, 'I wonder what the matter is.'

Taking the container, he opened it as quickly as possible. Hannah fell silent, mirroring the worried look on her husband's face.

The first thing he did was go to the bottom of the communication to see who it was from.

"Well I never! Despot Schmidt; that's a coincidence."

"Why is that? enquired Hannah, but he did not appear to hear the question.

His face lightening, he exclaimed, "Oh. That's interesting!"

"Care to share, my dear?"

"We've been invited to Capparathia."

"What's the occasion?"

"Um, I don't think it's a particular occasion as such, but he knows that I've been meaning to visit him ever since he was appointed. I've never got round to it, of course. It is a long way."

"Do you want to accept?"

"Yes. Things seem to be quite stable here. The Ladosan Civil War appears contained and Emil has a handle on the Norland acquisition. I fancy a trip down south."

"Do you want me to stay and look after things?"

"You stay? No, we'll all go. We'll take a good-sized retinue as well. I wish Alan was here. Still, I could take one of the other senators... which one would be most appropriate?"

He was talking more to himself by this stage. Meanwhile, Hannah considered the implications of them being away for a protracted visit. It was not that long ago that they were concerned about the Ladosan conflict spilling across the border. There were still Hoamen over there as trainers and advisors. Was this the most appropriate time to go off on what would be an extended holiday? It would take a good fortnight to get down to Capparathia at wagon speed.

"My dear?"

"Huh?"

"Do you think it would be a good idea for you to consult the senate first?"

"The senate?"

"It might be wise to speak to them first, get them onside."

Finally Frank focused on his wife's words and saw wisdom in them. "You're right. We've got a meeting due tomorrow anyway. I can tell them about this trip south we'll be taking. A good idea."

~ End of Chapter 11 ~

Prospects of Peace - Chapter 12

"I had to work for my privileges, but them youngsters today expect 'em by rights. I waited my turn to get my dues, but they want 'em straightaway. I were patient, knowing that I'd earn my reward. But these young folk nowadays want everything immediately. They don't know how lucky they are..."

Hulffan cropper Reuben was giving his friends the benefit of his considered opinion. The ever-faithful Amos was with him at a table in the Selerm along with brothers Tsodd and Rodd. The bar area was three-quarters full, but the noise level in there was relatively low that evening.

When there was no response to his words of wisdom on the youth of the day, Reuben decided to switch subjects. Being an expert on foreign as well as social affairs, he gave them counsel on events beyond Thyatira's northern border.

"Them Laodician bastards are a queer lot! We always thought they had funny ways with their constant squabblin'. Now they're all fighting amongst each other. Let 'em all go and kill each other, that's what I say. 'Tis better than when they come over 'ere and attack us."

"That's for certain!" exclaimed the Selerm's proprietor with feeling. With no problems that evening, he was enjoying a chat with friends.

Reuben knew that, unlike himself and Amos, Tsodd had been in the militia many years previously and was involved in a battle with the foreign invaders. He said, "Yeah, Tsodd, you encountered 'em at first 'and, didn't you?"

"That I did. We were in Bynar... or what was then part of Bynar, I'm not sure if it's part of Thyatira now. Anyway, we were making our way to the Mitas gap when we were attacked by a force of Laodicians. It was a big battle, extremely bloody. There was... I think it was Solly. Anyway, he was going crazy in the thick of it, slashing down his sword on the enemy like someone demented."

"Solly?" queried his brother, "are you sure? He's usually so mild mannered."

"Yeah, it was out of character. It was a bloody mess. Japhses was wading in too, slashing that great sword."

"A lot of good men lost their lives."

"Yeah, Gideon, and his son John. I remember Cragoop was upset about John..."

Reuben said, "An' you an' Bodd got injured as I recall."

"Yeah, I passed out. Bodd got hit on the head."

"Knocked some sense into him!" Amos joked.

Then Reuben asked Rodd, "You'd already joined the guard hadn't you? Were you in that battle with yer brothers?"

"Not that one," the current Captain of the Guard advised. "Despot Thorn sent me on to the Gap as part of an advanced party. I was involved later, of course, in the counter-invasion of Ladosa."

"That went on and on."

"We got bogged down, it's true. All the waiting around got boring, especially during the winter. Long periods of hanging about between the action."

"You preferred the battles?" Amos came back into the conversation with a twinkle in his eye.

"It was exciting, so I guess in some ways, yes, I did. That might sound crazy, I know, but living on the edge added a certain zest to life. Knowing that you were facing the prospect of dying at any moment does that to you. The war was not an exclusively bad experience as far as I was concerned. Of course I was involved in the Chogolt War since then. Life is sharper on the frontline, unlike anything else. It might have been bloody and horrible, but it helped me to see existence from a different perspective. I believed I learned from the experience."

"You're not saying you'd like to go through it all again, I 'ope," declared Reuben.

"I won't exactly invite it, but if called upon to do my duty once more, I shall not baulk."

"All I know," said Tsodd, "is something Bodd said afterwards. He says that anyone who says they weren't afraid, they're a bloody liar!"

With that, he went to pour some more practil juice from the decanter and managed to do so all over his other hand. Reuben laughed and said he should be drinking ale like the rest of them.

"I don't feel like it tonight," came the serious reply. The proprietor then left the table to get a damp cloth to wipe his hand with. By the time he returned, the conversation had moved on.

Reuben was complaining about some fresh immigrants to Vionium. "There's a family of Ma'hol moved into one o' them new houses that

232

Hanson put up. Typical of Hanson, he don't care who he sells to, as long as he gets the money."

"Have you seen 'em?" asked Amos.

"Naa, but I 'eard about 'em. They come over 'ere and take jobs from the locals. The shame of it!"

"What jobs are they doing then?"

"Who?"

"This new family."

"How the hell do I know?!" irascible Reuben replied.

Rodd said, "I had a conversation with Cragoop recently. He said that some Ma'hol were even moving into Castleton, the new, western end. He said that they asked Illianeth about schooling for their kids."

"Is she going to accept their children?" his brother asked.

"Sure, why not? As long as they speak the common tongue and can afford the fees."

At this, Reuben mumbled something incoherent and took a long gulp of his ale.

Meanwhile, at a table nearby, three other friends were having a drink and a chat. Flonass had all but given up on the idea of a fresh adventure to West Torravis. The two hundred stens would have to go begging. He had forgiven his two former crusader buddies and realised that they now had other lives to lead. This was their first get-together in a while. It was Vophsi's night off and Darda was enjoying a sudden extra day's leave. He was keen to explain why.

"The Despot has got an invitation to go down to Capparathia in the deep south. He's asked me to come along."

"Asked? Or commanded you?" Vophsi enquired.

"Um, he put it in the form of a question, but I guess it wouldn't have been the right thing to say no. Hey, I'm looking forward to it. It'll be a break in routine and it's certainly somewhere I've never been before."

"And," Vophsi came back, lowering his voice, "it'll get you away from the captain for a bit." As he said this, he indicated in a subtle way towards Rodd a few metres away.

"It wasn't him giving me a hard time, it was Stephen. He hasn't been so bad lately. I think he's getting used to me."

Flonass said, "Surely if Despot Thorn wants you to go with him that must be a good thing."

"Yeah, he's been good to me."

"I know why he wants you to go," his friend said with sudden certainty.

"Why's that?"

"In case you come across any of them lagua on the way. He knows that you're the best man to have around."

They all laughed and Darda finished his drink. He needed to leave before it got late and he made his excuses. Spending the night with his parents, he wanted to catch them before they went to bed. In the event, they had retired already, but they were up early to join him for breakfast the following morning.

"These are from the new butcher's wife," his mother told him as she placed scrambled eggs in front of him.

"What happened to his old wife?"

She looked puzzled for a moment before the understanding dawned. "It's not the wife what's new," she explained. "The butcher is a new one. He set up shop in the high street, but they own a smallholding jus' round the corner."

Darda was too busy eating to reply with words, so he nodded instead. It was at this point that his mother said what was really on her mind.

"Now you be careful going down south! It gets very hot down there."

"I'll be okay, mum, it got hot in Azekah sometimes."

"And watch out for them southerners and their funny ways."

"What funny ways?" Darda enquired before taking another mouthful.

"Oh, I don't know," Mother confessed before adding, "but you be careful anyway."

Father was on the point of telling his wife not to fuss. As it turned out, she had said her piece, so he did not have to speak. Darda himself had no real concerns. Unlike his trip around the world, this was merely to the south of his own country and he would be well-equipped and surrounded by his own men. He should be safe enough.

It was the morning of the important senate meeting when Frank would tell them his plans for his trip away. It had been put back until the afternoon to ensure the maximum number of senators could attend. He was happy, in the meantime, to stand to one side of the bailey and watch a food delivery being made. An efficient system was in operation with workers going to and fro like a column of ants.

Later, on the way across to the senate building, he bumped into Illianeth again and asked her about the Ma'hol children at her school. "How are they settling in?" he enquired.

"Surprisingly well, My Lord," she replied. "I did have my reservations, but all the other kids play with them nicely."

"I'm pleased to hear it."

"One or two funny comments from the parents at first, but the children themselves are too young to have learned prejudice."

Frank raised his eyebrows, commenting, "That doesn't say too much for adulthood does it!"

Illianeth laughed. "One mother said she'd changed her views on the Ma'hol since she had neighbours arrive from Rabeth last year. She said they are extremely polite and no bother."

"It makes you wonder what she'd been expecting."

"Wild orgies and riotous behaviour, with the occasional child sacrifice thrown, in I expect."

"You're probably right," Frank said with a smile. "We always think the worst of people we don't understand. Do you know why they moved here, the family I mean?"

"The father runs a butcher's shop in west Castleton. Following a slow start, I understand it's doing well. It's proving popular. I go there."

"I seem to remember someone telling me about a meat seller's stall they saw in Krabel-Haan which was covered in flies. I hope the one here has their hygiene to a better standard."

"It seems okay and I haven't heard of anyone going down with food poisoning."

"That's good to hear."

"And there's rumbling about a relative moving in and setting up a Ma'hol restaurant."

"I hadn't heard that."

"It would certainly give folk an alternative to their usual cuisine."

"Do you think the poor people in that part of town would be able to afford it?"

"I don't know, they'd have to pitch their prices right. I don't think anything's certain yet, My Lord. If it *does* come to town, Cragoop and I will certainly try it out. Maybe they will site it further up this end of town and it'll end up the haunt of the senatorial families."

"Stranger things have happened."

In the end, Frank dragged himself away, but it had been good to see Illianeth again and have a good conversation with her. The former unruly castle servant had come along way and was now in the upper echelons of Thyatiran society as a senator's wife. It was good to see how she was blossoming and, with her teaching job, making something good of her life.

So, following this encounter, he was in high spirits as he entered the building. He only hoped that his senators would not give him a hard time, because he did not expect them to be happy at him leaving for a protracted visit to the other end of the country. By now, the senators knew the reason for the delay in their meeting. They liked their Despot to be present and probably would not appreciate him being away, not with the neighbouring war unresolved.

In the event, Karl alone, his longest-serving black subject, questioned the timing.

"From the accounts we are receiving, My Lord, things are coming to a head across the border. Is this the wisest time for you to be going on such a long journey?"

"I appreciate your concern, Karl, but my interpretation of the intelligence we're receiving is different. I see no firm evidence that the war is about to conclude any time soon. Enter a new phase perhaps... but even if it did end, I'm not sure that my presence here would make much of a difference. The Ladosans would want to rebuild their country without foreign interference. That's the impression I'm getting from Alan."

"I hope that you are right, My Lord."

"Besides, I have confidence in you, in all of you, to manage in my absence. You've done so in the past, when I've spent time in Asattan for instance."

"Will the Despotess be staying then?"

"No, she will be coming with me, as will Joseph. He'll gain from the experience. I have been meaning to go to Capparathia for a long while now. It is high time I got on with it. Despot Schmidt needs our support. I believe that he is a good thing, and..."

"Certainly a lot better than Schonhost was!" Karl interjected.

"...and it will help his cause for us to be visible in our recognition of him. By strengthening this association, we also strengthen ourselves. Therefore I see it as an important diplomatic mission to be seen standing beside him."

After all these years as both a despot and Member of the Inner Council, Frank understood the subtleties of Hoame politics better than most. Schmidt was his protégé and, as a commoner made up to the despot class, his position was unique in recent history. Many of the other despots despised the man, but Schmidt had shown his skills in dealing with problems; his despotate's contaminated wheat crisis for instance. Frank was convinced that this man could be a valuable ally in the future. Many of the old despot houses were creaking at the seams. To court the friendship of the more dynamic ones, such as Lovonski and Schmidt, was a sensible strategy.

He continued, "You, Karl, will be in charge of defence here along with General Japhses. On the civilian front you, Otto, will be looking after things in my absence."

Frank had spent time thinking the night before making that decision. He would have chosen Emil, being the most senior senator, but he was busy sorting out the Norland assimilation. Hanz Drasnik was considered, but he was too volatile to put in charge.

"Thank you, My Lord," Otto responded before asking how long the Despot planned to be away.

"Well, it takes a couple of weeks to get there. Then we will need to stay a reasonable time to make the visit worthwhile..."

Just then a messenger entered the room. It was highly unusual for a senate meeting to be interrupted, but then he was carrying a despot's message tube.

'It must be further information from Schmidt,' Frank thought as the tube was handed to his personal assistant, Tristan, who passed it straight on.

"Wow!" went Frank in surprise as he read its contents. It was not from Despot Schmidt after all. "It's from Despot Heisler from Rilesia," he declared.

"South of Aggeparii," Freidhelm said helpfully.

"Indeed. He wants to discuss a trade agreement between us. Do we do much with them now?" Frank asked the last speaker.

"Not a great deal, no. But with the acquisition of the extra land from Aggeparii, the western border strip, we now have a common border with Rilesia."

"I see, thank you, Freidhelm."

"If I may be so bold, My Lord, you could travel down to Capparathia by way of Rilesia. You could kill two birds with one stone."

"Yes, I see it."

"If you stayed a couple of nights, it would only delay your journey by a week at most."

"An excellent idea, Freidhelm, and you're the man for the job!"

"My Lord?"

"Your portfolio is trade, is it not?"

"Yes, My Lord."

"I was thinking of taking you with me to Capparathia in any case, but it makes perfect sense if we are going to visit Rilesia on the way."

Frank gave the message back to Tristan who asked, "Shall I tell him that you're coming in person?"

"Yes, excellent. Plus another one to Schmidt accepting his invitation, but explaining that it might be several weeks yet before we arrive."

"Several weeks, My Lord?"

"I don't want to be too specific. Besides, it will take a while to get everything together."

"Yes, My Lord," replied Tristan, adding, "if we do down the western strip of Norland, we can pass directly into Rilesia. Then there's merely the Harradran despotate to traverse before we get to Capparathia."

This was excellent news for Frank and his assistant knew it. The fewer areas to go through the better, as far as Thyatira's leader was concerned.

"It's quite hilly in Rilesia, I understand," Cragoop said helpfully.

"Oh yes? And hot and sandy in Capparathia," Frank replied. "It will be a trip of contrasts."

The meeting continued for a while after that, but the one other matter of import was brought up by Karl. His voice as shrill as ever, he raised the matter of security.

"In view of last year's unfortunate incident, I must recommend most strongly that the Despot takes a sizeable escort this time."

Often in the past, Frank had scorned taking more than a minimum of soldiers with him. However, this time he had his entire family, plus several other travelling with him. Also, following the horrible kidnap ordeal, he was not going to go with a small escort again.

"You're right, Karl. Freidhelm, here, will be with me, plus Tristan and some senators' clerks. I shall ensure that I have a good sized military contingent to accompany us this time. Please rest assured of that."

The black senator relaxed visibly as he sat back in his chair. The general mood in the chamber was serious, but not too concerned.

Frank concluded the meeting, saying, "I have every confidence in you all. I'm sure you'll be able to hold things together in my absence. I shall be taking two of the superdakks with us, but the other two will remain here in the stables. On Karl or Japhses' authority, they may be used in an emergency to get messages through swiftly. That way, I shall be easily contactable when I am down south. Still, like I said, I have every confidence in you all.

"It will take a few days for us to get the personnel, wagons and equipment together before we leave. If, in the meantime, any of you need to see me, then please don't delay."

"Yes, My Lord," several voices responded.

"Good," said Frank with a smile.

Freidhelm was excited at the prospect of joining the Despot's party to Rilesia and Capparathia. He also possessed feelings of trepidation. He had taken over the trade portfolio following his predecessor's untimely death in the summer of 2618. That was almost three years ago now and Freidhelm had had a fairly smooth ride since then.

Now he was to be thrust into the forefront of negotiations regarding imports and exports with two other despotates. Thyatira currently did little trade with them, so there was certainly room for scope. He knew that Capparathia imported timber, so there was one possibility for expansion. Meanwhile, hulffan by-products were an ace card he would have to use wisely.

In the couple of days following that senate meeting, Senator Trepte was a busy man. For one thing he quizzed his colleagues as to what extra commodities their despotate should be bringing in. He ended up with a list which he hoped would be useful.

Funnily enough, his Despot's party would be travelling through the despotate of Harradran, between Rilesia and Capparathia. For Harradran was where he was born and spent most of his life. He had been a junior advisor to Despot Sandhausen when, in 2609, at the age of thirty-two, he made the big decision to emigrate to Thyatira with his family. It was during the time when many people from all over the country were migrating to the recently expanded northern territory. It had been a huge risk, but one which paid off handsomely. He now owned a large house in the exclusive eastern part of Castleton and a prestigious job. Nevertheless, the next few weeks would test his worth and he knew it. It would also be the longest period of time that he had ever spent away from his wife and children.

One of his fellow senators mentioned that it might be a good idea for him to get the financier Deejan Charvo to join the delegation. After all, the man's financial backing was helping many businesses start up and flourish in Thyatira.

He arranged for a private meeting with the merchant in the latter's impressive house from which he conducted his business. In the event, the meeting did not go according to plan. The reason for this was that Freidhelm did not actually have a plan. All he possessed was a vague notion that Charvo greased the wheels of industry with loans from his vast wealth.

"I'm sorry, Freidhelm, but I am a little uncertain as to why I am being asked to join you."

"Er...um..." the senator began. He was learning a valuable lesson, namely to come better prepared to a meeting. The embarrassed man managed to waffle something about money being needed to lubricate the wheels of trade, but it was a poor performance. He sounded like a twentieth century management consultant short on ideas.

Deejan did not want to give the fellow a hard time. He was in a good mood and did not have a busy schedule that day. Therefore he replied, "I am still uncertain as to what role you see me in. If it is to finance businesses from other despotates, then I'm afraid I must decline. It is simply not practicable. On the other hand, if your negotiations present a need to expand certain industries here, in the light of what is agreed, then that is something I would be happy to look at."

"Yes, that would be a good idea!" the senator gabbled with relief.

"Yet I don't quite see the need for me to actually be present in those places."

More "Er...ums..." followed before Deejan put him out of his misery.

"I tell you what; I will have a think about it, if that is okay."

"Oh yes, I..."

"I will let you know tomorrow."

A servant showed the senator out and Deejan sat at his desk considering the matter. While he did not see much mileage in his presence in the Despot's party from a business point-of-view, there might be another reason to go. That evening, he went to the Castle hall around dinnertime.

"My Lord, I wonder if I may have a word?"

"Ah, Deejan! By all means. Pull up a chair."

The Thorns were sitting together at their normal places at the end of one of the long tables. Retired steward, Natias, and his wife, Eko, had joined them for the meal.

"Thank you, My Lord. It's about your trip to Capparathia."

"Oh yes?"

"I believe you'll be leaving in a couple of days time."

"Something like that. We're heading to Rilesia first."

"Ah," the merchant looked crestfallen, "does that mean you will be going through Aggeparii?"

"What's left of it," Frank said with a cheeky smile. "No, we'll be heading down that westward strip of land near the border, part of the Norland deal. Why, did you want to come along?"

For Frank could understand that Deejan would not want to set foot in his old homeland of Aggeparii again. He had narrowly escaped the clutches of Despot Kagel and, although he felt safe under Frank's patronage, he wanted nothing to do with his former leader.

"Yes," the merchant answered, "I have been considering it."

"Good."

"Although I feel that my worth would be limited. I wondered if I could come along merely for the experience."

"Like a vacation?"

"To have a break. I've never done anything quite like it before."

241

Then Frank had a bright idea. "What about bringing the children?"

"Do you think that would be appropriate, My Lord?"

"Sure, we're all going," Frank replied, indicating to his family.

"I would want to bring some servants."

"Naturally, bring as many as you want. It's going to be quite a large convoy by the time we've finished. We need ten wagons simply for my wife's wardrobe!"

Hannah had been listening quietly, suddenly gave her husband a playful poke in the side.

He continued, "Seriously, I don't mind if we take a large contingent on this occasion. In fact, the more the merrier."

"Thank you, My Lord! I shall have a word with Sebastian and Keturah."

Back home, his two adoptive, white children listened in silence as Deejan explained everything to them.

"We will be travelling as part of a large, escorted convoy all the way to the deep south of Hoame. I have never been there myself before, but I understand that they have a different climate and different ways from us. Capparathia's southern border is the Great Desert itself which no one has ever been able to cross. As far as we know it goes on for ever. They say that you can see nothing but sand as far as the eye can see."

"How long will it take to get there?" Keturah asked, her face aglow with excitement.

"The journey usually takes two weeks, I am told. That is the most direct route. But we'll be going to Rilesia first. They are different again, lots of mountains."

"Have you been there before?"

"No, Keturah, I haven't."

"Oh."

Then Deejan addressed Sebastian with a question. Sebastian who did not look half as thrilled at the prospect of going as his sister. A crusade was one thing, but a sight-seeing tour?

"Do you have any questions?"

"Why?"

"Why what?"

"Why are we going?"

"Its a holiday for us. The Despot and senators who are going with us have business to attend, but we are simply going for the experience."

"So it's not for business then?" queried the young man, his expression extremely serious.

"No, it is purely for the pleasure," his father patiently explained.

"How will the business run in our absence?"

"I don't want you to concern yourself with that, Sebastian. I've spoken to Walter and he is happy to maintain a limited service here for the duration of our vacation."

"Oh, I see," Sebastian replied, slowly coming round to the idea.

His father was beginning to wonder if he had done too good a job in turning the former waif into a financial expert. It was with some relief that he saw the young man thaw out under the influence of his sister who possessed no such concerns.

"It's going to be great!" she declared. "Mountains and deserts, lots of adventures. I'm looking forward to it. When do we go?"

The south-eastern Buffs had been defeated. The army that was once the most powerful in the region was a spent force. It was true that mopping up operations were still taking place against pockets of resistance, but these were coming to a conclusion. Even the most fanatical Buffs would soon be either dead, or prisoners.

They were victims of their own hubris. At the commencement of hostilities, the Buffs had possessed a higher proportion of regular army soldiers than any other group. Yet even they suffered from an equipment shortage which was never fully resolved. They had taken on all-comers: Rose, Yellows, the Pink army as well as the Neo-Purples. Taken them on and been ground down as a result.

There were many factors involved in their defeat. For one thing, their cause failed to catch the imagination of fresh young men and women eager to find a cause to fight for. These flocked to the Neo-Purples in droves, but few to the Buffs. The latter were seen first and foremost as the old government who got the country into this crisis in the first place. Heavy casualties on the front line could not be plugged by fresh recruits.

Another hindrance was poor leadership. Disastrous frontal attacks and wasteful street fighting degraded them as a fighting force. They thought that they could take on every other faction at once, but the effort bled them white.

Perhaps the greatest factor had been the inability to break through to the central area of Ladosa, still owned by their fellow Buffs. In order to do this, they needed to seize the town of Wesold and its surrounding area. The tenacious Yellows died hard, fighting for every street and house. Their action allowed the Neo-Purples to build themselves up from an army so small it was held in contempt, into a major player. Meanwhile, the Roses had ensured a war of attrition that meant Buff reserves being thrown into gaps in their line and expended in never-ending fighting.

The Neo-Purples had, unconventionally, kept the pressure up even during winter. The Buffs, already plagued by disease and lack of food, were not given the opportunity to rest and regroup for the spring. Their fate was sealed with the fall of the strategic towns of Wesold and Fanallon. Now it was all over in this region bar the shouting.

Where did this leave the other players in this part of Ladosa? As so often in war, the situation was often confusing. Yet, as major hostilities paused for a moment, the fog cleared somewhat. The Yellows had been annihilated, the southern Pinks seemed to have melted away. That left the Rose army in charge of northwest and Neo-Purples southwest Ladosa. The two armies now comprised of battle-hardened veterans. They faced each other over a one hundred and twenty kilometre-long front. Much of this was taken up by the River Yar. At around two hundred metres wide for much of its length, it was a natural, if not insurmountable barrier.

Rose and Neo-Purples were anything but natural bedfellows. Yet even without a formal alliance they had worked together to defeat a common enemy.

The southern commander, Marshal Nazaz, spelt it out to her senior officers.

"We have grown greatly in strength since the outbreak of hostilities. Our army is far bigger for one thing. We are also well trained and equipped thanks to the assistance we have received." Although she had not mentioned them, those in the know got her reference to Hoame. She was keen to give them credit to those she could. After all, her lover was a Hoaman. The marshal continued,

"Plus, of course, large parts of our army are now seasoned troops and a match to the best soldiers anywhere in the world."

"Should we not try to find an accommodation with the Rose?" asked one of the majors present. "Much as I despise them."

Charlotta replied, "My thoughts exactly. I would ally us with the Ma'hol if I thought it would mean a defeat of the central Buffs. There will be no end to this conflict while they are still standing. The truth is we are not strong enough to do it on our own. We need help from the Rose if we are going to invade the centre. With that in mind, I am sending emissaries to the Rose to see if some kind of agreement with them can be reached."

Another officer asked for the latest news of the notorious Buff General Vap, now a fugitive somewhere in the southwest.

"No sign of him yet. I am writing a decree doubling the price on his head if captured alive. I want him brought before me to face public justice for his war crimes."

"Wasn't he dismissed as commander of the Wesold garrison?"

"Last year, yes. The latest we heard was that he was still commanding troops somewhere south of Fanallon."

Over the following week and a half, couriers were kept busy between the Rose and Neo-Purple camps. It bore fruit insofar as a six week non-aggression agreement was signed between them. The Rose hierarchy appeared a lot less taken with the idea of invading the central area though. The future of the war remained unclear. At least the Neo-Purples could pause for breath. During the lull they would rest, regroup, re-stock, recruit and train new volunteers.

Relegated to the rear, Alan kept himself busy helping out at a training camp east of Wesold. There were several black Hoamen there still and a steady trickle of new recruits to knock into shape.

Civilians still stayed away from the region and Wesold itself was something of a ghost town. In fact, considering the number of men and women who died fighting there, it was probably swarming with spirits bound to the physical plane.

That was of no concern to Alan as, one evening, he made his way back to his digs. His little cottage was no more than a kilometre from the camp, so extremely convenient. Charlotta had arranged a male servant to prepare his meals for him which made life that much easier. The servant stayed in an adjoining dwelling, so the Hoaman enjoyed the privacy he desired.

245

His role as military advisor had somewhat faded away. His lover insisted on him being nowhere near the fighting following his lucky escape. He did not argue, but threw his energies into the training programme which everyone agreed was producing first class recruits.

Why did he stay and not go home to Thyatira? He asked himself the question several times. It was the relationship with Charlotta that held him there. Not that he was sure in his mind what that relationship was exactly. He was new to this sort of thing. Endlessly he asked himself if this was really love. She would come and see him soon, but it was frustrating in the meantime. Was that love? The physical relationship they enjoyed was amazing and the pleasure unlike any other, but was that love? He could not be certain.

The days were longer now and it was still light when, that evening, she paid him a visit.

"I can only stay until the morning," she warned, but at least she had put herself out to come and see him. He could be confident of a night of hot lust, but first she had some news to impart. It was news designed to put a dampener on any sexual fervour for the moment.

"They've finally found that monster, Vap!"

"Oh, good."

"But it's not."

"Huh?"

"He was already dead. There were several Buffs at that place who caught a fever and died of it. It was in an enclave near the Rabeth-Mephar border. In their emaciated state they could not stand up to it. I hope he suffered."

"My friend would tell you that Vap is suffering now in the spirit world."

"I hope your friend is right. If there's no justice in this world, I'd like to believe there was a future one to redress the balance. I suspect it's wishful thinking, though, for this universe is short on justice."

"You're in philosophical mood tonight."

"My arse! I'd have liked to have watched him suffer for what he did to the marshal... and to you."

Alan shrugged his shoulders.

"I hope you don't forgive him!" she declared vehemently.

"I simply don't think about the man. That's the best response, surely."

"Maybe you're right. I'd like to know what those Rose vermin are thinking. They'd better not be contemplating a pre-emptive strike against us. Our front line is being kept on full alert for just such an eventuality. I don't think they will, but they are dragging their heels all of a sudden."

"They will have suffered substantial casualties too. It's natural for them to want to reassess the situation."

"I told them that the single way to end this war is to knock out the remaining Buffs. We can have another election then and all respect the will of the people. It's the only way."

"I know the future's unclear," he replied. It sounded like a pathetic response even to his own ears, but the last thing he needed was fresh election talk.

They fell silent for a while, sitting at opposite ends of the same sofa, but a thousand kilometres apart. The woman was lost in her thoughts for a good while, peering into empty space. It was as if her mind was processing data like a computer. Then she seemed to collect herself and come back to the present. With a sudden smile she edged towards him. It was a different Charlotta.

"All the more reason to make the most of the present moment," she said and put her arms around him.

Their lips met and the kissing began. It felt good... until there was a knock on the door. A courier had brought an urgent dispatch and she had to read it there and then.

"The village of Hemily has fallen. It was the last known pocket of Buff resistance in the southwest." Fully taken up with the news, she continued out loud, more to herself than Alan. "This marks the end of this phase of the war. I must convene a meeting tomorrow with the senior officers and iron out our next move. I'm increasingly ignoring the Committee, they're not where the action is. We must decide on our strategy for the next phase of the conflict."

Alan sat back, trying not to show his annoyance. His passion was dissipating by the second, to be replaced by frustration. Was this how his future with this woman would be? Even if the war ended tomorrow she would busy herself in an election. He suddenly was not at all sure that his future lay here.

A hundred or so kilometres to the east, the barricades were still up on the approach to Isson. These were to keep out the so-called plunderers from Braskaton. No effective reconstruction work had begun on the nearby Ladosan capital and some residents, desperate in their plight, came to the town seeking charity. That was the last thing most hill folk wanted to give. As a result, there was little debate and turning away all-comers was their firm policy.

A few people blamed Eleazar for having gone down to the city on a mercy mission. They said it encouraged the lowlanders to try their luck in Isson, but this was hardly fair. Most former city dwellers knew nothing of the priest's doings.

"Don't be soft in the head!" a local committee member told them when they complained. "Whether Eleazar travelled down there or not, these scavengers would have made the journey here. Stick to the barricades and don't allow such silly notions to enter your heads."

The man himself was unhappy with the barricades still being used. Auraura and Zebulon between them had persuaded him not to make an issue of it though.

"No point in making yourself a martyr over this," the elderly church leader had advised. "Best to choose your battles wisely."

The extraterrestrial cataclysm had effectively blown the flames of war out in this region. Life for the survivors was tough. Many of the capital's residents perished during the winter, even if it had been milder than usual. Those with relatives further west, within Buff-held territory, went there. Most did not have that luxury. Once the snows cleared from Braskaton's shattered buildings, many dead bodies were found.

Many Buff officials were wiped out in the initial blast and local government was a major casualty as a result. An interim parliament was set up in a village west of the city. It was clearly a temporary measure and designed to be seen as such. Little of any import seemed to go on there in any case. Trying to relieve their citizens' suffering was a full-time occupation. A few talked about pursuing the war, but it was all talk and no action.

The Pinks in the extreme north of Ladosa had been hit too. So badly affected were they, in fact, that their parliament decided to wait it out and not actively pursue hostilities.

Little of this was clear to the citizens of Isson. Communication with much of the country was non-existent, and besides, they were in a state of self-imposed siege in any case.

Eleazar went through to their children's bedroom to read a story following one particularly busy day. While Auraura ironed clothes in their living room, she could hear her husband's gentle voice talk of fairies and other mythical creatures.

He had been out from dawn to dusk. There was much to keep him busy: a funeral to preside over, sick to visit and Quinty's house to help with.

The late church benefactress' former home had twenty-five people working to restore and add to the structure. The work was coming on well. Eleazar was not a craftsman, but lent his hand with other volunteers helping out on the project.

The reconstructed building would be a great asset to the Church. A conference centre, an administrative hub, a base for training, its uses would be many-fold.

Auraura, meanwhile, had plenty on her plate. As well as running the household, she helped with poor relief and various fundraising enterprises. Isson was trying to keep a sense of normality going, even artificially.

She experienced one particularly interesting encounter that morning. A traveller arrived from the extreme east, across the mountains. The pass was open for the first time that spring. This individual told of terrible damage to their vines from the fireball in the sky. A whole industry was wrecked at a stroke. Auraura told him that she hoped they would able to rebuild. The man was not at all sure it could be and was seeking out a distant relative for help.

"Darling, are you there?" she called out, for the storytelling had fallen silent.

Putting down a shirt, she tiptoed to the children's bedroom and cautiously opened the door. There was her husband with the book open on his lap. The children were fast asleep... and so was Eleazar. She smiled and left them alone. He would wake up in due course and come out in his own time. Right now he needed the rest.

~ End of Chapter 12 ~

Prospects of Peace - Chapter 13

The morning came for Despot Thorn to leave for Rilesia. Sitting in his wagon with his family, he was quite pleased that they were getting underway so soon after breakfast. The previous few days saw a scurry of activity as Castle staff and others scrambled to get everything together for the journey. Frank insisted on all the wagons being in situ the night before.

The back of the column was within the Castle bailey, the vanguard some hundreds of metres down the road. Now everything was in place for them to commence the journey.

In spite of the cool, late spring morning, Frank insisted on his wagon being open, at least for the start of the journey, so that he could see what was going on. They could always raise the canvas later if desired.

Nestled into his seat with a faithful old toy and a book, Joseph observed the hurried comings and goings around him. Next to him sat his mother's new handmaiden, Sharin, about to travel out of her home despotate for the first time in her life.

A couple of soldiers ran past the leading wagon. One of the drivers was shouting at his dakks as he struggled to control them. Most of the beasts were standing patiently for the order to move out.

"Got everything?" Frank asked Hannah.

"Yes, I think so... um, Sharin, did you bring down that hat box I told you to?"

The young, white girl's eyes bulged as she realised it was still sitting up on the third floor of the Castle. She apologised profusely and was released to run and get it. Frank told himself to be patient, although he was eager to get going.

Eventually the servant reappeared with the large, but light box and gave it to a male servant to stow away in the relevant wagon. She fairly jumped back into the Thorns' vehicle and Frank indicated to a waiting guardsman to give the order to move out.

There were shouts from various people and some Castle staff and close relations lined the road to waive the convoy off. With a creak and a clatter, the Despot's conveyance began to move. It was quite a jolt, in fact, but they soon got used to the movement.

What a sight it was, over twenty wagons stretched out along the road. The leading one had been going a little while before the final vehicle began to move.

Squad Leader Darda and some of his soldiers led the way. The Despot and his family were second, followed by a wagon containing Senator Trepte, Despot's Secretary Tristan and some clerks. Next up were two superior conveyances carrying Deejan Charvo, his family and certain essential luxuries. Further wagons were carrying assorted servants, baggage, camping equipment, catering / food supplies and more soldiers. There were a couple of completely spare vehicles and one full of spare axles, other parts and tools to cater for any conceivable breakdown on the way. All the transports had been serviced over the previous days, but, following the kidnapping, Frank was leaving nothing to chance. It was, after all, a breakdown that started that terrible sequence of events and that was not going to be repeated.

For the same reason, he got Bishop Gunter to bless the convoy the night before. His request was for it to be done then, so as not to delay the start on this, the morning of their departure. Frank liked to think that he was covering every eventuality, but knew that fate could still surprise them.

"Comfy?" he asked Joseph who was high enough up to observe that was going on outside.

"Yes, thank you, Father."

Two enlarged squads of hand-picked soldiers were acting as escort. Squad Leader Paul, more experienced than his counterpart at the front, took up the rear. The final two wagons both contained soldiers and their equipment. A supply of spare dakks, plus a pair of precious superdakks accompanied them.

So they were underway. Frank wanted to make good progress that first morning. At the slow pace that the wagons moved, it would take a whole day merely to get to the pre-2620 border with Aggeparii. The road network throughout Thyatira was good by Hoame standards, with all the main routes mettled with hulffan tar. This particular highway led to Aggeparii City, so they would have to divert from it after they passed the old border. The convoy would travel down the recently purchased narrow strip of land bordering

251

the Rabeth-Mephar border, all the way down to the Rilesia despotate. Few of the travellers had ever been there before.

Hannah enquired of her husband, "How many times have you met Despot Heisler?"

"A few times. He reminds me of old Despot Hista of Bynar a bit."

"Oh?"

"Worries a lot."

"Why is that?"

Frank shrugged his shoulders in response before saying, "I've brought along some maps courtesy of those cartographer fellows. Rilesia looks like it's the smallest of the despotates."

"Aggeparii will be taking on that accolade soon, at the rate Kagel keeps selling bits off."

"You could be right," he replied with a smile.

"Can you see the day when there are fewer despotates?"

"Possibly, Thyatira is currently the exception in purchasing chunks of land from its neighbours. It's a conservative country, they don't like change. That's why we're having to be careful how we manage the Norland acquisition. Still, from what Lovonski tell me, most despots are more concerned with self-indulgence than anything else."

"What do you think?"

"It's hard to say. Most have appeared pleasant enough when I've met them. Well... if not pleasant, compliant. Who knows what goes on behind closed doors?"

They stopped for lunch outside Lowdebar, then got back underway fairly promptly. The dakks would not tire out at a steady, slow pace. Nearly every wagon possessed a team of either four or six pulling them. Whilst some emergency fodder was being carried, they would get most of their nourishment from grass along the way.

Back on the road, a number of soldiers were usually seen walking alongside the vehicles. It was not unusual for the passengers to jump down and exercise their legs for a while before climbing back up again. On one of his own perambulations, Frank found Deejan walking faster to catch up with him.

"Fine weather, My Lord."

"After a chilly start, yes."

The countryside looked fresh, with a thousand different shades of green. In typical northern Hoame manner, the land undulated gently.

Either side of the road was a drainage ditch followed by a wide green grass verge before the trees began. Lowdebar was no longer in sight.

"I had not imagined our delegation to be so large, My Lord. It stretches back as far as the eye can see."

"It's not so much our delegation as all these escort and support vehicles we need. You're right, though, it is certainly the biggest one I've ever been involved in. I did hint to both despots Heisler and Schmidt to expect a large contingent."

"I've met Despot Heisler."

"Oh, yes?"

"When I was with Despot Kagel."

"How did he strike you?"

Deejan hesitated, but he knew that he could talk candidly to Frank. So in the end he replied, "Businesslike, with an attention to detail. Not unpleasant."

"I see. I know Despot Schmidt better. The first time I met him, he gave me a present."

"Oh?"

"His predecessor's severed head!"

"My goodness!"

"I suppose it was a dramatic gesture, but at the time it seemed merely practical. It proved that he had dealt with Schonhost's rebellion. It saved a lot of bloodshed in fact. We simply have to look over our northern border to see what the effects of a civil war are."

Deejan nodded his head in agreement, but had nothing further to say on the subject.

The weather stayed fine that day, but the light was beginning to fail as they passed through a gap in the dyke which marked the old border with Aggeparii. Once the entire party were passed into Norland, they encamped for the night.

"Quickly! Come on men, put those tents over there. Bring the poles. Where's David gone? Fetch him now..."

Darda, with a burst of energy, seemed to be everywhere as he organised the camp for the night. Only the VIPs would be sleeping in the tents and he wanted to make sure that everything was just right for them.

Impressed by what he saw, Frank made a mental note to tell Captain Jonathan when he eventually returned. Back at the Castle, he got the impression that the captain saw young Darda as something of an imposition. Entering the guard straight as a squad leader was unprecedented and Frank had agreed it on the basis of the former crusader's testimony. But there was something about the young man that the Despot liked and it pleased him now to see such efficiency being shown.

"All is set for the camp, My Lord."

"Excellent, well done, Darda."

"I have organised sentries to patrol throughout the night, although I am not anticipating any trouble."

"Thank you."

The squad leader certainly knew how to hit the right note. His opposite number, Paul, was normally in the border guard under captain Rodd. He did not know Darda at all well and let him get on with seeing to the important passengers. There were plenty of other duties for him to organise and his men were kept busy.

"It's been fun today," were Joseph's last words before he fell asleep.

Hannah turned to Frank and said softly, "I don't know why I'm so tired tonight."

"Maybe it's all this fresh air. Or it could be the mental energy of getting everything ready." Then he began yawning himself and they both agreed it was time to settle down for the night.

Flonass was at work extra early and ran up the stairs to the first floor cabin where the mill office stood. He unlocked the door and went in. Picking another key, he opened the safe to check the petty cash. All was in order. It felt good being trusted by his employer. In return, the white was becoming fiercely loyal to Mr Onstein and would not have a word said against him behind his back.

Yet his dreams of fresh adventures to West Torravis were fading away. He simply could not find anyone suitable to accompany him. Mr O was insistent that he should not go without another, experienced traveller. The nephew would be left in peace to get on with the fresh life abroad he had chosen. Maybe that was for the best. That angle did occur to Flonass before, all he had thought about was fresh adventure and two hundred stens. He would simply have to put the notion behind him and get on with his routine. A steady job and an employer he was devoted to, it could have been a great deal worse.

"Ah, my boy! How are we this morning?"

"Very well, thank you, Mr O," Flonass replied, sounding up-beat.

"I saw the convoy leave a short while ago."

"Despot Thorn?"

"That's right... and quite an entourage they had too. I was told they're off to my old stomping ground of Rilesia."

"You could have joined them," Flonass suggested cheekily.

"I don't think so," Mr O replied in good humour. "No, I've been back but once since I left ten years ago. I have no plans to return again, not since my sister moved here to Thyatira. People say it's beautiful with all its mountain scenery, but it's often wet and miserable. I prefer the climate here."

"Let's hope it's not too wet for Despot Thorn," the assistant replied, thinking, 'That Tristan is on that convoy, the last possible person to go on an adventure with me. He didn't want to though...'

Later that morning, during a lull between visitors to the office, Mr O struck up a fresh conversation.

"I see they're digging a huge new pit west of the town."

"Vionium? Yeah, I've only seen it from a distance. I don't know what it's for."

"A rubbish tip, apparently. The old one is full, so they're covering it over apparently and are starting again. This one's going to be on a much bigger scale, I heard."

"S'pose it's better than it being dumped all over the place. That having been said, people are pretty good about that sort of thing."

"So they should be! There's no excuse."

While he was still speaking, a worker came in and handed the owner a letter which he read in silence. However, it was not long before he was divulging its contents to Flonass.

"This is a follow-up to a tentative enquiry we received. A drone from Ephamon contacted me regarding a potential order. It's quite substantial in size. If it comes about we will have to get them working overtime to fulfil it."

"Will that be a problem?"

"Not at all! It's good news, my boy, good news."

Flonass beamed in response. He might not be going on a further adventure, but life was pretty good nevertheless.

"Sit down, Darda, and have something to eat. You're giving me indigestion!"

The Despot's reprove was good-natured and Darda did as he was told. In his efforts to be efficient over breakfast he was overdoing it a bit. He sat with his bowl of porridge next to the Thorns as indicated. Frank engaged him in conversation.

"I understand it's quite hilly where we're going."

"Yes, My Lord."

"What was it like at Azekah?"

"Azekah City is built on a plain. Behind it is pretty flat too. There it is criss-crossed with waterways. Some are natural, but they've dug canals to join them up. It's a bit of a maze. In between are the fields where they grow their crops."

Frank was pleased that the young white was not too intimidated to chat with him. He asked if he had experienced a winter over there, on the other side of the world.

"Yes, My Lord. There was plenty of snow there too and the canals used to freeze over, especially the narrow ones. One was on the front line and we kept on having to smash the ice each day so that the enemy couldn't charge across it."

"I see. So it was a far more effective barrier when it was water."

"Yes, My Lord."

"Well, let's hope for an enemy-free journey on this occasion."

Soon they were back on the road again and working their way down the border strip between Rabeth-Mephar on their right and Aggeparii on their left. The standard of the road here was poor and several soldiers were employed in guiding the wagons round the largest potholes. They made a good job of it, but were relieved when the quality of the road improved somewhat further along.

The forest to the right accompanied them the entire way without a break. The closely-packed trees and undergrowth meant it was black and not a little foreboding. In any case, there were more pleasant sights to concentrate on. A sparsely-populated area, a lot of it was taken over for sheep grazing.

"Look!" cried Hannah at the sight of a shepherd boy following a small flock. "It looks like a scene out of the Bible."

A bit further on they passed through a seemingly unescorted flock of sheep on either side of the road. The sun was up by now and it was getting warm. Darda was walking alongside the Thorns' wagon at the time. Like the rest of the soldiers, he was in semi-armour. The sheep had red dye on them for identification purposes. The squad leader began laughing at one specimen. Its owners had got carried away with the dye and plastered it almost from head to tail. "It's got sunburn!" he declared and his audience laughed.

"Is there much further to go?" Joseph posed the classic question of children on a long journey.

Hannah looked to her husband to answer. He said, "We should enter Rilesia tomorrow morning, so I suppose we're almost half way there."

A scout was sent ahead on one of the superdakks. Late afternoon he returned and reported to the Despot that the border was a couple of kilometres away.

"All right, thank you. Darda, is it okay if we encamp here for the night?"

It may have been formed as a question, but it was taken as a command. The convoy halted and soldiers and servants began buying themselves. One wagon had, in fact, fallen behind. One of its four dakks was lame and was being exchanged for another one. They would catch up with the rest before night fell.

Purely by chance they had stopped next to a stream. They found its water unseasonably chilly, but it was still a useful resource.

The Thorns tucked into their beans and mascas supper with relish. They were in a larger group that evening which included Senator Trepte, Deejan Chavo and his children. As the sun was setting, they sat round a camp and, with the conversation light, it was a pleasant atmosphere.

"Did you see those hills up ahead?" Hannah asked Freidhelm.

"Yes, My Lady. It looks like we'll soon start ascending once we cross the border."

Frank joined in, saying, "I've been told to expect an escort awaiting us once we leave the current region. I'll send the scout along first thing to tell them to expect us." Then he betrayed what was on his mind by saying to Hannah, "I don't suppose they'll be quite so interested in Ladosan goings on either here or when we get to Capparathia."

"No," his wife concurred, "I expect it will seem somewhat distant to them."

257

Joseph, meanwhile, was keeping extremely quiet. Watching the fire and feeling its warmth, he was enjoying staying up late and hoped he would not be noticed. His parents, of course, knew the score, but saw no harm in it.

For a long time no one said anything, then Frank broke the spell.

"Well, it'll be an important day tomorrow, best we all try to get some sleep." With that, he led by example and made for his tent.

Washing in the stream the following morning, the water coming down from the mountains certainly did seem icy cold.

Still, they were soon underway and the scout returned to confirm that a Rilesian military detachment was, as arranged, a short distance up the road. Shortly before reaching the border they passed a large, derelict building whose original purpose was anyone's guess. With its roof caved in and trees growing up inside, it was long abandoned.

"Welcome to Rilesia," read a big, wooden sign at the border. It was pristine in appearance and Frank wondered if it had been erected in his honour. Either way, a local military escort on dakks was there to greet them.

"I am Colonel Kesselring," commander introduced himself. "We are to lead you to Despot Heisler's castle."

The visiting dignitary thanked him and enquired as to when they should expect to reach their destination. He was surprised when he received the answer, "By nightfall;" he had assumed it would be earlier. The colonel explained.

"We will be ascending through two-and-a-half thousand metres and progress will be slow with your wagons. I see you have brought extra dakks, good. I recommend you harness them up for added pulling power during the ascent."

"Oh, I see. Very well" replied Frank and the order was given before they pulled away once more.

Soon the ground was rising and the landscape changing. The road became narrower and began zigzagging up a mountain side. Small, shallow streams were observed flowing swiftly beside the way. There were many tall, evergreen trees on the hillside and the view became limited.

The local escort kept themselves to themselves and the level of talking dropped as the travellers took in the unfamiliar landscape.

Low, dry stone walls lined the verge before a drop into the valley. The occasional lone sheep was seen on the steep sides.

Onwards and upwards they went, the colonel certainly had known what he was saying regarding the wagons making slow progress. 'A snail could go faster than this,' thought Frank and hoped they would make it. Indeed, along one particularly steep section, the soldiers were all helping push the conveyances along. The gradient eased off after a while, much to everyone's relief.

They were progressing now with the mountain to their left and the valley to their right. When there was a break in the trees they noticed that the other mountains in the distance were becoming obscured by mist.

Eventually the road levelled out completely and they found themselves on a plateau. The area was a network of small fields demarked by stone walls. Many of these had either sheep or cattle in them, occasionally both.

Once the rear of the convoy had made it to the level ground, they stopped for a break. It meant a much-needed rest for the dakks.

"Is everything well, My Lord?" the colonel enquired as he rode up to the wagon.

"Quite well, thank you."

"If we take a breather now, that will be best."

"Of course," replied Frank. His view up ahead was becoming obscured by the low clouds setting in, so he asked, "Have we much further to climb?"

"No, My Lord. There is a bridge between the next two hills, so there won't be too much up and down to go."

It was cooler at this altitude, but the mist had a lot to do with that. Frank observed some agricultural workers with a wagon up ahead on a track at right angles to the road the convoy was on. The track possessed special passing places where the walls bent into the fields, so that two vehicles could get past each other.

Underway once more, after a while Hannah remarked, "Is it me, or is the mist starting to clear?"

She was right and, when they stopped midday for lunch, the sun could be seen struggling to get through the blanket of cloud.

No one wanted to dally and they soon got going again. They passed the entrance to what looked like someone's country estate. Two pillars marked the beginning of a long drive up to a house in the distance. One of the pillars was at an angle due to the ground having shifted a while ago.

The bridge they were to negotiate, that the colonel had mentioned, was something of an engineering feat. It spanned the valley at quite a height with a network of supporting wooden beams at different angles. Three hundred metres long, it was not easy to see the far end, for the mist still hung here.

Wide enough for two wagons to pass, the Rilesians said that no more than two of their heavily-laden vehicles should be on it at any one time. The Thyatirans were careful to obey this injunction and it took a long time before the entire convoy got across and lined up on the other side.

"Don't look down!" Hannah warned as their son peered over the side.

"How far down is it?" the boy asked, but no one offered an answer. The bottom was obscured anyway; many people felt that was a good thing.

Frank began contemplating the journey on from Heisler's castle. He did not fancy negotiating those steep roads on the way down. Going up was bad enough, but the wagons' brakes would be tested to the limit on the way down. If one was to fail... he shuddered at the thought. 'I wonder how the locals manage,' he pondered.

"Look, Father!"

His eyes followed to where Joseph was pointing. They had rounded a corner and there, a mere kilometre away, was Despot Heisler's castle. Stuck on a peak a couple of hundred metres up from the road they were on, its round towers with conical tops reached into the heavens.

'It looks impregnable,' thought Frank.

"It looks beautiful," said Hannah.

They carried on a short distance until they came to a massive, oval area covered in crushed, white stones. Several local vehicles were already parked there and the colonel explained.

"If you would be so kind as to park your vehicles here, My Lord, the guest house will accommodate most of your personnel. As I trust it was explained to you, we have room for twelve places available within the castle itself."

Frank was not sure that had been explained before. He quickly worked out that a dozen places would be sufficient for his VIPs, plus essential servants. He looked across and observed the building described as the guest house. It was a mini-fort in its own right by the looks of things, guarding the entrance to the walkway up to the castle itself.

Calling his squad leaders to himself, Frank gave them instructions to look after everything for the duration of their stay. With eighty or so personnel to care for, it was no mean responsibility. As Thyatiran ambassadors, he told them, their exemplary behaviour was essential.

Leaving them organising the parking of the wagons, Frank strode over to the party waiting to ascend further. Hannah, Joseph, Sharin, Tristan, Senator Trepte, Deejan Charvo and family plus a couple of essential servants; all the essential personnel could be accommodated. A posse of attendants from the castle suddenly appeared and began taking the guests' luggage. They each wore a smart uniform which included a plumb coloured cap which appeared curious in the eyes of the visitors.

The colonel led them up the walkway to the castle. It held a uniform width of some five metres, but it was not straight. Instead it curved first one way and then the other like a giant snake. Built on the top of a ridge with a sheer drop either side, it ascended at a constant, mild gradient to Despot Heisler's residence.

"Well," said Frank to his wife as they neared the castle's entrance, "we've made it."

"Yes," she replied, "we've arrived."

Hannah lay awake in bed the morning after their arrival at Despot Heisler's castle. Her night's rest had ended with a particularly active dream. She smiled at the thought that, following it, she woke up more exhausted than when she had gone to bed.

Maybe it was simply that her mind contained a lot to process after the night before. There had been a lot of introductions to new people, the great and good of Rilesia. She could not remember half the names now. They certainly seemed eager to meet their distinguished guests from Thyatira. Then her husband was something of a legend in these parts: the foreign prince who was now not merely a despot, but a Keeper as well. The hosts were as welcoming as they could, the visitors being treated like royalty.

Despot Lothar Heisler was in his early fifties. He had been in the role half his life since the death of his father. Hannah found his reputation for being fussy to be well founded. Smartly attired, he was somewhat on the small side and dwarfed by his large wife. Despotess Magda Heisler had formerly married Lothar in childhood, but did not go to live with him until her mid-teens. Nowadays, she was extremely overweight with thick legs that seemed to overflow her dainty shoes. Hannah considered that her counterpart wore far too much mascara and would look a lot better if less heavily made up. She also seemed overpowering in her manner. Host and hostess were trying a little too hard, but Hannah could forgive them for that.

The one other character who stuck particularly in the visitor's mind was General Muller. With jug ears and a toothy smile, he struck her as comical. His stuffy personality and awkward manners tended to accentuate this.

'The evening did not go badly,' she reminded herself. 'It can't be easy being hosts to the most powerful man in Hoame. I sensed that they were beginning to relax as the evening wore on in any case. What of today? We're being promised a brisk walk; not too brisk I hope.'

With her husband surfacing now, she decided to get up. Aided by their servants, the couple were soon washed and dressed smartly enough to go down to breakfast. Before they left their suite, Frank looked out of the window at the view. Immediately below was the rocky outcrop upon which the castle was perched. The walkway they had ascended the day before was not visible from this window. In the middle ground was a green, fertile valley with hills on the other side. The scene beyond was occulted by a thick mist.

Although not one of the largest of Hoame's castles, the inside seemed a maze of corridors to the visitors. They were grateful, therefore, for their guides. Breakfast was to be held in the Grand Hall, but the Heislers were not ready yet. Embarrassed by the poor timing, the head servant ushered the Thorns into an ante-chamber to wait.

A small, square room, it had plush leather seats which one sank into.

"I'm so sorry, My Lord, My Lady, but I am sure Despot Heisler will not keep you waiting long."

Frank was at pains to set the man's mind at rest and assured him they were unperturbed. Joseph, on best behaviour that morning, sat quietly with his parents. Before he disappeared, the head servant pointed out that there were sweetmeats available on the little tables next to where they were sitting.

It seemed a bit silly to spoil one's appetite before breakfast, but Frank was feeling quite peckish. Popping an almond-flavoured cake into his mouth, he then wondered how it would look if Heisler turned up and he had his mouth full. He therefore chewed it quickly and swallowed as soon as he could.

"May I have another one?"

Before Joseph's question could be answered, the head servant returned and they were escorted out of the ante-chamber into the Grand Hall. The bright colours struck them as they entered. High up within the building, there were proper windows here. In fact there were more, and bigger, glass windows here than Frank had ever seen in his time on this planet.

With the sun burning off the mist, a great deal of light was bursting into the room. It illuminated the fine, long, oak table, around which were seats upholstered with bright scarlet fabric. This blended in with the satin curtains and the brilliance of the scene almost took the visitors' breath away.

The table was laid out with much cutlery and a large selection of things to eat, from bowls of fruit to croissants.

'So much for a light breakfast!' thought Hannah. 'No wonder Magda Heisler is so large.'

The hosts appeared with an army of retainers and soon Frank and Hannah were sitting with them at one end of the completely full table. Glancing down, Frank noticed Deejan Charvo and his children seated around the half way point. The merchant was engaged in conversation with a local. A further peer down the table revealed Senator Trepte further along on the right-hand side.

With the exquisite furnishings, fine china and high quality cutlery, the guest of honour had to laugh to himself. What would Heisler make of his crude tables and benches? At least his internal castle walls had been redecorated fairly recently, but he was noticing now fine tapestries hung in the present room, far better than anything in Thyatira. He did not mind, but it might give Hannah ideas.

There was quite a din from the assembled breakfasters. An army of white servants were coming and going too. Then a strange sight caught Frank's eye. In the far corner of the large room was a black woman sitting on a rough chair by herself. She was busy knitting away. No on else paid her any attention and she seemed fully taken up in her task. "Yes, yes," she was saying to herself, if the observer's lip reading was any good.

The host noticed him staring and said amiably, "Don't worry about her."

"Who is she?" Frank enquired.

"Oh," Heisler sounded dismissive, "just a crazy woman. I wouldn't worry about her."

Deciding to heed this advice, the guest said, "It is a spectacular view from our room."

"I'm glad you like it," the other man beamed. "If you look again in a little while, the mist will have cleared. You will then be able to see a whole lot further."

"Right, I'll do that."

"We thought that you and Hannah might like to go for a walk down to the village after breakfast."

"Yes?"

"Magda will accompany us in her coach, but I feel that walking is the best way to see everything. Plus the exercise will be good for us."

It was nice to see the host starting to relax and Frank readily agreed. The meal was soon over and preparations being made for the trip out. Freidhelm stayed in the castle to commence trade talks. Both despots were happy to leave these details to their subordinates.

Before long the party was assembled, a large gathering of courtiers and their servants following the two despot families. Frank glanced back to see some of his fellow Thyatirans, but he did not have the opportunity to speak to them.

Heisler led the way with Frank, Hannah and Joseph alongside him. A crowd of come forty people came on behind in a mass. There was a babble of conversation from them, but it was respectfully reserved.

Back down the snaking walkway, they then hit a narrow road leading to a village at the bottom of the hill.

"It is no more than a kilometre and a half away," Heisler advised.

Tall hedges either side of the lane precluded the view beyond at first. When these stopped they were able to see the nearby mountain tops, although the further ones were still obscured by clouds.

The decline was quite marked and it was explained that Despotess Heisler's carriage was going by a longer route which was not as steep.

"She will rendezvous with us in the village."

The fields on either side were a rich green with interspersed rocky outcrops. The occasional sheep could be seen grazing therein. They passed a metre and a half tall brick wall which stretched for a couple of hundred or so metres. It was poorly finished. The bricks were of uniform size, but the mortar in between was haphazard. In some places it was sticking out like oozing mud, in others it was missing altogether.

The kilometre and a half estimation was about right and it did not take them much time at all to arrive at their destination. Narrow cobbled streets ran between the dwellings. Most of these were going either up or down, because little was flat in this hilly area. The place had clearly grown organically with no planning. Yet it was quaint, with steeply sloping grey slated roofs, wooden-framed buildings with small windows.

Villagers turned out in force and cheered the party as it passed through. It rather amused Frank, who turned to his wife and, in just above a whisper, said, "Ours don't do this for us."

Hannah thought of pointing out that they had done so when he returned from his kidnap ordeal, but she smiled rather than speak a reply. All that mattered was that the reception they were witnessing was a genuine one. There were no soldiers behind the modest crowd coercing them.

Magda Heisler had joined them by the time the guests were ushered through the entrance of a small shopping arcade. She said, "We thought you might like to see the wares that our local craftsmen make."

There was a big selection on offer, from trinkets to a two metre high cuddly toy. It was supposed to represent a bipedal animal of some sort. Frank wondered what in heaven it was, but was too polite to ask.

Joseph was staring avariciously at some intricately made toy soldiers. Spotting this, his father said he would buy them for him. At this point the obsequious shopkeeper said he would gladly give them as a present.

"Nonsense!" the visitor declared in determined fashion, "that would not be fair."

The only trouble was that Frank had not brought any money on this jaunt. Fortunately one of the Thyatiran servants could oblige and his employer made a mental note to ensure he was paid back. Hannah came away with an exquisitely-fashioned doll which fortunately was not two metres tall. They spent a while there looking round and Frank declared, "Such fine craftsmanship! I am sure that there would be a ready market in the Thyatiran towns for such wares."

They were in high spirits when they finally came away from the shops. It had been engaging to see such different items on display than were available back home. Despot Heisler was delighted at the obvious pleasure his guests were showing.

There was a visit to a small-scale distillery and a weaving demonstration before the party finished there.

"Are you okay to walk back?" Heisler enquired. "I have some conveyances on standby if you prefer."

Frank and Hannah looked at each other momentarily, as if communicating by telepathy. Then the former declared, "We're happy to walk back, thanks," guessing correctly that this was what his host would prefer. Magda Heisler again travelled in her carriage.

The ascent was taken slowly. Looking into the distance, the visitors could see a whole mountain range now. The scene on the mountainside on the other side of the valley was also clearer. Patches of gorse bushes were interspersed by grassy areas. The top was all rock, grey and pale purple in colour.

"So different from back home," commented Hannah.

"Yes, beautiful," responded her husband who was grateful that he did not have to tackle such gradients on a daily basis. On this one trip it was bearable, even enjoyable.

As they neared the castle, Heisler struck up a conversation about the previous year's superbolide.

"It was visible here in the northwest sky, travelling that way," he indicated with his hand.

"Yes, we saw it with our eyes too," replied Frank.

"What do you think it means?" the local despot asked earnestly.

"I believe it was a meteorite, a heavenly body that got caught in the planet's gravity and fell to the ground. The bright light was caused

266

by the intense heat generated as it travelled through the atmosphere at colossal speed."

This scientific explanation was lost on Heisler, who was on a completely different plane. He relied, "But what *message* did it bring?"

'Message...?' wondered Frank, but the man continued with his own theory.

"I believe it to be an omen of ill fortune. It could be a plague, or another war, like that terrible Chogolt invasion."

"Well," began his fellow despot, trying not to sound too dismissive, "it occurred the better part of a year ago, and..."

"Is it really that long?"

"Um, it was late summer. We're now on the cusp of summer again now, so it won't be long before it's a year. We haven't had a plague and I know of no other war currently than the Ladosan Civil War."

"Aren't you worried it will spill over into Hoame? You're on the border, after all."

"No sign of it doing so as yet. In fact the way things are going, it looks less likely."

"I remember the previous war with them, Frank, we suffered badly in that cold winter."

"In Ladosa?"

"Yes, we were besieging one of their cities..."

"Oh, which one?"

"A grey one; I don't recall the name. We didn't have enough men and our supply line was far too long."

Wanting to put an end to this, the guest-in-chief went out of his way to voice assurances that direct Hoame involvement in the current Ladosan struggle was extremely unlikely. He did not mention the covert operation in support of the Neo-Purples.

Heisler came back, "So you don't think the, um..."

"Meteorite?"

"Yes, that. You don't think it was an omen then?"

"Not at all; you may rest assured. Purely a random, natural phenomenon. Nothing to worry about."

They walked the final few hundred metres to the castle in silence, each lost in his own thoughts. Heisler did not look entirely convinced that the fiery phenomenon was not a harbinger of doom. On the other hand, Frank was amazed at this craziness.

'How superstitious can anyone get? I know the fellow is not a Christian. I guess he fills the space left by faith in the true God by all this superstitious nonsense. Oh well, I don't think I'll say anything more about it unless he raises the subject again.'

He did not. One they reached the fortress residence, Frank looked up at one of the high walls above him. It was rendered pale grey. Long, black streaks came down from where a gutter ended.

"Do you get much snow here in winter?" he enquired as they entered the building.

Pausing for a moment, a thoughtful reply then came. "We used to have a lot in years gone by. I can remember in my youth when the roads were blocked with snow. One couldn't get down to the village. We were completely cut off here at the castle. Some tenacious villagers struggled through the snow with a milk churn to keep us supplied. We haven't had a winter like that in many a year now. Last winter there was a dusting, but that's about all. I'm not sure why it's changed. I suppose the climate is getting warmer."

Hannah and Frank relished a bit of free time later that morning. They agreed that they were both enjoying their stay in Rilesia.

"I haven't had the opportunity to speak to Deejan since we arrived," he said.

"I'm sure you'll be able to catch up once we hit the road again."

"Yes. Our stay here is not meant to be a long one."

Frank did manage to catch up with Freidhelm shortly before lunch and learned that the trade negotiations were going well. The senator was interested to hear about the good quality toys being made here.

"They might be a welcome import," he declared. "They'd certainly be something different."

The crazy knitting woman was back at her station as lunch commenced. Meanwhile, it was Capparathia's recent history that Despot Heisler wanted to talk about.

"I never did like Despot Schonhost, or his son. The father was extremely rude to me on one occasion when we were both visiting Asattan. I've never forgotten it." He did not elaborate, but preferred to remind the Inner Council member of his support in crushing Schonhost's rebellion. "I did provide an army to fight alongside you, if you remember."

"Yes, of course," Frank replied. "It was a good thing that it never developed into a fight. We have the new Despot Schmidt to thank for that."

"Ah, yes," Heisler replied, but said no more. Frank suspected that the man despised Schmidt, the commoner elevated to despot, for most of his counterparts did. All the Keeper could do was spread the news that Schmidt was a good thing and that his ascension effectively saw off a crisis that had been threatening the country's stability. He only hoped that when he did eventually reach the deep south that everything was as good as he hoped it was. There was a lot riding on Schmidt's success for Frank's own reputation.

Meanwhile, Despot Heisler gave his final word on the matter with a muttered, "It's a funny old business and that's for certain."

~ End of Chapter 13 ~

Prospects of Peace - Chapter 14

Back in Thyatira, two senators were about to begin a meeting. Cragoop, in charge of production, had asked Otto, of the accounts portfolio, to discuss extra funding. The white did not, on this occasion, wish to commence the serious business straightaway, as something completely different was on his mind.

"I was discussing the morality of fairytales with my wife," he said as he took his place at the desk of the other man's office. His words certainly caught Otto on the hop.

"Fairytales? I would have thought they were the most moral of tales, surely. You have a clear distinction between the forces of good and evil. If my memory serves me right, good prevails in the end... nine times out of ten at least."

"Ah, I wasn't so much thinking of that angle. I was considering more of the lines of: is it right to tell little children about fairies, implying they are real, only to tell them when they are a bit older that they are not?"

"Please explain."

Cragoop thought his words had been clear enough, but he could not stop now. So he continued, "Illianeth says there's no harm in it, making up fun stories for little children. I must say she's extremely good at it. She can sit there and come up with all these tales about a fairy queen and certain other fairies, all off top of her head. The children love it. And of course for a while they believe that fairies actually exist. Then when they are older, they are told they were not real. Illianeth says it's harmless fun, but I have a nagging doubt."

"So you're working from the premise that ultimately fairies are unreal."

"Of course."

"And what if they are real?"

"What? Fairies?" asked Cragoop, starting to wish he had not begun this conversation in the first place. Otto was being so serious.

"Yes, fairies."

"Um, I suppose the situation would be different then." Then, trying to lighten the tone, he asked flippantly. "Why, you haven't seen any have you?"

"No, I haven't," came the earnest reply, "but someone close to me told me she did see some once, as a girl, and I believe her."

At which point Cragoop felt extremely awkward. Otto was not someone renowned for their jokes and he could not look more serious at that moment. How he wanted to change the subject!

"Shall we discuss business?" asked the black.

"Yes!" exclaimed Cragoop with an eagerness which betrayed his embarrassment. He thought, 'This is seriously weird. Make a mental note in future never to stray away from the real matter in hand with this fellow.'

"You wanted to talk about increased funding, I believe?"

"Indeed," began Cragoop. He was going to stick strictly to the point for the rest of the meeting. "The last time he was here, Emil spoke to me about the state of the roads in Norland. They're pretty poor apparently and must be completely re-built to bring them up to scratch. We're going to need a big increase in the amount of aggregate being produced if we are going to achieve this."

"The stone that forms the roads' under-layers?" Otto asked for clarification.

"That's right. The stone is quarried here and crushed first before the wagons take it to the site. There are several different layers, in fact, before the finished article is topped off with hulffan tar, but it does use a great deal of stone."

"I understand."

"And any project to seriously tackle such a large problem as Norland would appear to present..." here he paused to take a breath, "is going to need a significant increase in our quarry production. It will mean hiring more men, bringing in new machines; I have the figures here." He laid out some papers on the desk. "And I'm making a case for a further steam engine to be ordered. They are most efficient and save time and money in the long run."

"Hmm," went the other man as he began to study the documents in front of him. He took his time while Cragoop held his breath. It was an impressive presentation of the business case. Eventually he answered.

"As you know, the money is a lot tighter currently than it has been in many a while. Nevertheless, there are funds available for projects with the best business case."

"Exactly! To increase the standard of the roads there will have many benefits. Faster communication brings down business costs and encourages trade. It would raise the morale of the people down there and help them to feel part of Thyatira and accepted by us. So there are major social issues involved as well as economic benefits."

Slowly, Otto replied. "Leave these with me and I shall study them at my leisure. This will need to be brought before the full senate and I think it best that Senator Vebber be present to explain the background. After all, he is the one with first hand experience of Norland."

"Do you think it should be approved?"

"It would be foolish of me to say until I have studied all the facts carefully."

Cragoop had to leave it at that. As he left the office, he was quietly confident that the full senate could be persuaded. Emil would support him. 'One thing I won't be mentioning,' he considered, 'is fairies.'

It was with a sigh of relief that Frank passed out of Rilesia and across the border into the Harradran despotate. Not that it had not been a successful visit to Despot Heisler. It was simply that diplomatic niceties got a bit wearing after a while. They possessed little else in common with the Heislers to discuss. Maybe having to be on one's best behaviour was a harder these days. Back in Thyatira, Frank was his own boss and could relax. The same was true to an extent when he stayed at the Citadel in Asattan. With most of the Inner Council supportive of him, he did not have to try so hard.

'I wonder if being scrupulously polite is more of a strain as I get older,' he pondered. 'Maybe I'll grow into a cantankerous old man who is incredibly rude to all those around him and doesn't give a jot.'

Fortunately that time had not yet come and the Rilesian and Thyatirans contingents got on well. In the final two days of their stay the guests were shown other sites of natural beauty that were on offer. This included a particularly striking lake in a deep valley. The water was turquoise and frequented by a variety of fowl.

Meanwhile, Freidhelm's trade negotiations had born fruit and more goods would be travelling between the two parts of Hoame in the future. Frank was impressed by the senator's patience in achieving this goal. He wondered if the man's predecessor, the late Senator Shreeber, would have fared so well.

Heisler's castle was something of a warren inside and Frank experienced an unfortunate episode on his final day. Alone, and having lost his bearings, he had wandered into a bedchamber. No one else was present and it was furnished with the usual things one would expect to find in such a room. However, lying on a wooden trolley was a selection of metal utensils. It took the visitor a while to work out what they were. He cracked the puzzle when he recognised some thumb screws. They were instruments of torture. He exited the room immediately and not mentioned it to anyone, not even Hannah. The whole thing left an unfortunate bad taste in his mouth.

It was time to put that behind him. The Heislers' farewell had seemed warm and the Thorns were soon on the track heading south. They were directed on a route without any steep gradients as they slowly descended from the heights. The Rilesian military escort had turned back a couple of kilometres shy of the border and the convoy was on its own.

Safe in the knowledge that their own soldiers would ensure their safety, Frank and Hannah, as well as their entourage, were free to admire the view.

"Have you noticed how much hotter it is?" she enquired.

"I have. It was cooler at higher altitude, of course... and we're travelling south."

"And we're moving into summer."

"Yes. I remember the previous time I went down to Capparathia, it was very hot then."

"Look at that!" exclaimed the Despotess suddenly, pointing up at the sky.

A flock of large, pink birds were flying overhead. They sported long beaks and were unlike anything she had seen before. When asked, her husband could not enlighten her as to their species.

"I've never seen the like before."

"But I thought you'd been this way before."

"They must have been hiding that day."

Hannah gave a toothless smile at the sarcastic response. There were plenty of other sights to see. The terrain was good deal less mountainous here. Rather they were traversing a series of low hills on a road which was in a better state of repair than some the convoy experienced.

Cultivated fields covered the landscape, larger ones than back home in Thyatira. Some had workers hoeing in them and they stopped their work briefly to see the long caravan pass.

Frank realised that he had not spoken with Tristan since they left. Wanting to put that right, he made sure he engaged the young man in conversation one break.

"How did you find Ladosa?"

"A bloody mess!"

"I can imagine. It must have been a bad time."

"There were good times as well, My Lord. I made one or two firm friends during the time I was there, although I guess I won't ever see them again."

"No, I suppose not. The Neo-Purples, did they strike you as well organised?"

"I can speak for their ambulance service. I thought it was extremely well organised most of the time. Our job was simply to get them back to hospital as swiftly as possible. There were others whose duty was to apply initial treatment on the battlefield. Many of the injuries were horrible; women as well as men. I could never get used to that. It simply isn't right."

"Well, it's all behind you now," Frank said quickly, concerned that Tristan was starting to get emotional.

"Yes, My Lord, it is all behind me," came a mechanical reply.

Later that day, during the long, afternoon haul, Hannah was dozing when Joseph suddenly posed a question to his father.

"Do you think there are worlds other than ours?"

"Of course there are," Frank responded without thinking as he tried to swat a fly that was bothering him.

"I don't mean heaven. I mean other worlds with people like us."

"Yes I do, lots of them."

There were hardly any alive on Molten now who knew of Frank's origin from beyond the stars. He had never told Alan, or indeed his wife. As far as he was aware, she had no idea. It was too late to tell her now. Yet should he tell Joseph? Did he not have a right to know his father's origin on a far off planet? He was certainly not going to mention it now, but it might be a good topic for a death bed confession.

"What do you think they're like?" Joseph persisted.

"Other worlds?"

"Yes."

"I'm sure they vary a lot."

"But what makes you so sure they exist?"

"Well, you know that our sun is a star?"

"Yes, my tutor told me that."

"And Molten goes round it. There are other stars in the sky which we can see at night. It is reasonable to assume that they have planets going round them too."

"Oh," went the boy as he pondered the matter. After a while he came up with, "I could write a story about another world."

"You could indeed. An excellent idea."

The matter was left there. The convoy was soon passing a succession of towns and villages. The main road skirted these settlements rather than go through them. This was unlike Thyatira where the main arterial roads linked the towns rather than bypassing them. In the event, it suited Frank's purposes, because he did not want any delays if he could help it. Men were despatched at intervals to purchase fresh provisions, but the convoy itself plodded on at its slow pace.

A conscious decision had been made not to call in on Despot Sandhausen of Harradran. This was simply to get to Capparathia quicker, not because Frank did not like the local leader. Sandhausen was, in fact, one of the easier despots to get on with. The two men had accompanied each other on the march south during the Schonhost Revolt three years previously.

Sandhausen harboured no love for the Schonhost dynasty, calling it a tainted bloodline. He had not enjoyed having someone he was wary of on his southern border. As a result, he was a lot more supportive of Schmidt's appointment than some of the more snobbish despots. They were amicable neighbours.

As it happened, Harradran's leader was away at the Capital at this time in any case. There was already a good trade agreement between Harradran and Thyatira, the latter supplying a great deal of timber to the more southerly region. Even as he considered this, Frank noticed that trees were not nearly as thick on the ground here. The soil was beginning to turn sandy as they progressed.

Nearing the boundary with Capparathia, they stopped for the night. There was the usual bustle of activity as camp was set up and the evening meal got underway. The Despot and his wife kept out of the way while all this work was going on. Hannah was rootling in one of her luggage bags. Frank, meanwhile, was standing near a bush, admiring the setting sun on the horizon, when he was joined by Joseph. The lad was clutching a note pad and held a pencil in his other hand.

"I've started my story, Father."

"Ah, good."

"As there aren't many stars, I've decided to set it on a world without a sun."

"It'll be a bit cold there!" Frank said, quite amused.

"They'll light fires."

Deciding to be more serious, the father replied, "Without a sun it's unbelievably cold. I mean, even a gas like... methane would be a liquid, or a solid."

Science was not his strongest suit and he had no idea why he chose to mention methane. He simply knew it was a gas at "normal" temperatures and found on some hostile planets. In any case, it set his son thinking.

"Methane? The men in my story can be made out of that: methane man!"

Opening his mouth to respond, Frank then thought better of it. Why stunt the boy's originality? Let him write is story without too much outside interference. Methane man it would be.

Later that evening, round a welcoming camp fire, Frank sat with his wife to his right and Darda to his left.

Hannah asked, "Is it correct that we should be crossing the border tomorrow? Into Capparathia, I mean."

"Around midday at the best estimate. I'm going to send scouts on ahead, like we did when we entered Rilesia. No doubt Schmidt will not want to be taken by surprise. He knows we're coming, of course, but not exactly when."

He then turned to the squad leader who was busy getting the last bits of his meal out of his mess tin with his finger.

"You look like you enjoyed your meal."

"Yes, My Lord, I was hungry."

"But, from what you've told me, not as hungry as you got on the way back from Azekah."

"Oh no, we were starving then, especially towards the end when we were running out of money. I don't want to go through that again."

"No,"

"Vophsi exchanged his sword for a meal for the three of us. That might sound a bit crazy, but then you're starving you'd do anything for some food. Not much point in having a sword if you're dying of starvation, is there?"

"Indeed not. And at Azekah itself, what was the local cuisine like?"

"More spicy than back here. It was... different; different vegetables in particular. But you got used to it. We didn't eat badly at all."

"Tell me a bit more about life during the siege, Darda, I enjoy hearing about it."

The young man was happy to oblige. His audience was genuinely interested.

"Okay. Still talking of food, the central part of the city had been cleared of houses and given up to agriculture. That was done a long time before we arrived, when the city was more closely besieged. It meant they did not starve."

"Presumably the fighting didn't go on the whole time."

"No, My Lord, but it was quite active during the time we were here. I think we earned our money!"

"I'm sure you did."

Prompted by Frank, he spoke at length about different aspects of his stay in Azekah. While the two men chatted away, Hannah was feeling a bit left out. When Darda was eventually released, she spoke her mind.

"You men can't half talk a lot!"

"What do you mean? We were merely having a little chat."

The following morning, Frank woke with a start. There were noises going on in the camp, but all of a routine nature. He relaxed again. There was nothing untoward and he was pleased that his kidnap ordeal of the previous year was not precluding him from sleeping on the journey. It was warm already and he got dressed in light, summer clothes.

He managed to have a conversation with Deejan Charvo over breakfast, commenting that he had not seen much of the merchant the past few days.

"No, My Lord. The three of us enjoyed a pleasant time in Rilesia. I loved the scenery. There wasn't an extensive view first thing. However, as the day got going, one could see further and further. The mountains were quite spectacular."

"That's right, quite breathtaking. Although the dakks do struggle up those steep gradients."

"I'd be more scared going down; if the brakes failed on the wagon..."

"Yes, it doesn't bear thinking about. I think we were lucky the way we come back down. It was a longer, less steep decline."

"But those hairpin bends on the trail at the beginning..... we probably covered four times the distance to get from A to B."

"Mmm."

"But my two enjoyed it."

"Sebastian and Keturah?"

"Yes."

"Where are they at the moment?"

"Exploring... somewhere close by, I hope. They had early breakfast. In fact, now I've finished eating, I think I'll go along and find them."

Servants and soldiers were coming and going, collapsing the tents and undertaking many other essential chores before they could get going. Nevertheless, Darda, finding himself near his Despot, found time to ask him a question.

"You've been to Capparathia before, haven't you, My Lord?"

"That's right. It was a long time ago. I was working it out, it was thirteen years ago if I've got my calculations correct."

"May I ask what it's like?"

"Um, I remember snippets. There's a plateau in the northern part where a lot of wheat is grown. When you get down into Capparathia proper, it's quite different. Sandy soil and fewer trees, mostly palms. There was a lake near where we stayed, the biggest body of water I've seen on this pl... since I've been here. We were taken out onto it in boats."

"Wow, I'd love that!"

"Well, I don't know if we'll get the opportunity. That was at a previous despot's country retreat.

"But you enjoyed your stay?"

"Yes, I think so. Then I came home and found that conspirators had plotted to overthrow me back here in Thyatira."

Frank was dead pan as he made the last comment and Darda was not sure if he was joking. So the former added, "But that's another story I'll tell you about some time."

Soon they were underway again. Their ears were deaf to the creaks and groans of the slow-moving wagons, so familiar were they as background noises. Two scouts were sent up ahead on superdakks to make contact with the Capparathians before the main party got to the border.

Ten kilometres inside the region, Despot Norbert Schmidt sat within his tent with a temporary military encampment set up specially for the occasion. He wanted to personally escort Keeper Thorn from the border area to where they would be staying further south. This whole visit was a massive deal for him and his staff were under no illusions that everything needed to be just right. Not only was the most powerful man in Hoame coming to stay, but the very man who had defied convention and set Schmidt up in his present role.

When the previous despot, Schonhost, launched his audacious (some would say insane) revolt against the Inner Council, Thorn led a multi-despotate army southwards to confront him. It was Schmidt's decision to assassinate his despot which collapsed the enterprise and averted a civil war. Being offered the post in his former leader's place was his reward. It was by no means a foregone conclusion, he knew. He might easily have forfeited his own life for such a deed. Yet Thorn was a practical man and it had been a pragmatic solution. Either way, Schmidt held a debt of gratitude to him. As a youth, he never in his wildest dreams thought he would become a despot. It was not as if he grew up without any ambition, though.

He was born on his parents' estate in the village of Gelburn, eight kilometres from the regional capital Jazerlaffen. His father was a top advisor to Despot Schonhost, his mother also attended court. Norbert was given a classical black Hoame education. Following school, he spent a while in the army as an officer, although he did not see action.

Upon his parents' early deaths, he was made advisor himself. He found the reality of court life quite different from what he had been led to expect. All the backbiting and manoeuvring he found distasteful. Yet one must to get on, even if that meant playing the game. He liked to think he made more allies than enemies during his ascent up the ladder. He married well and two children quickly followed, a boy and a girl.

At thirty-five, in 2615, he was made Counsellor, the chief advisor to the despot. It was quite an achievement to obtain this post, in his father's footsteps, so young. Yet disillusionment with the whole court ethos was never far away. He had enjoyed the military life and the discipline it brought, but politics was radically different, with its behind-the-scenes wheeling and dealing. A realist, he resolved to make the best of it, after all it was the highest position he was likely to achieve.

Schonhost's revolt, late 2617, came against his advice and he was far from being the sole courtier to be shocked by the move. After secretly sounding out the top military men in Capparathia, Schmidt took it upon himself to assassinate the despot before an unwinnable battle took place. Not knowing how His Excellency Thorn would react, he took the severed head as proof of the deed. The subsequent offering of the vacant despot's role came as a complete surprise. The situation was unprecedented and he had acted in the face of the emergency. By averting a battle, he actually spared Hoame blood. Thorn's immediate concern was the stability of the region. If he had put it before the Inner Council it would have taken an age for a decision to be made. The power vacuum was plugged straightway.

From that point onwards, Schmidt recognised the vital nature of this Keeper's patronage. This was especially the case in the face of disquiet from a few of the long-established despots from other areas. The critics maintained their criticism behind closed doors with the powerful man having made his views plain. Schmidt's own fate would rise or fall with the Keeper's fortunes. He made sure that he pursued policies which would meet with Thorn's approbation.

Now coming towards the end of his fourth year in the role, Despot Norbert Schmidt reckoned that he had made a pretty good job of it so far. He could not pleased everyone, but as those who have wielded power across the centuries know, that is par for the course. He had been wanting Keeper Thorn to visit for some time and had sent more than one invitation. Now that it was about to take place, he was full of barely concealed excitement. If the Thyatiran enjoyed this visit, it would only cement his own position. It was the most important test of his tenure.

A messenger reported, "My Lord, His Excellency Thorn and his entourage are approaching the border now. We expect them to cross at midday."

"Excellent! Ready the dakks, saddle them up, get my uniform. We must go to meet our distinguished guests without delay."

Summer was in full swing in Ladosa. Daises and buttercups dotted the fields, while conkia adorned the hedgerows. Bees, dragonflies and other winged insects filled the air. Foliage on the trees was full and verdant. If nature was at full tilt, the human situation was on pause. The Civil War had finished its first full phase and it was not at all clear what the next would be.

With the defeat of the southwest Buffs, the Neo-Purples were in control of the entire south of the country. It took a while to reduce the last pockets of resistance, but that operation was complete now. Their top military commander, Marshal Charlotta Nazaz, was concerning herself with the future.

Supply lines were too long for operations further north, so new depots were being established nearer the current front. Field hospitals needed to be moved and fresh communication routes worked out. She discussed strategy with her senior officers. Hallazanad had been promoted to Major now and was included in on the deliberations. Unfortunately he did not see eye-to-eye with the marshal as to where they went from here.

"I say we should move the bulk of our army, presently here in the southwest, further east. We can then launch an offensive northwards into the Buff heartland. It is only through their defeat that we can draw this conflict to a conclusion."

"They have had a year to prepare their defences," Charlotta replied, "it would be a costly move."

"It is the soft underbelly of the beast. Strike there and we can fan out to attack Laybbon to the west and Lefange and Braskaton to the east. Victory will not come until the capital is taken."

"We have a large Rose army immediately north of here. They are far more active than the Buffs, far more offensively minded. If they see us thinning out our forces here, moving them east as you say, they could be tempted to attack southwards, non-aggression pact or not. All our hard-earned gains would then be for naught."

"You don't trust the Rose at all?"

"They've got to earn their trust. Dragging their feet is not gaining them my confidence."

"So are you considering a pre-emptive strike against them?"

"The Rose?"

"Yes."

"No, I want to get them to cooperate with us if possible, fight the common Buff enemy. It makes strategic sense. South of the Buff heartland, our scouts tell us, is a no man's land since vacated by the southern Pinks. The Buffs, concentrating on defence, as I said, are showing no propensity to move into that area. So that is a useful buffer zone, something we have not got here."

"I must confess to being surprised," Hallazanad confessed.

"How so?"

"I thought you were sanguine regarding an accommodation with the Rose. After all, we have signed an initial agreement with them."

"I was, but our recent communications have met with silence. It is not a good sign. We need to plan for every eventuality whilst hoping for the best outcome."

"Before the war we'd never have dreamt of allying ourselves with the Rose, they're even crazier than the Buffs."

Charlotta knew what he meant. She replied, "We have to be practical. If we can end the fighting with a commitment to allow the electorate to decide, then it is in everyone's interests. The Rose, for all their faults, must be democratic at heart. They are still Ladosans."

"So you're appealing to their better nature even though they might not have one."

The marshal could do without this. She was facing problems and tensions from every direction. The Neo-Purple Committee, the political heart of the organisation, kept sending her communications from their base far away from the action. "What do you know about war and strategy?" she would have liked to have replied. "They're eighty kilometres behind the frontline and have never visited it, or come anywhere close. They should wind their necks in and leave the strategy to me." Nevertheless, in practice she had to keep in their good books. She sent them bland replies in a bid to gain the time she needed.

Meanwhile, the common soldiers, almost immediately the fighting went on hold, formed their own debating circles. They discussed every idea under the sun as to what the Neo-Purples should be doing and not even the most outlandish idea was out of bounds. It was all very Ladosan, but most unhelpful in keeping military discipline.

In fact, the Neo-Purple reading of the situation in the rest of the country was a long way from actuality. The one thing that Charlotta got right was that the remaining (central) Buffs possessed no intention of attacking southwards. In fact, a little under a year since the superbolide exploded, they were like a rudderless boat adrift on the waters.

Braskaton still looked like an atom bomb had hit it with tens of thousands killed, including nearly all their top politicians. Desertions from the army were rife and the remaining troops spread thinly across the perimeter of their land. A huge lethargy overcame the central Buffs as if the stuffing was knocked out of them. Unable to undertake any offensive actions, their entire strategy was reactive.

Up in the north of the country, the Pinks were not doing much better. They came off badly in the early battles against the Rose and Buff factions. A rural area, many of the surviving soldiers had gone back to their farms once the first flush of enthusiasm subsided. The small Pink enclave south of the central Buffs had ceased to be due to attrition. This was now the no-man's land that Charlotta referred to.

The one other player was the Rose. Their heartland, and biggest area of control by far, had always been the northwest. Like the Pinks, they had held a subsidiary parcel of land which was no more. The eastern Rose area was at the epicentre of the superbolide explosion and blown to kingdom come. There were few survivors.

The northwest Rose fared a lot better, fighting the southwest Buffs to a standstill and giving the Pinks a bloody nose. Being ruled by a democratic committee, strategic decisions were made painfully slowly. At the beginning of the conflict they saw the Buffs as the major enemy to overcome. Their greatest efforts, therefore, were aimed against the former government forces. Together with the Neo-Purples they defeated one of their two powerbases. Even so, for all their battles, many of which could be classed as victories, the Rose territory barely changed.

The Rose were as undecided as the Neo-Purples as to what to do next. They recognised the latter as the most dynamic, rising power in

Ladosa. but their strategy of attacking the Buffs still held. Late spring, fed up with all the dithering, one of their generals had launched an offensive eastwards into the Buff heartland. The committee were furious and, in spite of spectacular initial gains, ordered a pullback. It took a threat of disciplinary action for the general to comply.

This, therefore, was the situation in Ladosa at the beginning of summer 2621. If an immediate political solution could not be found, then the fighting would recommence all too soon. The only two factions with any initiative were the Neo-Purples and Rose. They currently faced each other like a pair of gunslingers in the Wild West, waiting for the other one to draw first.

Alan was starting to feel like a spare engine part. A change in mood in the Neo-Purple camp meant foreign military advisors were now excluded from their deliberations. This was a poor response to some of the best ideas of their successful campaign to date.

Meanwhile, the flow of fresh recruits, which had been a feature of the spring season, all but ceased with the change to summer. The decision was made for the Hoame contingent to return home to Ephamon. Alan alone stayed.

Not that the drone enjoyed a purpose any more; his relationship with Charlotta alone kept him there. He had moved to fresh digs nearer the frontline. It was another picturesque cottage with marigolds out the front and silver mound artemisia predominating the back garden. While his lover discussed strategy, he kicked his heels in his gilded cage.

'I'm nothing more than a kept man,' he mused. 'This is all so topsy-turvy, typical Ladosan I guess. They always have things round the wrong way. Charlotta says that she loves me... maybe she does in her own way. Yet I am coming second to her political ambitions.' For Alan, the free spirit, this was a poor return.

One evening, she came to visit him. Her opening comments were not exactly the stuff of star-crossed lovers.

"Ah, my darling, you'll never guess."

"What's that?"

"The Rose lot have elected a new General Secretary for their committee. It's someone I know from my civil service days. I believe this is someone I can do business with."

284

It was clearly the issue on her mind, but a peck on the lips and a discussion on political dealings was not his idea of a good evening. Belatedly, she tried to make amends. Putting down her satchel full of papers, she tried to take hold of him, but he pulled away.

"My darling, let's go upstairs."

"No." he said, stepping back and pushing her hand out of the way.

"I'm sorry, but we're going through a difficult time presently and we have to make some important decisions. But... I tell you what: let's just forget about it tonight. Let's go to bed."

Alan was not in the mood. In fact he could not be less in the mood and told her so. She looked hurt, but he was not going to let her off the hook that easily. It was time to tackle some fundamentals.

"I'm stuck here for no purpose. You only see me when you've finished all your important business of the day. The whole situation is driving me crazy."

"But it won't be like this for long. I want you, Alan, I really do!"

If she could be in two places at once, the conference room and the love-nest, she would have. She did not want to lose him, but the war was at a critical point. The decisions made now would mean the difference between victory and defeat. If he could be a bit more patient then things would work out.

"I could make you..."

"I don't want to be made anything!" he snapped.

For Alan, this whole situation was bonkers. He was the adventurer, the free spirit. A lover of action, but able to give wise counsel when called upon. Now, however, he was reduced to a foreign woman's mere plaything. If this was what love was, then it was not all it was cracked up to be.

Patiently she tried to bring him round. She desired him more than anything in the world. The politics would not be this intense for ever, things would settle down. If only he could hold on a bit longer. Then they could be together.

He listened and, on the face of it, he calmed down and became more compliant. In the end she led him upstairs where they made love. Yet for Alan, this was a farewell gift. His mind was made up. He did not tell her that night. Charlotta held more meetings she absolutely had to convene the next day. It would be his opportunity to get his things together, take a couple of dakks and depart. His Ladosan adventure was over.

285

As they crossed the regional boundary into Capparathia, Frank was reminded quite what an alien landscape it was here.

The soil was yellow-ochre with little flecks of black in it. Unfamiliar trees lined the route, some palms, others with dark brown bark which was peeling off to reveal a lighter under-layer. The road was well maintained, but topped with large stones, it did make the wagons clatter as they progressed.

It was hot and they were wearing light clothing and hats to shield their heads from the fierce sun. A dry heat, even the breeze felt warm.

"Father, what's up there?"

Joseph was pointing to a high plateau about a kilometre away on their left-hand side. It rose suddenly from the plain and was several kilometres long.

"If I'm right," Frank replied, "that's where a lot of Capparathia's wheat is grown."

"How do they get up there?"

It was not as stupid a question as it sounded at first, for the walls were sheer along the side they could see. The boy's father assured him that there must be a road to the summit on the other side.

A welcoming committee came into view ahead of them. Shortly before they left Thyatira, Frank was suddenly concerned about the size of his entourage, so he had sent a message to Despot Schmidt to forewarn him what to expect. Now, as he peered through the shimmering heat haze on the road, he was glad that he had.

The Capparathian contingent was mounted, but held their ground as the wagon train edged nearer. As they got closer, Frank recognised his opposite number, tall in the middle. He had to chuckle to himself as he remembered their first encounter. It was hoped that the Capparathian was not about to present him with another severed head on this occasion.

"Ah, Your Excellency! I trust you've enjoyed a fair journey. It's nice to see you again," came the warm greeting. No disembodied heads this time.

"Frank, please." He wanted this visit to be in his fellow despot role. The less formal, the more relaxing he hoped the stay would be. "It's a long time since I was last here. I've been looking forward to it."

Soon the two were standing together, Schmidt considerably the taller man. With his narrow beard and long hair, flowing in the breeze, he was a magnificent sight.

Introductions were made and Frank ensured that his top men were all included. The host explained that they would meet his wife at the Schloss.

"By the lake?" asked Frank.

"Yes, that's right."

"That's where I stayed last time."

"Ah! We've had it spruced up a little since then, but it's still basically the same. It's a nicer venue than the castle. If it is acceptable to you, we'll go straight there for a late lunch."

"That would be lovely."

For the journey to the Schloss, Schmidt joined the Thorns in their wagon. The driver was given instructions to pick the pace up. With the road here a cinder track, it did not make so much noise.

"We have been looking forward to your visit," the local leader declared, totally unable to hide his enthusiasm. "I hope that we can make your stay a pleasant one."

"I'm sure it will be."

"We can take a boat out onto the lake one day."

They had done that on their first trip. Frank and Hannah were happy with the idea of doing it again. The latter certainly enjoyed her stay on that occasion, finding many of the people at court pleasant to get along with. She sat smiling as they proceeded, her ebony skin glistening in the heat.

Soon the Schloss, the despot's summer residence, was in view. Largely of wooden construction and mostly one floor, it possessed a long balcony that overlooked the lake. The shoreline was three hundred metres from the building and the water appeared flat calm.

Schmidt led their chief Thyatiran guests indoors. This group included Tristan, Deejan and his family. Darda and the military escort were taken on to another place a couple of kilometres further. The VIPs were ushered into an anteroom where they stood as their host explained.

"My wife will be coming down any moment, then we can go through to lunch once I've introduced her to you."

They waited in silence and with expectation. Frank got the impression that his counterpart was embarrassed by the delay and decided to say something to ease the tension.

"I noticed a burnt area shortly before we met you."

"Oh yes, we do get bush fires occasionally this time of year. It's important that we keep on top of them. Everything is so dry and in this heat..."

"Of course."

"We have watchtowers manned to spot any outbreaks as soon as possible."

"That makes sense; put out the fires before they can take hold."

Finally the hostess arrived. Despotess Rudella Schmidt sailed into the room, a group of female attendants in tow. She wore the most extraordinary outfit on. A lacy, gold top of elaborate workmanship. It had stiff, broad shoulders which stuck out and one of her servants was fiddling with the one nearest her as they entered. Her short, red/gold tartan skirt exposed thin, girl-like legs and leather lace-up shoes. On her head was an enormous, white hat with a flat, mortar-board type top.

"I suddenly feel under-dressed," Hannah whispered out of the corner of her mouth.

Rudella was certainly a lot older than her husband and had a round face with her greying hair fitting neatly over her ears and a fringe at the front. For all the aforementioned, it was the beaming smile that held one's eye, for it lit up the entire room.

"So sorry to have kept you," she apologised to the Thorns before taking her place by her husband. The top of her head was barely up to his shoulders.

"Not at all," Frank replied, "We're delighted to meet you."

Schmidt said, "Shall we go through? You must be hungry."

It was a light meal of cold meats and salad, but there was plenty of it and it tasted as good as it looked.

"This ham is quite delicious," Hannah declared.

"I hope you like the cheeses too," replied Rudella, her voice quite low. "We have two and twenty different varieties."

"My goodness, that *is* a lot."

"We imported some specially."

Meanwhile, Schmidt was saying a bit about the itinerary for the next couple of days that he had personally overseen.

"I thought that, once you have settled in your room and rested a while, we might take a walk out. There should be some clouds coming over in the late afternoon, so it won't be too hot. Then in the evening we have an entertainment arranged, some magic tricks which I think you'll enjoy. We have a longer walk set for tomorrow morning before it gets too hot. Following our siesta, we thought that a game of pétanque might be rather fun."

Frank had no idea what that was, but he responded by saying that he had brought along his Senator Trepte to lead some bi-partisan trade talks.

"Later, yes," said Schmidt.

"Ouch!" said Frank.

"I'm sorry?"

"Oh, nothing."

The conversation was suitably light for the rest of the meal. It was when they were alone together in their bedchamber that Frank got to ask Hannah why she had kicked him. She explained.

"Poor Norbert was trying to tell you about all the lovely entertainments he's organised for us. All you could respond with was trade talks!"

"Oh."

"He's clearly tried his best to arrange a schedule to amuse and interest us. Try to enter into the spirit of it, my dear."

"All right, I'll try," he replied in full contrition mode.

"And that Rudella is an absolute poppet. She has such a presence about her and is so easy to chat with. Intelligent and sweet with it. I'm sure I'm going to enjoy our stay here."

~ End of Chapter 14 ~

Prospects of Peace - Chapter 15

"Hey, mista, have ya got any spare change?"

The beggar woman appeared thin and hungry that morning, leaning up against a wall in the shade. With a pock-marked face, she looked a good deal older than her thirty-five years.

Alan was nearly home, but stopped off at a small town a short distance shy of the Mitas Gap. Strong Neo-Purple territory, this area experienced no battles in the current war. With the frontline moving ever further away, the conflict was not the first thing on people's minds. It was good to feel a sense of normality, with busy folk hurrying to and from their daily business.

Dressed still in his Ladosan clothes, the drone attracted no attention. He possessed plenty of money and had bought a couple of fresh dakks for last part of the journey. If he ate a quick lunch here, he could be at the other side of the mountain pass well before sunset.

Hesitating outside the tavern, he replied to the beggar woman. "I can do better than that; I'll treat you to a meal if you like."

She hesitated a moment to take the words in before quickly getting up and following the stranger indoors. It was cooler inside and quite refreshing. Before long she was eagerly tucking into a beef stew. Scoffing it quickly, it was as if she had had nothing to eat for a week. Alan was taking his time over his meal. Then, with a sudden movement, she put down her spoon and scowled at her benefactor.

"I s'pose you'll want sex in return for this?"

Stifling a chuckle, Alan replied, "No strings; just enjoy your meal."

The woman found this most odd, but soon she was scraping her plate clean. When her companion asked if she would like some more bread, she answered in the affirmative.

Later, over a cheesecake dessert, she began to open up a little.

"I'm escaping from my man," she said, "'e was goin' to slash me!"

"What do you mean?"

"'E threatened to slash my face if I ever leave 'im. But I got away an' I'm goin' further. Where ya headin'?"

Feeling safe to divulge his destination, Alan replied, "I'm travelling south, into Hoame."

"Hoame? I ain't been there. Are you from there then?" Her tone was a cross between curiosity and suspicion.

"From Thyatira," he replied. Then, to allay any fears that she brand him a spy, added, "We've been helping the Neo-Purple cause."

It was sensitive information, and maybe he should have been more circumspect, but he was close to home now and would soon be out of this foreign land. Besides, the woman's mind seemed more occupied with her own self-preservation than anything else.

"Are there any cheap places to stay in Thyatira? I'd be safe there, wouldn't I?"

"I'm not sure if there are cheap places to stay. I could put you up in a room for a week if you like, while you sort something more long-term."

"An' what do ya want in return?" came the slow, cautious response.

"I want nothing in return," he replied casually. It was up to her whether she believed him or not.

"Why would ya help me for noffin'? It doesn't make sense."

"In my universe people do kind things merely for the sake of it. A life without trust is a sad one."

She did not reply, neither did she look convinced. When Alan went to pay the bill, he returned to see the door to the outside closing and the woman gone. With a shrug, he got his things together and made his way to the stables where he had left his dakks.

'Heading home... it'll be good to see the Castle again: familiar scenery, familiar faces. I can't wait to have a good ride on a superdakk once more.'

Stepping out, the sun was bright and the street busy. Time to be moving on. The stables were a few blocks away and he made his way there at a relaxed pace.

A small crowd were gathered at a street corner to hear a political debate. Two speakers occupied a makeshift platform and were trying to convince their audience by force of argument. A middle aged man with a waxed moustache was giving his point of view, making dramatic gestures with his hands as he did so.

"Through his establishment of the Second Constitution, the Ladosan nation, after several years of decline, had again found an organic form that not only united the people, but gave the working classes an expression of strength that was as real as it was ideal in nature."

"Ah," his adversary came back, "but we know that this attempt ended in failure. You may say that the lack of genuinely brilliant leadership was the cause. But hardly less significant are the causes that can be found to some extent in the nature of the establishment of the new constitution itself."

The original speaker came back with, "That's all well and good, but you fail to make allowance for the internal political leadership of the people. The true statesmen of this great land have an unlimited inner development that is the true essence of democracy. It is this that we should hold dear."

Alan moved on, more confused than enlightened. When would these Ladosans ever grow up? The amount of effort they expelled with this nonsense seemed ludicrous to him.

'It will be good to get back to some sanity in Hoame. I will never again complain about Hanz waxing lyrical about the usefulness of chain gangs, or Cragoop's coal production figures.'

Entering a fresh street, he saw a group of male soldiers waiting outside the stables. He hesitated momentarily, then carried on, because he had no reason to fear the Neo-Purples. They were on the same side of the street. When he got close it became clear that it was he they were interested in.

"Are you a Hoaman?" asked their officer as he stepped forward.

"I am."

"Why are you dressed in Ladosan clothes?"

"I've been helping out as a military advisor for you, further north."

"See?" came a female voice from behind the soldiers, "I told ya he was a spy!"

The ungrateful beggar woman held out her hand for a reward, but the captain glanced at it contemptuously before addressing Alan again.

"We must ask you to come with us, to check your story out... and surrender your sword in the meantime."

There were six of them, Alan counted. He had faced worse odds in the past and come out on top. On the other hand, he was hopeful that this could be settled amicably, so he surrendered his sword and went quietly with the men. In return, he was not restrained in any way, but the armed group escorted him closely.

"What about my money?" a voice from behind shrieked.

292

"We have to check it out first," the captain replied. "Come back tomorrow."

'That's quick for a decision,' the prisoner thought.

The Ladosan officer then asked him, as they processed down the road, "So our Central Committee will know all about you, will they?"

"They should do," the drone replied, trying to sound relaxed. Communication of these things would not have been widespread; the complete opposite in fact. He was concerned.

"Good," the other man said with a note of sarcasm, "because they are in town today and I can ask them. You'll have to give me your details."

It was late afternoon by the time Alan was released. Mercifully the Neo-Purple politicians were in the know and vouched for him. The delay meant that he would have to hurry to cross the border before nightfall. Clutching his returned sword's handle, he was pleased to have that back again. The beggar woman's calculations had backfired. Instead of free lodgings in safety, she missed out on a reward which was not due. That gave Alan some satisfaction as he mounted up and galloped out of town. 'Bye bye Ladosa,' he thought, 'I shall not be returning in a hurry.'

Bishop Gunter experienced a difficult couple of days. Everyone seemed to be taking their problems to him and no one their solutions. It drained him of vitality and he decided to pay the monastery a visit. Muggawagga would understand, he was someone that Gunter could unburden himself onto. Why should he suffer alone?

"And then the woman had the effrontery to complain that *she* was the one who'd been treated unfairly! It was her responsibility to see that the flowers were arranged properly and all she'd done is left them in containers. All the other issues blew up out of that original dispute. Some people eh? It amazes me quite how self-centred some people can be. She should have more consideration for those around her."

His long tirade concluded. All he wanted now was for the abbot to agree with him and he would be satisfied. The little Ladosan had listened quietly while his visitor ranted and he remained in the same manner for some time afterwards. It was quiet. Gunter's words still seemed present in the ether, swirling round them in the silence, in a

293

decaying orbit. Eventually the other man spoke. His words were soft, yet piercing.

"Maybe it would help to see the situation from the lady's perspective."

More silence. Gunter waited for him to continue; he knew he would in time.

"Put yerself in their shoes for a while. From what you've told me, this woman is having difficulty in making ends meet. She lives in poor accommodation and that's probably a chronic worry, something always at the back of her mind. We are all the product of our experiences and her lot in life has not been an easy one. Perhaps if she was given some help at home, her attitude would ease a bit."

"I doubt it!" Gunter said automatically. He realised he was merely being defensive and wished he had not said it.

"Me ol' bucka, you don't know that."

"No, I don't."

"My advice is for you to think it over. Then leave it a couple of days for tempers to settle before you go and see her again."

"She came to see *me*."

"Okay, but you make the move this time. Reach out to her. And after you've talked it through calmly, see if she will take some practical help to improve her lot."

"Mmm, you're right," Gunter conceded after a while. "I should not be so quick to judge her harshly. I know better than that. I've been a fool."

"And *you*..." the diminutive man replied, "need to forgive yourself. Yer were caught up in the middle of all this business and found it difficult to see the wider picture. Be kind to Gunter."

Gunter smiled and thanked God for this good friend. He knew that Muggawagga would give him a helpful perspective.

The conversation moved on and the visitor brought up the subject of the Ten Commandments. He said, "There's debate as to how relevant they are today."

"Is there?"

"Yes, if we're saved by grace then surely they're redundant."

"Jesus didn't think so. He quoted them to the rich young ruler."

"But they come across as a negative approach to life. Telling us what not to do the whole time."

294

"Yer think so?" asked Muggawagga. "Maybe it's a matter of perspective. T' me they are a positive set of guidelines for life."

"How so?"

"Would yer like me to go through 'em?"

"If you like."

"You shall love the Lord your God with all your heart, all your mind, with all your soul and with all your strength. What could be a more positive start than that? If you love God that way, then you won't want to worship idols. There are so many idols folk worship: money and possessions for two. In Ladosa they worship the craziest idols possible: sportsmen and politicians! I would say it's an extremely positive thing to worship God alone, for he alone is worthy and won't let you down."

"Carry on."

"You shall use God's name worthily. There is power in the name of God and power misused is an exceptionally bad thing.

"Keep the Sabbath Day holy, because it will teach you the meaning of holiness. If we grow from spiritual babes, we will live to make every day holy, but we have to start with that first step, the Sabbath.

"Honouring your parents, what could be more positive than that? They are wonderful relationships to be treasured. Again, the wise man is he who has learned to honour everyone, but we have to begin somewhere.

"When you know God, you will not want to murder, to commit adultery, or to steal. For you know that life is sacred, that it needs to be pure and that all possessions are only temporarily in our keeping anyway. These commandments help remind us of these facts.

"Again, knowing God you will always shun falsehood. Lies have a power about them which must not be underestimated. It is best not to go down that road in the first place. Jesus came to give us the truth. so no false witnessing can be allowed. Lies are dirty, nasty and dangerous. They are away from the path that we should be treading.

"Coveting what others have? We possess nothing in reality, so it is a waste of energy, a negative energy. On the other hand, in God we possess everything. As Jesus said, to gain our lives we must first lose them. To cling onto the old, like the materialists do, is to live in illusion. We live in the light of Christ, it is a different universe.

"There, Gunter, me ol' bucka, I hope that's positive enough for yer."

"Alan, how wonderful to see you again!"

"Nice to have you back."

"Hi, Alan."

"Welcome home."

The greetings were many and varied as the drone entered the senate chamber the morning after his return. It was the regular weekly meeting and he was glad to get back into the swing of things straightaway. It would be good to be amongst rational human beings once more who did not worship at the door of the extraordinary idea of democracy.

Meanwhile, his peers were delighted to have him back. Otto had been due to chair the meeting, but immediately deferred to Alan. They were low on numbers that day as several senators were elsewhere. On the other hand, General Japhses was attending to give them a defence briefing.

The truth was that the general had received little intelligence from across the border recently. So, after giving a modest presentation, he let Alan take over.

"Thanks, Japhses. Our allies, the Neo-Purples, have secured the south of the country following a successful campaign. We can expect the war to continue further north, but currently on the other side of the border from here is in the control of friendly forces."

"Do you think," asked Japhses, "that we should reduce the number of patrols we run? Or even the number of men we currently have along the border?"

"I'd advise against it. As with all wars, the situation is unpredictable. The Neo-Purples have done well, but they're not the most powerful group there. We..."

The deep voice of Saul interrupted from the back, with, "I wouldn't trust any of them Laodician devils. We must keep on our guard."

"That's hardly fair," declared Hanz. "We've been working in partnership with these Neo-Purples we should be able to trust them to a certain degree. Isn't that right, Alan?"

"To a certain degree, yes, but Saul isn't entirely wrong. Whilst it looks like the situation has shifted in our favour, now is not the time to drop our guard. I thought I detected a certain sense of normality returning to the area on the other side of the border."

"Normality?" queried Hanz.

"What passes for normality in Ladosa. That usually means spouting nonsense, but it's better than warfare."

Otto asked, "What about the refugees over here? They are costing us money every week. We are having to tighten our budgets elsewhere, Norland sucking in funds like there's no tomorrow. It would be good to see the back of those refugees."

"The last time I spoke with the Despot he did not want to return them against their will. Once they feel safe, they will go back of their own volition. If I'm right and stability is being re-established in the south of Ladosa, then some will soon choose to leave us."

"How will they know?" Saul asked.

Japhses replied, "They seem to have a good intelligence system. It takes no more than a few of them to come and go in order to keep the rest informed. The refugee numbers have never been entirely static. Despot Thorn made is clear that we are to allow the occasional traffic both ways across the border as long as the overall number goes no higher than the original quota."

"That was set at five hundred, wasn't it?" asked Hanz.

"Yes," the general confirmed. "We do a count every now and then, but they are not popular and there is no point in unsettling them merely for the sake of it. The precise number was five hundred and fifteen at the last count."

Alan said, "We must follow the Despot's wish to make them feel as welcome as possible without releasing them into the general countryside. I believe that we will see a reduction here soon if present trends continue. Plus, Japhses, conditions across the border are ripe for us to try and re-establish the spy network again. I know it became increasingly difficult once hostilities broke out."

"You're right, I'm working on it."

"Good. With things changing over there we need to know."

The rest of the meeting was taken up with domestic issues of minor import. When it was over, Alan and Japhses continued their conversation in private.

With a frown on his face, the general asked if there was something extra the senators had not been told. He knew Alan too well and suspected he was hiding something.

"Naa..." he replied at first, then he considered the matter further. "Except that I do have concerns about the Neo-Purples. Most of the Hoame military advisors and trainers came from Ephamon and they've been sent back home now. I found myself sidelined and eventually chose to leave. The Neo-Purples want to be self-sufficient, that's for sure, and our presence (only known about within certain circles) was an embarrassment to them."

"So they've discarding us now that we've given them help?"

"We've helped them with training, advice and matériel. I hope they remember that, even as they choose to go it alone!"

"They should recognise the debt they owe us," the general declared firmly.

"You're right, but these political types are a strange lot."

"Ladosans in general, surely."

"There *are* some good ones."

"Hmm... have casualties been high?"

"Sure have. I know that some of our countrymen have rejoiced in that, but the Despot warned me not to think that way. He said that history teaches that countries generally rise from the ashes of a civil war far stronger. And with an army of experienced veterans who suddenly find themselves out of a job. They haven't reached that stage yet, of course, but I believe that there are grounds for concern looking at the future. A Neo-Purple victory certainly would be the best outcome Hoame-wise, but even then I wouldn't trust them fully."

"Never trust a Ladosan!" Japhses spelt out his philosophy.

"Yet I've made one or two connections there. I hope that, if it came to it, I can use them to see sense prevailing."

"A bloody business, war."

"Yeah. I had an interesting conversation with one fellow about his time in the previous war, against us. He knew that I was from Hoame, at least I think he did, but he was recollecting life under siege as if I hadn't been involved myself."

"You and I will never forget it," the general said. "In the winter, all that snow, the damp, the cold..."

"And the ash that came down on us from the volcano to add to our misery. Yeah, you're right. But this was seeing it from their perspective. I forgot which town he was in, but they were facing starvation shortly before our withdrawal came. He said it was like living in hell. Gangs roamed the streets and broke into houses where they suspected the residents were hoarding food. Folk were reduced to walking skeletons. The rich exchanged their possessions for a measure of corn smuggled into the town. They'd shut themselves into the darkest corner of the house to devour it before anyone could take it from them. Friends and relatives robbed each other for food. All social order broke down and people turned on each other like frasses. All reason and decorum was lost in their desperate plight. A woman would sell herself for a crust of bread. Meanwhile, dead bodies of the weakest lined the street."

"If we'd known they were in such a state, we could have stormed their strongholds."

"I don't think the Ladosan situation was as desperate where we were in the south."

"And the present conflict?"

"We besieged Wesold and..."

"The Neo-Purples, you mean."

"Of course. They besieged the town for a long time before the Buffs capitulated. Things were pretty grim there too, but with few civilians present, there were not the same number of mouths to feed. Still, as someone once said, all war is hell."

"That's for certain," came the general's earnest reply.

Frank slept extremely well on his first night at the Schloss. He woke early and found Hannah still sound asleep beside him. Quickly bored, he got up gently, washed and dressed.

Creeping out of their suite, no one else was about. Unlike Heisler's castle, this residence had a simple layout and he quickly found the stairs leading down to the main living room.

All was quiet except for a single male voice in the distance. As he got closer, he recognised it as Despot Schmidt's. He needed to get closer before could he make out the words.

"...With this shipment of goods arriving next week, we will expect payment within the next fortnight as per our agreement. Moreover, we... oh, hello Frank!"

The visitor had not intended to intrude, but the door to the speaker's office was wide open and he was easily spotted. A scribe was in attendance and was having a business letter dictated to him. Frank made his excuses and retreated to the other end of the large lounge area. From there he could overlook the lake.

With the sun on the ascendant, its light was shining on the rippling waters. The temperature at this early hour was pleasantly warm.

Schmidt quickly concluded his business for the day and swept through to join Frank. As he spoke, his tone was almost apologetic.

"I have to dictate; my writing is not fine enough."

Frank thought this was a strange thing to say. He was sure that many despots employed scribes. A good scribe would know how to set out and edit a letter, there was more to it than merely putting down the words as they were spoken. He tried to put his host at ease.

"I've only recently employed a secretary myself, Tristan, who is in my party here. Hannah says it is high time I did so and reckons the standard of Thyatiran communications will rise as a result."

These words had the desired effect and Schmidt relaxed noticeably. Picking up a new thread, he pointed to the lake and said, "I thought we could go out on the water this afternoon."

"I am entirely in your hands."

"And we'll go for a walk after breakfast, show you some of the local flora. Rudella is good with that. Back here for lunch, followed by a siesta, then out in the boats late afternoon. How does that sound?"

"It sounds wonderful! I'm sure we'll enjoy that a lot."

It was not long after this that the rest of the guests surfaced. Before they knew it, they were led through to a large dining room for the most sumptuous breakfast ever. The choice was amazing: full cooked meal, croissants and huge bowls of strawberries and mandarin segments in syrup. All was neatly laid out in spotlessly clean surroundings.

"I simply must try some of the fruit," Hannah declared.

"Me too!" exclaimed Joseph excitedly.

Despotess Rudella was late, but her husband bid them start, so they did. Frank liked to keep tabs on his fellow guests. Deejan Charvo and family were tucking in, some locals engaging them in conversation as they did so. Freidhelm was at Frank's table, but said little as he ate.

"After breakfast," began Schmidt, "I am expecting Councillor Arrandeck to join us for the day. I appointed him at the end of last year and he is proving invaluable to me."

"I look forward to meeting him," Frank replied cordially. He was thinking what to add when Rudella made her entrance. She sported another interesting hat on that morning, a navy blue tricorn with a red flower attached to the front. Again she had a group of servants in attendance around her. Her warm smile was still in evidence.

"I hope that you slept well, Frank, Hannah?"

They assured her of their good night and soon the despotess was beside them, tucking into breakfast.

"I understand," began Hannah, "that we will be going for a walk after we're finished here."

"A good idea to set off early in my view," the hostess replied.

"You try to avoid being outside during the hottest time of the day?"

"Always, this time of year."

Following the meal, the party gathered together in a group in the lobby. Hats were being put on and last minute preparations made, ready for their perambulation. Then Councillor Arrandeck appeared and was introduced to them.

Frank estimated his age round about the sixty mark, a little on the old side for a new confidante. Of average height, his huge belly stuck out in front of him.

"Greetings, Your Excellency, it is indeed an honour you bestow on us by your presence."

The visitor was getting tired of trying to get the Capparathians to be less formal. The Schmidts alone seemed to be complying with this request. So he merely expressed his delight at being there and his eager anticipation to see more of the countryside.

Soon the party was underway. Double-file, they snaked along the path. Tristan wondered if he should stay close to his employer, but the despot families were sticking together and chatting away. He therefore settled in with Deejan Charvo and his family, some fifty metres back in the procession.

At the front, the chief guests were enjoying the unfamiliar landscape. The sandy path took them between craggy rocks with overhanging creeper. The undergrowth possessed many plants not found in Thyatira. Some were long and thin, with leaves stretching up a metres. They passed twisted trees with silver bark, four to five metres high with narrow trunks. One or two areas they passed by had seen fires in the recent past. Already green shoots were springing up through the blackness. Councillor Arrandeck noticed the visiting Keeper staring at the flora and commented, "It behoves all the curious in our understanding of nature."

"Um, yes."

"Despot Schmidt is, of course, keen to patronise the scientific community."

"Is he?"

"Oh yes. Our botanists are currently cataloguing all the different species of plants in Capparathia. A large project, as you may imagine, it is seen as a first step to a better understanding of nature."

"I see."

They walked a little while before entering a clearing, around the edges of which were benches. Sitting on the ones on the eastern side, shaded by the trees, they continued talking while servants brought forth water to quench their thirst.

When he took on the role of despot, Schmidt had been told by Frank in no uncertain terms that support for the local Church was a firm duty. He now made clear his commitment.

"I have been funding the building of new churches and training of clergy. I hope to arrange a meeting for you with local church representatives later in your visit. They will affirm my support, I'm sure."

"I'm pleased to hear it, Norbert, well done."

Rudella then chipped in, "And we have been championing the cause of whites here in Capparathia. Schools and hospitals are being built for them."

They knew how to keep Keeper Thorn sweet, for these were both causes dear to their guest's heart. Rudella even went so far as to say she had begun reading a Bible.

"I thought I'd start at the back, to see how it ends. So I am reading Revelations now. I can't say it is the easiest of compositions to understand."

"I'm not surprised!" Frank exclaimed. "I would not advise that for starters."

"Oh!" exclaimed the despotess, looking a bit taken aback.

"Some parts of the Bible are easier to follow than others. If I may be so bold, I would suggest starting with the Gospel according to St. Mark. That's a good place to begin. It might help if you have a chaplain to help you with the interpretation."

"A chaplain?"

"A priest to guide you and help you to understand it. Not everything can be taken at face value. That having been said, it is the most exciting book to read. I'm sure you'll enjoy it once you get into it."

Before long the trek was recommenced, but it was heading back to the Schloss by another route. It was important for them to get there before the hot weather struck and they managed this. A light lunch was followed by a siesta for them all. Activity at the despot's residence apart from a few guards and servants ground to a halt as they took a rest from the worst heat of the day. It reminded him of an incident a quarter of a century earlier on the planet Columbus. Following the first election, everyone at Brok Oblonski's mansion slept in the next day. He had likened it to the enchanted castle in *Sleeping Beauty*. On this occasion, Frank was happy for a rest and Hannah soon joined in. She found herself nodding off after a while, despite her anticipation for their afternoon trip on the water.

They woke up in good time for the afternoon excursion. The schedule of events was a relaxed one. Hannah's feelings regarding the boat trip were as nothing compared with Joseph, who got overexcited at the prospect of going onto the lake. He had to be told off before he eventually calmed down a degree.

A flotilla of boats set off from the jetty near the Schloss. Of modest size and shallow draft, each was fitted with an awning to provide shade. The two despot families were huddled in the leading vessel along with a crew and attendants. Joseph asked lots of questions and tried reaching down to touch the water, but his arm was not long enough.

"Careful, sit down!" his mother directed.

There was no cooling breeze and despite it being past the hottest part of the day, it was still extremely warm. The boats were of an improved design to those Frank and Hannah had been in the previous occasion. These new ones had masts for sails, not currently in use, and stations for crew members to use their oars to propel the craft. Silently they glided along. The guests were enjoying the scene before them. The far shore was out of sight and they stuck fairly near the right-hand bank.

Schmidt explained, "Beyond the horizon, where the lake ends, is the impenetrable desert signifying the southernmost border of Hoame. Nothing grows out there in that inhospitable place."

Looking at the other, nearby boats, Frank asked, "Is Councillor Arrandeck not joining us for the trip?"

"I'm afraid he could not. Urgent business to attend to."

"Oh."

"Of course I brought in all new advisors since the autumn of '17. It seemed to be the right thing to do."

"Have a fresh start, you mean?"

"A new beginning, precisely."

Joining in, Rudella was eager to praise her husband's achievements. "As well as supporting the Church, my husband is a patron of the arts and sciences. He is a busy man."

"I can tell," Frank replied, matching the woman's smile.

"So it is nice for us to take time off to receive our honoured guests."

Hannah said warmly, "And we are having a fabulous time taking in all these sights which are so different from back home."

"We sure are!" cried Joseph, much to everyone's amusement.

That night, the boy asked his father to tell him a story before he went to bed. It was an unusual request, but Frank found a recollection come into his head, a tale from the late twentieth century he had been told as a child. It was about a man back on old earth and was supposed to be true. He hoped it was.

"There was once a man who led a bad life and got himself into a great deal of trouble. He owed money to some nasty people and he was due to pay them back or face the consequences. Unable to get the money by legitimate means, he decided to steal it from his employer. He obtained a duplicate key to the safe and, on a Friday evening when no one else was looking, he took out the money he needed so desperately. Immediately he had done so, he realised that he had left his fingerprints all over everything."

"Fingerprints?"

Following an explanation, Frank continued, "He was in a quandary. He felt he had to take the money, or else the nasty men would kill him. There was no other way he could raise the funds in so short a time. Then a plan came into his mind. He took a lot more money, in fact all the money that was in the safe..."

"All of it?"

"All of it."

"Was it a lot then?"

"A large amount, yes. He took it and, with a friend, went to a casino, a gambling house. He was not allowed in himself, so..."

"Why?"

"Um, I can't quite remember, I think he's had an argument or something with them before and was not allowed in. Anyway, his friend went in with strict instructions. He was to put it all on a bet with a 50/50 odds. If he won, the man would pay back the money he'd taken, pay his debts and keep the rest. If he lost..."

Here he hesitated so long that Joseph had to ask what the other alternative was.

"He'd made up his mind to kill himself. He even worked out how to do it."

"How?" asked the curious boy.

"Walk into the sea and drown himself. So the bet was made,... and he won! He was so relieved that he stuck to his intentions and kept what was left over. It was still a great deal of..."

"Did he give his friend any?"

"I'm not sure, I expect so. Anyway, the "theft" was never discovered, because he paid it all back straightaway before the loss could be discovered, He went into business himself and set up a successful company which employed a lot of people. He gave money to good causes and became a pillar of the community. His life was completely turned round and he never gambled again in his life."

"That's good," Joseph announced seriously.

"He married and had children and led a long and worthwhile life. No one knew how he started his business until shortly before he died. He was dying of cancer and told the whole story to his son. No one had any idea of the previous life of this man honoured by society."

"So what's the moral of the story?"

Frank hesitated. In real life not every story has a moral. However, he quickly found one as he answered, "That sometimes God can bring good out of a bad situation."

Fortunately that satisfied the boy, but it left Frank wondering why in heaven he chose this story to tell. It had simply been on his mind and it seemed like a good idea. The tale had been told to him as a boy and it always struck him as crazy how the man's life hung in the balance on a 50/50 bet. If it gone the other way... In any case, Joseph was going off to sleep now.

A while later, Frank and Hannah lay awake in bed, discussing how the day had gone.

"They're certainly trying to impress us," Hannah declared.

"Of course," he relied, "but then they've got some pretty amazing scenery to show us."

"That rock formation in the desert..."

"The pointing hand?"

"Yes, coming straight out of the sand as if a colossus was buried underground and sticking his arm out into the air."

"We could see it in the far distance, I wonder what it looks like closer up. The bleakness of that desert; an ochre sea as far as you can see. With that heat haze..."

"But I was more thinking of other things, " she said, "Trying to impress us with his patronage of the arts, supporting the Church, the whites... all that kind of thing."

"Don't you believe them?"

"Let's just say it would be nice to hear what the common folk around here have to say."

"I don't suppose we'll get the chance to hear."

"I'll be interested," she continued, "to hear what Darda, Paul and the others have to say when were eventually reunited for the return journey."

"Don't let's start thinking about returning yet, we're going to be here a while. Freidhelm enjoyed the boat trip, but he won't be with us for tomorrow's sightseeing. He's getting down to trade talks with his opposite number. While we enjoy our holiday, he'll be doing some hard negotiating."

With a giggle, Hannah replied, "A senator's work is never done."

"Well, he'll have to run it past me in any case before any deal is signed off. I get the impression that the Capparathians are bending over backwards to be accommodating. So there's every hope of a good, renewed and enlarged trade deal. That would help our economy."

"Let's hope so. Personally I'm looking forward to a ride out into the wilderness tomorrow. I wonder what we'll see."

Deejan Charvo and his family had enjoyed their day too. The children devoured a huge breakfast which included experimenting with several kinds of fruit not encountered before. They ate at a table with Tristan, Freidhelm and several other Thyatiran clerks. There were many more local court members milling about getting their food.

Having been told by his father it was rude for a man to wear a hat indoors, Sebastian found it curious that one of the Capparathians, a thirty-ish, skinny man, was sporting a cloth cap. No other male headwear was to be seen. He whispered to Keturah next to him, "Why do you think he's wearing that?"

"I dunno," she came back. "Probably forgot he had it on."

"Yeah, but..."

"Why don't you ask him?"

She made the suggestion in jest, so she was not pleased when her brother immediately got up and strode over to the man as he scooped orange segments into his bowl.

"Excuse me," came the rather loud question, "but why are you wearing your hat indoors? Is it a local custom?"

Hesitating but briefly, the man replied, "No; this is why," and he removed his headgear momentarily to reveal a large, ugly growth on his head. Sebastian was frozen to the spot, wishing the ground would open up and swallow him up there and then. The local popped his hat back on, finished getting his breakfast and went back to his table without either a glance or another word.

Red-faced, the young man returned to his seat. Keturah had been the sole witness to the incident and gasped at the sight. The other people at her table stopped talking and looked at her.

"Are you all right?" asked her father.

"I'm okay, it's nothing," she responded, playing it down.

Her tone-of-voice had a note of finality about it and those who had stared at her quickly lost interest and got on with their breakfasts. Sebastian returned to the table, but it was only later, when the pair were alone, that they could talk about it.

"How could you do such a thing?" she asked accusingly.

"I was curious," he responded defensively, "how was I to know he was hiding a deformity?"

Keturah pulled a face, but there was no point in pursuing the matter. Soon they were venturing out again, part of a group on a guided walk. The visitors were being shown a local beauty spot and advanced along a path with thick, tropical growth on either side. There was much to take in by way of flora and fauna unknown to the northerners.

"Where's Keturah gone?" Sebastian asked, more to himself than anyone else. He stopped and let the rest of the party go past before peering back down the track.

There, in a small glade they passed through, his sister was standing. She was bent forward, staring intently at something on the ground. The rest of them walked on to the viewing point a hundred metres further up, to see the valley scene. He, though, went back to see what she was up to.

"What are yer looking at?"

"Look at these ants!" she cried, her tone one of awe.

The insects were certainly a lot bigger than their counterparts back home. Further, they were carrying fragments of leaf across the path and into the undergrowth. Scores of them were visible at any one time, scurrying back and forth, seemingly with great urgency. Sebastian caught the mood and was soon watching them as intently as his sister.

"See that one?" she asked, pointing downwards, "it's got a piece of leaf far bigger than itself."

"Busy little fellows, aren't they?"

It was a mesmerising sight and the two spent a long time simply staring at the busy insects. Eventually they decided to leave them to their work and catch up with the others.

"I'm glad we came here," Keturah said warmly and unconsciously grabbed the other's arm.

"Yeah, I know father's enjoying it too."

"Not sure I'd want to actually live here though."

"Oh?"

"Too hot!"

"Phew, yeah."

"But there are lots of amazing places to visit. The folk seem friendly too."

"Apart from that man with the growth on his head!"

"I saw what happened. That was your own silly fault."

"I guess you're right," he conceded.

"After all," she continued, "I did warn you not to."

With a sigh he conceded, "Yeah, no one to blame but myself. I should listen to you in future."

"That's right, a lesson well learnt!" she declared and playfully pulled his arm.

~ End of Chapter 15 ~

Prospects of Peace - Chapter 16

Another warm morning and Frank did not hang about, but got up before Hannah stirred.

A number of servants were scuttling around at that early hour, making sure everything was ready for breakfast. Moving out onto the veranda, he found himself alone. There was a slight, welcome breeze.

'I wouldn't mind the temperature being like this at midday,' he considered. 'Goodness knows how hot it will be by then.'

The sun was a short way beneath the horizon, but its rays were playing on the underneath of several layers of thin cloud. They were a bright pink hue against a pale blue background. He was happy simply to watch the colours develop as they enveloped the entire clouds and became a slightly deeper shade. The sounds of the efficient servants in the background he ignored, but then a different noise came to his ears.

'That's Freidhelm... and Tristan,' he worked out from their distinctive accents. Although not as strong as the native Thyatiran dialect, it still sounded different from the locals here in the south.

"Good morning, My Lord," they greeted him as he re-entered the room.

Soon Hannah, Joseph and the rest joined them and they sat down together. Frank noticed that the guests were all sitting together, apart from the Capparathians. He did not like that, they should be mixing more.

"Something the matter, darling?"

"Oh, it's nothing," he replied to his wife, side-stepping the issue. It was best mentioned another time.

"I'm going to have some of the strawberries this morning," she declared "they're quite outstanding."

"Yes, both quantity and quality. Look at the size of those bowls!"

They collected their food. Frank looked round, not finding his host present yet. He was sure the Schmidts would enter soon.

Joseph was eating a cooked breakfast and his father asked, "How are you getting on with your story?" Faced with a puzzled expression, he added, "You said that you were going to write an adventure story about Methane Man."

Pulling a face, the lad replied dismissively, "No, I couldn't be bothered to do any more."

"Oh," went Frank, somewhat taken aback, "so how much did you write?"

"About a page... almost."

It was not worth pursuing, so instead he asked Tristan, sitting diagonally opposite, how he was enjoying the trip.

"To be honest, My Lord, I've felt at a bit of a loose end."

"I thought you'd make the most of an opportunity simply to rest and take it all in."

Tristan looked a bit guilty, for he knew that he should be appreciating an expenses paid vacation. He had expected to be involved in bi-lateral talks between the two regional rulers. In the event, both despots seemed more disposed to sight-seeing than anything else. 'Is there something wrong with me, because I can't simply relax and enjoy a pleasant time?' Eventually he replied unconvincingly, "Of course, the scenery is beautiful."

Then Freidhelm said, "My Lord, maybe Tristan would like to attend the trade negotiations with me today. I could do with the extra support."

Seeing Tristan perk up at this suggestion, Frank gave his consent. If the young man would prefer to sit round a table discussing business instead of sightseeing, why stand in his way? Meanwhile, Freidhelm went up in the despot's estimation. Not to be jealous of his role was a sign of maturity and Frank appreciated that.

The place was full now of people either getting or eating their meals. A loud chatter of voices filled the room. Scanning round once more for his host, Frank spotted two male servants assisting a blind courtier to a table. One was holding a plate piled high with cooked food which looked like an awful lot to consume for breakfast. Then belatedly he spotted the Schmidts homing in on where he was sitting. Norbert Schmidt was sporting a khaki outfit which looked the part for their upcoming desert excursion. Rudella was in a magenta ensemble, with gossamer sleeves and a conical hat so tall that Frank wondered if she would poke a few holes in the ceiling.

"Ah, Frank, we're a little late, my apologies."

"Not at all, the chief guest replied, standing up, "we haven't long started our breakfast."

There was a scraping of chairs on the floor and Frank looked round to see that Tristan and Freidhelm were leaving the table to make room for the Schmidts. The hosts smiled as they sat down and servants brought them some food.

"It's going to be another hot one," Norbert announced. "We will be taking plenty of water and shelters. Please make sure you keep well hydrated. You need to sip little and often. If you feel a headache coming on it's probably dehydration - try not to get to that point. With a few sensible precautions we can all have a good time."

They listened to this sage advice from someone who knew what they were talking about. The guests were resolved to try to keep it. The explanation continued, "We will travel south by wagon and, from a vantage point, we can gaze out across the desert. We will get closer than we were the other day. You might not think it much to look at, at first, but it has a mesmerising quality, I think you'll find."

Frank could have reminded him that they had visited Capparathia on a previous occasion, but it did not seem right to. The man was clearly proud of what his despotate had to offer and it was only kind to respond positively to such enthusiasm.

Before long they were piling into wagons and setting off. The vehicles possessed awnings, but were designed so that the travellers could still see out the sides. The dakks wore little shades over their heads. These were supported by spokes coming up from their collars. The visitors had never seen such a thing before, but it seemed an efficient arrangement to keep direct sunlight off the beasts' heads.

While Rudella engaged Hannah in conversation, Norbert had something on his mind that he wanted to discuss with Frank.

"Is it true what they say: that you have banned capital punishment in Thyatira?"

He spoke with an air of surprise and Frank knew that it was an unprecedented move within Hoame.

"It is true," came the reply. "I'm not asking other despots to follow suit. I'm not even setting myself up as an example. It simply seemed the right thing to do."

"I see," the other man said slowly as if trying to take it in.

"I've watched executions in the past, since I first became despot. It's not a pretty sight."

"No."

"I suppose it came to a head when..." and here he lowered his voice so it was barely audible amid the creaks and clattering of the wagon "... one of Hannah's friends was convicted."

"Of murder?"

"Well, planning her husband's murder, yes. I couldn't bring myself to sanction the death penalty. Then it didn't seem right to have one law for the privileged members of society and a different one for the others."

"Yet our society is uneven, it always has been."

"Naturally, but it seems only fair that the same punishment should apply for the same crime."

"So what sanction are you imposing instead?"

"Life imprisonment."

"I see. You see that as more humane?"

"Um, I could try to take the moral high ground and say yes, but that wouldn't be honest. Between you and me, I did it to please my wife, in the case of this woman. After that I continued the policy for consistency's sake. I am not entirely convinced it is a lot more humane."

"How so?"

"Well, is it humane to keep someone locked up for the rest of their lives without hope of release? Our law and order senator is keen on his chain gangs, so many of the prisoners do get to breathe the outside air... but psychologically... knowing that they will never ever be released? Never be free..."

"Which would you choose?" asked Schmidt.

"Between life imprisonment and execution?"

"Yes."

"In respect of myself?"

"Yes."

"I'd choose life, of course. We have but one life and we all want it to go on as long as possible. Only someone mentally unstable wants to die."

"And how is the policy working out?"

"How do you mean?"

"Are there more murders now?"

"Now there's no longer the death penalty as a deterrent? I'm not sure, it hasn't been in force long enough to tell. I doubt it will have any effect though: if you murder someone in anger, or out of jealousy or hatred, I don't think you stop to consider the legal sanction that is going to apply. You're well past that stage."

With a smile, Schmidt replied, "You're probably right."

"Plus, from the religious perspective, there is always the possibility of repentance."

"In gaol you mean? That's true, I hadn't thought of that. If someone is executed they probably have little time for remorse."

The despotess' conversation had concluded by this point. Rudella asked her husband what he and Frank were discussing.

"Um, not a nice subject."

"Tell me!" she demanded, her tone amused and playful.

"Murder... and whether one would be put off committing it by the knowledge it's a capital offence."

With a straight face, Rudella asked, "And who is it you're thinking of murdering?"

The men merely laughed at this and the conversation fizzled out at that point.

No signs of any clouds now and the sun beat down. Rudella was not wearing her hat inside the wagon which was just as well as it might have poked through the awning. A servant was fanning her and Hannah positioned herself to catch some of the residual airflow. Norbert reminded them to keep drinking and belatedly Frank took a couple of large swigs.

The road was made of crushed white stones, over which a thin layer of sand had blown over since it was last swept. It was not the worst of surfaces, at least there were no potholes. Either side was a sandy view with tall cacti at irregular intervals and the odd spinograss clumps. In the middle distance rocky outcrops sprung up.

Arriving at a small oasis, they were informed that this was to be their stopping point for lunch. The excursionists stayed on board the wagons until the servants finished preparing tables under canopies amongst the few palm trees.

"Gosh it's hot!" Hannah stated the obvious as they took the few steps to the sheltered tables.

The others were soon engaged in animated conversation as they awaited the food, but Frank took the opportunity to look around. From his position he could see into the distance, but a couple of metres away was an old wooden bench with slats painted dark green.

No one else was paying it much attention, let alone sitting on it. The paint was peeling off, exposing white wood underneath. Dozens of tiny flies we alighting on the pale areas. They would walk around briefly, then take off as one, before landing again on the same patches. The white parts must have held an attraction for them. It was intriguing to watch and he would have drawn it to the attention of the others if they had not been wrapped up in their discussions.

Back to the tables, he noticed that his knife was outside the shade of the canopy. He went to move it slightly as it was been laid at a slight angle. His hand recoiled in pain, for it seemed red hot exposed to the direct rays of the sun. He gave a little yelp, but, looking up, was pleased to see that no one had noticed his foolishness.

Joseph, he noticed, was being served and was concentrating on the food set before him. Soon they were all eating away and the conversation was light and relaxed. Frank was keen to hear what the schedule was for the rest of the day. Either they had not been told earlier, or he had not been paying attention. Fortunately, Norbert took this opportunity to tell him.

"We will rest in the wagons after the meal, then late afternoon we will proceed to the viewing platform to look over the desert. There is a concert arranged for the evening and... "

"A concert, here?" asked Frank, much surprised.

"Here in the oasis, yes. It is a perfect setting."

"How lovely."

"We will need to wrap up a bit late evening, before the chill sets in."

"I was forgetting it gets cold at night," stated the visitor.

"Indeed. The temperature drops swiftly once the sun is down. That's why I suggested shawls for the ladies to wear at the concert."

The rest of the day went largely according to plan. Following the siesta, they made their way to the platform to behold the panoramic view of the desert. To the best of Frank's knowledge, there was a wide band of desert around the whole planet either side of the equator. No one had ever tried to cross it and its effect was to keep both hemispheres separate. The former interstellar traveller had no idea whether the southern half of Molten was inhabited at all.

The scene shimmered in the distance from the heat haze. The air here was extremely dry and they made sure they kept topped up with water. There was no growth in this region, not so much as a cactus.

One or two rocky outcrops protruded, the most striking of which was the fist-like crag which Frank and Hannah discussed earlier. Slate-grey, it was north of their current position and stuck out of the sand ocean.

"Could anyone live out there?" asked Joseph.

"Not for long," replied his mother. "Fascinating to look at, but a terrible place to stay."

That evening, the guests of honour sat on comfortable chairs with their opposite numbers to watch a torch-lit concert back at the oasis. The rest of the audience stood behind them. While he recognised it as classical music, Frank had not heard any of the pieces before. It was not quite his thing, but he enjoyed watching the performers as much as anything. He was amused when he glanced over at Rubella who was concentrating hard on the performance. As she did so, her tongue was sticking out and playing with her top lip.

Following several pieces played by the entire ensemble, there were a couple of solo performances. The first was by a young man on a bowed instrument. Most of the audience was in raptures, but to Frank's ears it was a mess. More than a few notes were completely off key. He glanced over to Hannah who gave him a fleeting grimace before turning back. Joseph was sitting between them, fast asleep. A second soloist, a woman on a keyboard, was far more accomplished.

"That was a bit different," was Hannah's softly-spoken assessment as the applause died down at the concert's conclusion.

"It certainly was," her husband replied.

It was getting late and the VIPs returned to their wagons for the night. Joseph was woken up so that he could go to bed. Then Frank found himself wide awake and was happy to go for a wander around the perimeter of the oasis with Schmidt. While the servants cleared up, the musicians put their paraphernalia away and the guests retired, the two men walked and talked. The light of the torches fanned out into what otherwise would have been an inky dark night as only those on Molten know.

"Thank you for a memorable day, Norbert."

"I'm glad you've enjoyed it."

"We have... and I can see what a huge effort has been put into everything today."

"If you've had a good time, then it was all worth it."

316

When he eventually did retire, Frank lay in reflective mood. 'All this effort put in for me more than anyone else! It has been an extraordinary time since I landed on the planet. Let's see, we are in 2621 now, so I've been on Molten nineteen years now. That's longer than I was on Marmaris and considerably longer than my thirteen years on Eden. I can remember when the thought of the twenty-seventh century was a novelty, now we're in the third decade. I remember being on the planet Gan for the turn-of-the-century party. Pastor Robert, Hal Pascoe - where are they now, I wonder. Where are they now?'

Back in Thyatira, Alan was making sure things were running smoothly. Attending all the senate meetings, he led with a firm, but effortless style. Emil was still fully occupied with the Norland acquisition. Elsewhere there were no known crises on the horizon.

Late one morning, Alan was making his way back to the Castle following a brief visit to the senate building. He did not go the most direct route. With little on his schedule for the day, he chose to walk through a small wood. Summer here was warm, but not too hot. The green of the trees still looked fresh and there was a dappled light through the leaves. A few insects, including a large dragonfly, went past and birds sung in the trees.

As he approached the entrance to the Castle wall, a waiting servant ran out to meet him.

"Alan, you have a visitor. Baron L'Rochfort is here to see you, along with a drone."

The Castle resident drone wondered what this deputation from the Capital meant, but the Inner Council Member was quick to put his mind at rest.

"Merely a flying visit. I needed to see Despot Lovonski and thought that I may as well come the extra distance to see you. I realise that Frank is away at present, but I thought it would be good to catch up."

"Sure."

"But first I'd like to introduce Raymond here."

The two drones exchanged greetings, the one from Ephamon coming across as effeminate in his manner.

L'Rochfort explained, "Raymond has something he wishes to discuss with you in any case."

"Okay. Let's go into the Throne Room. It's nice and cool in there. Do you want refreshments?"

"We've just eaten, thank you."

Once settled in the small chamber, Alan asked the Baron how things were in the Inner Council.

"Much the same," came the answer. "Count Wonstein continues to plot. It's the usual manoeuvrings, but we may need to do something about him one day."

Alan did not press the Keeper for further explanation and soon it was Raymond's turn to speak.

"We've been most pleased with the surfacing work your Thyatiran workmen have done in the area surrounding the Citadel. Yet it is some years since the last repairs were affected. Through natural wear and tear several cracks have appeared and some holes are forming now. We need some remedial work done sooner rather than later, preferably before the autumn."

"That shouldn't be a problem," Alan informed him and a price for the work was sorted out there and then. He would delegate the task that afternoon.

Inevitably, though, the topic of Ladosa was discussed between L'Rochfort and Alan. The man from the Capital gave an overview from the Inner Council's perspective.

"The fighting appears to have stopped. I know for a fact that the Neo-Purples and the Rose have signed a truce. Faced with that united front, the Buffs are going to have to pay attention. Every effort is being made to set up a negotiating table and get down to the business of securing a peace."

"Good. Japhses' spies are reporting a succession of hostilities in the southwest of the country, but it's still proving difficult to obtain information further afield. I haven't heard from Charlotta since I got back, neither from my contacts in Isson, near their capital."

"I am more optimistic of a lasting peace within Ladosa than at any time since the troubles began. I gather that the central Buffs had the stuffing knocked out of them by that fireball landing on top of them."

"While their south-western counterparts were defeated by our allies, the Neo-Purples."

"Hmm," L'Rochfort responded thoughtfully. "I hope that they show their gratitude in the coming season and beyond. We put ourselves out for them and they should realise their indebtedness to us. I know that you have your concerns in this regard."

"Too right! I felt I had to leave after feeling sidelined by them."

"I know. I was debriefed by Captain Wulf upon his return."

"And I do wonder how good their memory will be. Our assistance tipped the balance against their enemies and they should not forget it."

They discussed this some more and the Keeper talked about them sending an envoy, but did not suggest Alan. He realised that the drone had had enough, concluding, "I hope that Field Marshal Nazaz is not too busy to receive them. We have heard nothing from her the last few weeks."

"Me neither," replied Alan, who still wondered at the bond between himself and the Ladosan woman. Charlotta had told him she loved him, but was that pillow talk? Quickly dismissing these thoughts, he chose to go off at a tangent.

"During all the time I was there, during the war, I mean, I only ever saw one Ladosan official in national costume. Baggy trousers and a thousand different, bright colours, it was quite a sight."

"Yes, a funny lot those Ladosans."

It was the stock judgement of Hoamen on their northern neighbours and concluded the topic of conversation. The Keeper then passed on a piece of domestic news.

"The former Autarch's Palace burned down last week."

"The Autarch's Palace..." Alan repeated slowly as he recalled distant memories, "...that hasn't been used in a long time surely."

"It used to be employed for Inner Council meetings twenty or more years ago. But since the office was abolished it hasn't been utilised a great deal. I remember we held a conference there five, maybe six years ago. Following that, everyone said it should be used more, but it hasn't been. Now the entire building is gutted, a dreadful sight."

"What caused it?"

"They think it was a lightning strike. There was a brief, but violent downpour that night. It's the first rain we've experienced in several weeks and everything has got extremely dry."

"Ah, we're lucky here," Alan replied, "We've had showers at night which have kept the river levels topped up. Anyway, are they going to rebuild it?"

"The Autarch's Palace? No. We held a meeting last week and the decision was unanimous. It's a piece of our history gone, I suppose, but it wasn't used much and it would be a waste of resources to try and resurrect it."

They chatted some more, while Raymond sat there quietly and impassively, taking it all in. L'Rochfort explained that they would be leaving early the following morning and that is exactly what they did.

Alan felt buoyed up by the visit. It was good to be kept abreast of developments. The news from Ladosa certainly sounded optimistic. Had these people finally come to their senses?

He imagined Charlotta busying herself with political matters and important affairs of state. So when, the following day, he received a long love letter from her, it took him completely by surprise. After reading a bit of it in the Castle hall when it first arrived, he retreated upstairs to his room to take it in slowly.

"My dearest darling Alan, I will begin by telling you that I stood beside my bed this morning... I thought of you... the covers were warm by the light of the sun coming in through the east window... as I smoothed them with my hands, I thought to myself, 'Ohhh... I wish Alan were here!' I imagined how wonderful it would feel to crawl back into that nice warm bed and snuggle up into your arms my darling... I love laying naked beside you... our fingers gently exploring each other's bodies... looking into your eyes... touching your face... your hair... gently kissing.

"What would you like me to do next my love? You want to hear about what I did a little while ago? Oh... I will tell you my dearest love...

"I was alone. The house was so quiet. To be safe I locked the front door. Then I came here to my bedroom... I imagined music was playing softly and I imagined you sitting there on my bed... I remember that you enjoy watching me undress myself...

"I kick off my slip-on sandals and walk over to you... overjoyed that you are here... I bend and give you a quick soft kiss and my hand traced down your face, enjoying the feel of its contours... you turn slightly and kiss my palm... I smile and back away, reaching up to undo my hair... it falls around my shoulders and you realise what I am doing and you sit back against the pillows to enjoy the show... I begin to unbutton my blouse and you watch, mesmerised. I have a

320

bit of a hard time not running back to you to cover you with kisses, but I know how much you enjoy watching me undress. I slip my blouse off my shoulders and my hands run down my neck and lightly over the lace of my bra... there is a delicious tingling sensation as my fingertips brush lightly back and forth over my nipples. You begin to rise from the bed and I shake my head and motion for you to stay put and watch me. I lean back against the wall and I run one hand slowly up my leg... catching the hem of my skirt where it falls just above the knee and drawing my skirt upwards on that leg... past my thigh... until you catch a glimpse of my lace panties..."

There was a great deal more, getting increasingly erotic. The letter ended, "Mmm, warm and safe together... Forever... I love you my darling. Charlotta."

'Phew!' thought Alan, 'that wasn't what I expected.'

Folding the letter carefully, he was about to secrete it away when he stopped to smell it. The paper was heavily scented. He paused before finally putting it away somewhere safe. He was not at all sure what to do. He had thought the relationship was over, but she certainly did not want it to be. But what future could there be in it? Charlotta was tied up with Ladosan politics and his home was firmly in Thyatira. Life would be miserable for her at the Castle as it would be for him in Braskaton, or whatever other Ladosan town she wanted to settle in.

'But is this love?' he asked himself, not for the first time. 'Is she not merely using me for her own fantasies? I'm certainly not going to reply in like vein, it would only encourage her and be dishonest.'

He thought further about it in the days that followed. While he could not bring himself to destroy the letter, he would not be replying to it.

A further week went by in Capparathia with the Thyatiran contingent enjoying every day. There seemed to be no end of sights to be seen, both natural and man-made, and they learned a great deal about the social history of these parts.

The roasting hot weather continued and it was still fairly oppressive at bedtime. Hannah, while enjoying her visit in general, was finding it hard to sleep at night. She kept on having to move her head on the pillow, because it got hot so quickly. Frank was amused when the locals referred to the weather as being "quite warm" when to the

321

northerners it felt baking hot. Nevertheless, the guests were determined not to let the climate mar their enjoyment and rose above it.

Sabbath came round and the whole party attended church in a nearby village. The Schmidts' attitude towards the faith appeared ambiguous. Rudella appeared interested in it, if on a superficial level. Norbert seemed to look upon it as a necessary duty if he was going to retain the patronage and goodwill of Keeper Thorn.

The service was a quiet one and not dissimilar to some held back in Thyatira. Frank was intrigued to see a trio of white nuns attending and afterwards engaged one, a short lady of about sixty, in conversation. She seemed keen to sing the local ruler's praises.

"Despot Schmidt is a great patron of the Church. He has encouraged ecclesiastical building and the observance of the Sabbath. He has even reduced taxes for blacks who come to worship."

'That's one way to get them to come!' thought Frank.

"Yes, My Lord, he has taken a heavy yoke from off our backs." This was clearly a reference to the previous Despot Schonhost, but she dare not criticise a black, particularly a high-ranking one, out loud. "He is also a patron of the arts."

"Really?"

"He is, encouraging music, painting and sculpture amongst other things."

A glowing reference indeed. Frank made as if to leave, but the nun was eager to raise a theological point with him. Although not particularly in the mood for such a discussion, he did not want to appear rude. Glancing up, he saw his family engaged in conversation in another part of the building with the Schmidts. He faced the nun alone.

"Consider this matter, if you will, My Lord. I was recalling the admirable reply of one of the saints when asked which he would rather do: convert sinners, or console our Lord."

The woman hesitated, but Frank had no intention of interjecting. He let her complete her point.

"'If it was a matter of choice,' the saint is reported to have said, 'then I would console our Lord.' Is that not a marvellous reply? With the saints, God always comes first, with others man comes first."

Frank knew that the easiest thing in the universe would be simply to agree with what the nun said, or even to say nothing and smile sweetly. The trouble was he disagreed so profoundly that he could in no way hold his tongue.

"Surely," he began, "the highest way would be to serve God by converting the sinners. If someone beside you in dying of thirst while you are reading the Psalms, you are not helping them and you are not honouring God. Give the dying person your water first and only then read your Bible. Otherwise your faith is a sham. You serve God by serving his creatures."

The nun's face went red and she did not look at all happy. Mercifully for both parties, the others caught up with them at this point and Frank could say goodbye and move on.

"An interesting discussion?" asked Hannah as they made their way out of the church.

"Um, it was different."

A slight frown flickered across her face before she decided to say something else. "They were showing us the architecture of this place while you were talking."

"Yes?"

"Did you know that it is over a hundred years old?"

"I didn't. It's big for a village."

"I should say no. The obvious question is how could the whites have afforded it? Apparently they had a mysterious benefactor, a Saint Hanasson who provided the funds. He was a white and left as mysteriously as he arrived, so the story goes. It is a popular legend around these parts."

"I can't say I've ever heard of him, ow!"

Frank exclaimed out loud due to misjudging a deep step on his way out and jarring his back. They were following close behind the Schmidts and Hannah did not want her husband to make a meal of it. "Don't make a fuss!" she whispered at him and he obeyed. As a result he soon forgot the discomfort to his spine.

"It's quite something, isn't it?" asked Rubella, turning round.

Hannah replied, "It a magnificent building, grander than any such ones in Thyatira."

"Is that so?" Rudella replied, obviously delighted.

"We are currently having a cathedral constructed, but that is a long way off completion and I'm not sure it will be as grand as this one."

It was the right answer, for the locals brimmed with pride over this unlikely architectural wonder.

That afternoon, Frank was shown another wonder of Capparathia, something altogether different and, a heathen might say, more practical.

The visitors were getting used to their siesta by now. All, that is, except Tristan who came out of his room early to find the Schloss completely devoid of life. He went through into the large, lounge area to see some men drawing up some wagons outside. Preferring not to be spotted, he scuttled back to his room.

A while later, the Thyatirans were lined up on the veranda with their hosts to see a demonstration outside.

"I want to show you these wagons. A group of our technicians have devised a more efficient, lighter design as I hope you'll see."

The vehicles did not look radically different from the standard Hoame ones. In fact Tristan was disappointed. He had wondered if they were like the smaller ones he managed to good effect in Ladosa. Nonetheless, once the demonstration started, he was as impressed as the rest of the observers.

One wagon went past at double the usual speed and was being pulled by a mere four dakks. Despot Schmidt enjoyed giving the commentary himself. "As you can see, unladen, we can dispense with the extra dakks. With a load of five hundred kilograms the vehicle can still be pulled by six."

The demonstration went on for some time and the guests were impressed to a man. Frank asked, "So are we allowed to ask the secret?"

"Arvawood is the secret, although there is no point in pretending it is a secret. That and a newly designed suspension system which gives a smoother, more comfortable ride."

'Not like Deejan's wagon that left me feeling sick!' thought Frank, who replied, "I'm not sure I've heard of arvawood."

"The arvan tree only grows in these parts and even here it is not prolific. Its timber is sturdy and extremely light. The trees grow exceptionally slowly, so we are having to manage them carefully."

Hannah said, "A most impressive demonstration."

Norbert replied, "We have four examples to give you."

"Are you sure?" asked Frank, who then thought it was a bit of a daft question. He had to say something.

"I am. You can take them back with you when you go, along with a team of six for each."

It was a most generous gesture, one fully appreciated. Frank mused, 'What with superdakks and extra-light wagons, I'll be the envy of all Hoame.' He then came up with the idea of granting Despot Schmidt a couple of superdakks, if the Mehtar would release them. He promised to speak to the foreign ruler and Schmidt was delighted at the idea.

The following morning they set off early for a day trip to the Malhall Valley. They travelled by conventional wagon to the place and it took most of the morning. Norbert let his wife explain.

"Recently some prospectors found gold here. Under Despot Schonhost, ninety percent of any such finds automatically becomes his property. But that was counter-productive, because it did not encourage people to try and find more. Norbert has wisely changed the law so that the finders keep a large percentage. Being mostly poor whites, even a modest find can mean a lot to them. As a result we've got something of a gold rush going on here this summer. There's limited room and we are having to restrict numbers."

"Something easier said than done," her husband added disarmingly.

"But it is attracting a lot of attention in these parts."

"I bet it is!" exclaimed Frank.

They arrived and exited the wagons into the full heat of the sun. Servants held parasols over the guests, but in any case they made their way to the shade of some nearby trees. It was hotter than ever, but the party was well prepared and even the guests were getting used to it by now.

An attendant brought Rudella's hat for her to put on. White, and rather like a mortar board, it was fully sixty centimetres square. 'That'll keep the sun off her,' thought Frank.

To be fair to the despotess, the others in the group donned headwear as protection from the sun coming through the branches. Their hats were not quite as ostentatious though.

Accompanied by several servants and a few soldiers, they worked their way down a track into the floor of a valley about three-quarters of a kilometre wide. Further down the track, the vegetation was more plentiful, with a large number of trees giving welcome shade. A two hundred and fifty metre wide river ran along the bottom. It was fairly shallow with sandy banks.

As they passed, Frank noticed a stack of thick logs. A large tree had been sawn up, piled neatly and then left. Over time the fierce sun bleached the wood.

Up ahead, another tree had fallen across the water and was providing a group of white children with a great place to play. They walked along the almost horizontal trunk and then jumped into the water which was a little deeper at that point. Norbert appeared slightly embarrassed by their presence until Frank pointed them out and commented cheerfully, "They're having fun!"

Moving upstream, they came to another area of activity, but this time it was adults panning for gold. Others were working at an assortment of contraptions slightly away from the riverbank. When they spotted their despot, the prospectors stopped what they were doing and bowed low. Upon receiving his master's sign, an officer accompanying the group told the locals to carry on. This they did and the VIP party watched them.

A black servant, who was a expert in the field, explained to the guests the various techniques being carried out. Norbert pointed as he added, "The geologists reckon that there is probably more in those cliffs. The gold is often found with quartz apparently and there is plenty of it there."

Hannah nodded, saying, "Yes, I can see a vein."

"And I am currently negotiating with Count Bodstein to see if we can order one of those steam-powered machines. It could speed up the drilling process and could even be utilised as a pump if we dam off part of the stream here."

They stopped for a while watching the scene. The workers were all volunteers and beavered away with great concentration and little chatter. All were whites apart from a solitary black couple who looked to be a husband and wife team. No one cried out, "Gold!" or anything similar while they were there.

A delightful picnic lunch was followed by a quiet journey back to the Schloss as they took their rest on the way.

Once re-established at the summer residence, Frank was alone with the Schmidts. Hannah was having time with Joseph.

"We have a treat for you this evening," Rudella told him with a twinkle in her eye. "I hope you enjoy it, but I want it to be a surprise."

"I see," replied Frank. What else could he say?

326

"But first we would like to discuss with you a topic dear to both of our hearts."

"Go on."

"As well as being patron of the arts and sciences, Norbert is keen to promote higher education here in Capparathia... and indeed in greater Hoame if possible."

"Oh yes?"

"We have already overseen the inauguration of six schools for whites in the despotate, but this is something altogether different. We are thinking in terms of a higher education establishment where students can get a nationally recognised qualification and where research into various fields can be carried out."

"A university."

"Exactly! There are none, at present, within Hoame as I'm sure you know, but we have read about the universities of old and that is the sort of thing we are talking about." Here she hesitated before continuing, "We understand that you attended university back in Oonimari."

"That's true," responded Frank. It was indeed true if one swapped a mythical land on Molten for the university at New Jerusalem on the planet Eden. The principle was the same.

"And we wondered if you could give us some pointers to help with the establishment of one here."

At that, she suddenly produced, as if performing a magician's trick, a scribe equipped with a pad of paper and writing implement. Both Schmidts sat on the edge of their chairs, ready to take in every word. Frank was hoping he could do the subject justice. After all, it was a lifetime ago and, even if he had been a cardinal's Special Organiser, he was not involved in running the education side of things.

"My university," he began, "was a specifically theological institution. I'm getting the impression that you wish to cover other subjects."

Norbert replied, "We would want a facility where scientific research was carried out, so science must form part of it. This all started out of necessity, and we already have a small group of scientists finding solutions to some of our problems. For instance, we were having difficulties with our hulffan-tarred roads in the summer. Not that we have many, but at the hottest time of year the tar was becoming liquid, making the roads impassable. Our technicians have been working on a solution and, while tests are on-going, we believe they are close to success."

"That's good."

"While a completely different team worked on the wheat blight problem last year and overcame it."

"Yes, I was amazed at how quickly that was done. But you're not talking solely about a research establishment are you? I gathered from what you said before that higher education is the frontline aim."

"That is correct," Rudella assured him, "and it is that aspect that we are asking your advice on."

There followed a long conversation on the basics of the physical needs such an institution would require: a convenient site, accessibility, accommodation, lecture halls, research areas and the like. However, it was more on other aspects that they most wanted Frank's input. The guest soon got the idea and did his best to help them.

He advised, "You need to set goals for what you want to achieve. It will be a massive enterprise, you would be best to start small and build the project up over time. There needs to be a team of committed people."

"I follow what you're saying," Rudella assured him. "We can have a theology department as well as science, adding further subjects / departments in time. It would be good if we can catch the imagination of the other despots."

"That's right!" Frank enthused. "You have to ask yourselves the question, do you want this to be the University of Capparathia, or the University of Hoame? I like the idea of publicising it throughout the eleven despotates, but a great deal of thought would need to go into how to do that and at what stage of the project."

Glad that their guest was entering into the spirit of the enterprise, the despotess came back, "We'll need some good people to lecture, obviously. I'd like to see us attract the best minds from across Hoame. In time, we could think of having a section for whites... separate, perhaps."

"If we are talking about a nationwide venture, based here in Capparathia, then central funding should be made available. You'd need to attract talent from across the country, both staff and students. You must get the Inner Council on board in order to do that. I am not planning on visiting the Capital this year, but I would be happy to write to them in support of your idea. I can think of a few Keepers who should be interested. In addition, I can pull a few strings to arrange an audience for you. I'm talking about you doing a presentation before the Inner Council."

"Both of us?" asked Norbert, glancing at his wife.

"Certainly. A convincing presentation should bring forth the funding that you will need. You've certainly convinced me!"

They talked for a considerable time, Hannah arrived and joined them for the last bit. Many issues were still not exhausted, though, when the hosts said that they would have to call a halt, for the evening would soon be upon them. It was agreed to continue the following day which was already designated as a rest day with no trips planned.

The evening's entertainment was participatory, being a dance held at the Schloss. Dancing was the last thing on Molten that Frank wanted to do, but fortunately he found himself taking part before there was time to think about it.

A spacious room was cleared and courtiers and their families took part as well. Joseph was by no means the youngest participant, while the eldest must have been well into their eighties. To the accompaniment of a band of musicians, a man called out the steps. To his relief, Frank found that a lot of walking was involved as well as some skipping. Hannah was having the time of her life, while a cooler evening than of late was welcomed by all who took part. There was much laughter and merriment and the fun went on well into the night.

"We don't have to worry about getting up early tomorrow," said Hannah when it was all over and they were walking back to their room. "Now admit it, even you had a good time!"

Frank was honest enough to concede the point, adding, "Although I can't see us putting on a like event back home any time soon."

"I wish we could!" cried Joseph, walking behind them along the corridor and still very much on a high.

"Well, when you're despot, Joseph, I'm sure you can hold a dance in the Castle hall."

"I will! I'm going to make sure we hold one every week!"

They laughed before retiring to bed, tired, but happy following a most varied, but enjoyable day.

~ End of Chapter 16 ~

Prospects of Peace - Chapter 17

Eko was in the sitting room of her large house in Castleton when a servant swept through with the two flower vases that she had asked for. Left on her own again, she considered her good fortune. Happily married for almost forty years, living in a luxurious place with a house servant and a gardener, there was much to be thankful for. Looking back on her life, she could never have imagined she would get to this point.

She was born to a relatively affluent white family in the Upper Village (as it then was), the sole child of loving parents. Her early years were spent at home, before being sent to the local school at the age of seven. Her first day was one she would never forget.

"Go and tell that boy to get down!" a teacher ordered the introverted, shy girl, pointing to a little hellion climbing up a fence.

"What? Me?" Eko's expression, if not her lips, had said. But if the teacher told her, she had to obey.

Off she set, in great trepidation. The boy was so busy concentrating on scaling the wooden structure that he didn't notice her until she spoke. Trying to make her soft voice audible against a background of other children playing, she called out as bravely as possible, "Teacher says you should come down."

The boy turned with a frown, but, liking what he saw, his face soon changed to a grin and he took delight in jumping down to ground level.

"What's yer name?" he asked in a friendly enough tone.

"Eko."

"Hi, Eko, I'm Natias. I was seeing if I could get weally high, as high as possible."

She giggled at his funny way of speaking and Natias found it infectious and laughed back. It was the beginning of a relationship that would last for the rest of their lives.

Years passed and soon their schooldays were behind them. The pair were married soon after he got a servant's job up at the Castle. Zadok the priest performed the ceremony.

Despot Rattinger senior was the local ruler, but he died soon afterwards to be superseded by his son. Natias showed a talent for numbers and was soon employed helping out the despot's elderly steward. The new Despot Rattinger took a liking to him and had little hesitation in promoting Natias to be the official steward's assistant. A higher position meant a room, albeit a pokey tower chamber, within the Castle itself and he and Eko moved in.

He tried to keep a low profile and quietly went about his duties. Eko also carved out an inconspicuous place for herself within Castle life. Flower arranging was always a passion with her and, given an official allowance thanks to her husband, she made sure there were beautiful displays on show within the otherwise drab building. Life was good, her single regret being that no children came forth from the bond of love she shared with Natias.

Time moved on and Despot Rattinger's behaviour became increasingly boorish. with drunken rages and evil mood-swings. Fortunately, the invisible Eko was not on the receiving end of these, but Thyatira's blacks left in droves. Natias was promoted again, this time to be the steward himself when that position suddenly became vacant. The couple moved into a much larger room on the second floor of the Castle. Vacated by the previous black occupant, this was luxury indeed. They realised that they were probably in a unique position of privilege for whites within the entire country.

Other people came and went. Out went the blacks, in came the drones who were very much a mixed bag. Adrian and Crispin fawned and flattered the despot and joined him on all-night drinking binges. They made her husband's life increasingly unpleasant. The third drone, Alan, was an entirely different kettle of fish. From an influential family in the Capital, neither despot nor the other drones dared make fun of him. A force for stability and common sense, he ended up effectively running the region along with a great deal of assistance from Natias. The steward and his wife were sorry that Alan needed to spend time away negotiating trade deals with neighbouring despots.

The situation was extremely wearing on Eko who was not at all happy with the direction things were going. It grieved her especially that her beloved husband was a constant source of mockery to those in charge.

Matters changed suddenly in 2602 with the despot's death and the introduction of a replacement in Despot Thorn. One of the new ruler's actions was to expel Adrian and Crispin, much to the Castle workers' delight. In fact, Eko felt as if a great weight was lifted from her shoulders. The new incumbent retained Natias as steward even after a new generation of blacks was enticed to settle in Thyatira. He stayed in the job a few years longer until the expansion of the despotate and a huge reorganisation which saw the introduction of the senate. This was a change too far and Natias retired. What was most pleasing for the couple was that they were allowed to retain their room within the Castle.

Yet needs change too. When, in 2618, a large house was offered to them in what was then called the Castle Complex, they were both interested. Indeed, Eko was keenest and it was she who persuaded her husband's friend, Laffaxe, to come and live in the mansion with them. There was certainly enough space.

Yes, it had been a long journey to a life of veritable luxury in retirement. How much she appreciated it. Still happy with Natias and able to pursue her hobbies of quilt making and flower arranging, it could not be much better. She got on extremely well with the Despotess and helped her out with arranging events such as the Christmas fair held at the Castle.

Eko took a sip of her practil juice. It was livened up with a splash of alcoholic gnass to make it more interesting. Lost in her thoughts, she did not hear the knock on the front door. It was only when her servant came through with the flower seller that she came to.

"Oh, thank you. Hello Suzanna, did you manage to get everything?"

"I truly did, here, take these!" came the reply as the flower seller deposited a load into the servant's arms.

She went to collect more and these were taken through to a utility room. Eko had brought the vases through and the pair spoke about the flowers for some time before Suzanna brought another topic up.

"How is Laffaxe?"

"Not too good," Eko answered, scrunching up her face. "He rarely comes out of his room nowadays. Natias is with him right now."

"Doesn't look good then?" asked Suzanna, but her friend saw no point in answering. Instead, she had a question of her own. "How's business?"

"Never better! It's coming towards the end of my busiest time of year. I haven't been able to sell any to the Charvo household lately. He's still abroad with his children, leaving that grumpy Walter in charge. You know what? He once told me he thought flowers were a complete waste of money!"

"Walter?"

"Yes."

"Oh well, never mind. I'm sure the rest will be back from their jaunt soon."

"Where is it they've gone?"

"Down south, with the Despot."

"Hmph!" exclaimed Suzanna with distain. "It's all right for some people. The rest of us have to work for a living."

"No, not in that column! That's for incoming expenses. Write the figure in that box."

"That's not what I've been told before."

"But these columns don't add up at all. These figures should not be here. They should be over here - look!"

Emil was inspecting the town's budget with the Mayor of Felsham in the Norland region, now part of the expanding Thyatira. The senator realised that the man before him had not compiled the figures. Nevertheless, the mayor seemed to have little or no understanding of rudimentary economics, let alone bookkeeping.

The scale of the mismanagement here, Emil found nothing short of scandalous. The fact that the local economy was actually doing rather well was entirely down to an entrepreneurial spirit at a low level, not the competence of those higher up in the region.

For the visitor it begged the question as to how such an incompetent individual could have got into such a position of authority in the first place. He was elected by a small cartel of local businessmen who formed an exclusive club called the Town Corporation. Maybe they wanted someone who did not think for himself, but rather a man they could manipulate to do their will. That would explain a few things.

With enough on his plate without wanting to rock the boat, Emil saw no point in getting heavily involved in local politics at this relatively early stage. If the local bigwigs wanted the man there, he concluded, it was better to work with him and get things sorted out that way. He got the distinct impression that the mayor's incompetence was merely that and the fellow was not deliberately involved in underhand dealings.

The mayor's office was beautifully furnished, no expense spared there. He had been in the post for a year and a half, perhaps he was simply a slow learner. Emil hoped so.

By the early evening, the senator was back at the hotel he was staying. A mid-town establishment, it was small at twenty-five rooms. Notwithstanding, it was convenient and not uncomfortable. The best room was reserved for him and he was content with it. There was much to ponder as he sat on his bed.

'I'm going to have my work cut out if I have to go into the finer detail in every town down here. It shouldn't come to that. Newton for one seems to have more competent personnel in charge.

'Still, I should look on the bright side, because we are managing to get some movement in Norland. It will take time to get the whole thing sorted out and this area
fully assimilated. Rome wasn't built in a day.'

The following morning, he visited several cottage industries on the outskirts of town: a potter, a furniture maker and a specialist enterprise making fasteners for clothes. With a great deal of enterprise going on at grass roots level, there was hope for the future.

The following day, Senator Vebber left to travel north once more. He should catch the main weekly senate meeting and give an update to his colleagues. It took two servants and a clerk to help him get his considerable frame aboard the wagon. Once this operation was complete, there was a collective sigh of relief.

'I must try to lose some weight,' he considered as his conveyance took off. 'The trouble is I feel so hungry if I stop eating!'

Munching a faltice root, he thought further about the Norland project. 'I can see myself spending a couple of years at least on this task. I've hardly visited the south-western strip of land bordering Ladosa. I have more than enough work cut out for me here. Besides, I understand the sparsely-populated strip is mostly made up of self-sustaining homesteads and hamlets, plus one or two quarries. If there are no problems there, they are probably best left alone, at least for the time being. I have enough on my plate without them.'

The holiday in Capparathia was coming towards its conclusion. At breakfast on the penultimate day, Deejan Charvo and his family were sitting on the same table as the Thorns.

"Have you enjoyed your stay here?" Frank enquired, looking at Sebastian and Keturah.

"Yes, My Lord," the boy answered slowly, taking care of his diction. "We have seen many memorable sights."

"We certainly have!" Deejan confirmed heartily.

Frank glanced up and noticed Norbert in earnest conversation with a messenger near the entrance of the large room. It looked to be something serious and he frowned as he watched the two men intensely. They disappeared into the corridor and the observer wondered what all this was about. He did not have to wait long to find out.

Re-entering with purpose in his step, Despot Schmidt made straight for his table.

"May I have a word in private, Frank?" he asked quietly.

By way of an answer, the other man stood up and left his fellow guests and disappeared with his opposite number. Not a word was said until they were alone in a room with a servant standing guard outside.

"Trouble?" asked Frank, wondering what in heaven's name had happened. Foreign invasion, a landing from outer space, his mind was working overtime.

Answering slowly, Schmidt said, "A week or so ago, a couple of foreign travellers were discovered. A man and a woman, they were in a poor way - dehydrated and thought to be delirious - and were taken to a town near here. It's taken them several days to recover, but they are telling a tale that they crossed the desert to get here."

"What! From the..."

"From the southern hemisphere, that's correct. We've never heard of such a thing before. In fact I'm sure it's never happened."

"My goodness!"

"And now they're feeling better, I'm informed, they're spouting all sorts of dangerous dogma."

"Really?"

"Yes, criticising our society, calling for a revolution."

"Are you saying they've been here before?"

"Oh no, Frank."

"I wondered how they knew about our society."

"I'm not entirely sure, although I understand they were most inquisitive as soon as they began to recover from their desert ordeal. The decision was made at local level to isolate them so that they could not contaminate our people."

Both despots were of a like mind. That mind entertained no thought of welcoming the strangers, but seeing them as a threat. Unlike his colleague, Frank had not been born and bred in Hoame. For all that, after nearly twenty years in the country he felt as keen as a native that dangerous subversives from the outside could only spell trouble. "I'd like to interrogate them," he stated.

"I thought you would," Schmidt replied, "so I've already ordered their transportation here. They should arrive early afternoon."

"Thank you, Norbert, well done."

"The officer who interrogated them yesterday said that they clammed up after a while. I hope you have more success."

"I shall have to try and gain their trust and not be too fierce with them to begin with. I shall stay here at the Schloss today and inform Hannah accordingly. There's no reason why she and the rest of them should not go on today's trip."

His wife was naturally concerned when Frank told her that he was having to remain at the residence "on state business," but she did not want to make a fuss. She therefore went with Deejan, Freidhelm and the rest of the Thyatiran contingent to a local beauty spot that had been reserved for the final full day of their visit.

Left behind, Frank paced up and down alone in his room. He had never heard of any exchange between the northern and southern hemisphere of planet Molten. The common understanding was that the Southern Desert, as the people of Hoame called it, was impenetrable. Not that anyone had ever been known to test that theory. That was not in the nature of Hoamen who, for the most part, and with few exceptions, were insular in their outlook. It was true that districts such as Thyatira and Ephamon were becoming more cosmopolitan, but that was merely a few Ma'hol, Sarnicians and Ladosa, nothing too far afield.

The idea that they should be welcoming these people from the south never entered Frank's or Norbert's heads, particularly when they were reported to be preaching revolution. There were, apparently, two survivors, a man and a woman, from a larger group that originally set out.

Norbert, too, stayed behind at the Schloss, but he had no desire to sit in on any interrogation of the foreigners. He would rather hand that responsibility to the Keeper and therefore, by extension, the Inner Council. That was the best protocol, he considered. The two men picked at a lunch together, during which little was said. Fortunately, they did not have long to wait afterwards before the prisoners arrived with their escorting soldiers.

Watching them being unloaded from the wagon, Frank noticed they were chained and manacled. He pulled back and said to Norbert, "If you have them put in the allocated room, still in their chains, then I can order them to be released. That should get off to a good start. Have you got their names?"

"Um, I *was* told," the other man answered, sounding a bit embarrassed, "but I can't recall right now. It was pretty unpronounceable."

"All right, well never mind."

Things went according to plan to begin with. The room picked for the interview was a pleasant one with a good view of the lake. Frank expressed suitable surprise at the prisoners' restraints and ordered them removed. The pair did not look at all threatening, but he retained a guard inside the door to be on the safe side.

The man, probably in his mid forties, was named Jan Wiejowki which, to be fair to Norbert, was pretty unpronounceable for a Hoaman. He wore a long face with blotchy skin, getting over the extreme sunburn he had suffered. His head had a fine down of hair over it and his brow wrinkled readily when he spoke.

"I must protest at our treatment so far!" he exclaimed. Ve come in friendship and have a great deal to offer. All ve have been met vith so far is hostility and suspicion."

"I'm sorry to hear that," Frank began, his voice as smooth as he could make it. "And where *have* you come from?"

"Our country is called Arcadia and ve have crossed right across the Northern Desert to get here."

"Indeed. And you are?"

The woman introduced herself as Cyla Knox and looked a decade junior to her colleague. She wore fairly short blond hair. From the dark streaks along her central parting, it was clearly dyed. To Frank, her face looked hard, with cold eyes, thin features and a pointed nose. In the event, she answered his questions politely enough, giving her name and adding that she was her expedition's "political officer."

"So you came all the way across the desert?" asked Frank with a faint smile. He was trying to sound impressed and bring forth more information at the same time. It worked.

Jan replied merrily, "Ve certainly have; the first people ever to make it! Others have tried, and ve are the sole survivors of a party of six. Ve decided to cast off from the Salient and made good progress at first, but then the going got harder. Nine days out some people..." he paused here to cough "... some vere for turning round."

The man was struggling with a dry throat and Frank ordered some glasses of water. Once there arrived, the tale was resumed.

"It became much hotter. Then a big sandstorm came up at dusk; you could not see your hand in front of your face. The following morning, when it was all cleared, two of our party vere missing."

"Did you find them?"

"No," Jan replied. He did not seem to mind the interruption. On the contrary, he was pleased to finally find a willing audience and told a long tale of hardship and struggle against the odds until the three remaining members finally reached the inhabited land in the northern hemisphere.

"Three?"

The woman broke in, explaining, "Carla died the first day we arrived here. Her body could not take it."

"Oh dear, I'm sorry to hear that. But how fascinating and how brave."

Jan came back, "Ve knew there vere people here and thought that ve could vork together for the common good."

As the ensuing conversation unfolded, Frank omitted to pick up on this comment about them knowing that there were inhabitants north of the equator. Instead, he was trying to find out more about the civilization down there. His relaxed manner meant that the pair were quite forthcoming in some respects. For instance it came out in conversation that they possessed more species of animal down there. Yet it was apparent to the questioner that no information of a sensitive nature was being divulged. It was understandable. Then it came out that the couple had barely eaten all day, so food was hastily provided in the form of a cold meat salad which went down well. Following the impromptu meal, the discussion was resumed.

It developed into a game of chess, with Cyla questioning Frank about matters northern and him answering without giving too much away, then the roles were reversed with a similar result. He found more luck with Jan, particularly regarding the expedition itself which he had led and, indeed, it was his idea in the first place.

"If you give us enough provisions to go back home once ve have recovered, ve can tell them about you. Maybe some of your people vould like to return vith us."

"That's a great idea!" responded Frank enthusiastically while in full lie mode. His reward was a tale that alarmed him greatly.

"Near the end of our journey, ve came to a large rock formation sticking out of the sand. Looking back at it from your side, Carla said it looked like a hand sticking out of the sea. Ve vere there vhen ve came across the remains of a ship."

"A spaceship, you mean?" Frank tried not to show too much surprise.

"The same, you know of such things?"

"I do."

"Good!" relied Jan with obvious relief, "the dullard I spoke to before on this acted like he knew nothing about such things."

"We've had visitors from other planets in the past, but not recently."

"No, they refuse to come out here now, not now a Chang Tide has established itself in this region of space."

"But you're from this planet, aren't you?"

"Ha, yes, there are currently no other-worlders in Arcadia, or elsewhere that we are aware of. It was one of these, a doctor, who told us she visited your land on a previous occasion. I must..." here he hesitated before continuing, but felt he had said too much to stop now "... admit that she preferred being with us."

"What was her name?"

Completely ignoring the question, he said, "Unfortunately she was killed when her craft crashed. It was completely destroyed."

"But you found the remains near that large rock formation that you mentioned earlier?"

"Ha, no! The one ve found the other day vas a military craft, left over from the Great Var as far as ve could gather. It contained a couple of battle robots in stasis vhich one of our party vas for trying to reactivate there and then. Vith our vater completely run out by this time, ve did not have the luxury of vaiting around. Ve had to try to make it to our destination. It was just as vell ve did, or else ve vould have all perished."

The conversation continued through most of the afternoon. Frank was alarmed by what he heard. These people of the South were unreformed in their outlook. They must have been cut off before the Great Reformation swept across the known galaxy. They were irreligious, amoral, with no respect for authority and, most shocking of all, thought humanoid robots were acceptable. None of the religion, moral revolution, or common phobia of robots of the civilised universe had got through to them. The few modern visitors from other planets had apparently not been able to change their ways.

That late afternoon, as they day trippers returned to the Selerm, the prisoners were reincarcerated nearby as Frank debriefed Schmidt. He was certainly not going to mention either robots, or spacecraft, but there were plenty of other grounds which he knew a proud Hoaman would condemn them for.

"They are most dangerous people, Norbert."

"Is it as bad as we suspected?"

"If anything, it's worse. You were absolutely right to contain and quarantine them."

"So what did they say?"

"Quite a lot. The man was more forthcoming than the woman at first. It was only later that she showed her true colours. He told me that a number of expeditions have set forth from their land, trying to reach us. There is a spur of land reaching out into the desert from which the journey would be at its shortest. All other attempts have turned back or disappeared, apparently, but this one went on doggedly and they nearly all perished in the attempt."

"What are we to do with them? If they return home it will encourage more."

"You're right," said Frank.

"But if they do not go back, their countrymen will conclude they all perished in the desert."

"And, one hopes, be put off trying to emulate them. You're right. I'll have to give the matter further thought overnight."

"Of course."

"I promise you a decision before we go home."

"Thank you, Frank. And what about the woman? You said that she spoke more towards the end."

"She did indeed. She suddenly tired of the polite game we'd been playing and began lecturing me on the errors of Hoame society."

Looking surprised, Norbert declared, "She made up her mind extremely quickly!"

Frank was not going to tell him about the other world doctor who had visited both hemispheres on Molten. Instead he replied, "These political types sow unrest wherever they go. They are not to be trusted. I would not trust them if they were sent back, neither let loose here."

"Which leaves us with a major problem," the local despot said before exhaling air slowly.

The two of them agreed to leave the issue there for the rest of the day. It was to be the visitors' last evening before commencing the long journey back home. Frank knew that his host was desperate to discuss his and Rudella's university idea some more before they left, so that had to be the priority for this final evening.

The Ladosan Civil War seemed to be over. The central Buffs, realising that they were at a huge disadvantage against a united foe, agreed with the proposal to end the fighting. The idea of a multi-party symposium was being floated. Chatter in the markets was of a new General Election. Maybe, the Buffs considered, they would do better with the electorate than in battle. An uneasy peace began, but at this early stage it appeared fragile.

In truth, the signing of an armistice was merely putting a rubber stamp on the reality that the fighting had ground to a halt. In the eastern half of the country, the conflict effectively ceased almost a year previously. The catastrophe of the superbolide in the late summer 2620 not only caused a huge amount of damage and large-scale casualties. It also knocked the resolve to fight out of the survivors.

The naturally suspicious hill-folk of Isson had kept their guard up for a long time afterwards. Most refused to take the relatively short journey to the devastated capital city of Braskaton to aid their fellow countrymen, although a handful did.

Isson's inhabitants held a large celebration on the evening that news of the armistice came through. Nothing was organised officially, but most of them joined in a wild night-long party. It felt good to let off steam. The overwhelming feeling was one of relief. In spite of them being surrounded by superior forces during the war, they held their ground and grasped a level of independence not known before.

Few on that night wanted to think too hard as to what the future held. In the days that followed, though, the more responsible residents started to face up to some hard questions.

The barricades were dismantled and free movement re-established with the lowlanders. The town had not been hit nearly as badly as the surrounding countryside and many more folk started coming into Isson than went in the opposite direction. Following an early spate of robberies and burglaries, the local militia was put to work patrolling the streets in an attempt to keep law and order.

Liberated from the worries of war, and without a common enemy at the gates, the local politicians could no longer find a consensus. Fracturing into a multitude of groups and sub-groups, they were soon squabbling over nearly every issue under the sun.

One faction, drunk on the power that the war provided them, were all for making a unilateral declaration of independence. This was considered extremely foolish by others who pointed out that there were many bigger towns in Ladosa and none of them was wanting to go it alone.

Another major bone of contention was to do with quite how much they reconnected with the lowlanders. Many did not like the idea of their resources being "wasted" on their capital's struggling citizens. Braskaton was still a virtual wasteland following the natural disaster the previous summer. So many of its inhabitants had been killed and a sizeable proportion of the survivors since moved away. It was by no means certain that the city would be rebuilt.

Eleazar the priest, a Hoaman yet highly thought of member of Isson's community, came under pressure not to help the lowlanders. He and Auraura saw it as their duty to assist those in need, but even they eased off their visits to the capital. In any case, those trips had born fruit in the shape of a fresh project for them to put their energies into. The pair were setting up an orphanage.

One day, working in his church in the poorer part of town, Eleazar had a visitor from the more affluent area. Senior priest, Zebulon, was enthusiastic about the new venture on the other side of town.

"Fourteen orphans, you say?" the elderly man sought confirmation.

"That's right," came the answer as the resident priest finished folding up a purificator and laying it carefully on the communion table. The main body of the church was a converted warehouse and, thanks to a huge amount of work done by the parishioners, looked pretty good now. The spacious, oblong area was filled with neat rows of wooden chairs. At least they looked as neat as possible where there were barely two exactly alike. The internal walls had been whitewashed and the holes in the roof mended. It was coming on. He continued, "They're due to come up from Braskaton tomorrow with their benefactor."

"Ah, yes, the gentleman you said is donating a legacy to make the whole enterprise possible."

"That's right," Eleazar said with a smile. "He himself is moving away and wants to leave it completely in our hands. I have employed a superintendent to be in charge of the orphanage, although I know that Auraura will be playing an active part."

"And where is your wife currently?"

A sound made them both look round. They turned to see three young men striding purposefully up the central aisle. Lowlanders from their dress, mean faces, long knives hanging from their belts, the way they walked - in short everything about them spelled trouble. They had not come to have their confessions heard.

"Give us your treasures!" their leader called out as soon as he felt close enough. "We want your treasures."

The last thing that Eleazar wanted was violence, especially as he did not want Zebulon hurt. Cooperation was the single rational response.

"I'll give you what I can, but we are not a rich ch..."

"Come on, now!"

The brass candlesticks were still on display after the last service, so he began with those.

Zebulon, meanwhile, could not contain himself. "Gentlemen," he began in the most authoritative voice he could muster in his terrified state. He did not get a second word in before one of the robbers shouted, "Shut up, old man!" which he did.

Trembling hands and quick-beating heart, Eleazar picked up the candlesticks. Meanwhile, his mind was issuing forth continuous prayers for help. He turned back to see, with horror, his wife entering the room from the opposite end with a huge bunch of flowers. The robbers followed his gaze, their leader starting to smile as the attractive woman paced steadily towards them, holding the bouquet in front of her.

The priests, frozen to the spot and dumb with terror, watched as the woman came on. She was not slacking her pace, neither was she looking up from her blooms.

Three metres away, the man to her right began saying, "Now what have we got...?" but a sharp knife severing his carotid artery ended his sentence as well as his life.

Faster than a bolt of lighting she moved. The other two, standing close together, suddenly found the flowers hurled in their faces as she despatched the first man. There now followed the briefest of melees. The second man was still extracting his knife from its sheath when Auraura's plunged into his heart. The sole remaining man, their spokesman, put up more of a fight and blade clashed against blade two or three times until, with a swift move, the former bladator kicked him in the groin. He went down, spilling his weapon. Immediately she was over him, with her own knife at his throat. Only her husband's earnest calls spared his life, but she stood over him while Eleazar sought and obtained something to tie him up with. Zebulon stood frozen, his eyes bulging, still trying to take in what had happened moments before.

A church worker entered at this point and was sent with haste to find some militia to take the one surviving robber into custody. Sporting several minor injuries and still smarting from that kick, he was not giving them any trouble.

"I must be losing my touch," commented Auraura as she inspected the tiny cut on her wrist. She sucked away the blood before adding, "I must practice some more."

Meanwhile, Zebulon had thawed out and was placing the candlesticks back on the communion table. He was shaking all over and soon had to sit down. While he could not condone violence, he was not going to start criticising his deliverer. The truth was he, like Eleazar, was both grateful and relieved at the outcome, even the bloody one before them.

"Oh dear, the flowers," the priest's wife exclaimed, seeing them scattered, broken and sprayed with blood on the floor. She added in a matter-of-fact voice, "I'll have to get some more. Don't worry, I have the funds."

She exited the room at the moment the church worker returned with a group of militiamen. Their leader was well know to the priests and asked the obvious question as to what had happened.

Lying, particularly in the House of God, was not something Eleazar could ever remember having done before. However, he did not want the truth to get out and make his wife an object of wonder. Yes, folk would be pleased that finally some of the robbers had been dealt with effectively, but he felt he needed to make something up to deflect attention away from Auraura.

"These three men," he began, "came to steal church property. They had no sooner taken the candlesticks before a disagreement broke out between them and they began fighting. This is the result."

"I see, thank you," replied the militiaman who looked down at the one remaining would-be robber who was not about to say, "Oh no, a woman beat us."

"Get him out of here," the order rang out," and dispose of these bodies."

The militiaman then enquired after the priests' wellbeing, but they assured him that they were all right.

That evening, Eleazar and Auraura lay in bed before going off to sleep. He had to go through the events, if only to make sure he had not dreamed it all.

"Did you have the knife within the flowers?"

"No, silly, in my boot, where I always keep it."

"But you were so quick. You didn't seem to notice they were there until that last moment when you struck."

"Oh no. I sized up the situation immediately. I was bringing in the flowers anyway, I thought if I continued walking with them they would be a distraction so that I could strike first; you gotta have an edge."

"Hmm... what do you think will happen to the survivor?"

"What do *you* think?" she replied. Even her husband must know that the failed looter was heading for the noose. Then, abruptly changing the subject, she announced, "The wine arrived this afternoon, after you'd left the church."

346

"From across the mountains?"

"No, our new suppliers. We'll be well stocked with communion wine for the next year."

"Good. It's as well I'd left the building by the time it arrived."

"Why's that?"

"I feel calmer now," Eleazar replied, "but this afternoon I might have drunk a couple of bottles straight off to calm my nerves!"

Frank and Norbert had made the decision to put the day's events to one side for the evening. Their unexpected guests from the southern hemisphere were most unwelcome. This was the final night before the Thyatirans headed for home, so a decision on the explorers would have to be made in the morning at the latest. Frank welcomed this in a way, because it meant there was no time for prevarication, he would have to be decisive. Yet that was for the morning; right now he owed the hosts his further considered thoughts on setting up a university.

"Have you thought about where you're going to site it?"

"In the north of the despotate," Rudella answered. She was sitting on a sofa next to Hannah. Norbert was on a chair opposite Frank.

"Is that in an existing town, or is it virgin land?"

"It's on the edge of a small town. It has a good road system already in place and plenty of room to expand. It's flat too, plus the weather doesn't get quite as hot as down here."

"Good. There are so many considerations; the climate being one of them. The semesters will have to be arranged so that the hottest time is between academic years."

While the Schmidts' scribe made copious notes, they went through some of the many issues that would need to be addressed, including accommodation for both students and staff, food, washing facilities, timetable, how long the courses should last and what qualifications would come out at the end of it.

Frank said, "You need to make sure that any awards granted are recognised countrywide to make the whole enterprise worthwhile. With that in mind, I suggest that that you consult the other despots beforehand."

"If we can make them listen!" responded Norbert pessimistically.

"Some will want to. I'd suggest a travelling 'show,' or presentation around the country. Ask the other despots for their ideas. What would *they* like to see studied and researched? If you involve them from the beginning, then they are more likely to buy into the whole enterprise. I see quite a lot of Lovonski. He's a go-ahead sort of man, I can enthuse and be positive to him about it."

"Thank you."

"You'll need people who are totally committed to the project and be able to sell it well. That's why you're going to have to go through the whole thing in great detail first. Then they will see that it has been gone through carefully and take it seriously. But above all, you need the backing of the Inner Council."

"Do you think we'll get it?"

"Yes, I do. I was thinking in terms of writing to them, but the more I think about it, the more I realise that a personal visit would be more effective."

Rudella said, "We'd be most grateful."

Then Hannah, who usually did not like the thought of her husband spending time away from her in Asattan, said, "What about a joint approach? Norbert and Rudella here can give the presentation and you can back them up."

They all agreed that this was the best idea. The Capparathians would have to develop their scheme more thoroughly first and then arrange a rendezvous at the Capital with Frank.

"I will await your message once I'm back home."

"That would be wonderful," Norbert replied. "We will give this top priority in the coming weeks. I have some court advisors whom I feel confident will help us."

"Funding is the key," warned Frank.

"I'm sure."

"Firstly, short-term funding in setting the enterprise up. This will be considerable."

"Let's hope that gold rush gets off the ground!" put in Norbert flippantly.

Frank smiled, then became serious again as he added, "That is where a grant from the Inner Council will be essential. So you will have to do your sums carefully and come up with detailed costings and projections to present to them. We must accept that the project will have to start on a modest basis, maybe with a couple of departments, then grow in time. Once it gets started, it will be a lifetime's work for you, I hope you realise that! The..."

"Yes," Rudella cut in, "It will be vital to sell it as the university for the whole country, not merely a Capparathian enterprise."

"And tell them that it will bring prestige to Hoame, that will go down well."

Further discussion ensued regarding on-going costs, salaries and what fees to charge the students. Would the other despots pay for the students they sponsored? Later on in their deliberations, they turned to the thorny issue of the whites. Norbert knew that Frank was committed to white rights and had responded enthusiastically when the idea of having some place reserved for Hoame's underclass came up. They went through the notion of having a quota for white students, but no firm decision was made. Even Frank realised that the white issue was likely to be a bridge too far at the inception of the project.

For the second time, the conversation on this topic continued well after midnight. All parties present were in favour of setting up a University of Hoame within Capparathia. Education was not normally high on the priority list of the country's rulers. There was little opportunity for people to improve their social standing in the past. That had changed in recent years; there was even a white Keeper, so this was probably the right time to introduce such an innovation. Hoame would not be converted to a meritocracy overnight, though.

The final part of the discussion was to do with the ethos that such an institution should have. Norbert, who recollected free discussions with his friends when he was a teenager, wished it to be more than a place of education. In his enthusiasm, he began to get rather carried away. He suggested it be more like an academy of old where unshackled debate could be conducted without fear of consequences. Frank was more conservative in his outlook and issued a note of caution.

"If it comes about, I am sure that the university will develop a life of its own. But the despots, and indeed the Inner Council, would be horrified by such talk. I would not try and sell it on that basis if I were you. Besides, we don't want to have a Ladosan talking shop on our own soil, do we?"

It was a loaded question and Norbert gave the appropriate answer. He realised that he had got a bit over zealous and would have to tone it down a bit.

349

While it was time for bed, Hannah did not want to end what had been a good conversation on a sour note. So she took it upon herself to provide a summery.

"We're all in favour of this excellent idea. The fruits of scientific research have already been seen here in Capparathia. If we can build an institution to encourage this, it will help our nation considerably. Also, a university will raise the stature of both the region and the country and give young men the opportunity to expand their knowledge and their horizons."

Frank, who had gone to a co-educational establishment, thought about mentioning the introduction of women students in time. However, it was late and that was a discussion too far. Besides, that would never be passed either by the Keepers, or the regional rulers. It would have to be one step at a time.

They said their goodnights and, as he went to bed, Frank remembered the southern hemisphere people once more. He had a decision to make in the morning, but he already knew deep inside what it would be.

~ End of Chapter 17 ~

Prospects of Peace - Chapter 18

The eastern sky over Capparathia was streaked with red. A weather front came over during the night. It brought with it cloud, a change of wind direction and cooler air.

While the Thyatiran legion made final preparations for their return journey, their leader had a duty to perform.

"I want to speak to them one last time," he told his opposite number.

"Of course," replied Norbert. "They have been brought back to the same room for interview." Then he added as an afterthought, "Ah yes, there was a priest here first thing. He had heard of the strangers' arrival and begged an audience with them, which I granted."

With a smile, Frank answered, "That's nice, give them some comfort in a land that's strange to them."

Norbert needed to put this misconception right.

"I don't think it was like that. He wanted to test their doctrine and found it seriously wanting."

"Oh dear."

"I thought I'd better warn you."

"Thanks."

"Maybe I made the wrong decision, I shouldn't have let..."

"It's fine, Norbert, don't worry. I'll have another conversation with our visitors and then make a decision as to what we should do with them."

"Thank you."

Frank proceeded to the chamber. When he entered, he found the atmosphere within much changed. The man, Jan, appeared extremely worried, but the woman looked angry. As he took up his chair opposite them, Jan asked, "Are you going to have us killed?"

"My goodness; certainly not!" replied their inquisitor with genuine surprise. What had been put that into the man's head?

"I'm obliged," he replied, showing a small degree of relief in his manner. "After all, we believe that we have a great deal to offer your people."

"Yes?"

"In technology, in... many things, but above all political science."

"Go on."

"Our society might not be perfect, but it has grown beyond rulers with power over the masses."

At this point, Cyla, who had been looking daggers at Frank, took up the baton. Only her tone was not as condescending as her colleague's. She clearly despised what she saw of Hoame's society and was not afraid to say so.

"We can help the common people to fulfil their potential."

This was a good opportunity to draw their philosophy out, so Frank, ignoring his own feelings for now, asked her to explain. This she was happy to do.

"We have representatives whose interests lie with peace-loving people. Our interests cannot be separated from those of the rest of the human race. Our fraternal policies ensure that the liberation of the masses, in their struggle for freedom, becomes a reality. A ruling class, such as you have here, is the arch-enemy of the freedom movement. Their reactionary approach ensures that the workers are downtrodden and exploited, their basic rights denied them."

"Go on."

There are bourgeois republics in foreign lands such as yours currently, but Arcadia cannot have a bourgeois republic because she was a country suffering under imperialist oppression. Democracy is practiced within the ranks of the people, who enjoy the rights of freedom of speech, assembly, association and so on. The right to vote belongs to the people, not to the reactionaries. The combination of these two aspects, democracy for the people and dictatorship over the reactionaries, is the people's democratic dictatorship. The single way is through a people's republic led by the working class....

"So you are Marxists?"

"We strive for a society where all are equal."

"What does that even *mean*?"

"A society where everyone is seen to be equal."

"Before God, you mean?"

"That's not what I mean at all! We should be seen in society as being equal, that is a basic right."

"How is that possible? Not everyone is of equal intelligence, that is simply a fact. Not everyone has equal ability. In fact every single person has unique abilities in a thousand and one different ways. To deny that is not to face facts. If you started everyone off with the same money, within a fortnight you'd have rich and poor."

"What I mean is equality of opportunity."

"But some people will take advantage of opportunities while others will not."

"But at least they will have started off on the same footing."

Frank could no longer contain himself. He said, "You would end up in completely different situations five minutes down the road. Political systems which, in the past, have striven to bring 'equality' have, in practice, been amongst the worst dictatorships of history. They have ensured that if anyone dares to raise their heads above the masses, it is chopped off. If that is the kind of equality you want, then at least be honest about it. I agree that we are all of equal worth in the eyes of God, but that is something entirely different. What you are talking about is entirely artificial and, if I am frank, dishonest. What is the point of promulgating an idea which is manifestly flawed? You would have to be either a knave or a fool to do so."

From then on, the session became a full-blown argument with neither side prepared to listen to the other. It would have been painfully obvious to an observer that both parties were coming from such fundamentally different mindsets that there was no common ground to be had. Frank then became aware of the need to wrap this up and so he pulled the plug on the proceedings and reported back to Norbert.

"They are political fanatics, every bit as dangerous as the Ladosans in their doctrines."

"Is that so?"

"And they wish to evangelise anyone within earshot."

"So it's as bad as we feared."

"It's some type of recycled political system that was tried out centuries ago with disastrous results." Then he added with a twinkle in his eye, "We could dump them on the Ladosans, but I don't think even they deserve them." Norbert briefly mirrored Frank's smile before the latter became serious once more, continuing. "I'm sorry, this is no time to make light of this. In short, the New Reformation must have passed by the people of the southern hemisphere and their beliefs are ungodly and poisonous. We must do everything we can to protect our people from them."

Norbert knew that the Keeper was against capital punishment, so he did not suggest that. Instead he stated, "They cannot be released into our society."

"No."

"And, as we said before, if we send them back it will the effect of encouraging more to attempt the journey."

"That's right."

"So I suggest, Frank, that I detain them indefinitely in gaol here."

"My idea exactly! The guards must be hand-picked men who will not be affected by the prisoners. The illness must be contained."

"I do understand the seriousness of the situation. Measures will be taken today."

"Good!" exclaimed Frank with a note of finality. It was time to turn to happier topics. Soon they were outside once more and remarked on the cooler temperature. The Thyatiran soldiers were reunited with their colleagues and were lined up by the static convoy awaiting the order to depart.

First, though, there were the goodbyes. Hannah and Joseph were standing nearby and, when Frank announced that it was time to go, they began their farewells.

"Goodbye, Rudella," said Hannah warmly, "and thank you so much for all your hospitality."

The Capparathian despotess was sporting yet another extraordinary headdress, a purple number with twin peaks this time. She replied, "We have thoroughly enjoyed your visit and it has been a joy to show you around our humble sights."

"Wonderful sights they were. One day you must come up and visit us in Thyatira."

"I'd like that every much."

Frank meanwhile was exchanging a few words with Councillor Arrandeck.

"Your Excellency," the formal gentleman replied, "it has been an honour. I prithee a safe journey and godspeed for ye all."

The final parting words were between the two despots. It was an important landmark in cementing the relationship between the two men. Each had already proved himself to be a useful ally in the past and that would surely continue now that an even stronger bond had been forged.

"Have a safe journey, Frank, and thank you so much for your help with the university idea."

"It's a pleasure... and I'll make sure I help you with the Inner Council in that regard. We must keep in contact between now and winter and see if we can progress the project as we hoped."

The Thorns alighted their wagon, whose canopy was down for the time being. The vehicles pulled away and the occupants waved for a long time at the slowly shrinking Capparathian group standing in a huddle outside the Schloss. The sun began breaking through the clouds and the heat rose accordingly. Eventually they turned away and verbalised their thoughts on how the visit had gone.

"An unmitigated success," was Frank's verdict.

"I was able to relax a lot more than I'd anticipated," replied Hannah.

They were alone in their conveyance, apart from their son and a few servants. The extra wagons gifted by Despot Schmidt meant that the travellers could spread out more for the homecoming.

It was a long return journey for the Thyatirans from the southern tip of Hoame to their northernmost region. Passing through Harradran, Reichmenn and Aggeparii despotates on the way, they kept their distance from major towns as much as possible. Once Despot Thorn set his sights on home, he did not want to be held up if at all possible.

The long convoy snaked at slow dakks' pace ever northwards. As they did so, the extreme heat was replaced by more pleasant summer weather. Sandy soil gave way to brown; strange flora was left behind and more familiar grass, flowers and trees seen.

It had been the longest vacation of Frank's reign and he had certainly taken the biggest entourage ever to leave Thyatira during his reign. The lengthy break meant different things to different members of the party. On that protracted journey back, each one had time to consider what it meant for them.

Freidhelm enjoyed the excursions, but his main personal achievements were around trade talks with both Rilesia and Capparathia. His home despotate's economy was thriving and producing large qualities of goods. Trade beyond Thyatira's borders was essential to keep the workers busy and avoid stockpiling. In return, the other despotates possessed things that the northerners craved, so his role as trade secretary was an important one. Some

355

useful agreements had been signed on this trip. In particular he was as excited as his leader was by the new lightweight wagons donated by the Capparathians. He was looking forward to showing them to his fellow senators. In fact, with some useful trade deals under his belt, he was very much looking forward to reporting back at his next senate meeting.

Deejan Charvo, meanwhile, was coming to the end of *his* longest ever break from his work. In fact, prior to adopting Sebastian and Keturah, he never had a proper holiday in his life. Now he had spent several weeks away from balance sheets, simply enjoying the company of his children. Part of him was looking forward now to getting back to work, but he was pleased that he had made the most of his son and daughter's company. They were growing up so quickly and this quality time spent with them was precious. What amazing scenery they witnessed too, from the mountain ranges of Rilesia to the sandy landscape of Capparathia. 'If I were a young man like Sebastian,' he told himself. 'I could easily get addicted to travelling and visiting far flung places.'

The young man himself held other ideas. He certainly enjoyed the sights and experiences, particularly boating on the lake, but he was more content with his lot as an apprentice businessman and heir to his father's fortune. His musings were far away from thoughts of foreign travel. 'What a long way I've come from the back streets of Aggeparii City! I feel like I've been re-born into a new life. I want to do my best in the business when I get back home. I'll show myself worthy of the good fortune I've been granted.'

The time he and his sister spent together was not much different from back home. Ever since their lives came together there had been an unbreakable bond between them. Not that they were never subject to the occasional sibling squabble. Their biggest fallout had been a few years previously. Keturah got her face disfigurement corrected by the miracle doctor who stayed with them for a while. Sebastian refused to have his large face birthmark altered as he felt it was an essential part of his being. It caused a rift between them for a while which was painful to both. In the long run, it made them realise how important their relationship was and they got over it. Ever since then, the pair were inseparable.

She was the sole person that he confided in these days concerning the strange visions of future events that still occurred from time to time. On one occasion, on the long journey home, she let something slip when alone with her father. He mentioned foreign ways and events north of Hoame and she found these words come out before she knew it.

"Sebastian foresaw the civil was in Ladosa in a vision."

Deejan had been speaking idly about international relations. His daughter's words brought him up short, but he did not want to make too big a deal about it.

"So he's still having visions then?" he asked, trying to sound as matter-of-fact as possible.

"Yes, father."

Detecting that she did not want to talk any more on the subject, he kept quiet. Keturah was grateful for this, although in her own mind she was recalling a conversation with Sebastian from a short time before.

"I saw you in a church leadership role, instructing people."

"What? As a nun?" she had asked.

"No, you will preach. Many people will come from far and wide to hear what you have to say."

"Individually?"

I mean crowds o' folk from all around. You'll be a spiritual leader."

Keturah was stunned. No woman currently held such a role in the whole of Hoame. Yet, as far as she was aware, her brother's visions always came true. So she kept these things and pondered them in her heart.

Darda did not have such an exciting time in Capparathia. For long periods he and the other soldiers were cooped up in a barracks some kilometres away from the Schloss. Conditions were not unpleasant, but there was not a great deal to do.

Eventually he had organised a football competition and that was well received. Local people joined in and he was careful to organise the teams so that they each contained Thyatirans and Capparathians. The rivalry was still fierce enough; people want to win, but it never turned too serious. Several girls from the nearby village took part and that helped the men not to get too physical in their tackles. Due to the heat, matches took place in the evenings. Great fun was enjoyed by all. It had certainly been a good distraction, but he was happier now they were on their way home. He took his role as squad leader extremely seriously and wanted to treat his soldiers as he himself would like to be treated.

Tristan was learning patience. He had not been long in the job of Despot's secretary before having to accompany him on this trip. So, soon after having established a routine for the role, all was put aside for the duration of the holiday. He wanted to ease Despot Thorn's considerable administration burden. Instead, he found himself sight-seeing and being polite to minor officials in the courts of two other regional rulers. He wondered if he would have been better off remaining at the Castle back home and working there. When he confided in Freidhelm, the senator had sensibly told him simply to enjoy the break. "There will be plenty of time to work when you are back. Learn to relax."

The Thorns did not seem to pay him much attention and he felt at a loose end for much of the time. When he was not accompanying Freidhelm at the negotiating table, he possessed plenty of time to think.

'Did I do the right thing in leaving Ladosa? My position was untenable after Ayllom discovered the truth about me. I don't like lying to people, but I guess it was the right thing to do in the circumstances. There were greater things at stake than my friendship.'

So Tristan did his best to follow Freidhelm's advice and enjoy the break. Nevertheless, this was one holidaymaker keener than most to get home and back to proper work.

Joseph would never forget his first trip on the lake. In fact he made sure he was taken on there several more times when he did not have to accompany his parents.

He was learning what it was like to be a despot and could see the friendship between his father and Despot Schmidt deepen the longer they were there. When he was despot, Joseph told himself, he would do state visits to all the other regions and make friends with everyone. He certainly took to the Capparathian leader and was most impressed by him to the point of imitating his walk. He did find it strange that the Schmidts' children were educated in a different part of their despotate and he did not meet them at all. Were they not allowed holidays?

Hannah had quite liked the Rilesia stay, but found it easier to relax in the southernmost region. Maybe it was because she spent more time there, but maybe not. Rudella was an absolute dear and her extraordinary headwear would stick long in the memory. What with breathtaking scenery, exotic-looking plants, the concerts, dancing and artwork, these southerners had it all. She had got used to comparatively rough Thyatiran ways, but these Capparathians certainly seemed more refined in their tastes and manners. Hannah liked it, but she was glad to get away from the oppressive heat.

Frank, meanwhile, looked at the investment of time and personnel into this venture and concluded it was well worth it. He had indeed cemented his relations with despots Heisler and Schmidt. All the regional rulers were, of course, on the same side, but Frank was savvy enough to know that allies were always needed in politics.

No news came from home while they were away. He had left instructions not to be disturbed unless it was anything important. So he took an absence of news as something positive. During his one previous stay in Capparathia, there had been an attempted coup back home. He was definitely not expecting a repetition of such a thing this time. Yet it was a measure of the stability of the situation in and around Thyatira that he felt comfortable being away so long. Little in way of tidings were coming out of Rabeth-Mephar these days, while the situation north of Hoame seemed to be improving. It would be interesting to get an update from General Japhses when he arrived at the Castle.

What of Alan? How much longer was he going to be abroad? It would be great to see him again if, he hoped, when his friend returned. All would be revealed soon. In the meantime it was good to have a break. He felt revitalised and ready to face the many issues which doubtless would soon raise their heads upon his return.

One thing he pushed to the back of his mind was the southern hemisphere people. They were best forgotten. Nevertheless, he was more than a little intrigued as to the identity of the other-world, female doctor they had talked about. Was it the same Yvonne Williams who had spent a time in Thyatira with Nakajima Jr. a few years back? He would never know.

On crawled the convoy, obtaining food from local villages as they neared their destination. It was mid-summer and still warm by local standards, but jerkins and coats were being put on in the evenings.

"We're not used to these cooler climes," Hannah joked. "Our blood has been thinned from all those weeks down south."

"I'm sure we'll get used to it soon enough," he husband replied.
"True."

Their wagon jolted at another rut. The road in northern Aggeparii was badly maintained. Frank looked up and saw a rider in semi-armour approach on his dakk. It was Darda.

"My Lord!" he cried excitedly.

"What is it?"

"See that town in the distance?"

"Yes."

"That's Newton, one of the places in Norland. We must be crossing into Thyatira round about now."

Some soldiers walking alongside the Despot's wagon began cheering and the cry was taken up right along the line. They were back, they would soon be home again.

Frank had been hoping to get back to the Castle in the daylight, but the sun set as they were still some kilometres off. With the light fading fast, Darda hurried up to his leader's wagon.

"My Lord, we need to set up here while we can still see. I'm afraid we'll have to finish the journey tomorrow morning."

"Can't we continue with someone leading by lantern? It's annoying being so close, but yet so far."

The squad leader thought for a moment before replying. "That would be possible for a single wagon, My Lord, but I wouldn't want to try it for a whole convoy."

There was limited time to make a decision. The wagon train was at a standstill, lanterns were being lit, men were hovering by the vehicle in front of theirs which contained tents. His wife looked sleepy, but expectant, hanging on his word. He said, "I'd so like to get home. We could go ourselves and the others follow in the morning." He felt selfish, but so longed to be in his own bed again now that it was tantalizingly close.

Hannah merely shrugged in response, as if to say, "It's up to you."

"Right!" exclaimed Frank in decision mode. "Darda, I'd..."

"Yes, My Lord!"

"I'd like you and your squad to lead and escort me and my family to the Castle now. Meanwhile, the others can pitch camp for the night and follow in the morning."

"Yes, My Lord," came the reply. He was not going to question his Despot's order.

The Thorns' vehicle was near the front of the queue, so there were a limited number of wagons ahead to move out of the way. It was a fairly narrow section of road there and a steep drainage ditch on either side, so it was not the easiest of manoeuvres, particularly in the twilight. Yet, with soldiers either side issuing (sometimes contradictory) instructions, the skilled driver managed to get past the other wagons.

A soldier then led the way in front of the solitary vehicle. His lantern created increasing illumination as the natural light failed to nothing. Darda and his squad followed on foot behind the vehicle, two further men carrying lanterns. No one spoke.

The awning was up in the conveyance. Joseph was asleep in his mother's arms and Hannah herself was dropping off. Frank, unusually, climbed through to the front and perched himself on the bench next to the driver.

'I suppose I'm being extremely selfish in insisting on this,' he told himself. 'Oh well, it's done now. It would be a bit silly having an elaborate goodbye to the other people on the trip, after all we'll see each other again in the morning...'

Soon a couple of lights appeared in the distance and he knew these to be torches on the castle wall. They were home. As they neared the entrance, two of Darda's men went forward to speak to the sentries. One tripped over in the dark and cursed before quickly getting back up again. There were no other mishaps and the dakks walked slowly into the courtyard.

It reminded Frank of the very first time he arrived there. That was also in the dark and a young man named Rodd was driving on that occasion. Now he was Captain of the Guard and one of his brothers a Member of the Inner Council. No one could have predicted that at the time.

Frank jumped down with surprising athleticism and soon the soldiers were helping Hannah and Joseph disembark. Few words were spoken as they were ushered through the door to the keep and up the stairs. The Despot himself held back and sought out Darda.

"Thank you."

"My Lord."

"Get the dakks safely back into their stalls, but you may as well leave the wagon until first light. Then have it unloaded and the contents brought in. There's going to be some leave for you all, so that you can go and visit your families."

He made his way inside the building and, once he had ascended the wooden stairs to the balcony overlooking the hall, a familiar figure appeared from the opposite direction holding a lit candle.

"Alan! You're back."

"So are you," was the wittiest reply that the drone could muster after being roused from his sleep.

"You didn't have to get up specially."

"Huh! Now he says."

"Seriously, are you all right?"

"I'm fine and so are things here. You've had a productive visit?"

"I believe so. I'll tell you more in the morning."

"Sure," Alan relied as the two men began making their way upstairs. "We'll have lots to tell each other."

The Buff Party's chief delegate was a picture of pomposity. Sitting there in his traditional costume, baggy and brightly coloured, he exuded a superior air. The stub of a faltice root was sticking out of the edge of his mouth and it bobbled up and down as he spoke.

"Negotiator Nazaz, I may as well take your counter-proposals back to my council, but I cannot guarantee they will listen. We have already laid out the way forward that we think is best."

"It's about time you faced up to reality!" Charlotta snapped back. "I'm tired of all your delaying tactics and prevarication. Your proposed electoral boundary changes are preposterous and designed to give you an unfair advantage. We will not allow that. Your party is no longer in any position to try and dictate terms to us. You are weak and you must open your eyes to see that."

"My dear..."

"I will give you a deadline of one week for you to get your council to ratify the Rose/Neo-Purple proposals. If you fail to do so then our joint armies will recommence hostilities and sweep away what remains of the territory you hold."

The Rose Party representative was nodding vigorously at this. If the Buffs had hoped to split the new-found alliance, they were failing to do so.

362

Eventually the meeting broke up and Charlotta found herself alone in her hotel room. She stared out of her fourth-floor window at the scene of central Laybbon. There were few people and little traffic out on the streets. The town, north of Wesold, was a short distance within the central Buff area. However, if she carried out her threat, the coalition forces would make sure it was one of the first places to fall. She was not bluffing regarding the use of force, but in her heart of hearts, she did not think it would come to that.

For the truce was holding and a new General Election must surely be held soon. Yet there were several matters to be ironed out first. Charlotta was quietly confident that the stalemate would be broken this week. As for any election outcome, that was a complete lottery. Would the Neo-Purple vote rise to reflect their current military power and land acquisition? There was no guarantee. Yet, as a good democrat, she knew it must be held. The will of the people was paramount as all Ladosans were brought up to believe.

She was alone, very alone. No reply had been forthcoming from Alan and she felt a fool for sending that letter to him. If he really cared for her, she would have heard back from him, unless the messenger had been waylaid...

It was no use, she would have to throw herself into her work all the more. There was a meeting with her Rose opposite number tomorrow and then, at the end of the week, an important one with the Neo-Purple Committee. If the General Election went ahead and she was chosen to be a parliamentary candidate, she certainly would have her hands full. Maybe it was best not to have a partner in life, but the evenings were lonely.

A knock on the door produced two of her political advisors.

"Come in, sit down."

As they did so, one of them spoke, "We have received a communication from the Duma of the Pink Party. It makes for interesting reading."

"Right, let's go through it. We need to know where they stand."

The politicians poured through the papers before them and Charlotta forgot her own personal problems for the time being.

Frank slept well in his own bed back at the Castle, but woke up early. He kept still so as not to disturb Hannah and thought about the previous few weeks.

'An undoubted triumph, but time consuming. I'd spend a couple of years on holiday if I did the same in every despotate! Still, bonds strengthened and no crisis either at home, or internationally as far as we are aware, so that is all right.

'Several species of flora and fauna are different in the south of the country than up here. However many different types did the early colonists bring to the planet? They must have packed in millions of insects, for instance, to help the soil and establish a viable food chain. I know that the Culpers counted scientists amongst them. Presumably these included ecologists who would know what to bring to get the balance right. Even so, it must have been an incredible gamble on a virgin planet and I bet some of the species must have died out.

'I wish I knew more about the creatures of old earth, but I remember being told there were millions of different species and sub-species. Didn't Trixi tell me there were 100,000 different types of grass? Something like that. We can't have more than a tiny fraction, here on Molten, of the species that once thrived on earth. Presumably modern mutations...'

"Are you awake?"

Hannah's question cut through the silence and stirred him from his thoughts.

"Yes, and I'll be getting up soon. I want to be there when the rest of them arrive back."

"That'll be a while. They'll have to go through all the rigmarole of taking all the tents down and packing them away this morning."

"Although they manage that a lot quicker now than when we first set off. Got it off to a fine art."

"And they won't have Darda's squad to help them."

"Hmm... do you think I was selfish in leaving the others?"

"It's your prerogative, my dear."

Deciding not to pursue this line of enquiry any further, Frank got up. Soon he and his family were eating breakfast in an otherwise almost deserted hall. A servant was departing from their table after leaving some bread and butter, when Hannah spoke.

"I'm hoping to meet up with Freya and Klara this afternoon. I can catch up with the gossip."

"I'm hoping to meet up with the senate today and do much the same."

"You saw Alan last night, you said."

"Yes, so I know that there are no major contentions to worry about. I'm quite looking forward to being brought up to date."

"And I want to get out and have a close inspection of the garden after breakfast. I could see from upstairs that it has come on well in my absence. Maybe they worked better without me hanging over them the whole time. Those women from the refugee camp were certainly a big help in setting it up at the beginning. They had plenty of ideas, although in the end it's turned out somewhat differently."

"Mmm."

"I expect they enjoyed being called upon to take part in something positive. It's a pity their enthusiasm waned in the end. I'm not sure why; maybe because the design diverged from the traditional set-up."

They continued chatting quietly for a while, before and after Joseph was taken away by his tutor. The boy was not too pleased that his holiday was over. He would have preferred to have played with his new soldiers up in his room.

A cry went up outside before a guardsman entered to tell the Despot that the convoy had arrived back. They shot out of their chairs and hurried down to meet them. By the time they reached the outer courtyard, the wagons were halted and the travellers bailing out. Word had got round to relatives and there was soon a confused mass of people all hugging and otherwise greeting each other.

Frank stood aloof from the melee and watched the action. He noticed Deejan Charvo's fine wagon looking a lot dustier than when it first set off. It seemed odd that his party had not gone straight on to their home. Sebastian was first out, followed by his sister. In playful mood, he declared that his hands were cold before putting one on Keturah's warm neck. She squealed and chased him round the side of the vehicle. The observer was still smiling at the sight when someone addressed him.

"Familiar surroundings once more, My Lord."

"Deejan! Yes, it's good to be back."

"No doubt we will both have a good deal of catching up to do."

"Yes, but we'll soon be back in the old routine."

Looking round and seeing his vehicle stuck between two others and scores of people milling round, he remarked, "I'm not sure why we came in here. I think we'll walk there now and I'll get the driver to bring it round later."

The merchant was soon replaced by Senator Trepte. Above the general din, Frank told him that a full senate meeting had been set for after lunch.

Later that morning, the despot was in his third floor living room accompanied by Alan. The drone had much to tell him about the Ladosan situation.

"No one would have foreseen a Rose/Neo-Purple alliance before the war, They are most unlikely bedfellows. Having a common enemy in the Buffs seems to have been a catalyst. I got a fresh report from Japhses a couple of days ago. His spies tell me that the truce is still holding."

"So what are the prospects of peace in Ladosa?"

"Good, I'd say. The Buffs are seriously weakened and some players are out of the game altogether. Negotiations are well underway for a fresh General Election."

"Oh no!" exclaimed Frank, "that's when they are at their maddest."

His jaundiced views on the Ladosans was not unusual, but Frank had his own life experience to draw upon. The sole election he possessed first hand experience of was back on the Planet Columbus. He had helped a new man get into power, only to see him change overnight once he gained control. There were no certainties in the politics game.

"Maybe they won't be so mad this time," Alan replied. "The momentum has been taken out of the fighting. I detect a certain weariness after all the bloodshed... and that thing coming crashing down out of the sky."

"I'm sure."

"But going back to Japhses, I had an interesting meeting with him to discuss tactics. Several things have come out of the war which I'm suggesting we adopt here. I believe that our frontline casualty treatment can be improved, for instance. The Ladosans used smaller, swifter vehicles for moving the injured back from the fighting area."

"Ah, talking of wagons..." Frank began. He then told his friend about the new Capparathian developments in that field. This certainly caught his lieutenant's imagination.

"I'd like to see these new vehicles."

"You can see them this morning, they're just out there."

366

"I wonder if we can combine the best of both designs, Ladosan and Capparathian, to come up with something ideally suited as a field ambulance. I'll have to look into this and discuss it with some of our existing wagon builders. I believe there's potential there."

"Sounds good."

"The wagon builders here are extremely conservative and not given to innovation. If these new southern vehicles are as good as you say..."

"I must caution you, the arvawood is in short supply and likely to remain that way."

"Still, you mentioned an improved suspension."

"True."

"I'd like to give them a thorough inspection anyway, see if we can come up with our own design. It's not as if there isn't room for improvement."

"All right, it sounds like a good project to give yourself."

"I'll keep you informed. There's something else: did I tell you L'Rochfort visited here while you were away?"

"No, about the situation across the border?"

"Yeah," went Alan before explaining all about it, particularly the hope of finally achieving a non-aggression pact with our neighbours. "The Keepers want to work on a revised wording and presentation to put to whichever Ladosan faction ends up on top."

"Do you think I should be there for that?"

"At the Inner Council meeting?"

"Yes."

"It's up to you, Frank. A pact has been talked about for so long. I simply hope that if it does come about it'll be worth the paper it's printed on."

"I hope so too. If the mood in that country is for peace, it must bode well."

"Sure. Anyway, how was Capparathia and your pet despot?"

"Don't call him that!" Frank responded in mock hurt. "Besides, we went to Rilesia first. They were both worthwhile visits." He then went into some detail, talking about the scenery and the personnel encountered. Facts and figures on trade agreements he kept away from; they would wait until the formal senate meeting.

"Did you go on that lake again?"

"We did!" exclaimed Frank with feeling. For both men could remember their previous visit when Despot Schonhost had been there. Alan ended up getting lost and had to trek back through the desert. "At least we didn't have a mist come down on the water this time. Our whole party was accounted for. Joseph certainly enjoyed the trip on the water."

"I bet."

"So was there anything else big that we missed while we were away?"

"You missed the Sarnician circus!"

"What was that like?" Frank asked with a frown.

"Lots of scantily-clad women. Jugglers, high-wire walking, scantily-clad women, fire-breathing, novelty acts... did I mention scantily-clad women?"

"Once or twice," came the reply. "I'm not going to take the bait."

With a laugh, Alan continued, "They were well received and, I must admit, I was amazed at some of the things they performed. However much practice they must put in to perfect it all?"

"I'm sure."

"They've moved on now."

"Where to?"

"I didn't ask."

"Further into Hoame?"

"I'm sorry, Frank. I didn't take note of what direction they went. I can find out for you, if you really want to know."

"It doesn't matter. I'd better grab a bite to eat before this afternoon's senate meeting."

"Good idea, there'll be a lot of catching up to do."

"Great to see you back again, Deejan, and you two!"

Walter was a lot more animated than usual, so delighted was he at seeing his master and the children return. The travellers had eaten a light breakfast and were hungry. Food, therefore, was a top priority. Following an early lunch, Deejan held a meeting in his office with his assistant.

Even though he was not one for small-talk, Walter made a point in asking how their journey had been.

"Splendid!" came the reply and the merchant spoke about some of the sights they saw.

Nevertheless, it was soon down to business and there was much to report.

"I've coped, but it has been more than a little busy."

"You've earned a few days off."

Deejan knew it was unlikely his assistant would accept the idea of a break, but Walter replied, "I might just take you up on that, but first, I'd better fill you in on some details."

"Okay."

"The Sardis silversmiths paid their loan back early, which was something of a surprise."

"It was a big one, wasn't it?"

"Four hundred and fifty sten. Apparently business has taken off quicker than expected this year and they'd decided to cut their weekly outgoings by paying it back early."

"It's their prerogative."

"Indeed. On the other end of the spectrum are the Lowdebar Carpenters Guild. Their loan, if you remember, was for some new lathes. The machinery hasn't matched their expectations, apparently, and they've been struggling with the repayments. At least they came to see me before things got out of hand, I did appreciate that."

"Good, so..."

"So I've re-scheduled the debt repayments. Here are the figures." He paused as Deejan took in the details. It all looked sound to Deejan. Walter continued, "I think this will be okay now. Perhaps I was a little optimistic when the loan was first made."

"Still, you've salvaged the situation by the looks of things. The problem has been nipped in the bud."

"And we have a new client."

"Yes?"

"From Norland. The Newton Mayor came to see me in person. It was his first visit to Thyatira apparently. He was looking for a one grend loan over five years. There's good collateral there and I've agreed it over a four year period. It's a big one, but safer than most. Our reserves are still within parameters."

"Good; well done with that. What happened about the underwear factory in Setty> When I left they were hoping to expand their business on the back of an order from the army."

"That did not materialise. I had to revise some of their figures to a more realistic level. I've granted them a smaller amount than first requested: three hundred and fifty sten. In fact the first repayment was due yesterday and came through on time. I'd say it's running smoothly."

The pair went through some further details, but it was apparent that Walter had managed the business extremely well in his employer's absence. Naturally, Deejan was delighted and told him so. After giving his report, Walter relaxed noticeably and, following a midmorning snack with the children, found himself asking more about their trip.

Alone once more with Deejan, he said, "Sebastian and Keturah are full of it; it sounds like they had the time of their lives."

"I'm sure they did. We all did."

"But extremely hot by their accounts."

"That it was. I could live with it knowing that the time was limited, but I would not want to stay down there permanently."

"Hmm. It's been fairly warm here too, but nothing like where you were down south by the sounds of it. The weather's been cooler the last couple of days."

"It seems most pleasant."

"So what do you want to do today? I've left these for you to have a look at when you're ready."

Deejan beheld the pile of paperwork awaiting him. Walter might have achieved a lot in his absence, but there was still plenty of work to be done.

"I think I'll rest today, Walter. I want to sort out our things and get settled first. I'm grateful for you running through these with me today, but I think I'll probably restart work tomorrow."

~ End of Chapter 18 ~

Prospects of Peace - Chapter 19

The senate meeting got underway with Frank telling the members abut the trip to Rilesia and Capparathia. He was keen to inform then that it strengthened the bonds between the despotates and emphasised that increased trade was one concrete result.

"More trade means more prosperity for Thyatira and will help to keep our economy on track. Freidhelm here will fill you in on the details in a moment.

"There is one other matter that I must mention. Alan has told me about Baron L'Rochfort's visit here in my absence. I shall be taking a trip to the Capital shortly to attend an Inner Council meeting. They wish to have my approval for the proposed non-aggression pact with the Ladosans."

Saul and Alan both looked confused at this statement. It was the former who got in first.

"My Lord, how can the Ladosans agree to any pact if, as you say, they have not found a national government yet?"

"Um..."

The drone then came to his rescue, saying, "What the despot means is that a draft wording needs to be agreed. This will then be put to the new government over there, whatever it is. It is important that we get off on the right foot with the new administration once their election has taken place."

Frank smiled and nodded his head, responding, "Quite; thank you, Alan. Are there any further questions before we move on?"

There was none. It was therefore Senator Trepte's turn to give his report. He had much positive to report regarding the outcome of the trade talks with both of the regions. In particular he enthused about the new Capparathian wagons and told the members all about them.

"They have stood up to the rigours of the return journey well. We will be undertaking further trials in the coming days to see what the optimum load is and what teams of dakks are best suited to them. Three examples we have received gratis. Any more we will have to pay for and at a hundred sten each, so they do not come cheap."

"Does that include the dakks?" asked Otto.

"I'm afraid not. So they aren't cheap, but the despot and I are of a like mind that they are well worth it. It's not as if we will be able to buy a large quantity anyway, because they are not going to be mass produced."

"Why is that?"

"Due to the scarce availability of the wood involved in their construction."

"Oh yes," said Otto, "you mentioned that earlier."

"I have arranged for one of the wagons to be put on display in the courtyard outside here this afternoon. You may inspect it after the meeting and there will be a demonstration of it being pulled by a team of four dakks."

"Sounds novel," Karl remarked. "What other things have Capparathia got to offer?"

"Precious metals, gold and silver, plus malachite, copper as well as semi-precious stones including lapis-lazuli. Brought to us in un-worked form, we have the craftsmen available to finish the job."

Otto asked, "And what are the Capparathians interested in with regards to our products?"

"I have a list of items here," Freidhelm answered, placing a sheet of paper into the middle of the table. "There are a great many things including wool, timber, slate and, of course, hulffan tar for their roads. They have even perfected a method of refining the tar so that it does not run so readily in extreme heat."

"Most impressive, Freidhelm, I would like to take some time to digest these figures."

"Of course."

"And," Otto continued, "please include me in on the wagon demonstration. I am intrigued!"

Another senator with an important report to communicate was Emil Vebber. The Norland acquisition was proving a greater task than anyone had imagined and the big man's trips to and from the southern region were on-going. Now he was standing to give his latest report on the matter.

"The Norland census results have been completed. You will see the figures on the sheet in front of you. It has come as something of a shock, but the population there is a lot bigger than we'd been led to believe. The gaining of this region means an increase in Thyatira's population by almost thirty percent."

That caused a stir around the room. First to recover was Saul, who asked, "Isn't it a poor area?"

372

"It varies greatly. There is a bigger gulf between blacks and whites."

"But there are some poorer areas than in the... er, old Thyatira?"

"That's true."

"Then it could be a drain on our finances for years to come."

"I don't want to look at it that way," Emil responded. "The Norland acquisition is a great opportunity for us. Of course there are going to be obstacles to overcome, but there's nothing we can't manage. The Church is already doing relief work there. They..."

Otto interrupted with, "Didn't they have a Church there already?"

"Of course they did, but it was not as wealthy, nor as well organised. The problems will need central funding too, but I don't want to go throwing figures about the room until we have completed our survey of the region. There is still much work to be done." Then, with a deliberately upbeat tone, he added, "There are a great many good things that Norland will provide us with. They have some extremely efficient industries, often complementing rather than competing with our existing ones. It could have been a whole lot worse. Cragoop has been telling me that we have begun to experience something of a labour shortage as of late. There is a ready workforce down there, currently under-utilised, which can fill the gap. The potential is there, it needs careful supervision and management at a high level."

The Despot asked, "When are you next travelling down there, Emil?"

"Soon; I haven't decided exactly."

"Mmm... before you go, I'd like to discuss having you as a permanent Norland Secretary. As permanent as the foreseeable future anyway. Your land portfolio can be dealt with by another senator. We'll discuss it first thing before you leave."

"As you wish, My Lord."

The one other item of import was Cragoop saying that the proposed increase in stone quarry production was taking shape. More men had been taken on and new machines purchased. All was going according to plan. Tristan sat impassively in the background throughout the meeting. He took notes, but Frank had not spoken to him since they got back. He was starting to have doubts as to whether the role of Despot's secretary was for him. What role? He was not being given much to do. It therefore came as something of a surprise at the conclusion of the meeting when Frank addressed him. They were crossing the courtyard on the way to the Castle, passing the new Capparathian wagon about to be demonstrated to the senators.

"Right, Tristan, when we get back, I want you to organise a messenger, the best we've got, to go down to Capparathia, to Despot Schmidt and urge him and his wife to travel to Asattan where I will rendezvous with them. This is the opportunity for them to make a presentation before the Inner Council regarding their university idea. There's no time like the present as I'll be there to support them."

"Yes, My Lord."

"You can help me compose the message to Schmidt. It is a matter of urgency. I also want you to write a letter to the Mehtar." Then, seeing his assistant's shocked face, he added, "We'll do it together."

"Yes, My Lord."

"I want to keep him abreast of our latest news of the Ladosans. It's important that we share intelligence. Also, I want us to ask for a couple of extra superdakks for us to pass onto Despot Schmidt."

"I see."

"We mustn't forget Despot Heisler, either. I'll need you to help me do a communication to him as well... But first shall we have a drink? I'm thirsty!"

Flonass was working late at the mill. In fact it was ridiculously late, well past sunset.

Business had been brisk over the past few weeks. The late summer order book was bulging. The owner's assistant was busier than ever, but he did not mind. That afternoon, though, round about the time Mr Ornstein left for the day, Flonass detected a mistake in his paperwork. He had duplicated an order number. By the time he finished double-checking the documents, the light was failing and the last of the other employees leaving.

"Leave the keys with me, I'll lock up. I'll drop the key off at your house on the way home," he told the man in charge of the front gate. It was an unusual request, but Flonass was a trusted employee by now and there was no resistance.

Mr O had granted him the following day off, so he must get the mistake rectified before he left. Paperwork corrected, all he had to do was change the number on the consignment in the yard. It would be heading for the quarry in the morning.

By the light of his lantern, he made sure the safe was locked and his desk neat. Then, after putting on his rucksack, he picked up a marker, keys and his lantern and exited the office. The door lock could be tricky at times, but the key turned smoothly on this occasion. He descended the stairs to the floor of the compound, holding his light firmly ahead of him.

Everything was deathly quiet, but Flonass was not afraid of the dark, or being there by himself, so he went about his business unperturbed. There were many stacks of timber to negotiate his way round, but he knew the plan of the area like the back of his hand. He soon found the wagon with the duplicate number on it. Squatting behind it, he put the lantern down on the ground as he made the necessary amendment.

The operation did not take long, but, the moment it was complete, his ears pricked up. For he could hear male voices approaching and something in their tone told him that something was wrong. He extinguished his lantern immediately and stood up.

Even the slightest sound carried in that stillness and he did not move a muscle at first as the voices got closer. The gate was still unlocked, but he heard it creaking on its hinges as it opened. His direct view was hidden by stacks of wood, but he saw moving lights flickering beyond. There was no good reason for anyone to be here and while he could not make out the words as such, their tone told him that the new arrivals were up to no good.

Stealthily, Flonass began working his way back to the office. The extinguished lantern might have made a noise, so he left it on the ground as he felt his way forward, bit by bit.

By the time he got within sight of the wooden stairs leading to the office, two of the intruders were at the top, conversing with a third man at the bottom.

"Bloody well stay where you are!" hissed one of the figures at the top in a false whisper to the one downstairs.

The observer now got a good view of the man speaking by lantern light and immediately knew he had seen him before. A white, he was Flonass' predecessor and left under a cloud. He had not heard anything of him in the intervening year, but knew him to be of bad stock from old Vionium.

"We'll drag the safe here and then throw it over the edge," the man called down. He was speaking in a fairly loud voice now, apparently confident that no one else was about. Flonass wondered why they had not waited until later in the night, but, to be fair, normally no one was about after dark. Besides, it would not be an easy journey back home in the dark. 'They probably waited until the last of the workers left,' thought Flonass. 'A good thing they did not see my light.'

The men at the top wielded an axe and soon smashed their way into the office. Meanwhile, Flonass was trying to find a weapon to use. Trying not to make any noise, he picked up a pole from a stack. Eight centimetres in diameter and a little over a metre long, it would have to do.

Creeping forward carefully, he homed in on the man at the foot of the stairs. The intruder never saw it coming. One huge blow on the head and the fellow dropped like a stone to the ground. He was not going to bother anyone again.

Flonass looked up, conscious that the lantern ablaze nearby would expose him if one of the other pair glanced out at this moment. They did not. He dragged the limp body away into the shadows and hid under the stairwell.

"Malka? Where are you, you son of a frass?"

It was the second robber, not the ex-employee Flonass had recognised. Following a pause, the man made his way down to ground level... to be met by a great "thwack!" as the pole hit him.

This time the blow landed in his midriff and he bet double, unable to make a sound. A further blow to the head rendered him unconscious.

At this point, the sole remaining thief came out and saw Flonass dive for the shadows. Pulling out a large knife, he charged down the stairs in pursuit.

Flonass had a decision to make; whether to fight a man with a knife with his pole, or hide. He chose the latter course of action.

"Come here, you bastard!" the man cried, but the current employee was easily able to evade him amongst the stacks of wood. The would-be robber never relinquished his light, so it was easy to see where he was coming from.

Soon Flonass was back at the wagon and, after a period of feeling in the dark, located his lantern. He hesitated a moment while he worked out a plan of action, then he put it into action.

The lantern at the bottom of the stairs had never been extinguished, so the courtyard, including the gate, was well illuminated. Flonass worked his way forward gingerly, keeping one eye on where the other man was moving between the piles of timber. He got the key to the gate firmly in his hand before he dashed across there. Before the intruder worked out what was going on, the gate was being closed and locked.

There was no time for a sigh of relief, for her knew that the robber would be able to scale the fence in time. At least it gave him the opportunity to get away down the road.

He was reluctant to light his lantern, for it would show for kilometres in this pitch black. Even so, after ending up in the ditch twice, he realised there was no choice. He pulled out his lighting equipment from his rucksack and knelt on the side of the road. It was at that point he realised quite how much his hands were trembling.

The steel was cold to the touch and the lighting operation seemed to take far too long. Eventually the lantern was lit and he fumbled his other things back into his rucksack, glancing regularly behind him for a pursuer. He had to get away from there quickly.

It seemed a bit ridiculous, trotting down the road, holding the lantern as steadily as possible out in front, yet he dare not loiter. Where to go, though? He did not want to go home and leave it until the morning. It did not seem like a sensible option. The constables would not be about at this hour. Then it struck him, he would go up to the Castle and see if some soldiers would come out straightway.

Then an additional thought occurred, for it was then that Darda came to mind. His friend was a squad leader there, surely he would help.

Midnight came as he progressed through Castleton, going at a swift walk now. One or two lights were on in the houses there, but the vast majority were dark. His own illumination was flickering and close to going out by now. It failed as the Castle entrance, with its flaming torches on either side, came into view. Tired, but with renewed hope, he picked up his steps and advanced on the duty sentries.

The two guardsmen at the gate were standing impassively. In a normal night-shift the most exciting thing was to catch a glimpse of a low-flying ulner. So it was with some surprise that they spotted the lone figure emerging from the shadows. His gait told of some purpose about him and they stirred as he got closer.

"There's been an incident at the sawmill," Flonass began the speech he had been rehearsing. "Two men have been injured in an attempted robbery."

He went on to ask for Squad Leader Darda, saying that he was a personal friend. Fortunately, the guards were not dismissive. Anything to relieve the boredom and if this individual was their officer's friend, then Darda should not be cross about being woken up at this ungodly hour.

The man was fast asleep in his quarters on the second floor of the castle.

"Uh? What is it?"

It must be something important to be woken at that time and when his friend's name was mentioned, he came to swiftly.

Whispering, so as not to disturb anyone else, he said, "I'll be down as soon as I've got dressed."

Soon he was in the hall, looking at the sight of his pal with one of the guardsmen. Bleary-eyed, he asked, "What is it, Flonass?"

The tale was told succinctly. He concluded, "I think one or more of them might still be there. I didn't know where best to come for official help, then I thought of you."

Darda raised a smile, for, to him, a friend in need was a friend indeed. Addressing the guardsmen, he ordered, "Go upstairs now," and he rattled off five names of guardsmen he wanted waking up. Semi-armour, swords and lanterns, get them to report here on the double."

"Yes, sir!"

Then turning to Flonass, he added, "Don't worry, we'll go along there and see what's what."

"It's a long way."

"Not as far as it is to Azekah," joked Darda. "Do you want to sit down for a moment?"

A few days later, Flonass and Darda were indulging in an alcoholic beverage up at the Selerm. The latter was enjoying the afternoon off, but would have to be back at the Castle before nightfall. He was pleased to have secured a superdakk for the day which meant he did not have to rush away too early.

As for his friend, he would not forget the time that had passed since they were standing by the Castle together on the night of the failed robbery. The most practical way for he and the soldiers to get back to the mill in the inky dark was on foot, so he was shattered by the time they arrived back.

Of the two intruders he had struck, one was dead and the other suffered multiple fractures. Their accomplice, David the former assistant at the mill was now in custody. Mr O was relieved and delighted with Flonass' actions. He was not alone in that regard.

"The man has outplayed his hand this time!" announced Senator Drasnik with unconcealed glee.

For he and the constables has been trying to tie down this David and his reprobate family for years. He saw this as his opportunity to come down hard on the man and his whole clan. It was a case to be heard by the constables, but the senator would guide them in this matter.

"The drinks are on the house!" announced Tsodd as one of his employees plonked a couple of ales in front of the pair at a table.

"Thank you," said Flonass, "I was..."

"You did the community a favour," the Selerm owner replied, to applause from the other people present.

"But I..."

"Vionium can do without their sort. You've helped us all with your brave actions."

Later, the two friends were left to themselves to chat. Darda was happy to bask in the reflected glory of his mate's five minutes of fame. "You did well, Flonass."

"I didn't mean to *kill* that bloke! I just needed him out of the way."

"Of course. You did what was necessary."

Back in Azekah, Flonass had killed men in battle, but this was different. Nobody blamed him for dispatching the robber, in fact his action was lauded, but he still felt bad about it.

"But if I hadn't hit him so hard, I might not have incapacitated him. There were three of them and only one of me."

"You mustn't feel bad about it. They had no right to be there and they got what they deserved. You did well, Flonass."

Senator Vebber was not the sole person taking regular trips down to Norland. Gabriell had made several such journeys on behalf of the Thyatiran Church. The morning after one such visit, he was reporting back to Bishop Gunter in the latter's ground floor study.

"There's great poverty in the white sector of town. I visited several houses there. They rent from a black landlord who, apparently, leaves them alone as long as they pay up on time. The houses are in a poor state of repair, although to be fair I've seen worse in my time. One little child let it slip that they have their coats on their bed at night, because there are not enough blankets to go round."

"I imagine," the bishop replied, "that we're talking about a sizeable problem here."

"It is. I thought that next time I went, I could try to quantify it. If we're going to try and bring some relief to these people, we first need to understand the scale of it all first."

"Quite."

"And I think that Senator Vebber's census is going to help us with that. I encountered some of the census takers, it was not merely a number-collecting exercise. They have got some data there which will be useful to us."

The bishop nodded before replying, "I'll have a word with the senator. Meanwhile, I have held conversations with Alan about it. He was most supportive. He reckons that there will be increased work opportunities for the Norland whites now that they are part of our despotate."

"That's good. That will help the situation in the long-term. I've been trying to imagine some of those tiny children come the winter. Some basic assistance with clothes and blankets will go a long way. That's for the short-term, of course. Beyond that we need to plan carefully and understand the scale of the task before acting."

Gunter replied, "I have a meeting scheduled for this afternoon before Senator Vebber sets off for Norland once more. I know that he has been interviewing the local authorities down there."

"I think you'll find they're more concerned with feathering their own nests more than looking after their people."

"I fear you're right. They must be told in no uncertain terms where their new Despot's priorities lie. Despot Thorn has made it perfectly clear to me that he fully supports the Church's mission down there.

He wants to see the lot of the poor people, which almost always means the whites, improved."

"I'm pleased to hear it."

"But I totally agree with your proposed strategy. In the short-term, I'd like you to set up relief bases in each of the main towns. I shall write letters to be delivered to the respective mayors informing them of our intentions. We are not asking for their permission. We can bring down the full weight of the Despot's authority upon them if they try to obstruct the Church's operation. We have the funds; this is our opportunity to put them to good use."

"Thank you, Gunter, I'm delighted to have backing both from yourself and Despot Thorn. Armed with that authority, I'm sure we can move mountains."

"You have enough Church volunteers?"

"I certainly have. We are working well as a team."

"Excellent! But tell me: I hope you had the opportunity to share in worship with local churches while you were down there."

"Oh yes, they can be a lively bunch."

"I'm glad to hear it."

"But there was one encounter that annoyed me somewhat."

"Oh?"

"There was an... um, event held one evening in the biggest church in Newton. A presentation was followed by a question and answer session. Asked to be on the panel to give answers and opinions, I was happy to accept.

"I'd been assisting with some manual work that afternoon, helping move stuff around the place. It'd gone on longer than anticipated and there was no time to change. So I was in my rough clothes. Anyway, the guest speaker was an elderly gentleman from Reichmenn. When we were introduced, he immediately began pressing me with searching questions. Was I born again? Had I been filled with the Spirit? I was able to answer both in the affirmative. He then began going on about speaking in tongues. I tried to tell him it was a gift I had neither asked for, nor desired. That was not good enough for him. He told me that I could not be a full Christian unless I spoke in tongues."

"How rude!" exclaimed Gunter, quite shocked.

"It was, but not the first time I've come across such an attitude."

"You should have told him to read 1 Corinthians. St Paul was completely opposed to folk who put that gift ahead of others."

"I know; you're right. I should have said something like that. As it was, I think I was too shocked to give him a coherent answer... but then I did not want to get involved in a theological debate at that juncture. It would not have been appropriate. Besides, it was clear that he possessed a closed mind and wouldn't listen to anything I said."

"Oh dear. I hope it didn't spoil your evening."

"Not quite, but I could have done without it. Like I said, it is not the first time I have encountered those who say you are a second-class Christian if you do not speak in tongues."

"It's a crazy thing for people to say," Gunter replied. "It is prideful, boastful and also plain unbiblical."

Gabriell then broke into a chuckle, adding, "Of course we won't be so intransigent in our beliefs and not listen to anyone else when we get old, will we?"

"Of course not," the bishop replied, smiling.

Later in the conversation, the ecclesiarch raised a fresh topic, saying, "Azikial came to see me the other day."

"Ah, everything okay at the hospice?"

"Ticking over nicely, I gather. Then we got to discussing new ideas for services. I'd like to have your opinion on them."

"Okay."

"While we have a good number of lively services, I'm trying to introduce a few more contemplative ones. I must confess that Abbot Muggawagga has been an inspiration here."

"A godly man."

"Indeed. I've been thinking of introducing an evening, or night-time service of contemplation. We could start with the church being well lit with many candles to begin with. Then we could extinguish the candles one by one while a lament psalm is read out."

"Hmm, sounds like a good idea for Lent, or Holy Week."

"Then choristers could come in from the back, each holding a candle, bringing in light. The symbolism is clear: we'd be saying that God is here, therefore there is hope, and so on..."

After a pause to consider this, the priest said, "You could also use a psalm as an intercession, with pauses for reflective silence."

"I like that idea! Thank you."

"Although we'd have to think carefully where to hold it. If folk are having to walk home in the dark following the service... that is the way accidents happen. Lanterns have been known to go out, leaving the poor people stranded if they're not careful."

Both men had only ever known the pitch black, moonless, Molten nights, but Bishop Gunter rather overlooked this valid concern in his enthusiasm for the finer points of the service itself. "Maybe," he eventually replied, "it would be something to be held up at the Castle, in the new chapel there. I'll speak to Despot Thorn when he has a moment."

"Yes, a good idea. I'm certain he'll be sympathetic to the idea."

It was late summer and nature appeared tired. Shrivelling nettles stood amongst the long, yellow grass. The spirit of growth had slowed and the vegetation looked dusty and worn out. The mornings were cooler, with heavy dew which showed up on little spiders' cobwebs on the grass first thing.

While her husband prepared for his up-coming visit to Asattan, Hannah was overseeing the finishing of her garden project. She was quite pleased with the unique way it was turning out, a departure from the original Ladosan formal garden.

Upon her return from Capparathia, the head gardener had given her a full progress report. She told him, "It may be somewhat unorthodox, but I'm happy with the result. Funny how it started from the idea of a herb garden. At least that is up and running."

"It certainly is, My Lady, the kitchen staff have come to rely on it."

"So they should."

"The wild flower section is well past its best, as you can see, but it looked a mass of colours when it was at its best."

"I have high hopes for it next year, with the able assistance of you and your staff."

"Thank you, My Lady," the head gardener returned, with a slight bow.

A row of young apple trees were planted beside a pathway in the centre of the garden. These would be trained along a frame in due course as they grew. The grass labyrinth was not a great success. In fact it was a muddy mess at present and the head gardener suggested extra drainage be put in.

She had already heard of an increased reluctance on the part of the Ladosan refugees to get involved. The gardener explained.

"They are playing hard to get. In fact, there was little choice but to give up on them in the end and rely on locals instead. Fortunately there have been plenty of them sufficiently inspired by your project to lend a hand...."

"That's good," replied Hannah.

"Plus the criminals, of course, and occasional assistance from the guardsmen for heavy lifting."

"Indeed."

She had heard that the women were put off by the locals, but decided to say no more. If the Civil War was over it would be but a matter of time before they returned in any case.

Mid-morning, she was back there with her friend Freya Ronenvink.

"The grass is still wet," the senator's wife complained, "my shoes are getting saturated! I should have worn my boots. It's too late now."

Hannah smiled by way of an answer, then asked her friend what she thought of it. As she spoke, Darda was on site, directing his men to put some large, heavy, ornamental pots into place.

"I like it," was the simple verdict.

"Good."

"Obviously there will be more to do in the coming years. I realise that. One can't have a fully-developed garden overnight. Nevertheless. you've got off to a good start."

"I'm glad you like it."

"I do indeed."

Meanwhile, another squad of soldiers was making its way back from Ladosan border duty. The track had recently been raised, widened and mettled with hulffan tar. It was a whole lot better than before.

Looking back at her own project, Hannah remarked, "Once these pots are in place it should finish it off for now."

"They certainly add something."

"Yes. I don't see any sense in spending too much time on the garden for the rest of the year. We will see how it beds in over winter. Then in the spring we can launch a new campaign."

"You make it sound like a war," Freya replied and they both laughed.

384

Darda and his squad soon finished their work, aided by the head gardener. Hannah inspected it all and instructed them to make a few minor adjustments before pronouncing her satisfaction.

Back at the Castle, Darda entered the hall to find the Despot and his assistant standing in front of him.

"Ah, just the man!"

"My Lord?"

"We're travelling down to Ephamon first thing tomorrow, to Asattan. I want you and your squad to accompany us as our escort."

"Yes, My Lord."

"I've spoken with Captain Jonathan and he is happy for you to pick five additional men to accompany us, so you'll have a larger command than usual. Tristan here will go through the requirements for the trip."

With that, the Despot left, leaving his assistant to fill in the details.

"We will be taking the three new Capparathian wagons and two superdakks..."

"Nothing but the best!" quipped Darda.

Ignoring this, Tristan continued, "We want to see if we can do the journey in two days instead of the normal three. Matthew is organising the catering. I need you to get your men together, ensure they have all the necessary equipment. We will need spare parts for the wagons, including two spare axles, and..."

"Do they have the same type of axle as the normal wagons?"

"Um, I don't know. You'll have to find out. Plus a total of twenty-four dakks for the journey, so you'll have to speak to the stable master."

Darda therefore found his hands full for the rest of the day getting everything in place for an early getaway the next day. He would have liked to have visited his parents before the departure, but it simply was not possible. He sent them a short note instead.

The following morning all was ready and the party for travelling southeast was assembled in the bailey. The wagons had been cleaned and looked fresh and new. A couple of the dakks were making loud coughing noises in the cool air. Hannah, after wishing her husband a safe journey, was standing back, watching him embark. She had hoped that he would not have to travel down to the Capital this year, but it had not worked out that way. Following his kidnapping the previous year, Hannah knew that she would be on edge while he was away. At least he had ensured a larger than normal guard accompany the small convoy.

"Bye bye" Frank called out as he took his place next to Tristan. The curtain sides were down so that they could see the people seeing them off. As well as the Despot's family, there were relatives of the other participants and a contingent of Castle workers.

Slowly the vehicles processed out of the exit and onto the road to the Capital. Once free of the Castle, the lead driver obeyed his instructions by getting the dakks to go at a faster pace than usual. With six dakks per wagon, it was hoped that they would be able to sustain this speed over a long distance. Time would tell.

Usually much of the escort ambled alongside the wagons. This time all the soldiers were seated inside the following vehicles. Relief dakks and the two tethered superdakks took up the rear.

"Right!" announced Frank, looking at Tristan with purpose. "I want to stop in good time tonight while it is still light."

"It'll be interesting to see how far we get."

"It will, but tonight I want you to help me with my speech to the Inner Council. The main point of the meeting will be to do with the pact with the Ladosans, as you know. However, if Despot Schmidt has received my message and can get to the Capital in time, before the meeting, then I want us to put forward this university idea. We are having to think on our feet, somewhat, but I have the notes from our discussions with the Schmidts. I want to use them to form the basis of a speech to inform and inspire the Inner Council Members. It will be a first for Hoame, and I realise that some of the ideas are radical, but if we don't do it now, I fear it will get delayed until next year."

"Which might, My Lord, give you all more time to perfect your ideas."

"You're right, of course, but at the very least I'd like to sow the seed on this visit. We're unlikely to be discussing the fine details such as funding, but to get them aware of the idea, and start to come to terms with it now, will save time in the long run. They will take a lot of convincing, some of them at least, so we will have to make my speech a good one."

"Yes, My Lord," replied Tristan with sudden enthusiasm. He relished the challenge and, besides, he thought a university was an exciting idea. "I am confident that we can come up with something that will grip them."

"Good, that's the spirit!"

"We will spark their enthusiasm as a first step to a University of Hoame."

"Excellent!" exclaimed Frank before sitting back contented. It was good to see the scenery going past at more than a snail's pace for a change. He was going to enjoy this journey.

Hannah's wagon drew up at the monastery. With her husband away at the Capital, she had made a snap decision to visit her friend Wanda Shreeber. As she disembarked, her driver and handmaiden helping her down, she realised that she was arriving unannounced.

Walking the short distance to Muggawagga's office, she met a monk coming out.

"Is the abbot within?"

"No, My Lady, he's out on a visit today."

"Ah."

"Was it anything I could help with?"

"Um, I was wanting to visit Madam Shreeber."

"I see. I can lead you to the women's quarters. A nun can take you from there."

She thanked the man prettily, but said that she could find her own way. That was exactly what she did. An under-abbess was on duty and, deferring to the Despotess, bid her go through to visit her friend. A handmaiden followed, holding a small bunch of flowers.

For the entire journey from the Castle she had been wondering how to start the conversation with Wanda. The last time she had asked, "How are you?" only to blush at the crassness of the question. How would anyone feel being incarcerated for the rest of their lives? Was it going to be an "on" day, or an "off" day?

As she rounded the last bend in the corridor, she took the flowers off her servant and bid her stay there. With delicate footsteps, she covered the last fifty metres to the cell. The wall on the outside was painted off-white with a dark green vine pattern. She peered through the grill of the locked oak door to see inside.

The walls within were bare, but a couple of barred windows brought a reasonable amount of light in. There were several items of furniture, including a well-stocked bookshelf. The bed was over to one side and a latrine was hidden by a thick curtain. In the centre of the room sat its occupant on a wheel-back chair reading a book.

Wanda looked up from it and, seeing who it was, gave a huge smile. Putting the slim volume down on a side table, she came straight over to the grill. This opened on a hinge and Hannah said, "I've brought you these," as she passed the flowers through.

"Thank you, they're beautiful," she said with feeling. As she took them further into the room, she continued, "I have a vase... and water. Give me a moment..."

"Of course," replied her friend, pleased that the visit was getting off to a good start. It was an "on" day.

There was a stool outside for the visitor to perch on and soon the conversation was flowing. Inevitably the news was all one-sided, but it did not seem to matter. Wanda enjoyed hearing all about the trip to Rilesia and Capparathia and listened intensely while it was described to her.

"So you liked Despotess Schmidt then?"

"I did. She was down to earth without being coarse. I don't think I'll be taking a leaf out of her fashion sense though."

Wanda giggled, then became more earnest as she asked, "Did you say Tristan went with you?"

"He did."

"How is he getting on?"

"As Frank's assistant? Extremely well as far as I can tell. Frank seems pleased with him."

"Good, that's good," Tristan's mother said wistfully before adding with a note of urgency, "but don't tell him I asked after him."

Hannah agreed not to. It was a pity that the young man had not been to visit his mother at all, but maybe it was understandable in the circumstances. A delicate subject, that much was certain.

"And Frank?" asked Wanda, "he found the visit worthwhile?"

"Yes, he did. Although now he's taken a trip to the Capital. I hope he's not too long this time."

"Joseph?"

"It was a holiday and an adventure for him. I'll never forget his reaction as we went on the lake in a boat. He was amazed by it all."

They discussed further things and the conversation flowed. Then Hannah said, "My dear, if I can find Frank in a good mood one day, I will try again."

"Try....?"

"Asking if he will grant you a pardon."

"Don't!"

"But..."

"Don't give me hope, Hannah. On a day like today, with the sun streaming in, I can be at peace with myself. Hope would be a dangerous thing in my situation. For every peak in my moods there is a trough. Far better if I can live day by day and not consider what might be. Imagination is an enemy, my dear, I do not want to give it rein."

Hannah realised that she had gone too far and was annoyed with herself. Desperately, she thought of another topic to turn to. Mercifully, she found it.

"My garden! My Ladosan garden at the foot of the Castle, it's finished. Or, I should say, finished as far as this year is concerned."

"That's wonderful," the other woman replied, regaining her composure. "Describe it to me."

Which is exactly what Hannah did. She was there a long time before finally dragging herself away. In the wagon on the way home she replayed how the visit had gone. Favourably, she concluded, but that did not hide the fact it was a tragic situation. Wanda was not an evil person, she told herself, but had succumbed to a moment of madness that ended her husband's life and, in a different way, her own.

She looked up from her daydreaming. The wagon was passing Deejan Charvo's fine house and there, in the middle-distance was the imposing edifice of her home, the Castle.

~ End of Chapter 19 ~

Prospects of Peace - Chapter 20

Despot Schmidt and his wife were well within the Ephamon region, nearing the Capital. They were passing a field which was covered in weeds, obviously left fallow that year. Up ahead was the largest city Hoame had to offer, Asattan, the central hub of their country and home to the ruling Inner Council. It looked grey and not entirely inviting at this distance.

For Norbert had not been to Ephamon many times in his life. He had only visited Asattan once before as an adult. Whilst advisor to Despot Schonhost, he was not once called upon to leave Capparathia.

Now, though, he was on a mission; to sell the university idea to the Keepers themselves. He was delighted to have the most powerful Keeper of all onside, the one who would back him up, the one they were going to rendezvous with shortly.

Rudella, meanwhile, was extremely nervous. It was one thing having an informal chat about it within the confines of one's summer residence. It was quite something else to support your husband as he made a presentation at the Inner Council.

They were forced to travel in one of the old style wagons. Three of the new arvawood ones had been given to the Thyatirans, two were out of commission with teething troubles and the others destroyed in an unfortunate fire. Ironic perhaps, certainly a setback, but not one that would not be overcome in time. Their existing vehicle trundled slowly through the busy city streets. There was not much in the way of other traffic, but it was still crowded with pedestrians.

The tall, imposing, black edifice of the Citadel was visible on occasions through gaps between buildings. The area around the fortress was off limits to vehicles and they skirted round it to get to an inn. This was the establishment recommended by a courtier and, if the servant he sent on ahead had done his job, there was a room booked for them there.

As soon as the wagon wheeled into the courtyard, the couple disembarked. The servants hurrying about were invisible to them, but the couple standing to greet them were not.

"Frank! Tristan!" Rudella exclaimed as she surged forward to give them hugs. The assistant was surprised she remembered his name, let alone this show of affection. In truth it was the relief of seeing familiar faces that prompted it. Norbert, too, was generous in his greeting.

Once these were over, Frank said, "We got your message in good time, but you do realise that you can come and stay within the Citadel itself?"

"I'm sure," replied Norbert softly, "but to be honest we'll be more comfortable here."

The Keeper did not press the matter, but asked if their journey had been a good one. It was then that the tale of the wagon fire came out. Wanting to play it down, he added, "It's a piece of ill fortune, it's true, but one that we will soon recover from. But tell; when did you arrive here?"

"In Asattan? Yesterday. We made good progress in the wagons you gave us!"

They had to laugh at the irony. Then, while Rudella engaged Tristan in animated conversation, Norbert updated his counterpart on another matter.

"I can report that the southern hemisphere people are safely under lock and key. They are securely held and, as you said. I am making sure they cannot influence anyone from where they are."

"Good! I can't stress how dangerous they are. Oh, and best not mention them to any of the Inner Council members. There's no need to worry them unnecessarily."

"Right," Norbert replied gravely.

The mood was a good deal lighter over dinner. Tristan made up the fourth at their table and was enjoying being included. They touched briefly on the university issue and the Schmidts' forthcoming presentation. Most of the conversation was on other matters.

"I have delivered a request to the Mehtar for a couple of superdakks for you. They are in short supply and he may not be able to spare any, but it's worth making the enquiry."

"Thank you, Frank, it would be great if he can release a couple."

"Hmm, well don't broadcast that too much either, or else everyone will want one."

The food was good and the conversation flowed. Nevertheless, they were careful not to stay up too late, for the important Inner Council meeting was due to take place the following morning.

Frank woke with a start and was so disorientated that he briefly checked for his TRAC, As the confusion dissipated, he realised that it was close on twenty years since he last wore a wrist computer. He shook his head and went for a wash.

Breakfast was brought up to him and he ate alone. A whole suite of rooms to himself while Tristan was having to slum it in the servants' quarters. Still, a certain etiquette needed to be observed.

He left for the meeting in good time as was his habit. Even earlier were the Schmidts, sitting in an ante-chamber. Norbert said, "A clerk told us that we would be called when it was our turn."

"That's fine, I'll see you in there then. Good luck."

Within the Council meeting room, Count Birkent was firmly established at the head of the table. The man was frowning as he sifted through the many papers in front of him, but looked up when Frank entered and his countenance lightened.

"Ah, hello Frank. I'm so glad that you could make this important meeting."

"Oh?" replied the other, not sure what this was a reference to.

"The wording to be put to the Ladosans," said Birkent by way of explanation.

"Of course," Frank said dismissively as he sat next to the one other Keeper in the room. Yet inside he was wondering at this. L'Rochfort, Alan and company had been trying to thrash out an agreement with their foreign neighbours, and former enemies, for years. Why the sudden rush?

Count Bodstein - Bodd - was next to arrive and gave his fellow Thyatiran the warmest of welcomes.

"You're not having to dash home immediately afterwards, I hope."

"Up north, you mean?"

"Yes."

"I don't want to hang around too long. I was thinking in terms of leaving tomorrow morning."

"I wondered if you and I could have lunch together here in the Citadel afterwards."

"Of course, I'll have time for that."

The room filled up fairly quickly after that. Baron Raseberg alone sent his apologies; all the others were present. Count Birkent did not delay in getting proceedings underway.

"Gentlemen, as ever the situation in Ladosa is far from crystal clear. Our best analysis is that the civil war is over and a new central government is about to be formed. Baron L'Rochfort here has been working on a revised proposal to put to the new administration. You have the floor, Baron."

L'Rochfort stood up and addressed them. "We all know how unpredictable the Ladosans can be. All the same, our network of informants from within that country has never been better and I believe we have the clearest picture possible of conditions there. This morning, I wish to concentrate on how it may affect Hoame / Ladosan relations."

A presentation followed about the foreigners' strange political system and the various big players involved. He concluded, "So while the General Election has not taken place yet, we have reason to believe the new set-up will be more amenable, indeed more reasonable in its reaction to our overtures. I have therefore drafted a proposed wording to be put to their new government as soon as it is in office."

Papers were handed out and the Members proceeded to go through it clause by clause. It quickly became apparent that this was proposing far more than a mere non-aggression pact as had originally been the case. This included some formal trade links and even the idea of setting up of embassies in Asattan and Braskaton. While it was radical, it was well received by most. L'Rochfort saw Frank raising his eyebrows as he read it and pressed him for his reaction.

"It's good, Oskar, but has more scope than I was expecting. It is prop..."

"Not appropriate," Count Wonstein interrupted stiffly, "not appropriate at all. An embassy for the Ladosans in our Capital? I can't even imagine such a thing!"

Frank took it upon himself to respond. "We'd have said that about the Embassy of Rabeth-Mephar a few years ago, but now we're used to it. No one thinks anything of it."

"But the Ladosans..." whined Wonstein.

The count, though, was out of step with the mood of the other Keepers. There was an overwhelming feeling in favour of L'Rochfort's proposal and it was passed with no other dissenting voices.

Meanwhile, in the ante-chamber, the Schmidts sat in silence. They waited patiently, although it seemed like an age. Eventually a clerk collected them and brought them into the room.

It was up to Frank to introduce the couple and he did his best to enthuse about the forthcoming proposal without stealing the Schmidts' thunder. He also kept it brief, so it was soon the Capparathian doing the talking.

"Our proposal for a university in Hoame is to bring about excellence in education and advancements through research," he began. "This establishment should bring together the best minds in the country. It will further our knowledge, advance the competence of the despot houses and be a unifying force for the whole of Hoame."

The Keepers sat in silence, for the most part riveted by what was a novel concept to them. Novel to planet Molten, that is, for they knew about universities of old. Norbert allowed Rudella to address the assembly for certain sections of their presentation and together they gave a thorough picture. Frank felt that they got the right balance with their pitch.

"A ridiculous idea! It's not something we need. I can't see the other despots going for it. Erect a new school for Capparathia by all means, but I for one will not vote for central funds towards it. It is simply not on."

Count Wonstein got his stringent views in first, hoping to sway the opinion of some of the other Members. Frank wondered if his motivation was to get at himself. He knew that Wonstein was not his biggest fan.

In the event, he had once more miscalculated badly. The Count again ended up looking out of touch, completely isolated in his conclusions. The others quickly rallied round Despot Schmidt and declared the idea an excellent one. Frank did not have to say a great deal more, but left it to the Members to enthuse.

"I like the idea," declared Count Schroder, "I like it a lot."

"This could help the country in so many ways," Baron Tastenberg enthused.

In the normal run of things, Hoame's Inner Council did not move so quickly. Yet the decision made there and then was that Baron Moffer would head a commission to look into the whole question. The Schmidts would have to be content with that.

There were a few other, relatively minor, issues discussed before the meeting concluded. The most exciting of these was the need for the Grand Canal to be dredged due to a build-up of silt.

Soon Frank and Bodd were exiting the meeting room. The former asked, "I hope you don't mind if Despot Schmidt and his wife join us for lunch?"

"Of course not, Frank, I'd like to get to know them a bit better."

Tristan caught up with them at the canteen, so it was the five of them together for the meal inside the Citadel. They enjoyed a table to themselves, but it was still quite noisy from the hundred or so other people eating their meals.

Frank was surprised to find Norbert somewhat deflated.

"They listened to what I said, but what did they do in the end? Set up a commission. Isn't that the same as pushing it to one side?"

"No, no!" both Frank and Bodd assured him. The latter went on, "Baron Moffer is a good man, He's open to new ideas. With him on the case you'll get things done."

"You reckon?"

"Absolutely! Plus there was a clear consensus in the Council. You will get your university, of that I am sure."

"I guess we'll have to be patient," replied Norbert as he glanced at his wife. The two Keepers present reaffirmed their belief that it was merely a matter of time.. and commitment; and planning; and promotion... In short, a lot of hard work, but their dream should come to fruition.

Not a great deal had been said by Tristan, but as the topic seemed to be edging towards an end, he made an unexpected contribution.

"Maybe one day, students from Rabeth-Mephar and Ladosa could be invited to come to the University of Hoame. It could be a force for world peace as well as all the other things you've said."

This was a bridge too far in Frank's eyes, but he did not want to slap his assistant down in public. He merely stated, "One day, perhaps, Tristan. It seems that the potential for this university idea is endless."

The others smiled at this, but before long, Bodd was asking Frank about some of the personalities back home.

"Have you seen my brother Tsodd lately? I received a communication from him not long ago."

"Um, no, I haven't in a while."

"He and Katrina are always on the lookout for new ideas for the Selerm. They want to try and keep it fresh now that they have competition."

"But surely there must have been other drinking establishments in what was the Upper Village before Katrina set up the Selerm?"

"They did, but they were pretty dreadful dives, on a much smaller scale. Their place offered something altogether more cheerful and trendy. But what was shiny and trendy ten years ago can soon lose its lustre. They have to work hard to keep it popular."

"Are they succeeding?"

"I think so, although they still have some of the old regulars from day one."

"I see."

"Anastasia and I are thinking of going to Thyatira with the children for a long visit, maybe this autumn."

"Really? It'll be nice to see you."

"Thanks, we've been discussing it. We're thinking of spending the winter there. We thought that a change of scenery for a while might be a good thing for us and give the children a chance to get to know their uncles better."

"Well, you'd be most welcome to come and stay at the Castle you know, Bodd, although the rooms aren't that spacious."

"That's most kind of you, but we'd be staying with Tsodd."

"At the Selerm"

"Yes. If it comes about; it won't be for a few weeks yet."

"Well, if you do come, make sure you call in at the Castle at least."

"We'll do that. Anastasia is keen to meet up with Illianeth again. They continue to correspond regularly you know?"

"I can't say I did. That's nice."

The Schmidts had been listening to this conversation with a detached interest. It did seem strange to them having a white Member of the Inner Council. Then the short figure of Barron Moffer suddenly appeared and spoke to the Capparathians.

"It turns out I have a free afternoon. What say you we make good use of the opportunity for a first discussion about the university idea of yours?"

Norbert and Rudella could not contain their delight and jumped at the chance. The meal was over, so Frank gave his blessing and they got up to go off with the baron. Once they left, Frank said to the to remaining men, "What, with the possibility of better relations with the Ladosans and a university, there could be some big changes on the horizon."

"I hope so," went Tristan, "I'd like to see some change for the better in this land."

Darda and his men were staying at a barracks on the outskirts of Asattan. As on the trip to Rilesia / Capparathia, once the escorting to the destination was accomplished, there was spare time to fill. Their digs were not too far for a healthy young man to walk to the centre of the city.

The squad leader gave his men a brief talk on the need for good behaviour before working out a rota. Six of the soldiers would have to stay at the barracks at all times. The wagons needed to be serviced ready for the return journey and the dakks exercised. Above all, the two superdakks they took to the Capital would have to guarded from outside interference. It was more than Darda's life was worth if, for instance, an Ephamon squaddie tried to take one on a joy ride. "Look after them as if your career depends upon it," he told his men, "because it does!"

Darda spent his fair share of time at the barracks while the others enjoyed a bit of rest and relaxation in the city. He got on well enough with the local officers, despite the fact that they were overwhelmingly blacks, and enjoyed a meal or two with them. For all that, when it was his turn for time off, he chose to walk alone to the centre.

He drank little alcohol these days, unlike some of the soldiers at the barracks. The last one he imbibed was back at the Selerm with Flonass. He had not particularly enjoyed it. Maybe he was changing. The sight of inebriated guardsmen staggering home no longer amused him. His strength of will was such that he did not feel a need to join in. Besides, the truth was he no longer found alcoholic drinks palatable and would sooner have a fruit juice. Who cared what the others thought? Despot Thorn was delighted with his handling of recent escort operations and had told him so. The praise encouraged him all the more to be an exemplary officer.

So it was away from the fleshpots of Asattan, the less salubrious districts, that he went. Instead, he found himself in a small bookshop a stone's throw from the Citadel. A new printing press had started up that spring, a couple of kilometres south of the city. Its produce found a ready retail outlet in this shop to augment its meagre supply of antique volumes. Unfortunately, while the paper quality was not too bad by Hoame's poor standards, the binding was certainly inferior. Darda found one starting to come apart in his hands as soon as he opened it, so he hastily shut it up and placed it back on the shelf.

One of the old volumes was a maths (trigonometry) book It brought a smile to the young man's lips. For memories of the early days in Azekah came flooding back to him. They went for adventure and fighting, but had to begin with extra school lessons and Pythagoras' Theorem. Not that they hadn't ended up with adventures galore, night raids, flaming projectiles... Then there were the funny instances, such as getting stuck in a drainage ditch and having to be rescued by a girl, or sneaking back through the enemy camp in his underpants...

"Are ye gonna buy that? Or perhaps stand there and read the whole book for free?"

Without answering the shopkeeper, Darda replaced the book and walked out. He had seen enough.

Then there had been the poignant moments in Azekah, such as the expression on the enemy prisoner-of-war working in the quarry. He wondered if he was still alive; still showing that defiance in his eyes.

The sun was lower than he expected when he got back out into the street. It was time to head back to the barracks. He stopped at a vendor on the street corner to buy a bag of sweetmeats for a sten. They tasted good. He chewed them one by one as he strode back to base. It had been a good trip out, even if he did not have a huge amount to show for it.

The next day he received a message that the Despot would be heading back to Thyatira that morning. There was much activity as the dakks were teamed up with the wagons. Darda breathed a sigh of relief when he saw that the superdakks were fit and ready to go.

It still seemed novel for the wagons to travel faster than walking pace on the way back north. These new conveyances were worth their weight in gold, it was a pity that they could not be mass produced due to the scarcity of the wood.

Used to ambling alongside the convoy, Darda found it strange sitting out the journey. Some of his men were in the wagon with him, laughing and joking with some friendly banter. Yet the squad leader was apart, sitting up one end. Gone were the days when he could join in with them. He knew that it was no longer an option. Captain Jonathan had made it perfectly clear that his status dictated that he was not "one of the boys."

He watched the trees as they passed. One was a large, long-dead oak. The trunk displayed a cavernous opening, exposing its hollow interior. The wood was bleached by the sun. Meanwhile the grass verges were yellow and dry.

'It would be good to have another get-together with my friends,' he considered. 'The last time I had a drink with Flonass, Vophsi was busy working in the kitchens. We'll have to pick a time when he's not on duty.'

As on the outward journey, the distance was covered in two days, to the delight of Despot Thorn. When they got to the Castle in Thyatira, the squad leader went about his duties with a quiet efficiency. His men appreciated his light style of command these days.

The following week passed quickly. One mid-morning, after to seeing to matters in the courtyard, Darda sought out his Captain to report to him. An agenda for the day's work was swiftly agreed.

"Well done, Darda," Jonathan said in parting, "keep up the good work."

This was something of a surprise, but he was not going to mind if his superior's attitude towards him had changed for the better.

Meanwhile, Frank, after lunch, decided to get straight back to work and walked over to the senate building. There, Hanz Drasnik was itching to give him a report.

"This David fellow had been a thorn in our side for some time. We were as sure as we could be that he and his family were involved in various criminal activities, but we could never pin anything on them. Now, however, he and two of his gang have been caught red-handed trying to steal a safe from the sawmill out of Vionium. A quick-thinking employee summoned some soldiers."

"Excellent!"

"We held the trial while you were away. David, the ring leader, has been given a ten year gaol sentence, followed by exile from Thyatira."

His tone-of-voice here seemed to be seeking approval, so the Despot was quick to support him.

"A good job, Hanz. And the rest of the gang?"

"Also sent to gaol, apart from one who perished. We've searched David's home and come across other stolen goods. Never managed that before; maybe they were getting complacent. Either way, that has given us the ammunition to come down hard on the family too."

Frank did not ask for details. He was simply pleased that the senator was dealing with it.

Later in the day, as he sat in his senate office going through some papers with Tristan, he had another visitor.

"My Lord, are you busy?"

"It's all right, Japhses, come in, sit down. How are things?"

"Busy as usual, but not a lot of excitement. I had a long conversation with Senator Vebber last week regarding the Norland acquisition. I needed to know how it will affect the army."

"Go on."

"There's obviously a larger pool for recruits. We have compulsory training for militia members in old Thyatira, but the senator was telling me that he'd like to hang fire on rolling that out to Norland."

"Mmm, he's probably right. We don't want to introduce too many changes all at once for our new citizens. Something for the future."

"Yes, My Lord. A modest enlargement of the guard has already been agreed by the senate. I would like to recruit some of these from the Norland towns."

"Marvellous idea; it'll help the integration."

"Senator Vebber agrees and with higher unemployment down there, I am hopeful for a positive response."

"What about the men from there who were already in the Aggepariian army?"

"Most seem to have opted to stay with Despot Kagel. A few agreed to be assimilated into our force."

"I see," replied Frank.

"There is one other small thing, My Lord."

"Yes?"

"An incident that occurred yesterday and has been reported to me by Captain Jonathan."

"All right."

"It was in the hall and..."

"The Castle?"

"Yes. Jonathan saw our new squad leader, Darda, handle a situation with great professionalism."

"Oh yes, what happened?"

"A young lad, a kitchen worker I believe, was creating a disturbance. He was upsetting a lot of people with his behaviour. Then Darda came over and ejected him without a fuss. He reminds me of Alan a bit. Jonathan was most impressed by how he handled the situation."

"That's good, he should be praised for that."

"My Lord."

"We took a bit of a gamble taking Darda on, but it's one which seems to have paid off. It goes to show that we should take a bit of a risk sometimes."

Autumn was heralded in Ladosa with several days of high winds and showers. The temperature was noticeably cooler and folk began stockpiling fuel for the winter days to come. Many went nut collecting too.

Nature looked tired. The flowers were wilting, the nettles sagging and the grass had lost its lustre. The hedgerows were suddenly thick with bright red berries.

The peace was holding. In fact no one now believed that the war would recommence. There was no will for such a thing on any side. The country was as tired as Mother Nature appeared to be. Each political party fared differently in the war. The conflict left only four viable players standing, the Buffs, the Rose, the Pinks and the Neo-Purples. The Buffs, who formed the pre-war government, had not fared well. Following a bitter struggle, their south-western enclave was annihilated. Meanwhile, their central bastion was in poor shape. With enemies every side, their troops found themselves spread too thinly around their perimeter to take the initiative. The catastrophe of the superbolide knocked them hard as well. What was left of their leadership now made the hard decision to abandon Braskaton. The capital city would not be rebuilt. The Buff Part still functioned, but it was a shadow of its former self.

The Rose Party, too, was a radically different organisation from that which began the civil war. Their eastern enclave was wiped out at a stroke by the fireball from the sky. It was no more. That left its stronghold, and main centre of operations in the northwest. From there they engaged Pink and Buff armies. Casualties had been high, territorial advances minimal. Many of the party's radical voices were no more. A more sober, conciliatory leadership had emerged, one which saw real benefit in an alliance with the Neo-Purples. Sage council within Rose ranks was for developing this tie-up. "Only together are we are strong enough to stand against the Buffs," was the motto of the hour.

The Pinks started with two centres of operation at the outbreak of hostilities, much like the Rose Party. The Pink's southern area had been squeezed between no less than five other factions and was not able to withstand the pressure. They were completely overrun. Their larger, northern area had been hit hard by the superbolide on one side and the Rose army on the other. Whilst they remained intact, they suffered terrible casualties and were but a shadow of their former selves. Sidelined in the talks being held by the other three remaining factions, they sat and watched for the outcome. Their overwhelming desire was a fresh General Election and a return to Ladosan normality.

Which left the Neo-Purples. Through excellent generalship and skilful strategy, they completely overran and defeated a superior Buff force. The war transformed them from bit-part to major players. They gained in strength like no other party. They also felt they held the moral high-ground, broadcasting the atrocities perpetrated by some of the Buffs, There were squabbles aplenty within the Neo-Purple political committee, but that was to be expected. They were good Ladosans after all and one thing they can do is squabble about politics.

Winning the war was one thing; winning the peace quite another. Since the armistice, the factions got together and agreed that a new General Election must take place. They needed to thrash out the conditions and organisation required. Mutual mistrust had to be overcome in order to achieve this, but achieve it they did. A six week election campaign was agreed upon. The new, temporary parliament would be based in Lefange, northwest of the devastated former capital Braskaton. The election was to take place against a pretty chaotic social backdrop.

Many people had been displaced from their homes as a result of the conflict. These were now heading home. Under the election agreement all prisoners-of-war not implicated in war-crimes were released. On top of that, the field armies were trimmed drastically. Many soldiers wanted to go back home to their loved ones. Others were simply tired of fighting, or had found military life lost its sparkle. In any case, the party coffers did not need the drain of having to pay large numbers of soldiers sitting around doing nothing, or worse, engaging in barrack room politics. That money could be better spent on electioneering.

As a result, the roads and byways of Ladosa were awash with humanity going in every direction. What with that and the superbolide, it was a country in upheaval and shock. A strange time, an observer might think, to be holding a General Election. Yet this was Ladosa, where the political system was paramount.

"These are the leaflets to be distributed in Laybbon," stated Charlotta as she pointed to several boxes stacked up against a wall inside her operations centre. "They need to go out within the next couple of days. Our representatives there are all ready, so I am told."

"It'll seem strange crossing enemy lines to get there," Captain Hallazanad replied.

Having survived the war, he was now acting as election campaign manager to parliamentary candidate Nazaz. He had been involved in elections before, but this would be like no other. The country was still in a state of upheaval and hatreds were raw. Some wanted reprisals for alleged atrocities, others had seen their possessions looted and their homes destroyed. Tales of rape abounded and folk had scores to settle. Yet the election must go on; most Ladosans saw it as their best hope for a lasting peace. All the parties signed a solemn declaration to abide by the will of the people, but what that will was going to be was anybody's guess.

More than a few in the Neo-Purple Party were fearful of the result. They suspected that many would revert back to old voting habits and that the Pinks, and especially the Buffs, would profit as a result. The population may consider them to be a safe haven, a force for stability in a time of upheaval. It did not matter what the truth of the matter was, for image was everything.

"Let's Win the Peace Together," was the Neo-Purple autumn 2621 General Election campaign slogan. It had taken many days to thrash this out at the party's Central Committee, but Charlotta was pleased with it. "It strikes the right positive note," she declared, "while hinting that we only got to where we are by our hard won battles."

The next few weeks would see a different kind of campaigning than had taken place the previous couple of years. These battles would be won with words, both spoken and written down. If she was successful in this, Charlotta would be transformed from a civil servant, by way of military commander, to a Member of Parliament. There was no higher accolade to be held and, if she played her cards right, she could attain it.

"We must move beyond thinking in military terms," she told Hallazanad. "We have to appeal directly to the citizens in what we call the Buff heartland. It needs to be got across to them that the Buffs do not own them, or their votes. Our job must be to force the message that the Buffs started this disastrous civil war and are not to be trusted. The..."

"But I thought it was more the fault of the Roses."

"Not when we're in Laybbon it isn't! If we're in Tracana we can tell them it was the Roses' fault, but within Buff territory we have to undermine the Buffs."

"Ah, I see."

"Then we hit them with a shining vision of the new future that awaits them when they vote in a new Neo-Purple government. So our strategy is two-pronged: blame the others for the past and look..."

"Look to us for a rosy future," the captain finished off her sentence."

"Perhaps not the best choice of words."

"Sorry?"

"A *rosy* future?"

Hallazanad laughed, it was an unfortunate choice of words. "Maybe," he tried again, "a *purple* future."

She replied, "Either way we need to inject some life into the election. Early polls are suggesting a listless electorate. That's not the Ladosa I know! We must force some energy and vigour into our campaign."

Speaking more practically, he replied, "The banners are on order and the placards are being made. I'm commandeering a couple of wagons to take them there in good time, with some soldiers for escort."

"Is that necessary?" she looked surprised.

"I wouldn't put it past some Buff scum to try and hijack us. They'll think twice with an armed escort."

"Be careful! They must not wear full uniforms, that would be in violation of the armistice agreement."

"Don't worry, we'll be careful."

"Thank you."

"Earlier, you mentioned a neo-Purple government," he said with a note of wonder. "It seems amazing that we can even speak in these terms. Before the war we were very much a minor party, like the Yellows."

"We must keep our feet on the ground," Charlotta warned, "for we still have a mountain to climb. General Elections are difficult to predict at the best of times. This one is totally impossible. Let's be realistic, 15% of the popular vote would be a major step forward for us. Time will tell. All we can do meanwhile is campaign hard to get our message across loud and clear."

That evening she was alone, working on a revised draft of a speech she was planning on delivering soon. It felt good to be back in the thick of a political campaign again, this was what she really loved to do. After a while, she put her pen down as her mind began to wander.

'I'm glad that no foreign powers sought to capitalise on our country's disunity. It was said that Oonimari had entered our soil before being hit by that fireball. I don't know if that's true, but if it is, then it serves them right! The Ma'hol have gone extremely quiet while the Hoamen have secretly aided our cause. No doubt they will be calling in the debt once the dust has settled.

'And Alan? I have not received a reply from him. Maybe it got lost of the way, it does happen. Should I write again? Perhaps it would be better to wait until the General Election is over. After all, I am going to be more than busy over the next few weeks.'

Flonass was walking to work. The days were starting to draw in and, with the overcast sky, it was taking a long time to get light that morning.

He was in an excellent mood. The evening before, he contrived to bump into the nurse at the Vionium hospital whom he had taken a shine to. On this occasion they enjoyed their longest ever conversation. For one thing he learned her name, Marie. That was a major step forward. She was a trainee, apparently, but was enjoying learning her trade. Apparently her father was previously a soldier in Despot Kagel's army and, once his hometown of Carnis became incorporated into Thyatira, he elected to transfer to Thyatira's guard. A move with his family to Vionium followed and that was when Marie got the job at the hospital there.

'She's cute!' was Flonass' verdict. 'Shy, but sweet. Not as brash as most of the girls near where I live. I'll have to try and get to see her again soon.'

Rabbits scurried away from his path as he progressed along the road to the sawmill. He saw his destination up ahead and a couple of early birds opening the gate. There was a permanent guard on duty throughout the night these days and he greeted the young man as he arrived.

"Morning, Flonass, a gloomy day by the looks of it."

"Hi Narry; yeah, I hope the rain holds off."

He trotted up the stairs and unlocked the repaired door to the office. Mr Onstein would be along soon, but he possessed plenty of work to get on with in the meantime. A couple of orders came in late the previous day and they needed to be entered neatly into the register. Some dockets needed seeing to as well.

It did not seem long before his employer arrived. Mr O was full of smiles and gave him a warm greeting, adding, "It's a bit gloomy in here isn't it? I'm surprised you can see to write!"

"You get used to it quickly."

"I could light a lantern..."

"You don't have to on my account, Mr O, I'm managing okay."

"Hmm. Don't be afraid to change your mind."

"I won't," replied Flonass, looking up briefly and smiling.

The room fell silent again as he got on with his work. Mr O was fiddling about with something at his own desk and Flonass did not pay him too much attention until he found the man standing at his desk, holding out a purse full of coins. Thinking it was to do with an order, the white asked if it was money to be banked.

"Not at all," came the answer. "It's a bit late, for which I apologise, but it's your reward for thwarting the robbery. Fifty sten."

"Fift...? Oh, Mr O, thank you so much!" Flonass exclaimed as he got to his feet.

"Not at all, it's well deserved. I meant to bring it sooner, but something else came up... but never mind that. You were exceedingly brave and did an excellent job in stopping those reprobates in taking our hard-earned money."

Flonass thanked him again. He was already starting to think what he could spend the money on, but the older man was speaking again.

"I feel a lot safer now the gang has been convicted and given exemplary sentences. I was most pleased with that. Still, it doesn't harm to have a guard on patrol during the hours of darkness from now on."

"No."

"Until the winter at least."

The familiar sound of the steam engine starting up in the yard came to their ears. Soon it was augmented by the much louder screech of the circular saw cutting into the logs fed to it. It was not too loud, though, through the closed door. They got back to their work and nothing more was said for a while.

A little later a customer arrived to disturb the relative tranquillity of the office. A short, white man with a wispy beard, he waved his arms about as he spoke.

"Where's my boss's order? Them folk out there in the yard ain't got a clue. Not a clue I tell ya!"

Mr O looked over to his assistant who immediately took change of the query.

"What's your boss's name?"

"John."

"Um, which John would that be?"

"John the smith, over at Lowdebar. He ordered forty, five-by-tens. They should be there in the yard, I was told, but your flunkies can't see t'find 'em, they can't."

Peering hard through his papers, Flonass declared, "Sixty-nine B. They should be there all right."

"They can't f..."

"Come with me," the younger man said firmly and led them out. A short while later he came back alone. Mr O was craving to hear the outcome and it was not long in coming.

"Order Sixty-nine B standing there larger than life. It was all aboard the wagon and awaiting delivery, exactly as had been arranged. Everything was in order. I don't know what all the fuss was about."

"So who," enquired Mr O, "told him they couldn't find it?"

"I don't know. All the workers I spoke with denied speaking to the man."

"Hmm, he was a bit of a strange fellow; perhaps it was all in his mind."

"Anyway, it's all resolved now."

At that moment there was the loudest of bangs, followed by shouting. Mr Onstein and Flonass dashed out to see what had happened. As they hurried down the stairs, the steam engine spluttered to a standstill.

"It's Mark," explained one of the worried-looking workers milling about. The small crowd parted to let the owner through to see what was going on. Flonass followed in his wake. There, near the machinery, was the man himself, sitting on a tree section as a makeshift stool. Pale-faced, a colleague was holding his arm tightly as blood tricked through his hands and onto the ground. Another man was sorting out a bandage to bound round Mark's wound.

It was not long before the injured employee was taken off to hospital. One of the other workers said to Mr Onstein, "The saw blade shattered without warning, pieces flew everywhere. One cut Mark's arm. It was a miracle that more weren't hurt. Look at this!" and he pointed to a jagged fragment embedded in the shed's wooden wall. "It could have killed someone easily."

Mr O turned round and ordered all those not directly involved to get back to work. Seemingly reluctantly, most of the men present slunk away. Flonass realised that the order probably applied to him as well, so he turned to go, but his boss called him back.

"You may as well stay. Let's have a look; see if we can work out what went wrong."

It did not take long for the investigators to ascertain the cause of the accident. A mature tree was being cut into lengths when the saw blade encountered metal nails deep within the wood. They had obviously been hammered into it when it was much younger and the tree's growth hid them over time. So they were completely invisible when brought to the mill. Mr Onstein put it down as a freak accident and just one of those things. He was pleased to hear that Mark would make a good recovery from the gash he received and would be back at work within a week, if only on light duties. Then there was the financial impact.

"We have a spare blade," he told Flonass later that day, "but we will have to order a fresh spare for the future. They do not come cheap."

"Will fifty sten cover it?" asked the assistant, holding up the bag of coins.

Fortunately Mr Onstein's sense of humour did not fail and he took the gesture for the joke it was intended to be. "Put that away, my boy, before I accept the offer!"

Not for the first time, laughter could be heard coming from the office. Then Mr O did like to run a happy ship.

~ End of Chapter 20 ~

Prospects of Peace - Chapter 21

The large frame of Emil Vebber waddled towards the senate building one morning, three weeks after the Despot's trip to the Capital. He passed through the entrance to the courtyard which was surrounded by a high, whitewashed wall.

None of these buildings existed in the spring of 2609 when Emil first arrived in Thyatira. It had been a time of social revolution in the country, nowhere more so than in this northernmost despotate. Inhabitants from the rest of the country were flocking to the brave new world there. These were mainly whites, but a fair sprinkling of blacks joined in.

It was an exciting time. Despot Thorn had effectively pulled off a bloodless coup at the Inner Council and established himself in a position of power there that no one sought to challenge. Laws were passed regarding the treatment of whites and freedom of movement. Thyatira annexed sizeable tracts of land from its neighbouring despotates. Before the other despots knew what was happening, a proportion of their most able subjects were upping sticks and making for this promised land.

Emil was caught up in the frenzy. A minor courtier to a southern despot, he concluded that at the age of forty-four this could be his last opportunity to start life again. With his family and possessions in a single wagon, he made his way north and presented himself at the Castle.

This was in the era when Despot / Keeper Thorn was spending a good deal of time in Asattan. There he was consolidating his position and weeding out Council Members who did not toe the line.

In Thyatira, the Despotess was in command. In practice she entrusted matters to one of the few other blacks already there, Karl Vondant, and the drone Alan. Emil was well received and made a good impression on them. Along with another new arrival, Hanz Drasnik, they began forming their ideas for administrating the new, rapidly expanding despotate. The Despotess insisted on there being white representatives and Natias the steward and Saul, the village head, were included in the newly instituted senate.

Unfortunately, this radical change proved too much for Natias and he announced his retirement. Nonetheless, before he left, he provided an invaluable service in explaining to the newcomers how the existing set-up worked. Money was not a problem and soon a huge programme of building works was taking shape in the shadow of the Castle.

The first senate meeting actually took place in the Castle hall and it was more a matter of the delegates introducing themselves rather than discussing business. For all that, there was one major, pertinent topic on the agenda: immigration. It was forever present on the agenda over the next few years. With people pouring into the region, and many of the whites spontaneously building houses for themselves in the existing villages, the situation was chaotic at times. The blacks gravitated to the centre of Thyatiran operations and what became known as the Castle Complex and eventually Castleton, began to grow and develop.

On a rare, brief visit back home, Despot Thorn told the new senators that he had no objection to their running matters, but laid down a few fundamentals for them to adhere to. One of these was to treat the whites fairly and retain white representation in the body. The other was to leave them in no doubt that, in the final analysis, his word was law above anything they might pass. For all that, in practice he usually left them alone.

As the oldest black member of the senate, and with a wealth of experience behind him, Emil found himself cast in the role of elder statesman early on. In the distribution of responsibilities, he found himself in charge of land allocation, a hot topic at the time. It was a role he held until recently with the acquisition of Norland. He was now in charge of organising the assimilation of this sizeable, populous area into the rest of Thyatira. With their different ways of doing things, it was proving quite a task. He found himself on a regular commute between Norland and the senate, where he would keep his colleagues appraised of the situation.

On this occasion, however, it was a private meeting with Despot Thorn that was in the offing.

"Hi there, Emil!" hailed a cheery Alan as they passed on the stairs leading to the entrance.

The big man returned the greeting and asked if the Despot was in the office.

"Yeah, I think so," came the reply.

A little out of breath after making it to the top stair, the senator paused for a moment to get his breath back. Soon, though, he was at the door to Despot Thorn's senate office.

"Come in," Frank cried in response to the knock. "Ah, Emil, nice to see you. How are you this morning?"

"I am grand, thank you."

"Do sit down. You brought some papers with you I see."

"I have," confirmed the other man as he placed his large frame on the seat provided and his folder on the edge of the desk.

"It's still quite nice weather today," the Despot commented.

"Indeed. A little windy, but not as much rain as we're used to this time of year."

"You're right, it's usually wetter than this. No doubt we'll be getting some rain soon."

The niceties of the weather out of the way, they got down to business. Emil began by recounting tales of some business practices going on within Norland.

"I've heard so many such accounts that I cannot dismiss them. I'm convinced they're true. If a tradesman puts in a tender for public works, they know that they will have to hand a bribe to the powers that be, usually the mayor, in order to secure it."

"Didn't we discuss this before and express our disgust at this practice?"

"I was wanting to build up a body of evidence before tackling it, Frank. The mayors have been extremely cagey, while some of the contractors were reluctant to speak to me about it. I needed to gain their confidence, their trust. I told them that a change is coming about and it is in their best interests to tell me everything. I now believe I have enough evidence to confront the mayors."

"Good," said Frank.

"What I did not want to do was go off half cock and, faced with a denial, have to back down. I've established the truth now beyond a shred of doubt, so I can put a stop to it."

"Good, they must comply with the same business principals as the rest of Thyatira. No bribery and better rights for the white community. Yet, as we've said before, we don't want a complete revolution. We are willing to work with the existing local power structures in place."

"That's the basis I'm working on."

"All right."

"The local governments are not short of money. In fact they have been stockpiling reserves for no good reason. It's been a bit of empire-building and accumulation of public wealth for the sake of it. Meanwhile there are public works which need to be tackled, some with urgency. I'm compiling a list, a full picture, but I fear it's going to take all their money and more."

"Funds will be made available, you know that."

"Yes. Many of these projects will take several years to put things right. I think we should start next spring. In the meantime, have worked out a list of priorities. I could go through one or two of the bigger issues if you like."

"Of course."

"In Felsham the drainage system needs a complete overhaul. I am concerned about the effects on public health, particularly in the summer. The drains run down the centre of the road of the town. They are covered by large concrete slabs, but many of these are missing. I think they have been taken away by... shall we say enterprising individuals? to help with their own buildings. So much of the drain is left open and it is most unhealthy. Also, it does doesn't stretch to some of the poor, white areas. There the housing is utterly sub-standard and squalid. It reminds me of the conditions in the Upper Village a dozen years ago. If anything, it's worse."

"I see," Frank returned gravely.

"That is one area to prioritise, I'd suggest. Meanwhile in Newton the public baths are in danger of collapse."

"Public baths?"

"They were erected a while back using stone from a local quarry to keep costs down. It's proved a false economy, because they're crumbling away now and in urgent need of repair. I spoke with an architect from Newton about it. He said that any repairs should be with the same kind of stone in order to stay in keeping with the original. He was quite insistent."

"Why, he didn't design it, did he?"

" I believe his father did. But any repairs will be faced with the same problems a generation from now."

"I agree. Look, Emil, we've got to get across to these people exactly who is the boss. Despot Kagel might have had a light hand on the tiller, but we need to integrate these towns fully in the long run with our old ones. Don't let them distract you; you know that you have the authority of the senate and myself behind you."

"Thank you, yes, I realise that of course."

"Good."

"In general," the senator continued in lighter vein, "there is a good mood within Norland I'd say. I don't want you to get the impression that all they're presenting us with is problems. They have some excellent industries, complementary to ours, plus morale amongst the whites in particular is high. They are pleased with the takeover and are looking forward opportunistically to the future."

"And the blacks?"

"A degree of trepidation within their ranks. Although most are willing to give us a try. I have heard tales of the capriciousness of the administration they have moved away from."

"Despot Kagel, you mean."

"Er, yes," Emil replied carefully, not wanting to bad mouth a member of the ruling class.

"I see."

"They're hopeful of more stability, knowing where they are. Plus the level of taxation has come down and that's always going to be popular."

"I'm sure."

"In fact I have heard factory bosses talk of increased productivity this year; they have noticed a difference."

"That's nice to hear. So it's not all a gloomy picture."

"Not by any means. I did not want to give you that impression."

"It's all right, you didn't. I know from your previous reports that there is much to celebrate with regards to Norland. What we need is a inventory of tasks that need to be undertaken there; urgent, important and those that are both. If you can add costings as well..."

"I am working on such a list, Frank, but I would like to include another category."

"Very well."

"Desirable things."

"All right."

"For instance the road system there needs upgrading. Commuting between Norland and Castleton I notice the difference. I have discussed increasing hulffan tar production next year with Cragoop

414

and he is confident it can be done. Yet I do need to pay another visit to Carnis shortly."

"I see."

"Carnis is the biggest town in Norland, as I'm sure you know and there are some things I need to see with my own eyes that I've been unable to up until now."

"Well, you have the freedom to come and go, you know that."

"I want to work on some paperwork later today, but I'd been hoping to leave tomorrow. Squad Leader Stephen usually provides the escort, we work well together. He's come down with a nasty sore throat. I can't drag him along."

"Take my young man Darda," Frank urged. "He provided excellent escort service for me since we took him on. He seems to thrive on it. He's up at the Castle. If you have a word with him, let him know exactly what you want, I'm sure he'll do a good job on this one occasion."

"Thank you; that's grand. I'll do that."

Tristan was starting to feel settled back in Castleton. The house was overgrown when he first arrived back. He spent some time getting the garden restored to a semblance of order. He also employed some workmen to redecorate the inside. Somehow the better state of the property reflected in his own mind and he felt more ordered in life.

Just as it had taken a while for him to come to terms with the house, his job as Despot Thorn's secretary also taken some getting used to. In the early stages he was not entirely sure what was being asked of him. To be fair to Tristan, his employer had not been certain either. It was becoming clearer now. The Despot was a keen correspondent, but needed help with the composition and neat writing of his epistles. This was a strong ability of Tristan's and he soon learned to write in a way that pleased his new boss.

He was also a sometime messenger / go-between from the Despot to senators, the Ma'hol consul and others within Castleton. The demands on him were varied, but not overwhelming. There was also a fair amount of travelling within the country involved: Rilesia, Capparathia and Ephamon. For someone who had visited five foreign countries in the past few years, this was nothing he could not manage.

Above all, much-needed stability was returning to his life. His early adult life, he now realised, had been one full of searching. Leaving on a crusade, but not staying the course; being involved in Alan's quest for missing pieces of an ancient device; time spent as an ambulanceman in Ladosa; he certainly experienced his fair share of adventures. The civil service job down in Asattan, inside the Citadel, had not worked out. Now he wished for nothing more than to settle into a routine for the next few years.

The house still looked unsightly from the outside to his eyes. His father's unfinished extension ensured that. He made sure he regularly saved some money from his wages and deposited it with interest at Deejan Charvo's. One day he would have enough to get it completed.

As for a female companion, there was none on the horizon. He had loved and lost the Lady Dionora in West Torravis and held onto the memory of her fondly. He did not know if he would ever love again, or indeed whether he was worthy of someone nice.

There were few people he could count as friends. Alan was someone he was on good terms with, but then the drone got on well with everyone.

Meanwhile, there was one big, unanswered question in his life: would he go and visit his mother? The mother who had been such a centre of love in his childhood. The mother who arranged for the murder of her husband, his father. How could such a deed ever be forgiven? Yet one day he might travel to the monastery to see her, but not yet.

One bright, autumnal Sabbath, he was up early and dressed in his best clothes. Attending the morning service was a duty that Despot Thorn insisted upon. It was not a hardship for Tristan who was trying to deepen his Christian faith. With all the things that had happened to and around him, he liked the anchor in his life that God gave.

"The Lord is my stronghold, my fortress and my champion; my God, my rock where I find safety," sang the psalmist. Tristan needed a rock in his life more than most and belief in this God was proving a great comfort to him. He had a couple of Christian books that he was reading to deepen his understanding of the faith. Yet, without a guide, he found them difficult to follow and his mind wondered.

Still in good time, he walked briskly towards the Castle. He got there well in time for breakfast and tucked into some fine porridge.

Content that morning to eat alone up the end of one table, he was nevertheless pleased when Alan appeared and made a point of sitting down next to him.

"Hi, Tristan, how are you this morning?"

"Fine, thanks. Are you staying for the service?"

"Er, no, I don't think so. I'm going to take one of the superdakks for a ride."

"I bet they like being put through their paces."

The drone, who was eating, merely smiled by way of a response. Tristan began eating his toast. As he did so, he spotted an attractive servant girl walking past. She seemed to hesitate. Their eyes met and they exchanged momentary smiles before he looked back down at his plate, slightly embarrassed.

"That's the third time she's been past here," stated Alan without looking up at all.

"Is it?"

"It is. She's got her eye on you."

"No, I'm sure she hasn't."

His friend glanced up and flashed a brief, knowing smile. He added, "You aught to get in there before someone else snaps her up. She's ripe for the picking."

A while later, Deejan Charvo, his family in tow, entered the large room and, upon spotting the Despot's assistant, made directly for him.

"Tristan, good morning."

"Good mo..."

"I was wondering if you could tell me where the service is being held this morning."

"Er..."

"We usually start having it indoors round about this time of year, but with it being such a fine day, I wondered if it was still going to be held in the bailey."

At this point, Alan said his goodbyes following his briefest of breakfasts and left them to it. Tristan did not know the answer to the merchant's question. He was deciding what to say when he spotted Bishop Gunter, his wife and two priests enter the hall. With some relief he pointed out the new arrivals to Deejan who turned and went to address them.

In the event, that Sabbath's morning service was held outside in the bailey. It could well be their last opportunity to enjoy the fresh air for such an occasion this year.

The bishop's text was John 4 and Tristan enjoyed hearing the tale of Jesus' encounter with the woman at the well. He was amused at the cross-purposes the two people were speaking about and considered how amazing it would be to have a personal encounter with the Son of God. What would he ask him? What amazing words would he hear?

However, there was one thing that baffled him. In the general melee that followed the service, people hung about and chatted to each other. Seeing a young priest unengaged, he made a point of going over to him for answers.

"Isaac, the bishop's talk..."

"Yes?"

"There was something I couldn't quite understand."

"What was that?"

"Why were the disciples so surprised to find Jesus talking with the woman at the well?"

"Hum," Isaac paused as he assessed the question and how to pitch his answer. "Like it says in the text, Samaritans and Jews didn't get on with each other. It was a racial thing. On top of that, she was a woman and pious Jews tended to despise women as inferior."

"That's narrow-minded isn't it?"

"We can't judge people from two-and-a-half thousand years ago by our standards. The disciples were the product of their upbringing, as are we."

"But Jesus wasn't affected?"

"He was able to rise above the conditioning, because he was so wise. It takes wisdom to recognise ingrained prejudices and courage to work against them. Jesus had both."

"But we're more enlightened nowadays," Tristan stated without emotion.

"Is that that a question, or a supposed statement of fact?"

"I'm not sure."

"We probably have at least as many prejudices as the people of the past, but we can't see them."

"But *we're* overcoming them!" Tristan cried with the enthusiasm of a child. "Here I am, a black, talking naturally with you, a white. That would have been unheard of not so long ago."

"True, although many blacks, and whites for that matter, still have their hang-ups in that department. People are prejudiced against immigrants, against foreigners."

"That's true."

"But they don't realise it most of the time. We all have them. More than half the battle is recognising prejudices within ourselves. For we can't hope to tackle a problem if we don't know it's there. In Jesus we have the perfect example of someone who rose above prejudices. It is up to us to emulate him."

"What about women?" asked Tristan.

"I'm sure they're just as affected as men."

"No, what I meant was, are men prejudiced against women?"

"Not in my experience," answered Isaac, slightly baffled by the question. "In my experience most men are rather fond of women."

"But we don't allow them to be in charge of despotates, or Members of the Inner Council."

"Of course not."

"Why?"

"That would lead to confusion. We each have our role to play within society for its good running. I could not be a despot, for instance, a free-for-all would lead to anarchy. Look at the Ladosans with their crazy political system. It leads to civil war."

Tristan was already thinking of his next question. "Isaac?" he asked.

"Yes?"

"You lead a Bible study group don't you?"

"I do, weekly. Next one is tomorrow night."

"I already attend one with Deejan Charvo, but you seem to have the answers. Would you mind if I came along?"

"Mind? Of course not; we'd be delighted to have you. Although please don't say I have all the answers!"

The priest gave details as to where and exactly when it was to take place. This exchange was concluding when the Despot came over.

"Ah, Tristan!"

"Yes, My Lord."

The crowd was beginning to thin out. Hannah and Joseph were hovering in the middle distance, waiting for Frank to finish.

"We've had a positive response from the Mehtar concerning the superdakks for Schmidt. I'd like us to compose a thank you letter."

"Now?"

"Before lunch."

"Is it urgent, My Lord?"

"Um, not exactly."

"It's simply that I thought we were not meant to do unnecessary work on the Sabbath."

An awkward silence followed. Isaac wished that he had made himself scarce, but it was too late now. He waited for the Despot to explode. In the event, a smile broke out across his face.

"You're quite right, Tristan, quite right," and he patted his assistant on the shoulder. "First thing tomorrow, in the Throne Room."

"Of course, My Lord."

The Thorns left and Tristan and Isaac exchanged looks.

"I wanted the ground to swallow me up!" exclaimed the priest. "The words just came out."

"He took it well."

"He did indeed."

"He must like you."

"Let's hope so," replied Tristan.

Isaac then departed to go with the bishop. The other man walked slowly back home by himself. He had a smile on his face.

Bishop Gunter sat in his living room with Esther. He was expecting a visit from Gabriell shortly; there were several things to discuss. In the meantime, they read a letter from their old friends at the church in Krabel-Haan.

Once they had both digested its contents, Esther said, "It's nice to hear that the old crowd are doing well: Joktan, Simon, Andrew... such dear souls... but what's this about another letter?"

Her husband fished about in the tube and found a second one which had become stuck inside. After glancing at it, he declared, "It's for you," and passed it over.

"Kat-pas'ara," she said with a note of surprise, "there's someone I haven't heard of in a long time."

Gunter waited patiently until she finished the second letter, addressed specifically to her.

"A bit extraordinary," was her verdict upon completion.

"How so?"

" Kat-pas'ara is someone I knew in my pre-Christian life. She says she has become a Christian now."

"She hasn't adopted a Christian name," he retorted with a slight note of accusation.

Ignoring this, Esther went on, "I'm pleased for her, but I'm surprised at the chatty tone. It wasn't as if we were ever particularly close. I mean, listen to this:

'I must check about the food supply for the Dionora Kitchen. I promised Loran'pta

that I would call about those this morning. I've been busy cleaning and doing

laundry since yesterday - I do believe laundry breeds if left to itself!'

And she addresses me as, 'My dear Esther,' although we were never particularly dear to each other."

"Maybe you're an inspiration to her," Gunter offered.

"Maybe..."

"And in her mind the two of you are closer as a result. Either way, I don't believe in slapping down a friendly hand reached out to one."

"I'm not going to slap anyone," Esther replied petulantly before saying more calmly, "but I'm not sure how to respond."

"Send her a chatty response, that would be kind."

"But what do I say?"

"If she can talk about laundry to you, I'm sure you can respond with some mundane stuff which would satisfy her. Besides, an account of your visits to the Ladosan refugees I'm sure she'd find interesting."

"And what about Joktan's invitation for us to go and visit them all?"

"I can't go! Not in the foreseeable future; I'm far too busy. You could go, Esther."

"By myself? I don't think so." After a pause, she added, "Maybe in the spring we could both go. It might do you good to have a break. Even the Despot enjoyed a holiday this year."

"A working holiday by all accounts... but you're right. We could consider it next year. It would be nice to see them all again." Then, satisfied that the topic was exhausted, he changed tone as he asked, "So what have you got on today?"

"I told you! There's a delegation of upper class ladies from Newton coming this afternoon. They want to talk about help for the homeless this winter."

"I didn't think we had homeless in Thyatira," Gunter replied dryly, "we call them dead."

With a deep frown, Esther replied, "That wasn't very nice!"

"No, I'm sorry," he backtracked, even if what he had said was broadly true.

"They want us to help these poor souls. Have a bit of compassion."

Suitably admonished, he apologised again for his comment and wished her a successful meeting. Not long afterwards, Gabriell arrived and Esther retreated to another part of the house after welcoming the priest.

"Come in, sit down. Would you like a drink?"

Soon Gabriell was reporting back on his latest fact-finding mission to Norland on behalf of the Church.

"I attended a seminar in Carnis last week. There was a lecture on Biblical ethics being given by a local theologian."

"Many people attending?"

"Almost forty, I'd say. I was most put off by what he said, though."

"Oh?"

"Talk about a liberal interpretation! It seemed to me to boil down to this: if there's a Biblical injunction which you don't agree with, then just say it applied to a different culture, thousands of years ago. It doesn't apply to us now."

"But that pulls the rug from underneath the entire Bible!"

"It does indeed."

"What did you say to him?"

"Not much; I didn't think it was the time or the place. Anyhow, we will have to do something about it."

"We will indeed," agreed the bishop. "What's the point of having a Bible at all if you're going to use that logic?"

"I wasn't at all impressed. The trouble, it strikes me, is that the Church in Aggeparii has been leaderless for many years. Priests and theologians have had no guidelines or proper training and this free-for-all in their thinking is the result."

"It can't all be that bad, surely."

"No, it's not. Many churches are doing a fine job in the community, both spirituality and practically. They have been tackling some issues head-on. In Newton, for instance, there was a scandal surrounding some white landlords."

"Whites as landlords?" asked Gunter, surprised, "I thought the whites were having a hard time in Norland."

"Many are, it's true, but there are exceptions to every rule. There's an area of Newton with some ghastly, substandard housing. Some better-off white men got together and snapped them up cheaply. Now they are offering the houses to desperately poor women on a sex-for-rent basis! The local church demonstrated against the practice and have managed to put a stop to it. It's one success story, but the whole of Norland seems to be awash with corruption.... it seems to me."

"I've heard Despot Thorn say that he is aware of some abuses of power in local government. It is his aim to put an end to it."

"I'm pleased to hear it, but the Church has a part to play in this."

"Of course."

"And we need to establish your authority, as Bishop of Thyatira, more firmly in the region. What we really need is an envoy, an emissary to impose your will upon Norland, bring the churches there into line with sound doctrine and practices."

Gunter simply looked at the priest and smiled. Eventually Gabriell realised that he was in prime position to fulfil such a role. He said, "You want me to do it, don't you!"

He was right. The pair spent some time thrashing out exactly what the role entailed and what delegated powers he would have for the mission. The priest did not mind undertaking the task as long as he knew where he stood with regards to authority and how exactly they wanted the Church in the south of the despotate to look. It was a lengthy, but fruitful discussion.

By the time a servant came into replenish their drinks, they were able to move onto other things.

Gabriell asked, "Did you tell me last time that you were thinking of setting up a printing press for Bibles in Thyatira?"

"I did. I'm still looking into it. There are a number of potential sites. That's not the problem, it's a lack of expertise. That's been the case in the past, in any case. Now a couple of brothers have moved into

Thyatira, up from Ephamon. They've got experience together of producing books."

"Good."

"I am hoping to save us some money in the long run. Books are expensive, as you know, but if we can produce our own..."

"Is money a problem?" asked the priest. For the previous few years, the Thyatiran Church had been fairly awash with money, but then a number of capital building projects had been undertaken in that time. It was enough to empty many a despot's coffers, although this northernmost despotate possessed the healthiest of economies."

"I wouldn't say money is a problem," retorted the bishop, "but we are having to be a little more prudent. Despot Thorn has had to cut the tax concessions to the Church a bit. The acquisition of Norland is proving to be an expensive business. I feel confident that with a bit of careful housekeeping we will be okay."

"Do you mean the Church, or the secular authorities?"

"Both, but to return to what I was saying, we are still trying to thrash out the best way to produce Bibles. It might not be best to print them here in Thyatira."

"We currently import them from Ephamon; that's right, isn't it?"

"Yes. We're looking into all the options, but the most economic plan might be to have the pages printed in Ephamon still, but then transported here to be bound and made into books."

"I see."

"I've made an initial order of ten copies on this basis as something of an experiment. It is likely to take several weeks. If they are up to standard, then we can see about ordering more next year."

"Ten is a modest number. Have you seen a proof copy?"

"Naturally. I haven't got it here to show you, unfortunately, but I am hopeful that they will be good quality. We want as many people to have access to the scriptures as possible."

"A noble aim."

"To allow everyone to be able to read, mark and inwardly digest them. So even the plough boy will know the scriptures well, as someone once said."

"Oh dear!" Gabriell suddenly exclaimed. When asked why, he explained, "I meant to bring you something, but forgot."

"What's that?"

"In an old church building in Newton I came across some paper sheets with poems written down on them. I think that they might be songs. There is a Christian theme therein and I believe them to be ancient carols, first sung hundreds of years ago. Some of them are quite beautiful and I thought we could incorporate them, or at least a selection, in our Christmas festivities."

"Spoken, do you mean, or sung?"

"Um, I'm not sure. I haven't been able to trace any music for the words as yet and the folk at the church know very little about them. I might see if someone with the right skills could compose some music to go with them, something cheerful."

"What an excellent idea."

The time came for Gabriell to leave. He said his goodbye and set off back to his Castleton parish. As he understood it, his Norland role would be a part-time, temporary one, so he still hoped to do justice to his ministry to the whites of Castleton. There was always much to do in the Lord's service. The harvest was plentiful and the labourers few, such as it had been from the dawn of the Church.

Back at the Castle, Hannah received some unfortunate news. The head gardener reported to her that several stone pots from her garden had been stolen. She went outside, with a handmaiden in tow, to see with her own eyes.

"How annoying!" was her verdict when she saw the evidence for herself. The round, bare patches where they had been were as plain as could be.

Turning to her servant, she ordered, "Go to the senate building and fetch me Senator Drasnik. I shall be in the Throne Room to receive him."

"At once, My Lady."

The girl hurried off and Hannah strode back to the Castle, extremely annoyed. How dare anyone see fit to steal her ornamental pots? She was going right to the top to ensure a proper investigation was made.

She knew that the Throne room was available, because Frank was across the road in the senate. Hanz was hurrying across to meet her, having been left in no doubt by the hand maiden that she was not a happy Despotess.

"It's probably immigrants, whites," he told her.

"Whoever it is, I want a thorough search made to find them. The gardener will give you a full description. If you need to employ some guardsmen to quicken the search, then commandeer as many as you need. I want them found."

"And the perpetrators punished."

"Of course."

"I will get to it straightaway, My Lady."

He could not remember the last time he saw her so cross and he was left in no doubt as to where his priorities lay for the rest of the day and goodness knew how long afterwards. What if a Sarnician trader had stole them and even now was in his wagon half way to Aggeparii City market? He would do his best.

The following morning he needed to attend the senate meeting. The subject of the stolen pots did not come up, but it was still on his mind. As he sat there, he knew that the constables had put their workload to one side to make enquiries and soldiers were hunting high and low for their whereabouts.

Joseph Thorn, soon to be a teenager and heir to the Despot, sat in on the meeting. It was a fairly routine one and a good opportunity for the lad to observe what went on. One of those giving a report was Senator Trepte.

"You may recall, early last spring, that I was charged with looking into the state of the housing in Castleton. I am, of course, referring to the white properties about which concerns have been expressed.

"The town continues to expand apace, and not merely houses. Permission has been granted to a group of investors wanting to build a hotel there. Several of the black residents expressed a desire for this and the idea is for it to be aimed at visitors to Thyatira. Understandably, they do not wish it to be up the far end. Some sub-standard white houses nearer this end would require demolition to make way for it. Of course usually this would be within Emil's remit, but it has been passed over to me."

Saul was not entirely happy about this, but he had seen the poor state of some of those white dwellings and knew this was not a wise battle to try and fight. Instead, he asked, "Is there actually a demand for it?"

"Apparently so. In any case, it's a private enterprise; no public money is involved. They merely require our permission where to site it. I understand it to be an up-market venture, so only people with a certain purse are likely to be able to afford to stay there."

These were coded words for "blacks as opposed to whites" and everybody in the room understood this, but nothing more was said. Freidhelm then realised that he was rather swinging off track and set about getting back to the point.

"In any case, I was charged with inspecting the standard of the general white housing in Castleton. Helped by various experts in the field, we concentrated mainly in the south-western district where a lot of unauthorised housing was thrown up. I'm afraid some of it did confirm our worst fears and some shockingly poor buildings were discovered. Most of the structures we will be able to strengthen through remedial work. But there were a few extreme cases where they are having to be demolished and a completely new building erected. The work is currently in progress."

Karl asked, "And who's paying for all this?"

"Um, it is coming from the public purse."

"But why?" Senator Vondant pressed, "why should it?"

"Otto and Despot Thorn here felt that it was in the public interest. It won't do to have our new town with buildings fit to fall down at any moment."

"I hope that this does not set a precedent. It's rewarding the careless."

Freidhelm glanced at Frank, but the latter was happy to let him continue to field questions.

"It is not considered a precedent. We have got our building schedule on track now. No one starts a new building without first getting permission. They will have to comply with standards that are set out."

"I'm glad to hear it," was Karl's final word on the matter, although it was clear that he was not entirely convinced.

With a change of subject, it was mentioned that some of the Ladosan refugees staying in Thyatira were volunteering to go home. The news was welcomed.

There were no other contentious issues and afterwards, as the members drifted away, Frank asked his son if he had enjoyed the meeting.

"Yes, Father," came the formal answer. He was not going to say he found it boring, but he did add, "May I go and play now?"

"Of course," Frank answered with a smile. As his son disappeared, he wondered if the lad was somewhat immature. Had he, as a father, mollycoddled him? Still, he considered, it was a difficult age, pre-puberty. Joseph would have to grow up quickly soon enough. Allow him a bit of innocent fun in the meantime.

By now there were three men left in the chamber. Tristan was on his shoulder and Hanz was hanging about, apparently wanting to have a word.

As the senator stepped forward, Frank addressed his secretary softly, "If you go back to the Castle, I'll catch you up there."

"Yes, My Lord."

Once they were quite alone, Hanz began to speak.

"There is a matter I need to have a quick word with you about, if I may."

"Of course, the Despotess' pots. How's it going?"

"We are making every effort to retrieve them, My Lord."

"I'm sure you are."

The Despot's tone was quite amiable, but he had not allowed Hanz to say what was actually on his mind. Now he put that right.

"It is another matter that I wanted to draw your attention to. The senate is currently presiding over a criminal case which is due to conclude tomorrow."

Frank knew that the senate only presided over capital offence cases. He let the man speak further.

"It is a sex offence involving a couple of men from Setty. I won't go into the details unless you particularly want me to."

"Not unless it's totally necessary, thank you."

"It's that I don't think the offenses warrant death. If they are convicted, and I think they will be, I'd rather impose a lighter penalty. Under Shreeber's Law, there is a mandatory death penalty, as you know."

"So that's what they're calling it now, is it? Shreeber's Law."

It was named after its proponent, Tristan's father, who lost his own life shortly after it came into force. Hanz explained that there was a general feeling amongst the senators that the law should stand as their late colleague's legacy. The Law and Order Secretary, however, had never been happy with it. He continued, "It ties our hands, even when there are mitigating circumstances. I do not believe it to be appropriate in the current case."

"Very well, Hanz. I'm happy to be guided by you. Senator Shreeber meant well, I'm sure, but we must have flexibility in the administration of justice. I therefore use my executive powers so that the death penalty is at the senate's discretion and not compulsory in every case. That way you won't have to pass a formal motion which might embarrass, or upset some of the senators."

"Thank you so much, My Lord," said Hanz with obvious relief. He was a great believer in the law being fair, but firm and that meant flexibility was vital. He was a happy man.

"Let me know if you wish me to sign anything."

"I will."

Frank went over to the Castle where he ate in the hall alongside Tristan and Alan. The other two were engaged in a lengthy conversation about music which did not particularly interest Frank. The people at the next table were talking about the up and coming harvest. Again, not the most riveting topic for him. He, instead, tucked into the delicious stew in front of him.

'Carrots, potatoes, parsnips, all these fresh vegetables, quite delicious. To think, on most inhabited planets in the galaxy, people live under great domes and have neither fresh air nor properly cultivated food. They are produced artificially in hydroponics. None of the people here know quite how lucky they are. Then none of them know about space travel, or the fact that I was born many light years away. It barely seems real now; it was a lifetime ago.'

~ End of Chapter 21 ~

Prospects of Peace - Chapter 22

Emil's wagon trundled through the narrow streets of Norland's largest town, Carnis. He had found the journey with Darda most pleasant. This young man wanted to chat and it passed the time in an amiable way and was something of a contrast with his journeys with his regular squad leader, Stephen. Not that the conversation was erudite most of the time; more light and amusing.

"I hate it when you stub your toe," the young white was saying, "then there's that briefest of moment before the pain gets to your brain. You know it's going to come, and you brace yourself for it... and sure enough, suddenly bang! The pain hits you."

The older man smiled.

This was an old part of town and a proportion of the buildings were two hundred years old. Many of them looked it: timber-framed and with uneven tiled roofs, they exuded a certain charm about them. It was late afternoon and other wagons with various loads, such as barrels of beer, or furniture, passed by in the opposite direction. There was a steady flow of pedestrians as well.

The senator explained, "We're going to be staying at a hotel called The Chequers. I have not stayed there before. My usual stop-over place has got some... er, problems, so we can't stay there. I've been told that this Chequers place has a certain charm about it."

His companion wondered what the "problems" were, but felt it best not to ask. Emil was embarrassed to come straight out with the fact that a major infestation of bed bugs had been reported. All being well, there would be no such problem at the alternative accommodation.

Following their wagon was a second one containing their guardsmen escort and a clerk. These men were to be housed above a nearby stable three quarters of a kilometre away. Only Emil and Darda would be staying at the hotel.

Turning right at the next junction with a wagon and six dakks was no easy feat in these narrow streets, but the driver managed it. Soon the hotel came into sight.

Sited half way along a fairly busy road, it was flanked by private dwellings flush up against it on either side. The street widened to an open, cobbled square and there was a round, public fountain opposite the building, although no water was cascading from it on this particular day. The Chequers was long and tall by Thyatiran standards, having four floors. Some huge timbers formed a major component in its construction, but these were not particularly straight. From the small bricks used in some sections it was apparent that the original building had been smaller and extra parts built on over time. It gave the edifice either a rickety, or quaint, old world look about it, depending upon one's opinion. Out the front hung a hotel sign with its name and a picture of a black and white chequer board. Darda wondered if this was done deliberately to indicate that all levels of Hoame society were welcome to stay, but he did not say anything.

He helped his overweight compatriot down from the wagon and there was some frenetic activity while the soldiers unloaded the baggage and took it inside. It did not take too long for the pair to register themselves. The hotel manager, gushing and obsequious, showed his VIP guest to his room on the first floor. On Emil's request, Darda had been booked into the adjoining chamber.

A single flight of stairs for poor Emil to negotiate, but he was still puffing heavily by the time they reached the first floor. After taking a breather, the manager led them to their rooms. The inside looked clean and tidy, but it was an absolute warren of corridors, or so it seemed to the first-time guests. Up a step, round a corner, down a step, along another corridor... eventually they arrived. The soldiers took the cases in and then were dismissed for the night. They went to find the stables where some of them had stayed before. The clerk went with them, a decision Darda thought curious, but did not query. Presumably the senator was not planning on doing any work that evening.

The manager explained that the hotel's restaurant was on the ground floor, but perhaps Senator Vebber would prefer their meal brought up to their rooms. He did.

Darda was amazed at the size of his own room, with a large double bed and plenty of floor space all to himself. Alone, before supper, he bounced on the bed a couple of times in his excitement. Being a senator's escort certainly held its perks. This was far better accommodation than he had stayed in either Rilesia, or Capparathia. He peeked out of his window and saw that darkness was already beginning to fall. There was the novelty of street lights in this part of Carnis and the town lighter was going about his job with his oil-fuelled illuminations.

Having been asked to accompany Emil in the latter's room for supper, they tucked into some fine fare: venison pie, potatoes and gravy.

"This place seems pleasant enough. Do you like your room, Darda?"

"I'll say! It's lovely."

"Grand. My first appointment tomorrow is with the Weavers' Guild. I can expect a demonstration of their skills, but I'm more interested to see where their industry fits into the greater economic picture."

Darda nodded as he chewed. He was enjoying the way in which the black senator was being so casual with him. In his brief dealings with some of the other Thyatiran senators, most noticeably Senator Drasnik, he found them not quite so friendly.

At the end of the meal, Emil declared, "There's a busy day ahead tomorrow, we'd best get an early night's sleep." Darda took this as a sign of his dismissal and said goodnight as he made for the door. As he did so, a couple of servants arrived with lit candles for their distinguished guests. That saved him the bother and he gladly took one as he retreated to his own room.

Once inside, he closed the door and, for the first time, noted how ill-fitting it was. There was a huge gap at the bottom and, when he reached down and put his hand there, he felt quite a draught coming through. The idea crossed his mind of putting clothing down there to halt the flow of air, but then he got distracted by other thoughts and forgot about it.

Night was falling fast now and he took a look out of the window before going to bed. The traffic was thinning out and soon the last wagon of the night clattered by on the cobbles. He learned earlier that they were not allowed to move after a certain hour and now he was grateful for that. With their rooms at the front of the hotel, the noise would have been intolerable.

Soon he was abed, but too excited by it all to sleep at first. His parents would love to hear about this place. He could tell Flonass and Vophsi too, but he must be careful not to be seen to boast. Eventually his mind calmed and he drifted off into a deep sleep.

Darda awoke, feeling confused. After a brief moment of disorientation, he quickly realised three things: where he was, it was still the middle of the night and smoke was pouring into his room through the gap under the door.

In the pitch black, he jumped out of bed and threw on some clothes over his night ones. Quickly putting his shoes on, he made his way towards where he thought the exit was, arms outstretched ahead of him. He found the wall and worked his way sideways to the door which he opened. He was met by a bigger blast of smoke and, in the distance, heard the first cries of, "Fire!"

He made his way immediately to Senator Vebber's room. The door was not locked and he went in straightaway without knocking. Fortunately, the senator had left his lamp alight on the bedside locker. It's failing light still provided vital illumination at that moment. The big lump in the bed indicated that the man was still asleep. Without ceremony, Darda roused him and told him there was a fire.

Emil did not stop to question, but got out of bed and, hurriedly, like Darda before him, slipped on his shoes and a coat. Soon they were making their way out.

In his panic, the white did not think to shut Emil's door and the room was soon full of smoke. As they exited into the hall, it seemed to affect the older man worse and he was soon coughing badly and leaning on Darda for support. The latter lent him a clean hanky to put over his mouth. Then the lantern went out.

In the inky black, a smoke-filled corridor, shouts and screams in the distance and an unfamiliar maze to negotiate, Darda was extremely worried. It was quite possible they would not get out. He had not seen or heard any flames as yet, but from the rising din of voices, this was a major incident.

In the confusion they turned the wrong way down a corridor. Then the squad leader bumped into another young man who shouted, "Follow me!" Not needing to be told twice, they did indeed follow the man, whom they later found out was a hotel employee, as he led them to safety. A thick, acrid smell was all around them and there were blasts of hot air. Rounding one corner, they saw flames reflected off the wall at the next bend. Fortunately they turned down another way before they reached that spot, but the heat there was unimaginable. For the first time they could actually hear the blaze and it was uncomfortably close.

Down the stairs they went, a steady light was visible up ahead. It was less smoky here, but Emil was still choking badly. The trio were moving in a flow of people now. With great relief they found themselves in the well-lit, and currently unaffected, entrance hall. From there they evacuated onto the street. The hotel employee left them at this stage and Darda led the stumbling, coughing Emil across the road to the non-functioning fountain and sat him down. Standing close beside, he could feel the smoke within him and tried not to cough himself. He scooped his hand down to the dormant water, not caring at that moment what condition it was in, and took a few draughts. Turning back, he was a safe distance to watch the rest of the tragedy unfold. They were far from alone as a crowd soon began to gather in the square. Streetlights radiated the whole scene, to be joined by the even greater brilliance of the flames as the fire took over.

Some windows, especially in the middle section and the second and third floors, had huge flames pouring out of them by now. Others to left and right had a glow from further inside their rooms, others were black. The fire was obviously out of control and nothing short of a miracle would save the building. The question was how many occupants could be saved? As Darda watched, he could feel the heat on his face, even though he was a good distance away. Some at the front of the crowd began retreating. Meanwhile, people were running out of the entrance in dribs and drabs: two women together; a man and a woman with a child; another man by himself...

Sounds there were aplenty: the roar of the flames, muffled cries, cracking and bangs from within the building. There was a huge amount of shouting going on, but little in the way of coordinated action.

"Isn't there a fire brigade?" Darda asked a group of women. Most ignored him, but one turned and said, "They've been called." He looked down at his charge and found the big man hunched up with the hanky held firmly to his face. He was not sure whether or not to say anything to him.

A new man, a black, came out of the building. He stumbled onto the road and others went to help him. Getting to his feet unaided, he took their arms anyway as they led him away from the intense heat. His face and clothes were blackened and, between coughing fits, he said, "There's folk inside, on the fourth floor!"

At this point, the fire intensified as part of the front of the building became one continuous sheet of flame. There was a tremendous roar as it took hold, bits of debris were falling into the square and sparks flying off into the sky. No one else seemed to be making it out of the front door now. To the right, some men arrived with buckets. The crowd made way for them as they dashed for the fountain and filled them up there. Darda helped Emil move along to one side, so as not to be in their way.

"How are you feeling now, senator?"

Emil put a hand up in acknowledgement and nodded his head. He dared not speak lest it start another bout of coughing.

The would-be fire-fighters were not having much luck. The intensity of the inferno was such that they could not get close enough. They threw the water as best they could, but it fell short, onto the pavement. 'It would take a whole river to put that fire out anyway,' thought Darda.

The blaze had not fully taken hold on the left-hand side of the building. There were figures up there, trapped. They hung out of the third and fourth floor windows, gasping for air for all they were worth. Those on the ground made desperate attempts at coming forward, holding some equipment. It was not clear to Darda what it was. In any case they were beaten back by the heat and bits falling off the blazing building. As they looked, there was a roar as one of the big support beams in the centre gave way and sagged down. Sparks flew everywhere and little pieces of debris fell down, forcing the crowd back still further.

Harrowing screams issued forth and cries for help could be heard above the roar of the flames and the buzz of the assembled throng. One woman leant out of a fourth floor window holding something in her arms. She shouted down, "I'm about to throw my baby, please catch my baby!"

A man went forward and the crowd held their breath at what happened next. The mother tossed the baby out of the window. The small shape fell quickly and the man got right underneath and caught

435

it cleanly. A cheer went up, it was a small victory on a night of tragedy.

This left-hand side was starting to catch alight. If any were to be rescued from there , time was of the essence. People were still hanging out of the windows, trying to gasp for fresh air.

Another mother was about to throw her precious young offspring out. A group of women came forward with a sheet between them and caught the infant in it before retreating hastily once more.

At this point a makeshift rope-ladder from tied sheets appeared out of a window and a young woman began climbing down it. Unfortunately she was still at the second floor when she lost her grip and fell onto the unforgiving cobbles. She did not move and a couple of helpers dashed forward and dragged the body away from the conflagration.

"I can't breathe, help me, help me!" another trapped person pleaded piteously.

"Oh my eyes," declared a woman in the crowd next to Darda. "I ain't seen nothin' like it, ever."

"Look, look!" shouted another.

They had seen a man come forward with a long wooden ladder. In the absence of the town's fire brigade (where in the universe had they got to?) it was enterprising individuals trying their best to save lives. With the help of a colleague, he set the ladder up and, with a saturated cloth wrapped round his face, and defying the heat, he scrambled up to those trapped on the third floor.

Flames were licking nearby as a couple of people overcame their fears in desperation for their lives and transferred to the ladder. Onlookers held their breath as they watched the operation. "He's a hero!" one elderly man declared and others nodded.

The hero came down with two hotel guests, a man and a woman. He prepared to go up again. Yet, looking up, he saw the flames spreading quickly and the top of the ladder was now alight. It had to be abandoned.

"Help me, help me!" came pitiful cries above the roar of the flames and crashing of beams as the internal structure in the central section gave way. The crowd had swollen and all was confusion. A man on fire leapt from the building to his death. Others were screaming. The eye witnesses watched in horror. People could still be seen at a window and their shouts heard. There was a massive explosion and they were no more.

By now the entire structure was a wall of flame, spreading to the adjoining buildings. No one else would get out of the hotel alive. Amongst the new arrivals were the soldiers under Darda's command. They were lost for words at the distressing sight, but relieved to see their two compatriots alive.

"I wish to go," Emil announced quietly and Darda helped him to his feet. With the assistance of a couple of soldiers, they moved the senator away from the scene and towards the stables above which the men were billeted for the night.

On they went, away from the disaster scene. Round a corner it was cooler in the night air and a lot quieter. Emil began coughing again; he did not look well. Eventually their destination came to view, a couple of soldiers were standing outside with lanterns.

"Not long to go now, senator," Darda urged him on. "You can make." He certainly hoped he would, the big man looked fit to drop at any moment.

Through the collective efforts of the soldiers, Emil was transported indoors, upstairs and to a fresh bed for the night. As they breathed a sigh of relief, Darda peered out of the window at the huge orange-red glow on the horizon. He just hoped that the blaze would be contained and not spread to where they were staying. He put a soldier on sentry duty to keep an eye on the fires progress. One thing they could do without was a further evacuation.

"We certainly meet some strange people in the course of our ministry, don't we?" Eleazar said to his wife.

Auraura was pleased that he referred to their mission to the poor in Isson as "our" ministry. For it was, after all, a joint venture, even if it was the priest doing all the preaching.

The remark was prompted by an unusual visitor they entertained earlier that morning. A strange-looking man had drawn up his dusty wagon outside the church and come in. His load appeared to be limestone rocks, but he was offering to sell them opals.

"I come over the mountains," he declared.

"To the east, you mean?"

"O' course!"

"Okay," the priest had replied.

437

"You want to buy some o' the finest opals ever?"

He then produced examples of his real load. The opals were hidden in the rocks. After discovering them on the other side of the mountains, he had re-stuck the limestone together again to hide the semi-precious stones. They were a myriad of colours, all swirling into each other. Quite beautiful, but he was barking up the wrong tree.

"You should try someone else," Eleazar had declared. "We don't have money to spare... and besides, I don't know what we'd do with them if we bought them anyway."

The seller then tired to convince him that he should adorn his beautiful wife. While her beauty was not in question, the lady herself wore the simple wear of poor folk and the last thing she was into was jewellery. He went his way, leaving the husband and wife team to have a chuckle between them.

"I hope he finds a buyer," said Auraura.

"I expect he will. They're fine stones."

"Quite useless to us."

"Listen! What's that?" asked Eleazar.

It was a small, political procession going past the church building. For the General Election campaign had come to Isson. The hill-folk could hardly exclude people now that the end of the war was officially declared. Canvassers and candidates walked past the remains of barricades that had kept them at bay for more than a year.

Buff representatives, others from the Pinks and Neo-Purples, were all vying for votes in this enclave. Some came a long distance to tell the townspeople how much better things would be if only their party was voted into power. Some older citizens were highly cynical of the whole process. Others were more in tune with the usual Ladosan enthusiasm for things political. Lectures and debates were held in the town hall, but Eleazar and Auraura kept well away from them. It seemed that all Isson's independence during the war was now being handed back to the very politicians that had drawn the country into conflict.

That afternoon, Auraura went to the local market to stock up on provisions for the family. When she came back, she was full of an encounter she experienced whilst out.

"I met a young woman from a village a little way north of Tracana."

438

"Your old stomping ground."

"She was telling me about the conditions they're having to put up with over there."

"Following the war, you mean?"

"No, it was well within the Rose sector. I don't think they were affected by it directly. It's to do with a repressive landowner. He treats the tenants appallingly, making them work on the land for an absolute pittance. They're virtual slaves! No one seems to be standing up for their rights. The girl I met had escaped from there and travelled right the way across the country to get out of the tyrant's clutches."

"What's she going to do now? Has she got a job?"

"I don't know; I don't think so."

"We can't afford a salary for a church worker."

"I know that, my dear, but I was pondering doing something about the landowner."

"Huh?" went Eleazar, concerned as to what she was going to say next.

"If I went along there, I could sort that landowner out. That's what we do, isn't it, right wrongs?" Then, more to herself than anyone else, she continued, "I could call in on Ballianaza in Tracan while I was at it; I haven't seen her in a long time."

"Are you out of her mind?" asked her astonished husband. He knew that his wife enjoyed the occasional flight of fancy, but this new idea needed nipping in the bud. He put down what he was doing and sought to bring her back to reality. "It would be a long journey at the best of times, but it would be incredibly dangerous at present. The war might be over, but I'm hearing daily reports of lawlessness in some parts of the country. Robber bands roaming at will in some places."

She hesitated, then, as if a spell had been abruptly broken, broke out into a laugh. "Mmm, well, it was a nice idea anyway."

Eleazar breathed a sigh of relief, but it got him thinking. He said, "Talking of long journeys, there is one place I'd like to go."

"Oh?"

"I'd like to pay a visit back to Thyatira. There are lots of friends whose faces I'd enjoy seeing again. Although I realise that I'd have to wait until next year. I don't think any long journeys are wise right now."

"You're right," she conceded with a sigh. Then, suddenly more upbeat, she continued, "let's throw a party instead!"

"Instead of going away, you mean?"

"Yes."

"What's the occasion?"

"Does there have to be one?"

"Um, it's..."

"Let's hold one here, in the church. We could have a feast, or something. It would take a while to organise, it would be in a few weeks time. There doesn't have to be a reason, surely? If you need a reason, call it an end-of-war party, or an election party. Call it what you like, I don't care. It would be a break in routine, something happy, something away from the humdrum."

Her enthusiasm was infectious. Eleazar said, "Okay then, but if we're going to have a grand feast, let's do it properly. Do it for all the regulars here and those who have helped us throughout the year. Our funds are not great, but we do have some money saved up that we can use to buy food. After all the worry about the war, and our near-miss from that fireball, maybe we should throw a party to celebrate life itself."

The morning after the fire in Carnis, Emil was in no condition to be moved. A doctor was called for at first light and, with the senator's blessing, Darda was allowed to go back to the site of the fire and see what the situation was.

A large pall of lazy, dark grey smoke hung over the rooftops as he approached. Once the place came into view, he was not completely surprised see that what had been The Chequers Hotel was a burnt-out husk. Some adjoining buildings were burnt out too, but the fire had not spread beyond the immediate area. That was something of a miracle, Darda considered, considering the scale of the conflagration the night before.

There were considerably fewer people in the square, but small groups hung around. Darda quizzed the nearest one for information.

"The fire brigade arrived too late," an old man told him, "'tis a scandal. The fire marshal should be sacked!"

"Nevertheless, they seem to have stopped the fire from spreading," said Darda.

"But what about the hotel guests who were burnt alive?"

The hotel itself was a mass of broken beams and blackened debris. Pockets of smoke were ascending and a couple of men in uniform were going about with buckets of water, dampening these area before they caught fire again. The building was a shell and what little remained in the way of walls looked likely to collapse at any moment. The properties on either side, and a way up the street, were all gutted. These were private residences. Brick buildings were scarred with black streaks up from the windows from where flames poured out. The heavy smell of smoke was all around.

Some people were walking around in a daze. One middle-aged man came up to Darda. His face was blackened and his clothing was in rags.

"I lost my wife on the stairs," he said pathetically. "I couldn't go back."

Darda looked down and saw the man was barefoot and those feet were bleeding. He was still thinking what to say when a lady came along and led the man away.

He overheard many fractured conversations from the gathered observers.

"I spoke to a youth who still can't find his parents."

"I've never seen anything like it. I can't even describe it. People came out without their children. Others were throwing themselves out of the windows."

"I heard something, I looked up; the next moment they'd jumped out and were on the floor."

"Once it all started, it spread incredibly quickly."

"Horrific!"

The listener moved on. There was a gaggle of survivors, all of them blacks, wrapped in blankets, sitting on the edge of the fountain. The nearest one was shivering, more in shock than cold. Speaking about it seemed to be helping them.

"If we'd been there a moment longer we would never have got out."

"I heard banging on the door. Someone was shouting, 'Fire!' There was thick smoke along the whole landing. 'Get out, get out!' someone yelled. So we rushed down the stairs."

"The stairs? I remember climbing over bodies on the stairs, folk who overcome by the smoke. I couldn't stop to help them, I couldn't."

"I wrapped a wet towel round my face. There was so much smoke. I got lost in the stairwell."

"Smoke everywhere, literally everywhere. The smoke was so thick you couldn't see anything."

Darda was starting to realise quite how fortunate he and Senator Vebber had been. Waking up early saved their lives, along with help from that hotel employee. He wondered where the man was so that he could give thanks - not that he would have recognised him.

No local government officials were present, no one was taking control of the situation. He heard some angry comments about the lateness of the fire brigade in turning up. Maybe the people in authority were deliberately staying away now. Having concluded that there was no point in him hanging about any longer, he turned to go back. Besides, the smoky atmosphere was setting off his cough again.

When he arrived at the stables again, the doctor was in with Emil, so Darda stayed outside in the corridor with his soldiers. A young man, a stable employee, was a witness to the night's proceedings and was regaling them with what he had seen.

"I couldn't believe what I was looking at. Heard folk screaming and calling for help. The fire took hold so quickly. The firemen were struggling. Before they arrived, I saw children banging at windows, men, women screaming for help. Everyone's shocked. It's unbelievable; I still can't take it in."

He was finishing off his sentence when the doctor came out of the room. All eyes turned to him as he gave his verdict.

"He should make a full recovery, but right now he needs rest and plenty of drink."

Once he was gone, the squad leader gave his orders.

"John, you go to the mayor's office and tell him about Senator Vebber. Tell him we need the best accommodation for him to stay and recover. Try to get word to the Weavers' Guild that there'll be no meeting today."

He coughed a few times in response to a similar sound coming from the other side of the door. Then he turned to another soldier in his charge.

"Matty, take a dakk back to the Castle and inform Despot Thorn what has happened. Tell him that Senator Vebber is expected to make a full recovery, he must not be unduly alarmed. You could also

442

tell him that there has been loss of life in Carnis as a result of this fire."

The soldiers sped off to do his bidding. there was then a pause then another of them asked, "Would you like a breakfast, Darda? We have some food here."

So wrapped up in events, he had rather forgotten about breakfast. He replied in the affirmative, adding, "That sounds like a good idea. What about the senator? Has he been fed?"

"I don't think so."

"He may not feel like anything, but there again he might do. Go through and speak to him... maybe some warm soup? Make sure he has plenty to drink as per the doctor's orders."

Darda sat down. He felt tired. His mind was still trying to process the night's events. How many died in that inferno? The sight of people at the windows, as the flames were coming closer, haunted him. He witnessed some grizzly sights in the Azekah battles, but this was something altogether different.

One of the soldiers asked him when they would be travelling back to the Castle.

"When Senator Vebber is well enough to travel, not before."

After a while, John came back and reported that the mayor was too busy to be seen and no one else was available. In truth, he had met with nothing but contempt due to the fact that he was a white.

Darda, who had finished his breakfast by now, was furious. "We'll see about that!" he declared, standing up. Right, you two stay with the senator and see to him. The rest of you don your weapons. We're going to demand an audience with the mayor. I don't care who he thinks he is, we have the authority of the senate and the Despot behind us. I'll make him pay attention; make no mistake!"

"When did we last hear from Gabby?" Frank asked.

Tristan looked a little puzzled, "Er, from..."

"Our ambassador to the Ma'hol."

The pair were in the Throne Room on a bright afternoon. The Despot continued talking.

"I know he's the ambassador to the whole of Hoame now and not merely Thyatira. Even so, he's supposed..."

He cut off at the sound of a knock on the door. It was a soldier with a message.

443

"My Lord, the Ma'hol consul is outside and asking to see you."

"Oh," expressed Frank in surprise, "Well, send him up; we can entertain him here in the Throne Room."

"I think, My Lord, he would prefer it if you met him in the bailey."

This was an extraordinary thing for the guardsman to say, but without a word the room's two occupants got up and followed him out. It was only once they emerged from the Castle's keep entrance that the truth of the matter became apparent.

Harn'an-Fors, the Ma'hol consul to Thyatira, was standing in the middle of the bailey, beaming from ear to ear. Frank thought he had never seen such a huge smile on his face, but then he possessed good reason to be happy. For, standing behind him, was a servant holding the reins of two fine-looking superdakks. Magnificent-looking specimens they were. The sun streaming in over the castle wall bathed the creatures in bright light. One of them, a mottled white and grey, stamped the ground with a front hoof and let out a loud coughing sound.

"I'm delivering what you asked for, My Lord."

"Wonderful!" Frank replied, stepping forward and admiring the impressive beasts. I am most grateful, thank you so much."

"They arrived this morning, along with this," and he handed over a communication tube with the Mehtar's seal.

Eagerly opening it, Frank saw that it was a brief note from Rabeth-Mephar's supreme ruler.

"To my dear Frank Thorn, Order of the Royal Friend, Autarch of Hoame, Despot of Thyatira, greetings. I have great pleasure having these dakks delivered to you as a personal gift from us. May they be of good service to you. Sincerely Mehtar Arumah-Ru (followed by half a dozen grandeurs titles)."

"Will you come in, Harn'an-Fors, and share a drink with me?"

"I shall with pleasure."

The superdakks were passed to Castle stable hands for the time being as the men ascended the stairs towards the hall and then into the Throne Room. Beverages and sweetmeats were brought and the consul confirmed that he had no objection to the Despot's secretary remaining in the room.

After Frank expressed his thanks once more, Harn'an-Fors spoke.

"There is little news of worth coming out of my homeland as of late. Following the disasters of previous years, however, it is something of a relief to have a period of silence. I understand his Magnificence, the Mehtar, is personally involved in the designing of a new cathedral for Krabel-Haan. He wants it as something more magnificent than the world has ever seen."

'I bet he does!' thought Frank, who then asked about the Mehtar's health.

"He is well, thank you."

"And yourself? Are you able to keep yourself occupied in these quiet times?"

With a chuckle the consul replied that he understood matters were not so quiet with their mutual neighbour, Ladosa, adding, "Although it would seem that hostilities have been suspended."

"For good, I hope!"

"Indeed, but to answer your question on a personal level, I have taken up marquetry as a hobby."

"Really? How interesting."

"Only in a small way currently. I would like to think that I am gaining in proficiency at it."

"Well, that should keep you going through the long winter night."

"Quite so."

"And about the superdakks; I hope I made it clear that they are for a fellow despot, Despot Schmidt of Capparathia. I promise not to make a habit of asking for more of them for all and sundry, because I know they're in short supply. I do take it as a huge compliment that the Mehtar has agreed to let us have these two. They will help me cement an alliance within Hoame that I am keen to foster. I promise that it will not be setting a precedent."

The consul looked relieved. They chatted a short while longer, but then the Ma'hol was back on his way. Frank got Tristan to organise the transfer of the Mehtar's present down to Capparathia. He chose Squad Leader Stephen, mostly recovered now from his illness, to lead the expedition along with a full squad of soldiers. Their cargo was so precious that it was felt necessary to have a substantial armed escort. Wagons pulled by ordinary dakks with supplies and suchlike were needed for the journey. There was much to be sorted out, but it was hoped they would leave the following day.

Later on, Frank was back in the Throne Room with Tristan.

"Well, that's good news! Despot Schmidt will be delighted. All right, then, I'd like your help with composing three letters."

445

"Three, My Lord?"

"Yes. In order of urgency: one to send as a covering note with the present to Despot Schmidt; a second to thank the Mehtar for his most generous gift and a third to our Ambassador in Krabel-Haan to wake him up and let him know we still exist."

Early the next day, Frank was up on the third floor of the Castle walking past the instrument cupboard when he thought he heard a sound coming from it. It contained the inter-space communication devise left him by his brother, John. It had not stirred in years and he surmised it was no longer working. He hesitated.

"Frank, is that you?"

Hearing his wife's voice from the sitting room, he forgot about it and went to see her.

"Hello my darling."

"Joseph's tutor saw me this morning, he said he's been doing well lately, applying himself."

"That's good to hear. I think we need to step up our training for him in preparation for when he becomes a despot."

"I hope you're not thinking of resigning," she said flippantly.

Her husband, however, was in earnest, and continued, "He has already started attending senate meetings."

"Not every one from now on, surely, my dear."

"Um, you don't think so?"

"No! He'd be bored silly. Start off in a small way and work up, that's my advice."

"Hmm, all right then... but I think he should have his swordsmanship lessons increased."

"He's doing, what, one a week presently?"

"Yes. I haven't spoken to the sword-master lately. I think I should get a progress report from him."

Hannah wondered if it was strictly necessary for a modern despot military commander to be able to actually join in the fighting themselves. She then remembered that her husband had, in fact, personally led a charge into battle early in his career. Perhaps it was best not to challenge this.

"Yes, dear," she replied.

Shortly afterwards, he walked across to the senate building. A thin layer of morning mist hung over the grass in the middle distance. An elderly man passed by pushing a wheelbarrow load of fallen leaves. He wondered idly where the fellow might be going. Entering the building, he was met by an unusual sight, his defence secretary in full armour.

"Karl?"

"Yes, My Lord, I'm going to join General Japhses for the military exercises today."

"Oh, I'd forgotten about that."

"Two squads of guardsmen along with some militia from Vionium. It's a refresher with the general wanting to put them through their paces."

"I see."

"It's keeping the men on their toes whilst reminding the militia that they are needed in times of war. We want to try out some signalling equipment and see how the regular soldiers and the militia can be coordinated."

"Very well. Let me know how it goes."

Frank went on to his office and was sitting there alone when a clerk opened the door. His serious demeanour was disconcerting.

"What is it?"

"A soldier from Darda's squad, My Lord, returned from Norland with a message."

"Show him in."

It was now that the Despot heard the news of the catastrophic fire and, in particular, Senator Vebber being affected by it.

"Is he being cared for?"

"A doctor is in attendance, My Lord, and Squad Leader Darda is arranging better accommodation and seeing after things."

"So he's got a handle on it."

"I believe so, My Lord."

"But there have been fatalities in the fire?"

"Yes, My Lord, but we don't know how many."

"I see," Frank said slowly, wondering what to do. 'Who do I rely on when there's a crisis.' "Guardsman..."

"Yes, My Lord."

"Fetch me Senator Alan without delay."

"At once, My Lord."

447

The following day was wet in Castleton. It was the first substantial rain for a while and rivulets trickled down the streets as passers by hurried past. The wheat harvest was nearly completed, but now had to be suspended. Farm workers cursed. The land was community owned and there were not many privately-owned farms in the whole of Thyatira. Fortunately the hulffan crop was in. A bumper crop too, thanks to the new areas successfully planted in the spring. A notoriously fussy plant to grow, they were lucky this year in their choice of extra sites. In the sheds, the croppers skilfully applied their fassons, or specialist knives used for cutting the fibrous material.

Rain battered on the window of Deejan Charvo's study. He was in conference with his trusted deputy concerning an unusual development which concerned their business.

"We should not be too surprised, Walter, after all it's what happens in life. Be thankful that we have enjoyed a clear run up until now. We might have expected that the acquisition of Norland would have had unexpected results."

"Maybe," replied his dour, long-term employee and confidante, "but this bank did not exists a few years ago when Aggeparii was our home and Felsham part of it."

"Times change."

"Where did this bank spring from? That's what I'd like to know. It has come out of nowhere to threaten our existence."

"Profitability, maybe but we're big enough to fight our corner."

"Offering depositors four percent interest is going to attract a lot of people and drain us of capital coming in, Deejan."

"Unless we fight back. I've been working on some figures this afternoon. Look," he added as he passed them under the other man's nose. "We can offer five percent on deposits if..."

"Five percent? More than double the existing."

"We must face realities. We can add the condition that, in order to obtain this figure, the money must be held with us for a term of at least a year. That will produce stability and help us to plan long-term. I said look at the figures. There is still a profit to be made. Our average interest rate is twenty-five percent these days, so there's scope for us to make money."

"I wish we could go back to the days when we could charge two hundred percent," said Walter.

"I'm sure you're right, but it's no good living in the past. We are now in a different world from the Aggeparii days. In many ways it is a lot better. Defaults are fewer and we have the goodwill of the Despot. I wouldn't trade places with the old Kagel days. Would you, honestly?"

The assistant had to concede he would not. He then raised another aspect.

"We will have to make sure it is a level playing field. If we are hampered by Despot Thorn's injunctions, then so should this bank."

"You're right. I shall have a word in the ears of one or two senators, that should do the trick. If not, I can always appeal to the top again, although I am loath to bother him with such a matter. In the meantime, Tristan Shreeber has an appointment with me tomorrow morning. He's going to be the first customer that I shall offer the increased rate to. Word will soon get round."

A while later, Walter left. He could but agree with the points that his boss was making. It had been the initial shock that provoked his strong reaction. He was coming to terms with it now.

His presence in the study was taken over by Keturah. She had been waiting a long time that late afternoon for an opportunity to speak to her father alone.

"Ah, hello, my sweet girl," Deejan greeted her cheerfully as he looked up from his desk.

"Father, may I have a word with you?" she asked, closing the door behind her.

"Of course, what can I do for you? Is everything okay?"

"Yes, father. It's a personal matter, nothing to do with the business."

"All right, sit down. What's this all about?"

Clearing her throat, she began cautiously, "For a while now I have been feeling that God has been speaking to me."

"Ah," went the moneylender; he had not been expecting that.

"It's more of a feeling than anything else... but it won't go away. Also, things one or two people have said to me have gone to confirm that I am on the right track."

"Which is....?"

"I feel God is calling me to preach his word. In public, I mean."

"Um..."

"I don't mean just reading the Bible, I mean deliver messages about it that God had given me. I've started writing ideas down that have come to me, not from any human source."

Deejan thought deeply in the hush that followed. She was sixteen, a mere girl. Yet more than once she seemed the wisest member of the household and he included himself in that. Keturah was saintly in many ways, her devotion to him, the way she had nursed Sebastian during his illness... But there were no women preachers in Thyatira. None in the whole of Hoame as far as he knew. On the other hand, these were still times of social change in the land. Maybe this should be another one, or was it a step too far? On the other hand, if she actually was getting these promptings from the Almighty, they should be listened to...

"I know what I'll do," he eventually spoke, breaking the silence. "I shall have a word with Bishop Gunter. I will try to do your cause justice, but if I do not convince him to find you some sort of a role, I shall invite him to have a word with you directly. Is that good enough for you?"

He said it with a smile and, in response, she worked her way round the desk to give him a big hug. If this was, as she believed, really from God, then doors would open and barriers disappear. She possessed the faith to believe that firmly.

~ End of Chapter 22 ~

Prospects of Peace - Chapter 23

The burnt-out shell of the Chequers Hotel was a testimony to the ferocious power of fire as well as the folly of man. The cause of the fire was not known, but answers were being demanded as to why the fire brigade was so slow in arriving on the scene.

It was a catastrophe that caused huge psychological effect on the town. The scale of the blaze was bigger than anything within living memory. A substantial number of lives had been lost, although an exact toll was not possible. The injured were swelling the local hospital. While people were grieving over their loved ones, all were struggling to comprehend the scale of the disaster.

Numb with shock, relations trawled the church-run hospital wards trying to discover if their kin were there.

One white man said, "I've been looking all day for a friend who's missing. Someone told me that casualties have been taken elsewhere, but no one is giving me a straight answer. I went to the main hospital, but they don't know nothin'. Don't know if they're alive or dead. I can't take much more o' this."

Others came from afar merely to gawp at the scene of the tragedy. A short, white woman stood in the road staring at the blackened ruins. She said to the stranger standing next to her, "Everyone's in shock, y'know? The building must've gone right up, no stoppin' it."

The hotel was not alone in being lost, for several private houses on either side were destroyed too. Some residents, who barely escaped with their lives, found all their possessions incinerated. While the townsfolk were shocked and distraught, the community pulled together in the immediate aftermath. With the local government on the defensive, it was left to ordinary citizens to fill the vacuum. With blacks and whites equally affected, they came together in this hour of need like never before.

Well-wishers donated food, blankets and clothes. The churches in particular offered temporary accommodation for the displaced. Usual town life was severely disrupted in the wake of the tragedy. Adversity was bringing out the best in the community and that heartened those affected. Neighbours opened their doors and emptied their cupboards, but why was the mayor and his deputy not visiting the scene, or the casualties in hospital?

One person whose house was gutted, said, "I won't get over this; I've lost everything. I escaped in my night clothes. People gave me their clothes today; I'm grateful. Lots of ordinary folk offered to help us, both blacks and whites."

By the afternoon, volunteers were coming in from Newton. A messenger arrived at the hospital on superdakk to tell them that the Despot had organised a convoy of emergency aid which should arrive the following day.

At the scene of the fire, small columns of smoke were still rising in places. The air was full of it while blackened bits of debris were scattered over a large area. Fine ash was still falling a distance away. No one had organised a clear-up. Most onlookers were keeping a distance from the remains of the structure, for the few walls still standing looked fit to collapse at any moment.

Men and women milled around, staring in disbelief. For many it helped them to voice their thoughts, even to other bystanders they had never met before.

"The flames spread so quickly."

"I saw figures jumping out of windows, it was a nightmare."

"I heard that the woman from that house was escaping with five children. She could only find three when she got out. I dunno if the others survived."

"I don't know what's happened to my grandfather. I spoke to a lady who was hoping her relatives were alive."

A singed child's doll lay amongst blackened beams and other burnt debris. It was a poignant symbol of the tragedy that had befallen the town.

Nonetheless, soon the shock to turn to anger. There was a well-established fire brigade in Carnis. It was their job to put out fires speedily. Why did they not turned up until late? Why had the local authorities gone to ground? Where was the fire marshal? Where was the mayor? The fact that the deputy mayor was originally from Gistenau despotate was being held against him. There were murmurs about mounting a protest at the town hall. Fortunately this was all forestalled by the arrival of the convoy from Castleton.

Alan managed to persuade the Despot that the latter did not have to visit the scene of the disaster himself. He would do so as his representative. He had been busy on the trials for new wagon-plus-dakk combinations, but dropped that straightaway to head the relief effort. First step for the drone was the main hospital where the generous supplies he brought were gratefully received. However, it did not take him long to discern the mood of the people. Filled with resolve, he marched on the town hall, accompanied by some of his soldiers. A rag-tag group of local, concerned citizens were in tow.

"Take me to the mayor's office!" he demanded upon arriving. The soldiers were keeping the people outside. As yet the small crowd was preparing to wait a while and see if this drone's appearance made any difference.

The mayor was sitting at his desk when Alan stalked in, followed by a couple of worried clerks. He sat there as if frozen and it seemed to take him a while to comprehend what was happening. This was the second time in a couple of days that a northern Thyatiran had marched in and overturned his authority.

"What are you doing about organising relief for the fire victims?"

"Um..."

"I'm told that they are getting no assistance other than from their neighbours and that you are doing nothing."

He paused to let the man have his say, but not a word came from his lips. The mayor seemed utterly dismayed by the whole event and incapable of action.

"Get him out of here!" commanded the new man in charge and the clerks came forward to led the uncomplaining, pathetic mayor out of his office. "Right, now let's get down to business."

As he walked, Tristan noticed that some individual deciduous trees had changed colour ahead of the rest. It was good to notice details such as this to keep his mind off where he was going.

He felt stability in his life. It had taken a while to grow into the role of the Despot's secretary, but he thought that he was getting to grips with it now. He was settling into the house, although the unfinished extension looked something of an eyesore. Attending regular church services and Bible study were helping him to anchor his life down. This is something he needed and his mental state was stable.

The conditions were as good as they would ever be for him to do it. He was walking to visit his mother. The mother who, he could scarcely believe it, had arranged for his father to be killed. Anger

453

was not present in his heart, more a numbness. It would not be an easy meeting. 'What do I say?' He did not even know why he was going, except that an invisible force was compelling him. God perhaps?

It was not a short walk to the monastery, but lost in his thoughts he welcomed having time to reflect. He could have ridden, but that would have got him there too quickly. Yet he found his anxiety levels rising alarmingly as he neared his destination. Pace slowing, more than once he considered turning round. In the end, he told himself that he must go through with it.

"Good morning, my name is Tristan Shreeber. I have come to visit my mother."

With barely a word, the unemotional nun on duty at reception led him the way. He had not sent a message on ahead of his impending visit, because part of him was not convinced he would go through with it. Was it unfair to arrive unannounced?

His guide took him to the cell, indicated with her hand, then walked off without saying anything. Heart beating, dry mouthed, Tristan stepped up to the grill. He was pleased that the nun was gone and there was no one else about.

There she was, sitting reading a book by the light of an east window. Oblivious to his presence, it gave him the opportunity to study her. Her hair was shorter than he had see in and her face thinner. Then it was a while since he last saw her.

Plucking up courage, he took a deep breath and said, "Hello Mother, it's Tristan."

"Tristan?" she echoed in disbelief as she dropped the book and hurried to the grill. "Is it you?" She half believed it was someone having a joke at her expense. When she peered through, though, there was no mistaking who it was. "You came!"

"I was, so..."

"How are you? How are you doing? You look well."

He did not look at all well at this point, but the questions released him to speak of his job and recent trip to Rilesia and Capparathia. She listened, attentive to his every word, while he described the trip in some detail. There had been Ladosa before that, but it seemed like old news. It felt good merely to be able to talk, but inevitably he eventually ran out of things to say.

She studied him intensely, tears in her eyes. Even when he finished speaking she continued to stare at him. For so long she had dreamed of this moment; dreamed until she did not think it would ever actually happen.

The long silence was eventually broken when she said, "I know that I deserve to be here."

Pausing, she wondered if he might leave at this point, but he did not. she looked at him, his face difficult to interpret, so she went further.

"What I did was terribly wrong and I regret it now. If you could manage one day to tell me that you forgive me, it would mean the universe to me. One day..."

Wanda was afraid that she had said too much, but she was afraid that he might never visit again. It could be her sole opportunity to say these words in the hope of receiving forgiveness from the one person in the world she most needed it from.

Tristan did not hurry to give an answer. His last few years flashed before him: losing the one woman he had ever loved; his brother getting killed in battle; betrayed by someone he trusted; his mental breakdown in Asattan; finding friendship in Ladosa, only for it to collapse when his own subterfuge was exposed. So much pain. Now he wanted to rebuild his life and indeed he was doing so. Having unforgiveness in his heart would be like a ball and chain around his foot. Forgiving his mother would liberate them both in some way.

"I forgive you, Mother," he said softly.

He stayed for much of the rest of the morning. They were undisturbed and many tears flowed between them. "I will come again," he promised at his final goodbye.

Face red from crying, he hurried out of the monastery with his head down to avoid contact with anyone. There seemed few people about and he heard chanting coming from the main chapel.

Soon he was out in the courtyard, alone. It felt good. The visit had gone well and his spirits were uplifted, although there was no one he wanted to confide in. He decided to walk home a longer way to give him more time to think. He skirted round the southern end of Vionium, past cultivated fields. The farmers were ploughing with oxen, post harvest. Dakks were too weak to pull ploughs. He, like the farmers, had no idea what a miracle it was that the oxen survived the journey through space. It was in embryo form, courtesy of the

Culpers hundreds of years ago. Such transportation was strictly illegal in the twenty-seventh century.

After a while, Tristan found himself smiling and he was a bit surprised. It was then that he realised what a weight was lifted off his shoulders. He had not realised the scale of it until now. he would keep his promise to visit his mother again. The monastery did not appear to be keeping any restrictions on visitors. She might never be free again in this life, but they could still have a relationship again.

Having second thoughts about sharing this experience, he resolved to tell Deejan next time they met. Yes, it was a good day to be alive.

In Ladosa, the General Election had finally taken place. The collection and counting of the votes was done as quickly and efficiently as possible, but it still took a full three days. Nevertheless, with their passion for the democratic process, this was Ladosa at its best. A complex system of checks and counter-checks ensured that electoral fraud was kept to a minimum. The various party officials were satisfied that the vote had been as fair and free as was humanly possible.

The final overall figures were declared at the opera house in Lefange, a venue large enough to contain the delegates from across the country. Charlotta was very much in evidence as the results were called out. When they were, there were gasps of astonishment around the hall. Some were stunned by their party's good fortune, others devastated in defeat.

In round figures, the Neo-Purples achieved 45% of the vote. This was beyond their wildest dreams and a better result than the old Purple Party ever got. One factor which had helped was their releasing papers during the campaign which showed that the Buffs were negotiating to bring in Sarnician mercenaries during the war. Fortunately their own secret arrangement with the Hoamen had not leaked out.

Their new allies, the Rose Party, got 30% which again was better than they had hoped for. The Buffs' vote collapsed and the Pinks were almost wiped out.

The new leader of the Rose was on the moderate wing of the party and inclined to work together with the Neo-Purples. With a 75% block in parliament, they would have an unassailable working majority.

The people had spoken; the word "stability" was on everyone's lips. This was what most of the population earnestly desired and, with such a strong mandate, they hoped that the new coalition government would provide it. There was much reconstruction and reconciliation to be done across the land.

Many breathed a sigh of relief at the decisive result. Even the Buffs went strangely quiet and their leader, in his resignation speech, told his party to heed the voice of the people.

For Charlotta, a seat as a Member of Parliament was assured. That would be the bare minimum reward she could look forward to. There would be much wheeling and dealing over the next few weeks as ministerial positions were filled. This would form the governing nucleus to run the country. She was widely tipped for a senior post.

News travels fast and soon the refugee camp within Thyatira was awash with the tidings. In recent weeks there had already been a steady trickle of Ladosans leaving there for their homeland. Within days of the election details coming through, that turned into a torrent. The Hoame authorities were not unhappy with this development. The soldiers and volunteers staffing the camp began making plans for shutting down the establishment. The senate would have to discuss what to do with the facility. Some on the spot argued for it to be demolished. After all, to make it into a viable long-term community would take a lot of work. The despotate had always expanded organically and not by imposition. Whatever was the case, nothing substantial would be done before the spring. By that time, without heating or maintenance, many of the huts would only be fit for pulling down in any case. It was one decision that could be deferred.

Back in Lefange, Ladosa, Member of Parliament Nazaz sat in the office she recently hired. The new, smaller capital was having to get used to a huge influx of politicians, aides, advisors and civil servants. Without the many government offices that Braskaton possessed before the disaster, it was up to individuals to make their own arrangements. She had got in quickly and secured a prime site as a result.

Neo-Purple Party Committee Chief Borrazzan was due at any moment. He would be coming to see her following key negotiations with their Rose allies. She knew him to be one of a new breed of politicians in the country, pragmatic and always looking to secure a deal rather than stand on principle. She heard his distinct footsteps coming up the hall and tried to brace herself. About to learn her fate, she hoped not to be disappointed.

"Ah, Charlotta!" he declared with a politician's smile and handshake. The latter seemed a mite formal to her, it was not as if they had not met before. He held a small briefcase in his left hand.

"Come on in," she said, beckoning to a chair.

Taking a seat, his eyes roamed around the room. "A fine place you've found yourself here."

"Thank you."

"If a little empty at present."

"Um, I..."

"We will soon put that right."

"Yes?"

"I'll come straight to the point. I am able to offer you the job of Foreign Secretary. You will be our top person with regards to relations with our foreign neighbours. We on the Committee see it as recognition for your huge contribution in bringing about the alliance we have with the Rose Party. We hope that you can put your skills to good use when dealing with the likes of the Ma'hol and the Hoamen. What do you say?"

What could she say? To be offered one of the most senior and prestigious positions in government was an honour. Foreign relations was something she could really get her teeth into. The status she would enjoy in this role was greater than anything she experienced before.

"Yes! Yes, I am delighted to accept."

"Very well; we hoped you'd say that. It's getting late now, so we'll have to discuss your staff, budget and suchlike tomorrow. For now, I'd like to leave this with you."

As he spoke, he took out a sheaf of papers from his briefcase and laid it on the desk in front of her.

"What is it?" she asked, reaching out to pick it up as she spoke.

Standing up and wheeling away as he answered, he said, "A communication from our southern neighbours, the Inner Council of Hoame. It makes interesting reading. It will be your job now to decide how our nation responds."

With that, he was gone. She began perusing the documents. It was a new, revised offer of a compact between the two nations. As she read on, she realised it was far more comprehensive than a non-aggression pact. There were proposals for the exchange of ambassadors with the establishment of full diplomatic relations. Charlotta liked the idea; if ever there was a time to pull this off, it was now. Her country cried out for stability, what could be better than this?

Reading on, she came across a clause suggesting the public acknowledgement of the role that Hoame had played in the Neo-Purple military victory. That might be a sticking point. On the other hand, nothing remains secret forever in politics. If the news of the wartime pact could be released within the greater announcement of a deal with their former enemies, that might work. It would minimise any possible political damage. Indeed, if managed correctly it would turn what some might see a negative into a positive. Politics was a game and Charlotta Nazaz would prove herself to be a grand master of it. The woman had served a long enough apprenticeship, now she would put into action the skills she had learned.

Skipping to the end, she scanned down the list of signatories. Baron L'Rochfort was there, but Alan was not. Then she reminded herself that Alan was not in the Inner Council. She had still not received a reply to her letter and doubted he would write now. The message was clear and it did hurt her a bit, even now. What if she came across him again in the course of this new role of hers? She must not let that distract her.

Recognising this for the historic moment it was, she began reading through the document again slowly. This time she was making notes. If she was going to get this passed by the new government, and she strongly believed it should be, it was necessary for her to know exactly what the proposals being put forward were. In her view, a foreign alliance with this former enemy was within reach. There would inevitably be resistance to it in some quarters. She would need to be well prepared in order to carry the day in parliament.

A few days after the fire, Emil was fit to travel home. A couple of soldiers helped him into the wagon and he gave a token cough as he got on board. He was feeling a lot better now, following his ordeal. Darda gave the command and they pulled away, quite glad to leave Carnis and head for home.

The senator was delighted with all that the squad leader had done for him and was looking forward to giving the Despot a glowing report. The young man had earned it. The day after the fire, he marched up to the town hall to demand the best possible accommodation for Senator Vebber to convalesce. Finding the local authorities paralysed, and quoting the authority of Despot Thorn, he secured rooms in a good hotel, not merely for two, but for the entire party.

Regular visits from a doctor monitored the invalid, but in truth his condition had never been as serious as some of the poor souls involved in the tragedy. When Alan arrived, Darda reported briefly to him. The drone could see that he had the senator's care under control and let him be.

Now they were on their way back to Castleton. It was not a long way and Emil found a need to talk most of the journey. Fortunately, it did not seem to set off his cough again.

"It was a horrible experience, Darda, but it seems we were a lot luckier than many others."

"Everyone said how quickly it spread, but we were woken up early and that was..."

"The key thing," Emil finished off his sentence. "I was fast asleep. If you hadn't woken me I'd have been burnt alive!"

"I'm not sure about that, I..."

"Nonsense! You saved my life without any doubt. I am going to tell Despot Thorn as soon as we get back."

Whilst pleased, the recipient of this praise was also embarrassed and tried to direct the conversation away from himself.

"I heard one survivor say they were woken by screaming. They mentioned the baby being thrown down to folk below in the street. Also they said that a second staircase was unusable due to it being on fire. I don't know how they got out."

"Some people experienced a lot worse than we did."

"I went back the next day; the smoke still hung around. It got to the back of your throat. I saw some people trying to calm a young lad who'd lost his family."

"Tragic."

"Someone else said they got separated on the second floor. The mother was walking down the stairs, but all the flames and smoke meant they got separated. Another man was missing his brother-in-law and sister-in-law. They were in one of the houses next door, I think. He'd no choice but to leave everything behind simply to escape with his life."

Darda was finding it helpful to talk about it. Emil certainly did not mind. The white continued, "I sent a message to Alan to say that we were leaving this morning, but I didn't want to bother him, 'cos he's busy enough as it is."

That was true. The Despot's representative had had to hit the ground running upon his arrival, but he rose to the challenge. Based in the mayor's office, he opened his doors to ordinary victims of the catastrophe who wanted to air their grievances and get answers.

The key question was why the fire brigade turned up so late. A purpose-built station had been in existence long before the old Thyatiran towns got theirs. They were not badly equipped for the level of technology on the planet. So what happened?

Alan's investigation soon came up with the answers. Early on, a concerned citizen ran to the fire station and banged on the locked doors, but received no response. He assumed that, for some extraordinary reason, no one was present. In actual fact the duty firemen were indeed there, but deep in slumber! It took a later attempt by some further enquirers to wake them up. They moved into action then, but the delay was fatal.

It was small wonder that there was widespread anger when the story got out. Alan knew that heads would have to roll, but he interviewed the men involved first to get their account, their rather pathetic excuses.

With the help of the superdakks, he was able to keep Frank up to date with developments. Calls for the mayor's head were loud and vociferous, but Frank would not countenance that. At this time of great change within Norland, some stability was essential. So, instead, the unpopular deputy was dismissed. The fire service leaders were also sacked, along with the duty firemen, in spite of their belated efforts. Some townsfolk wanted further action taken against them, but that idea, rightly or wrongly, was dismissed. A trial would take time and Alan wanted the whole issue settled as swiftly as possible so that things could return to normal. Not that it ever would for those who had lost loved ones, or received serious injuries. In this society there was no provision for injury compensation. They had to rely on the acts of kindness from strangers and general assistance from the Church and Thyatira's rulers in Castleton. Indeed, a large-scale relief effort was put into motion. In the short-term this meant food, clothing and temporary accommodation. Churches swung into action here with great energy and enthusiasm, helping the dispossessed. For the long-term, central funds were promised to demolish and re-build the properties beyond repair. It was an unusual step for Hoame, but it struck the right mood and simply seemed the right thing to do.

Due to his swift actions and decision-making, Alan calmed the mood and forestalled any violent action being considered by some. Life quickly returned to normal for those not directly involved by the event.

Late afternoon, Senator Vebber and company arrived at the senate building in Castleton. A crowd went out to meet them. Fellow senators, plus ordinary blacks and whites, hurried to the scene. A message was sent to Frank who had been upstairs in the Castle. He came straightaway. There was much cheering and relief at their safe return following reports of the terrible holocaust in Carnis. When this died down, Emil held a private meeting with the Despot within the latter's senate office.

"Was it really as bad as the news we've been receiving? People throwing themselves out of upper-floor windows and suchlike?"

"I'm afraid so, it was a bad business."

Frank had been wanting to hear a first-hand account and sat riveted while the big man recounted that terrible night from his own perspective.

"Have they discovered how the fire started?"

"I haven't heard. I doubt if they will," Emil replied before spending a while praising Darda for his actions during and after the blaze. He concluded, "I believe, My Lord, that it would be appropriate for him to be recognised in some way for what he did."

"Excellent idea! I shall give it some thought."

"If I may be so bold..."

"Yes?"

"Let it not be too long. I would favour an early acknowledgement of his achievements."

"Quite right. Leave it with me."

A week passed and, one morning, Hannah went out with friends. Frank decided to have some time off and sat alone in his living room, musing.

'I haven't been on a spaceship for almost twenty years now. There was a time when I did so many interplanetary journeys that I thought nothing of it. People out there take for granted something that is mere fantasy as far as those on this planet are aware.

'I've been extremely lucky in my life. I was given the means to travel and see half the galaxy. I witnessed some amazing sights and met interesting characters. They weren't all interesting. That fat oaf Boz on board the *Cassandra* for instance. He was boasting about supplying military robots to both sides in the Third Intergalactic War. We both knew that didn't happen, but I couldn't be bothered to challenge him. He was trying to impress me. If he'd known all the places I'd visited then he might not have told me such nonsense. As far as I know, no more than two passengers ended up evacuating the ship before the operation was aborted. The other man died and I'm still here, nineteen years later, to tell the tale. Not that I *can* tell the tale, of course.

'Maybe I should write it all down, what I can remember anyway, and leave it for Joseph to read when I'm dead and gone. Then he'd be cross that I hadn't told him while I was still alive. It might be best if I allow my secret to die with me.

'The last time I saw my own parents was when I was eighteen years old, on Marmaris. I wonder what they'd have made of the dark Molten nights. I'd always hoped they would visit me on Eden, but perhaps that was a bit much to ask of them. They never went off-world in their lives.

'As for me, I travelled across the known universe and landed on my feet here. I have much to be thankful for.

'Talking of thanks, we've got the presentation to Darda today. It doesn't look like rain today; we could hold it outside. I'll have a word with Jonathan.'

He was still pondering this when a servant came up with the news that Alan had arrived back from Carnis.

"Ah, that's good. I'll come straight down."

His friend was in the hall, having a discussion with Japhses. The pair stopped and turned when he came down the stairs.

"Alan!" he greeted enthusiastically. It seemed a little over-the-top considering the drone was not long gone. "Tell me all about Carnis. It was a terrible tragedy from what Emil told me. Thank you for your communications, it sounded like you needed to knock a few heads together."

His lieutenant gave him a full up-date, ending, "It's all on track now. I had to spoon-feed the mayor a bit, but I think he's going to be okay. He's got his head together again. I've told him that his position is on the line if he messes up again."

"Good... and I gather that the victims are being cared for as well as possible."

"Volunteers are doing an excellent job."

"I'm pleased to hear it," replied Frank, who then realised that he had not spoken to the general standing there and sought to correct that. "Good morning, Japhses, I'm sorry, I should have said it earlier. Have you come to do the presentation to Darda?"

Hesitating at first, he replied, "I shall attend, although it is Captain Jonathan's show. But the real reason I am here is with news of the Ladosan election result."

"Is it good for us?"

"The initial signs are that it is. The Neo-Purples are forming a fresh government along with another faction. They have done rather well, I gather."

"So better relations with them are on the cards then?"

"With the Ladosans you never can..."

Alan interrupted, "Yes, Frank, they have some pro-Hoame figures in key positions. If the Inner Council don't blow it, we can seize the opportunity of a lifetime right now."

"Well, we've got Baron L'Rochfort looking after our interests. I trust him to do a good job." Then, seeing Jonathan enter the hall, he addressed him, "Captain, are we holding the presentation outside?"

"In the bailey, yes, My Lord."

"Is everything ready?"

"It is, My Lord."

A large contingent of Thyatira's military were on parade for Darda's award ceremony. The senate was well represented, plus some civilians, including Vophsi, Flonass and Darda's parents. Prior to the commencement of proceedings, Jonathan stood near the Despot. He finally conceded in his mind that he had been wrong about this squad leader and that he was making a fine soldier now that he had grown up a bit.

The ceremony was brief, the climax being when the captain made the presentation. Darda received a medal, one to go with his Azekah ones, a fine sword, plus a bag of money. Medals, although a long-established military tradition, had been used sparingly in Hoame. Frank thought that they were a good motivation. The sword was his idea too, one of a limited edition produced by the swords-smith and better quality than the regulation weapons. Frank had thought that the cash would also be well received as a practical gift.

"... For your bravery, initiative shown and coolness in the face of adversity," spoke the captain.

Darda was not certain where the bravery came in, he had just wanted to get out of the burning building. There was no way he could have left the senator there, that was not an option. His actions were more out of instinct, or necessity. Anyhow, the last thing on his mind was to contradict his commanding officer's words of praise. Glancing round, he saw his proud parents to one side and, with the other dignitaries, Senator Vebber grinning from ear to ear. It was the recognition from everyone that meant the most to him, but the money would always come in handy.

Once it was all over and the hero exchanged words with each of the VIPs, as protocol demanded. The rest of his day was free. He went back to his parents' house for a party. His friends were delighted for him, but could not resist making a joke of it.

"I don't know," said Flonass, "wherever you go, be it Azekah or Norland, you can't help being the centre of attention."

With a laugh, Darda replied, "I'm glad you could make it, and you, Vophsi. We'll have to have another session up at the Selerm some time soon."

"Yes," agreed the chef, "and you'll be paying for the drinks with all that money."

Next day, Frank was awake extra early and decided to get up. Before breakfast, he went for a walk outside the Castle, towards the woods north of Castleton. The sun was still under the horizon, but cast pink streaks along the bottom of the clouds against a pale blue background.

The grass was damp with a heavy dew and the wind was coming from the west. He made his way inside the woods and it felt good to be alone for a while. There was no senate meeting set for that day, but he did have some paperwork to tackle later. Maybe he should delegate more things to Tristan. That was a discussion for another time. Right now he found himself by a stream and stopped to observe the scene.

On either side of the water, the trees were fast shedding their leaves. He watched them descend. When one hit the current it was as if it landed on a slow-moving conveyor belt. Those midstream moved inexorably out of sight. Others nearer the banks got stuck, some to be released again after a while. The whole scene was mesmerising.

The breeze suddenly got up and a huge cascade of leaves came down. It looked like a golden snowstorm. He spotted a couple of rabbits further upstream and a squirrel descending a tree nearby. It was beautiful to watch, but he had to drag himself away.

Returning by a different route he was passing what was once Madam Velentua's house, now inhabited by Natias and his wife Eko, along with...

"My Lord!"

Coming out of the front door was Illianeth, Cragoop's wife and someone he had known from the very first time he arrived in Thyatira.

"Good morning," he said cheerfully, but her expression told him all was not well, so he stopped to hear what she had to say.

"I have some sad news, My Lord, Laffaxe has died."

"Oh, when?"

"Last night by the looks of it. Eko went into his room this morning and found him on the floor."

It was not the most unexpected news. The retired physician had been going downhill for some time. He asked, "Are Natias and Eko in there?"

"Along with the physician, yes. I'm sorry, My Lord, but I am going to have to go. I need to make sure everything is in place for my first lesson of the morning."

"Of course, and thank you for telling me."

Frank hesitated. The town was beginning to wake up and there were wagons out on the street. He decided to call at the house. Once inside, he saw Natias who was sitting down, shaken by the news.

"I spoke to him last night, My Lawd, only last night..."

"But I gather he hadn't been too well of late."

"He was not ill, My Lawd, but he did speak of being tired a lot. He'd lost a lot of weight, it's twue. I think he was worn out in the end."

"Yes."

"But he didn't suffer. If he's been in pain, he'd have called out and we'd have heard him."

"I'm sure," said Frank. The man was clearly in shock and needed all the comfort he could get.

It was certainly the end of an era. Laffaxe was another person who had been around from the beginning of Frank's time in Thyatira. The physician's brusque manner scared him at first. He kept on in his role to a fine old age and only retired in recent years. The arrangement of his living in the fine mansion with his best friend and his wife had worked out well as far as Frank was aware.

"Where's Eko?"

"Up in Laffaxe's room with the young physician. He looks young enough to be my grandson." Then, with a change of tone, he asked, "Did Illianeth come and tell you?"

"I met her in the street."

"Ah, I thought you awwived quickly, My Lawd."

"We'll have to give him a fine funeral. He was such an important figure in the old Thyatira. We will give him a good send-off."

The people upstairs were showing no signs of coming down any time soon. Frank thought that Hannah might be wondering where he had got to, plus he was extremely hungry, so he decided to head back to the Castle.

Bye bye, Natias, I will speak with you again soon."

"Thank you, My Lawd."

Back outside, there was a mini-drama going on. Two wagons, travelling in opposite directions, had somehow come too close to each other and locked wheels. It happened but a moment before, but already a small crowd of passers-by on their way to work were stopping to gawp. Both drivers were swearing at their dakks and each other in terns. The poor animals were starting to panic and pull, locking the two vehicles even closer together. Frank was pleased to be invisible with all this commotion going on and departed the scene with haste.

"Oh, there you are!" exclaimed Hannah upon catching sight of him entering the hall.

"Sorry, my walk took me rather longer than I'd intended. I went round..."

"Have you heard the sad news?"

"About Laffaxe?"

"Yes."

"I have, I was passing the house when Illianeth came out."

"Oh; a servant was sent here."

"I went in to see Natias and Eko."

"How are they coping?"

"I saw Natias; Eko was upstairs. He was a bit shaken up, as you can imagine, but not too bad."

"I'll have to go over there and speak to Eko."

"Let's have breakfast first."

Hannah frowned briefly at this before deciding it was not such a silly, or heartless suggestion after all. "Okay, then I'll go over there and offer my condolences and any practical help."

They settled down to eat, after which Frank went to the senate building and Hannah undertook her pastoral visit.

The morning passed quickly and productively for Thyatira's Despot. He read a report on the latest military exercise to take place. Senator Vondant was pleased with the state of preparedness of their armed forces by the sounds of it. It did not harm to be ready for all eventualities.

"My Lord?"

Frank looked up to see a clerk addressing him round his partially-opened office door.

"Yes?"

"Count Bodstein and his wife have arrived at the Castle and wondered if they might see you."

"Oh, right!" exclaimed Frank, who got up straightaway and hurried out to meet them.

Bodd and Anastasia's wagon was parked in the bailey and the travellers were in the hall. Soon greetings were being exchanged.

468

"It slipped my mind that you were coming. I hope you know that you're welcome to stay here at the Castle."

This was the same invitation he had made whilst they were all in Asattan. It received the same answer from Bodd.

"That's most kind, but we've already arranged to stay with Tsodd at the Selerm. I hope to see you again during our stay, though."

"You must! How long are you with us for? There was talk of your staying for the winter."

Glancing first at his wife, Bodd replied, "It's open-ended, it's still not decided. I think we'll see how it goes."

The news then came out about Laffaxe. Bodd said with a twinkle in his eye, "So the contentious old sod has finally gone to meet his maker. I hope God's ready for him, if not, Laffaxe will soon put him in his place!"

They laughed before Frank said that he first heard the news from Illianeth. Anastasia replied, "Ah, Illianeth, I want to see her soon and catch up."

"Are you going to have lunch here?"

Bodd replied, "I think we'll go to the Selerm now and eat there. Thanks anyway. We'll get settled, then catch up with my brothers if that's okay, but we'd love to see more of you and Hannah soon."

The doctor concluded that Laffaxe's death was caused by a sudden, massive heart attack, but most put it down simply to old age. He had had a long life and the end, when it came, was swift.

It was a bright, autumnal day when the funeral took place within the stone church outside Vionium. Bishop Gunter presided over the service with priests Isaac and Azikial in attendance. There were no known living relatives of Laffaxe. Frank and Hannah, of course, were in prime position, with Joseph seated between them. It was thought to be a good learning experience for him. Natias and Eko also sat in the front row, as did Bodd and Anastasia.

Gunter had known the deceased only in recent years. He relied on the testimony of old friends in order to learn something of the man's life. As a result, he was able to recount in his talk about Laffaxe's highly unusual medical education amongst the Ma'hol, at a time when the foreigners were anything but allies. That advanced learning put him in good stead for his lifetime's work. With the departure of the last blacks from Thyatira, Despot Rattinger had called upon

Laffaxe to be the Castle physician, a post he held until his retirement towards the end of his life. He was often to be seen experimenting with new remedies in his house, mixing up concoctions with his mortar and pestle. Gunter dared to say something about the deceased's strong personality. "He did not suffer fools gladly," he declared, "and the worst sin in his eyes was stupidity." There were many knowing smiles around the church at this stage. "That's for certain!" mumbled Bodd under his breath.

The bishop finished his oration with a message of Christian hope.

"Laffaxe is at rest now, following a long and illustrious career caring for other people. Jesus spoke about the many mansions, or resting places, there are in heaven waiting for those who would come after him. Jesus was speaking at a time shortly before his own death, a death that he would overcome with his resurrection. He gave hope to his disciples that not only was he going to his Father's, to God's house, but they would also be going.

"So we too can hold onto this wonderful hope that, in Christ, death is not the end. In him we have someone who conquered death and showed that it is not the end of all things.

"Whilst we may not have the answers to all our questions now, we can have faith that, in Christ, death is not the end, but the beginning of a new and better life."

Before the service concluded, Natias stood up and said a poem. His voice began to crack once or twice, but he kept going while the entire congregation wished him to carry on to the end. Some prayers were said and, finally, a hymn.

There was no party held after the service, apparently in keeping with the deceased's wishes. People stood around both inside and outside the church building chatting for some time. Many Castle employees were present, especially the long serving ones. Matthew was one of these. Frank noticed Hannah making a beeline for the head of the kitchen and engaging him in conversation, but did not think anything of it.

Gunter was hanging around Frank and more than a few people came up to the bishop to say what a lovely service it had been. "So moving," said an elderly woman whom Frank did not recognise, "it was exactly the sort of religious ceremony he would have loved." As she disappeared into the throng, Karl, who was also nearby, muttered, "That's not true, Laffaxe had no time at all for religion as I recollect." Frank tried to suppress a smile at this point.

"Have you had enough?" asked Hannah.

He husband turned to see her back with him once more. He asked for Joseph's whereabouts and was told that he was already in their wagon, waiting for them. The parents then departed and headed for the vehicle. They boarded the new, light-weight conveyance from Capparathia. Soon the dakks were trotting them back to the Castle.

"That went well," announced the Despotess.

"It did; one of the old guard gone," he replied wistfully.

"Don't worry," she told him, "the time to concern yourself is when you are the old guard."

~ End of Chapter 23 ~

Prospects of Peace - Chapter 24

Bishop Gunter was alone with Frank in the latter's living room on the third floor of the Castle. They had come up there following an evening service held in the chapel.

"A fine service, Gunter, something a bit different."

"We'd been planning on holding a contemplative one for some time now. It seemed to go well."

"It certainly did. I feel spiritually refreshed after that. Gabriell spoke well."

"Abbot Muggawagga first came up with the idea of extinguishing the candles during the confession. It was a pity he couldn't attend."

The evening was cool and Frank took a sip of his warm brankee before changing the subject.

"I hear that the refugee camp is almost empty now."

"It is. We are shutting up shop as the last one departs. I seem to remember when it was first mooted that we'd allow Ladosan refugees into Thyatira, that folk were worried at the idea."

"They were!"

"They thought they'd want to stay, but it hasn't proved to be the case. I think that the church can be proud of its record here. We provided aid, spiritual conflict and counselling as and when it was needed."

"Yes indeed, the Church is a real force for good here."

"I'm having difficulties with a renegade priest down in Norland though."

"Oh?"

"Preaching heresy. If he can't be stopped, I'm afraid I'm going to have to have him removed from his post."

"What's he been saying?"

"It's the old stuff about no one but whites can be Christians and all the blacks are damned. He was quoting Revelations chapter one to prove that Jesus is a white."

"Really?"

"It contains the only description of his hair in the Bible. It says that his hair was white as snow-white wool. It's the perfect description of one of our whites."

Frank was astounded. "Oh my goodness, I'd never made the connection. I've read that passage no end of times, but never thought of it before."

"Based on that half verse, this troublesome priest has built up an entire philosophy excluding the blacks from heaven. It's silly, it's tiresome, but it's something I've got to deal with."

"I'm sure you'll manage," Frank replied with a smile.

"I don't like being too heavy-handed, but if he is infecting the people around him, then he's a danger. Being a priest means you are in a position of influence. If you approach the role in humility and the fear of God, then there's nothing wrong with it. When individual priests' egos get in the way, it becomes a dangerous thing."

"Well, you know you have the full authority of the law behind you should you need it. We can always have him arrested on a charge of subversion you know."

"And make him a martyr? He'd love that. Thanks, but I want to deal with the situation with a less heavy hand."

"As you wish, as long as you know you have my full support, Gunter."

"I do, thank you."

Later in the conversation, they talked about the following week's service in the Castle chapel.

The bishop said, "It's going to be a harvest festival service, held in the morning. There's going to be a guest speaker whom you won't have heard before."

"Oh? Who's that?"

"I want it to be a surprise... but I've heard them speak and I think you'll like it. In fact, I think you will be impressed."

Intrigued, Frank was nevertheless happy to wait for events to unfold. He said, "Well, if you recommend him, I'm sure that he will be up to scratch."

Gunter smiled.

Then Frank continued, "Talking of next Sabbath, Hannah advised me to keep the evening free. That's not like her, she must have something planned."

At this, the bishop's eyebrows raised. He was feigning surprise, but not entirely convincingly. Frank did not press him. It was something else which would unfold in due course.

Katrina and Tsodd were entertaining the latter's brother, Bodd, and his wife, Anastasia, at the Selerm. They were sitting at a table in the corner, a short distance from the loudest drinkers on a busy night. Katrina did not mind the clientele making a bit of noise, as long as it did not get out of hand. Her staff were well drilled on ejecting anyone who crossed the line and her customers knew it.

Their head chef, Vophsi, was enjoying an evening off and sat at a table in the centre of the room. Nearby were some of the older regulars in the form of Hulffan croppers Reuben and Amos. A lone woman sat in the far corner breast-feeding her baby. No one was paying her any attention.

"So," Tsodd was saying, "How are matters of state going then, Bodd?"

"Busy as usual. I've finished of my round of mine inspections for the year. The hottest news is what's going on across the border. The Ladosans have held a General Election and..."

"That's enough, darling," his wife interrupted. "We were coming here to get away from politics, remember?"

"Oh, yes," the Keeper mumbled.

"So, Katrina, what's the news here in Thyatira?"

"I don't have time for such things."

Tsodd helped out with, "Our physician, Laffaxe, has died. He..."

"I know!" shouted Bodd rather louder than was necessary, "I was amazed. I guess nobody lives for ever. He's always been around... How old do you think he was?"

"Dunno," answered his brother, "in his late seventies, I think."

"A good age then."

"Yeah."

With average life expectancy in the primitive society in the low sixties, it was good by their standards. It was a harsh manual life for many; poor accommodation by modern standards and medication not nearly as good as on advanced planets. Small wonder that people did not live so long.

"Poor Laffaxe," Bodd said wistfully.

Tsodd laughed, "It's funny how folk look back at him fondly now. When he was alive many couldn't stand him and everyone was afraid of him."

"Would you like to be at your own funeral? Conscious, I mean, and hear what folk said about you?"

"No, I would not!" replied the proprietor with feeling before getting distracted by the conversation at the next table.

"I don't wanna go t'some silly party!" declared Reuben aggressively.

"There" be free drinks there," Amos told him, food too - lots of it."

"Mmm, will there?" the other replied, his manner suddenly mellowing.

"I'm assured of it. Tsodd's going to be there. I reckon there'll be plenty of folk you know."

"Free food? I'd want to take Brogg, give him a trip out."

"I'm sure that won't be a problem."

"Maybe we *should* celebrate the harvest's in," Reuben continued, clearly coming round to the idea. "Still a lot of work to be done in the sheds, but then we can't work on the Sabbath in any case. Yes, I'll be there."

"We'll go together."

"O' course."

At the next table along there was much frivolity as the former crusaders reminisced about their journey back.

"Whose silly idea was it to steal that canoe?" asked Vophsi. "It almost got us killed."

Flonass, with a smile on his face, recalled, "I've never paddled so fast in my life."

"You've never paddled a canoe before or since," Darda reminded him.

"That's not true. When I was little, my father took me out in a little boat on the river."

"I never knew that."

"It sank after a couple of goes."

"Were you okay?"

"No, I drowned," replied Flonass dryly. Then, not wishing it to be interpreted as a sarcastic comment, he added, "Seriously, I was in shallow water at the time and we gave it up. The boat was unstable. Going back to our journey, I thought we managed okay with that canoe. We were flying down the river... but I guess we can only laugh at it now 'cos we got away."

Vophsi enquired, "What about you, Darda, when we were buying extra provisions at the settlement? We were trying to get an idea of what lay ahead of us. Then you said, 'One more question?' and he said, 'Okay.' And you said, 'How big are your feet?' I almost collapsed laughing, but he didn't look pleased."

"Did I say that? I don't remember."

"That's convenient."

"Anyhow, while it's fun to talk about old times, I've got to be heading back to the Castle."

"In the dark?" asked Flonass, surprised.

"I've done it before; I'll be okay."

"Good luck."

"Thanks," said Darda, downing the last of his drink and standing up. "I'll see you both up at the Castle on the Sabbath."

"Yeah," went Flonass, "mustn't miss that!"

The friends said their goodbyes and Darda stepped out into the blackness of night.

Next day, a young man in simple attire walked towards the Castle along the Setty road. It was with some trepidation that he neared Castleton. For in the previous town he endured enough dark looks to last a lifetime. He knew that his mousy coloured, spiky hair and distinct clothing would mark him out as a foreigner here, but it had been most unpleasant. True, no one had actually shouted at him, or thrown stones, but he thought he detected a xenophobic hostility.

'Am I being oversensitive?' he asked himself as he neared the large, stone fortress. 'For two bronze coins I'd turn tail and go back,' he mused before correcting himself, because it simply was not true. He had come this far and would go through with the mission, even if there was rejection at the end of it.

Walking past the courtyard entrance, he noticed a large market in progress, going at full swing. Deciding to carry on, he made for the second entrance a little further round the tall, defensive wall. This was nearer the main Castle building, the keep. A couple of guardsmen at the entrance looked bored, but perhaps they would assist him.

"Excuse me, I am looking for a Tristan Shreeber. I understand he lives near here. Can you help me?"

The soldier he addressed seemed amused, but in a cold way from the look in his eyes. "Why should I help your sort?" he asked in a lazy, mocking voice.

"Yeah!" exclaimed his colleague in support.

The stranger was about to give a polite reply when an officer sprung onto the scene, seemingly from nowhere, and addressed the first guardsman angrily.

"Harka! That's not how you address a visitor!"

"But he's..."

"I know what he is, but unless you tighten up your act, you're going to be mucking out the stables for the next two weeks! As the sentries snapped to attention, the officer addressed the newcomer more calmly. "Who is it you're looking for?"

"Er, Tristan Shreeber, I don't know if you know him."

"Sure I do. I'm pretty certain he's over at the senate building. I'll take you over there myself."

"Thanks."

"No problem," the officer replied amiably before setting off at a fast pace. "My name's Darda, by the way," he continued as the other man caught up.

"I'm Ayllom, I've come from Ladosa."

"I think we all guessed that," the squad leader said with a twinkle in his eyes. "Ah, here we are."

They began ascending the wide external staircase when none other than Tristan came out of the building. Recognising the visitor straightaway, he called out his name in astonishment before declaring, "I can't believe it!" He turned to Darda and added, "We were together in the ambulance corps in the Civil War."

"Okay, I'll leave you two to it."

Tristan paused as he scrutinized his one-time friend. "Did you come to see me?" It sounded like a daft question, but in his mind he was trying to think of another reason for him to be there. After all, they had parted on bad terms.

"Of course I have."

"Listen! I've got the rest of the day off. I'm going over to the Castle hall for lunch. Come with me and we can talk over our meal."

That was exactly what they did. The conversation was kept light until they came to sit down in a corner away from staring eyes. Ayllom was dying to get something off is chest.

"I'm sorry, Tristan. I behaved badly, I know."

"I think it was the shock. I did deceive you after all, you were right about that. I'd been sworn to secrecy. I'm sorry."

"Hey, I'm the one apologising!" pointed out the Ladosan. "I felt bad about it afterwards. Then the more I found out about your mission to help the Neo-Purples, the worse I felt. My mother knew a lot about Hoame's help for our cause and I got the information out of her. So I'm sorry for the way I reacted; I hope you'll forgive me."

"Forgive you?" said Tristan, tears in his eyes, "of course I will. Did you come all this way to say sorry?"

"Yes, of course, it's been a burden on me for a long time. Now the war's over and everything's been revealed to me, I..."

"I'm glad you came," said Tristan with feeling. "I hope you'll stay for a while."

"Your countrymen aren't all as welcoming."

"Damn them! I'll sort out a change of clothes for you."

"And dye my hair?"

"Don't be silly, you'll be fine. There's no excuse for racialist attitudes. We do get the occasional Ladosan trader over the border anyway. In any case, you'll be my guest and any fool who abuses you will have to answer to me. Stay!"

"I don't want to impose."

"There's nothing I'd like more. I've got a large house and it would be great to have the company. Please stay!"

"Of course I will. I'd love to."

"We can talk about old times."

"What?" asked Ayllom, "you want to re-live all that blood and guts again?"

"There were fun times as well, like when we smuggled that prostitute into the camp and the commander opened the doors of the ambulance to find her sitting there!"

"That's not quite how I remember it. No, I'd rather hear about how you have got on since you came back here."

So Tristan recounted some of his exploits, talking about the trip to Rilesia and Capparathia and being directly employed by the Despot.

"Me old bucka, you've landed on your feet!"

478

"Life's pretty good, I can't complain... Listen! I don't have any work this afternoon. You can come back to my house and I can show you around."

That is exactly what they did. Then, in the comfort of his living room, Tristan declared, "Right, now you tell me what *you've* been up to."

"Okay. I carried on with the ambulances for a while, but it was never the same without you. The fighting ended. Some kept saying it was going to start up again, but it never did. It was getting boring simply hanging about. In the end I resigned and..."

"They let you?"

"Yeah, other units were being disbanded by that time. The people in the know obviously believed that hostilities were over. I first of all went down to visit my family and stayed with them a couple of days. I then went wandering around the country... on a bit of a quest, actually; met some good people. Then there was the General Election and I made sure I voted like a good citizen. I'm pleased with the result."

"Good."

"I see a better future for my country now."

"I'm pleased to hear it."

"You didn't ask me what my quest was about," said Ayllom and he reached down for something on his person.

"My mistake!" responded Tristan with a grin. "What was your quest about?"

"You remember the mansion we stayed in?"

"Of course."

"I set out on a personal mission to try and trace the owners once hostilities ended and we could move about. After all, I was still holding onto their stuff. We'd been told that they were Buff sympathisers, but that turned out to be a lie. They were an old couple, as apolitical as a Ladosan can be. They'd bought the mansion, along with its contents, off ex-Prime Minister Banzarrip when the latter fell on hard times. It was merely an investment to the new owners."

"So you found them? The old couple, I mean."

"I found their graves. In truth it was tragic. She died of shock after being turned out of their home with barely a bean. Her husband didn't last much longer. They left no heirs. I contacted the authorities

479

about the contents of the mansion that we had saved from the elements. There was a bit of argy-bargy about it all, but in the end I was officially granted possession of them."

Tristan surprised the storyteller with his reaction to this tale, for he let out a huge laugh. When this eventually ended, the Haman cried, "So you've been granted a few pieces of fine furniture plus a whole load of funny portraits! I hope you can buy a house that's big enough to accommodate them all."

He clearly still saw it as a big joke. Ayllom had to enlighten him. Speaking seriously, he said, "Didn't I tell you that those portraits were part of our country's inheritance?"

"Yes, I'm sorry, I didn't mean to offend you," Tristan hastily retreated. Another falling-out was the last thing he wanted.

"It's not that. But as soon as the peace broke out there was a surge in pride in Ladosa for our country, its heritage and history. I couldn't have picked a better time to take the paintings to the main auction house in Lefange. Folk were falling over themselves to bid for them. I held onto the furniture, but the paintings, they raised a fortune. This is your half."

With that, he produced a bag of money and plonked it onto the table in front of the astonished Tristan. The top was not tightly done up and the glean of silver could be seen.

"Oh my goodness! Ayllom, I never..."

"Take it then."

He did, saying, "A bag of silver coins, I'm speechless..."

"Open it up."

Tristan did so. The silver turned out to be merely on the top. The bad contained over fifty gold coins. "You weren't kidding when you said a fortune, this must be a king's ransom!"

Then he hesitated, so Ayllom, guessing what was on his mind, said, "Yes, it's genuine gold. I got it from the finest auction house in Ladosa. Besides, I had it independently verified."

Remembering the previous time he had been given such a princely sum, then given it away, Tristan resolved not to repeat that act. Complete the extension to his house, a new wagon... ideas were already forming in his head, but first there was something he needed to say to Ayllom.

"Thank you! Thank you so much. You won't know this, but I've been trying to save a bit of money each week and putting it away on deposit with a local moneylender. This, though, is in a different league. I'll be able to buy the moneylender if I want!"

"Spend it wisely, my friend, many are those who have come to grief through sudden wealth."

"You're right. I'll be sensible, don't you worry... but Ayllom, I can't find words sufficient to thank you."

"I gave you my word that if I ever able to sell them I'd give you your share. My own half is safely in a bank in Lefange."

"But you must have crossed the mountains with all this wealth on you; you could have been robbed!"

"I came through the Mitas Gap, not across the mountains. I hid them and dressed down, so that I would not attract attention. Anyway, I've made it now and fulfilled my obligation to you."

"But you'll still stay I hope!"

"If you want me to."

"More than anything. This money..." he paused to clear his throat "... will make a huge change. I'm going to stick with my job, it gives me an identity, an anchor to my life and it's interesting being involved at the highest level in what's going on. Nevertheless, this money will help me in other ways."

"I'm glad."

"But none of it is worth half as much as your friendship. It's so wonderful to see you again."

The two of them went for a walk shortly after this, calling in on a surprised Deejan Charvo. He had the security measures to keep the riches safe. Tristan told the financier, "I haven't got time now, but I'll tell you the full story on another occasion."

Once back in the confines of his living room, and with a couple of drinks between them, he said, "I hope you'll stay for a good time."

"I'm not in a hurry to get back."

"Good. Next Sabbath there's going to be a big party up at the Castle. I've recently started seeing a young lady who works up there, but she'll be on duty that evening. I'll make sure I get you in there if it's the last thing I do. The Despotess is organising it, I'll have a word with her tomorrow. I know she'll say yes."

"Party it is then," replied Ayllom with a grin on his face and his glass raised in salute.

That evening, Despot Frank Thorn, the one person in Thyatira unaware of the party being organised by his wife, was entertaining Muggawagga in his living room. It was quite late and Hannah, feeling tired, had gone to bed. The two men, although tired themselves, were in philosophical mood and harboured no thoughts of retiring for the night just yet. The abbot was talking about meditation.

"There is power in stillness. I don't mean personal power...maybe I used the wrong word. With the stillness of your body, your soul is in harmony. After all, we are body, mind and spirit."

"In harmony with God, you mean?"

"I do, but it's not an 'us' and 'him' situation. If we've to take seriously our being made in the image of God, we must realise our potential as creative beings. We are creating our reality, and indeed our future, at every moment. A lot, if not all of what we are is due to our choosing to be that way, whether consciously or unconsciously. So if we realise that, we can use it to our advantage. Not for personal gain, of course, that would be too absurd. But we can ensure that we are on the right path (the Narrow Way that Jesus spoke about) simply because we are choosing to be so. Nothing will be impossible if we use our creative will to consciously steer the right path. This is an astounding truth, one to be grasped if we really want to."

"Don't you think," began Frank in response, "that as time goes on, you realise that truth is not a simple matter of two plus two equals four?"

"How d'yer mean?"

"Well, as a child you want straightforward, concrete answers for everything. Naturally there are some things for which concrete answers are okay, but we carry that need on to higher things and give these precise explanations for things which are not suitable. We try to define God in the definite terms of the Trinity and the creeds. I'm not saying they're entirely wrong, but we should be honest enough to admit that we are never going to fully understand the infinite in terms of formulas. In the old days there used to be a debate as to whether God made the world, or there was evolution. It seems absurd now, of course, but it did happen. Now we know that they were both true. The truth can be fluid, even seemingly contradictory the higher you go."

"I follow yer."

"Man used to believe that atoms were little solid building blocks, out of which everything was made. Now we know that they're nothing of the sort. There is more empty space than "stuff" in an atom! In fact sub-atomic particles are made up of energy and not matter as anyone understands it. So solid things are made out of stuff which is anything but solid. You realise that simple answers won't do."

"And the mystics had it right all along."

"Exactly! The Holy Spirit can never be tied down, but is the creative force throughout the universe. He leads us on the merry dance of life."

"The dance of life? I like that. It gives our existence proper meaning, we are not mechanical beings, for our essence is spirit." Then Muggawagga changed tone when he went on, "But it's a bit much at this late hour. I think I'm going to go off to bed now, if you don't mind."

"Of course not," confirmed Frank, "I'll go too. You're in your usual tower room?"

"I am."

"And you have enough lights to get you there?"

"I can take this?" asked the abbot as he picked up a candlestick on the table with a lit beeswax candle in it.

"That's fine."

"I'll be off early in the morning."

"Right."

"So I'll see you on the Sabbath."

"Oh," went Frank, somewhat surprised. He was not aware that the other man was going to attend the weekly service. "All right then, see you on the Sabbath."

A couple of days later, Frank was in his senate building office with Emil. The latter was about to give a progress report on Norland.

"I expect you're going to tell me about more problems," Frank said pessimistically.

This took the senator by surprise.

"Oh, I hadn't realised that was the way I'm coming across. I probably highlight the problem areas, because those are the ones which require our attention. It does not do to sweep them under the carpet. No, the truth is that Norland is proving a brilliant acquisition and I believe that Thyatira will go from strength to strength because of it. A change like this was never going to be without hiccoughs, but in the greater context it's going remarkably smoothly. Keeping the existing government structure in place has ensured a smooth transition on the whole. Indeed, I believe that most ordinary citizens will have experienced little impact on their lives. Apart, I hope, from the lowering of taxes to bring them into line with the rest of us."

"But I thought there were problems with some of the town mayors. Carnis has been mentioned."

"I'd prefer to say, 'less than satisfactory business arrangements,' but we've smoothed these out now. They realise that we've got our eyes on them and they are behaving themselves as they know they have to in order to stay in office."

"Mmm."

"If I have concentrated on matters for improvement, then I have perhaps distorted the balance. But I hope my reports have shown the plus side as well. Norland will make us, not merely equal in size with the bigger despotates, but the economic powerhouse of Hoame."

"I like that!" declared Frank, "an economic powerhouse." Then, with a change of tone, he asked, "And what is the latest on the fire aftermath?"

"I'll be visiting Carnis again next week."

"I see."

"I'll travel after the Sabbath, following the party."

"Oh? What party is that?"

Emil had not realised that Hannah wanted it to be a surprise for her husband, but he looked so guilty now that he felt he had to say something.

"Um, the one the Despotess is holding in the Castle on the Sabbath evening."

"Ah, of course," returned Frank, trying to bluff his way out.

Once the meeting was over, he went over to the Castle and found his wife in the hall, talking with Matthew. He hung back, but as soon as she finished, he went up to her.

"What's this about a party here the day after tomorrow?"

"Oh," replied Hannah, realising the game was up. "It was going to be a surprise."

"It is."

"What I meant was... oh, never mind. I simply thought it would be nice to have a party and I thought it would be fun to have it as a surprise for you."

"Well, I could pretend I don't know."

Hannah gave him a look. "Anyway, I hope you approve."

"Of a party? Sure, why not?"

She almost said, "Because you can be stuffy sometimes and I thought that it would be safer to tell you at the last moment." However, some things are best left unsaid and this was one of them. If he was in a good mood, then all was well.

He asked, "Is there a special occasion?"

"I thought we'd call it a harvest supper. After all, the harvest is in, it looks to be a good one. That's a celebration in itself, but simply to show our appreciation to the community before winter sets in. Not that we can invite everyone, but we've got a cross-section coming. The Castle staff have been given priority to invite families and friends. The Norland mayors should be coming too. Blacks, whites, rich and poor, they're all invited."

"Are there enough spaces?"

"It's going to be, er... rather full; it's true, but I don't care."

He laughed at this, then cheekily asked, "So where's Hanson going to sit?"

While he was amused at the thought of inviting a notorious recluse, she was puzzled at the suggestion, facetious though it may have been. Then she spotted a messenger enter the hall with a communication tube.

"Your Excellency," said the messenger as he held the container out, "this is for you."

"Ah, the Inner Council," he said to himself, inspecting the tube. Then to the messenger, "You go across the bailey to the kitchen and get yourself some refreshments. Then report back to me."

"Yes, Your Excellency, thank you."

Sitting down next to her husband there in the hall, Hannah was hoping this would not require another trip to the Capital for him. "Not bad tidings, I hope," she said.

After quickly reading the covering note, Frank handed it over and looked at the rest of the papers he had fished out of the container.

"Not at all," he said, "arguably the best thing that's happened on the international scene in a decade."

It was the news that the new coalition government in Ladosa had accepted Hoame's proposals almost unaltered. Frank called upon a passing servant to fetch Alan, which he did straightaway. Soon the drone was sitting with them in the hall, giving his verdict.

"Signed by Foreign Secretary Nazaz, I see. So all those years of negotiations were not wasted after all. A pact with Ladosa, the establishment of full diplomatic relations and a willingness for further talks to increase trade and cooperation. That's a brilliant result."

"Yes," agreed Frank, "and I'm sure your efforts were largely responsible for it."

"I don't..." began Alan, but Frank interrupted him.

"But have you seen the funny bit at the end?"

"Eh?"

"The Keepers have decided on Count Wonstein to be our ambassador to Ladosa. It will get that troublemaker out of their hair. He'll be stuck with those Ladosan lunatics from now on. That'll put an end to his silly schemes."

"Are you sure," asked Alan, "that you should be referring to our new foreign friends as lunatics?"

"Maybe not, but I'm not alone in having to adjust. I wonder if the Mehtar has been informed, it doesn't say. I'll have to get something off to him. I'll speak to Tristan after lunch. Nonetheless, it's good news."

Hannah said, "Yes, it is, even your lunatic wife is pleased."

"I didn't mean..."

"It's okay," she replied with a smile. She had only been teasing him about her Ladosan roots.

Then Alan, putting the letter down after reading it a third time, commented, "We've been working towards a genuine peace with them for a long time. I hope that this lasts. I can barely believe it."

"Well," replied Frank, "we should believe it: peace in our time."

"Yeah."

"For everything there is a season, for every activity under heaven has its time. A time for war and a time for peace."

"Thank goodness the civil war is over and that it's brought about something good in the end. A strange birth."

With a deep sigh, Frank agreed. Then, getting up, he said to Alan, "Will you tell the other senators please? I'm going to try and find

Tristan now. I think he said he'd be in the Throne Room this morning."

He handed over the tube to Alan and left him sitting there with Hannah. Nearing the Throne Room, he saw a male servant come fairly flying down the spiral staircase before making straight for him.

"My Lord," he said with a note of urgency, "the locked cupboard near your living room... there are funny noises coming from it."

Frank stood for a moment taking the words in. The then penny dropped and with a tone that matched the servant's, he replied, "I'll see to it; leave it to me. You are not to mention this to anyone. Do you understand?"

The servant confirmed he did. Concluding that the Despot, who was quickly ascending the spiral staircase, would prefer to be unaccompanied, he went about his other duties.

Up on the third floor, Frank was alone. He always kept the key to the instrument cupboard on him and today was no exception. Quickly unlocking and opening it, his suspicions were confirmed. For the lights on the communication device his brother had left him, were extremely active. A whole bank of them were flashing and the noise started up again.

Picking it up, he took it out of the cupboard and carried it to the living room. Entering cautiously, he found it devoid of cleaning staff, or anyone else for that matter, and went in. Settling down in a corner chair, he blew some dust off the device before setting it down on the small table in front of him.

It was coming back to him now how to operate it. He leaned forward for the machine to take his retinal scan. The alarm stopped immediately and, before he knew it, a thirty centimetre hologram of his brother was standing above the communicator.

"Hi ya! I've been trying to contact you for a long time."

"John," replied Frank hoarsely, "are you all right?"

"Never better, big brother! How are things with you?"

"Fine. It's been such a long time."

"Yeah, the Chang Tides, it seems, mess up commutations as well as deep space travel. But never mind, they appear to be passing away from this sector. I've got a bit of time off, I wondered if you'd mind me paying you a visit soon?"

"I'd love to see you again," Frank replied to the man he had actually seen little of since growing up. Yet blood was thicker than water and he possessed but one sibling. "When can you come? Will you be alone?"

"Only a short hop from here... and I'll speak to the others. Is that okay with you?"

"As long as they know the score, it'll be fine. You'll have to land in the woods north of here and cloak your craft as before. Oh, and you're from a far off land here on Molten of course."

"Sure. You still in that old castle?"

"I am!" Frank exclaimed joyfully. The prospect of meeting John again after all these years was exhilarating. They then began a conversation about each other's lives in recent times, but this had to be cut short when the link showed signs of failing.

"See you soon then, big brother. We'll come dressed appropriately, like you said."

"Yes, I'll look fo..."

The link was broken. It did not matter unduly, for the important things had been said. John was alive, well and paying him a visit. What a wonderful prospect to look forward to.

The machine appeared as dead as it normally did. He seized it in his hands and hurried to the instrument cupboard where he popped it away amongst the guitars, horns and other things. Once the door was locked again, he breathed a sigh of relief. How wonderful it would be to see his not-so-little brother again.

The Sabbath came and, after breakfast, Frank was with his family in the hall. They were standing around with the other exclusive people, mostly senators and their wives. Deejan Charvo and family were there too. Soon they would file into the chapel.

Meanwhile, an army of servants behind them were busy working. Tables needed to be re-positioned, new ones brought in. Fresh candles were put in the holders and the floor swept amongst other chores, all in preparation for the evening. The non-surprise Harvest Supper party would soon be all set to go ahead.

The signal was given and the congregation shuffled into the much smaller chamber that was the chapel. The Thorns took their place of honour at the front and the other people soon filled all the available chairs.

Bishop Gunter introduced the service as one of special harvest thanksgiving. It was an old tradition that was being re-established at the Castle that year. Following a hymn and confession, priests Isaac and Azikial came up to do Bible readings. As they sat down, Keturah stepped forward. Frank wondered if she was going to do a third reading. Then, belatedly, and to his astonishment, he realised that this was the guest speaker that Gunter had mentioned. 'Well,' thought Frank, 'here's one surprise that was successfully kept from me.'

She looked nervous as she mounted the dais and unfolded her notes and spread them on the lectern. Her voice quavered at first, but confidence spread the longer she spoke.

"Harvest festival is an opportunity to say thank you to God for all the wonderful blessings he bestows on us. Above all, it is a time to show our gratitude to him for all that he does for us.

"Gratitude is an important thing. It's only fair that people say thank you when someone gives them something, or helps out. And how we take offence at ingratitude!"

Frank smiled; it was true. As the talks progressed, Keturah gave examples of kind deeds and anecdotes about ingratitude. She spoke about the many spiritual blessings bestowed on people before commencing her conclusions.

"So let's make sure we give God all the respect and thanks that are due, living lives of cheerful gratitude."

The talk was over. As Frank's tutor back on Eden might have said, "It was short, succinct, came to the point and left you with a message. A pass."

In the aftermath of the service, Keturah stood by her father shyly as, one after another, people went up and congratulated her on her talk.

"Did you write it yourself?"

"With the help of God, I did."

"Do you hope to preach again? I hope you do"

"If Bishop Gunter agrees, yes."

Frank stood from afar and decided to leave his congratulations for another day, for it seemed she might be overwhelmed by it all. 'Yet I could be wrong,' he considered, 'because she's certainly tougher than she looks."

Late afternoon and the guests were arriving in droves, ready for the harvest supper. Black mayors from Norland and white croppers from Vionium, it was certainly an assortment. Apart from the top table, the actual seating was on a first-come basis, so folk tended to sit in little gaggles with the people they knew.

The Thorns were amongst the last to enter the hall and took their place at the centre of the head table. This was at a ninety degree angle to the other long tables in the room. Bishop Gunter said grace and the feast began.

It had all been Hannah's idea and she found herself smiling as she looked across at the various groups of people enjoying themselves. The food and drink were top quality and everyone seemed to be having a good time.

Deejan Charvo sat proudly with his children on either side, chatting away to some senators. Walter was not present, having decided not to come.

The loudest table was undoubtedly Count Bodstein's. With his brothers and their wives there, plus a detachment of whites from Vionium, they were certainly having a good time. Frank took a glance at them too: Amos and Kim, Reuben, Mary and Brogg. They had been very much in evidence during his whole time in Thyatira.

General Japhses and Captain Jonathan sat with their wives. Further up that table, the former crusaders were having fun. Flonass has his new girlfriend, the nurse Marie, alongside him. They were listening to his colleagues' conversation.

"We're both thinking of buying houses," Darda was telling Vophsi.

"What, you and Flonass?"

"Yeah; we've both come into money recently and it seems the right thing to do."

It was the season for financial windfalls, for Tristan too had recently received an even larger amount of money. As the Despot's secretary, he managed to procure a couple of places on the end of the high table for himself and Ayllom.

"You certainly know how to have a good time!" exclaimed the Ladosan with a smile. "Do you have these events regularly?"

"Not at all," his friend assured him.

Meanwhile, Frank had finished the main course and was sitting there with a great grin on his face, watching the proceedings.

"We could do this every year," he told Hannah.

"Good," she replied. "I'd like that."

Trying to seize on her husband's good mood, she saw a good opportunity to raise a delicate subject.

"My dear."

"Yes?"

"About Wanda... do you not think that a pardon would be a good idea?"

The smile vanished from Frank's face faster than you could say, "knife." Then the sudden hardness of his face softened a bit and he said quietly, "I'll think about it."

It was a good deal better than a flat "no." She decided it was best not to push her luck and she said no more on the subject. At least a seed has been sown. She swiftly moved to another matter.

"You do realise that it was in this very room that we first met?"

"Of course, you were here with your mother and a bodyguard."

"Warshazzap, that's right."

"I wonder what became of him; he was Muggawagga's friend wasn't he?"

"He was indeed... and I can tell you exactly what's become of him."

"Oh?"

"He was recently elected as a Neo-Purple Member of Parliament. I heard word of it the other day."

"I didn't know he was the political type."

"My dear, most of us Ladosans are! He doesn't come from a particularly political family, it's true; but I'm told he feels he's getting a bit long in the tooth for fighting and wants to make a contribution another way."

"Let's hope he gets on well."

The ale that evening turned out to be a potent brew and a lot stronger than normal. Alan and Karl were sitting next to each other and both were feeling merry. The former was proposing a toast for the two of them.

"My old buddy, you and I've been through a lot together over the years. I prop..."

"Yeah, we 'ave!" Karl slurred.

"I propose... here's to absent friends: Eleazar and Auraura."

"To Gabby!"

"To the Mehtar!"

"And Despot Kagel... and Hanson."

Alan laughed at this before crying, "And Vanda Hista!" He glanced over to Frank and Hannah who, fortunately, were otherwise engaged.

"I'm sure," shouted Karl above the general din, "that Laffaxe is still with us in spirit; so... to Laffaxe!"

"To Laffaxe," repeated the drone with a guffaw before taking another swig. The alcohol was going to his head and, more giggly than anyone had ever witnessed before, sought even more absurd toasts.

"Tomas Shreeber!"

Fortunately, Tristan did not hear that one. Not to be out-done, Karl came back with, "Count Zastein, Baron Schail!"

"Zadok, the priest."

"Crag, the gaoler."

"Gideon, the village head."

"Madam Velentua!"

"Adrian and Crispin," said Alan.

Karl looked puzzled, "I don't remember them."

"Before your time."

"Oh."

Towards the end of this exchange, Hannah looked over and witnessed the pair. With a disbelieving frown, she nudged her husband and declared, "I'm sure I've never seen Alan drunk before."

"Well, there's a first time for everything. As long as people are enjoying themselves, that's all that matters."

The evening wore on and while Alan and Karl were not alone in becoming inebriated, the party never got out of control. Food was in plentiful supply, but Amos had to stop Reuben from secreting away a few chicken drumsticks on his person.

"No one'll miss 'em."

"I don't care! Put them back."

The old cropper complied and the incident was soon forgotten. He inspected his disabled son's face and wiped excess food from Brogg 's chin.

All were sated by the time the festivities concluded. Most of the guests departed fairly promptly. Those with further to go than Castleton were being put up for the night. Alan and Karl both needed help getting to their respective destinations.

A few people milled around rather than leave straightaway. Frank found himself standing with Natias and Bishop Gunter. His memory went back almost twenty years to his first arrival at the Castle. This same Natias, then steward, had welcomed him to his new home.

What a lot had happened in the meantime: wars, adventures, marriage, a son, plots, visitors from outer space, a kidnapping, murder and foreign treaties. He had come through it all more or less in one piece. What would the future hold? A visit from his brother for one thing. Gunter was talking.

"Before I agreed to her delivering the talk, I chatted with Keturah at my house. She said that the highest way to live is with passion, but without expectation."

Said Frank, "A profound statement from one so young."

"I'm not sure age comes into it. She's an old soul and no mistake."

At the other end of the hall, Darda was playing with Joseph. He was giving him an impromptu, and not too serious, sword-fighting lesson.

Natias laughed at their antics and said, "Your son will gwow into a fine Despot, My Lawd."

"Thank you, Natias. And that Darda is proving a first-class fellow too. In fact, with the future of Thyatira in the hands of the like of them, and Keturah, I see bright prospects looking ahead."

Then the bishop added, "It is a time for optimism, both nationally and internationally. Let us thank God for it."

"I agwee. It is a new ewa of peace and pwosperity. We are gwateful for our Despot here and, down in the Capital, the Keepers of Hoame."

As he spoke, a loud noise could be heard passing overhead, audible even within the stout walls of the Castle. Gunter and Natias looked puzzled and concerned at the sound. Frank, though, gave a slight smile. He knew it was a spaceship coming in to land.

~ The End ~

The Keepers Series

Printed in Great Britain
by Amazon

70771095R00293